The Fruit Tree

Sabir Ahmed

Grosvenor House
Publishing Limited

All rights reserved
Copyright © Sabir Ahmed, 2024

The right of Sabir Ahmed to be identified as the author of this work has been asserted in accordance with Section 78 of the Copyright, Designs and Patents Act 1988

The book cover is copyright to Sabir Ahmed

This book is published by
Grosvenor House Publishing Ltd
Link House
140 The Broadway, Tolworth, Surrey, KT6 7HT.
www.grosvenorhousepublishing.co.uk

This book is sold subject to the conditions that it shall not, by way of trade or otherwise, be lent, resold, hired out or otherwise circulated without the author's or publisher's prior consent in any form of binding or cover other than that in which it is published and without a similar condition including this condition being imposed on the subsequent purchaser.

A CIP record for this book
is available from the British Library

This book is a work of fiction. Any resemblance to people or events, past or present, is purely coincidental.

Paperback ISBN 978-1-83615-033-6
Hardback ISBN 978-1-83615-034-3
eBook ISBN 978-1-83615-035-0

Front and back cover by Zrhio (https://zrhio.com/)
Additional artwork by Madirune
(https://www.instagram.com/madirune/)

Contents

Dedication v
Chapter 1 1
Chapter 2 13
Chapter 3 26
Chapter 4 32
Chapter 5 40
Chapter 6 52
Chapter 7 62
Chapter 8 73
Chapter 9 82
Chapter 10 89
Chapter 11 99
Chapter 12 106
Chapter 13 113
Chapter 14 121
Chapter 15 130
Chapter 16 139
Chapter 17 152
Chapter 18 167
Chapter 19 174

Chapter 20	183
Chapter 21	189
Chapter 22	197
Chapter 23	204
Chapter 24	213
Chapter 25	222
Chapter 26	227
Chapter 27	238
Chapter 28	249
Chapter 29	256
Chapter 30	270
Chapter 31	277
Chapter 32	288
Chapter 33	296
Chapter 34	304
Chapter 35	316
Chapter 36	332
Chapter 37	342
Chapter 38	353
Chapter 39	364
Chapter 40	381
Acknowledgements	391
Resources	392

Dedication

For Megan,

Thank you. For more than you know, and for more than I have the time to explain. I finally finished it.

Chapter 1

She was so young, her innocence reigned over her face with the moonlight.

"Get ready for bed." He called to his little angel.

She jumped behind the folded corner of the duvet and sat upright. "Can you tell me a story?"

He sat by her covered feet. "What story do you want tonight?" He smiled.

"The one of Adam and Eve." She completely wiped off the smile on his face.

"Are you sure? There're many other stories you haven't heard like the prin-." He looked at her stubborn face. "I'm guessing you don't mean the holy version either?" he laughed as she shook her head.

His head bounced off the wall as his collar dug into his neck, marking its anger. He reddened, panicking, arms flailing to the side. He could hear the flapping wings of pages as his books plummeted to the ground, loose sheets fluttering in the surrounding air. The cold knuckles pressed into his throat as the shadow of the nearing head enveloped his face.

"Leave him alone!" A yell from behind following by hurried pats against the floor. "You walked into him, you fucking idiot." She strained as she pulled at the larger, trying to get between them.

The jock and the heroine locked eyes as if they were bulls locking horns. After a few long seconds, a grunt and then some angered stomps marched away down the hall. She looked to her right, to see a wall but nothing else. The frantic scraping noises on the floor helping her realise he was kneeling, scrambling to grab his books so he could scamper away into a dark hole.

She knelt beside him to offer a hand. "I'm sorry about him, he's just... air between ears sometimes."

He remained looking to the ground. "It's okay."

She held a book in her hand as she watched him. "Are... you okay?"

He had somewhat collected himself enough to look at her. "I'm sorry. I'm fine, thanks for your help."

She smiled at him. "You're... Ste...phen? Right?"

He chuckled lightly at the ground. "I- I'm Adam. Thanks, Eve."

"Oh... well now I look like a bitch." She half-heartedly laughed.

"It's fine, you can't know everyone." He smiled at her forgivingly. "Heroes can't remember everyone they've saved."

The smile returned to her face. "Well, I'll make sure to remember you, *Adam*."

She retrieved a pen that was tucked into the outside pocket of her bag. She grabbed the book in his hands, pulling his attention with it. He looked puzzled for a second but there was no denying his intrigue. He tried to stop her, but she cut him off. She wrote quickly. First numbers, then a few letters. She handed it to him.

"Call me." He read aloud. "Smiley face?" He stared at it for a few seconds, deciphering the scribble.

She laughed. "You don't have to if you don't want to." She shrugged. "Just in case you ever need saving again."

"N- No, I'd love to. I just... have to..." He paused a few times as he stared at the book. "...memorise the number 'cos this is a library book." He tried to stop himself from laughing, biting his lip to poorly conceal a smile.

She immediately grabbed the book from him and crossed it out, the force of her pen whipping the air around it. "You could've told me!"

"I did try to stop you, but you stopped me from stopping you!" He retorted, trying not to burst into laughter.

She lightly threw the book back at him as he smiled. They smiled at each other. He stared into her eyes. Blue, like a clear sky. A blank canvas that he was dying to paint onto. His mind drifted into dreams. He travelled in time. Years ahead, he smiled to himself. And then his dreams were crushed by a flashing barrier.

"Heeellooooo? Anyone home?" She quizzed him, her hand jumping in front of his eyes.

He came back down to Earth. "Hi... yes... sorry."

"Are you sure you're okay?" She looked confused.

"No," he paused as he grabbed all his things, ready to scuttle away into the darkness. "I'm Stephen. With a p h." He smiled to himself.

She looked at him for a minute. He was definitely different. Not what she'd expected from first impressions, but that wasn't his fault. He'd left some sort of mark on her, and she intended to repay it.

She grabbed his right hand and pulled it towards her. Her hands were warm, just like her smile. He just observed her, the warmth of her fingers burning their impressions onto the back of his hand. Then a hard, cold point crushed his squishy palm. It didn't hurt, but she made sure it left its mark.

The cool air enveloped his hand as she released it, replacing the hug with nothingness. He brought his hand to him, palm down. He could see the outline of her hand though there was none. Then he slowly turned it. There sat eleven digits. He looked up at her. Eve just winked and walked away. He knelt there, alone and mystified.

He looked down, completely bewildered. The conversation replayed in his head like a broken record. He could still feel the cold pen pressing into his palm. He was considering getting it tattooed – the template was already there.

When Adam returned home that day, he wondered what to do with that number. It was fading on his hand so he went over it, tracing it very carefully so as not to change the handwriting. He hadn't noticed it before but she'd even drawn a little winking face. He instantly saved the number in his phone, but then just stared at it.

He just sat there and thought of all the possible outcomes of what would happen if he did call her. Should he even call her? Maybe she meant text instead of call. Were calls too forward? Would he even remember how to speak? What would he even say?

The good thoughts lit him up, he could feel them hugging his insides. But the bad ones just dug into him. Deep wounds filled with bitter tears. The new scared him. He was a creature of habit. Can't be disappointed by familiarity. The comfort of the known was all he knew.

What if she gave me someone else's number and I look like a fool? What if she doesn't respond? Does she even want to talk to me? What do I say? How do I keep my cool? A whole bunch of questions yet he sought no answers. He just wanted to wonder. He just wanted excuses.

"What's that on your hand?" His mother broke his drifting mind, having noted the only break in silence to be his fork toying with his food.

He instantly pulled back his hand, knowing she'd seen it. "Noth-..." He looked up at her, those stern eyes reminding him there was no point in lying. "Someone..."

He couldn't find the words, wishing only to return the room to silence so he could focus on the chaos in his mind. He relented with a troubled sigh, lifting his hand and holding out across the table.

His mother received it, the inspection quick. "Who's this, Adam?" The corner of her mouth betrayed a slight joy.

He shrugged. He didn't really know, he realised. He'd never spoken to her before, just seen her around. The unknown. Unfamiliar. Scary. But her smile was so welcoming.

"Have they got your number?" She could see anxiousness painting his face.

He bowed his head, shaking it slowly. If he had just given his number in return, he could've shifted the burden onto her... How did he not think of that?

"Well, you'll never know at this rate. Don't miss out on something overthinking what *could* happen. Do what you want to do and regret it later if you must. It's easier to live with something that went wrong than it is to be haunted by regret. And this little smiley face doesn't seem very scary to me!" She rubbed the back of his hand with her thumb.

He managed to break a smile, nodding with thankful eyes. "When this goes wrong, I'm blaming you."

She scoffed with a grin, her hand throwing air towards him. "You'll be thanking me."

He finished his meal, the room returning to a silence it wasn't used to during this time but the weight of the air seemed to vanish. He'd been invigorated with a confidence he'd never known before.

The faint patter of haptics as he began typing. *Hi, it's Stephen. Note the p h.* he read to himself. He spoke the words aloud, as if it would make them sound different. It was a bold opening, he thought, bolstered by his new form.

He stared at the screen. Pondered on it for a moment. The thoughts came flooding back. The false ego dissipated before his eyes, as he failed to catch the flying pieces. He deleted the characters and threw his phone on his bed. This wasn't what he did, this wasn't his world. Maybe it was for the best.

He was used to being alone. The lone child, few friends, never doing much after school. It was a constant battle to convince himself he wasn't lonely. He was just alone. By choice. And happy. It was closer to teetering in comfort being uncomfortable, to the point where what he wanted became what he feared.

A couple of days passed. He'd put it behind him, just a fleeting moment that had run its course. He kept to himself, as usual. Out of the way, out of trouble, out of sight. Surviving, but never living. The tortuous days of school.

He was walking down a hall when he saw her again. She was in a group, the bull amongst them. He watched her smiling and laughing. His mind went crazy, replaying that event from a couple days ago. He couldn't escape it now.

Wrestling with his dreams for control of his mind, he tried to ground himself again but her electric smile gave his pulse the shock he hadn't expected. How did she have such a hold on him already, after mere minutes? There were barely enough words spoken to write the chorus to a song and yet the orchestra of his organs kept playing to her beat.

Click click. "Are you lis'nin to me?"

He blinked a few times. Back to reality, the large ape and a couple of his mates were in front of him. He started to slowly back up.

"I- I'm sorry, I won't do it again." He didn't even know what he was apologising for, but de-escalation is what you're meant to do, right?

"We can make sure you don't do it again." He gruffed.

Before Adam could react, the gorilla's shoulder started twitching. "Come... on... Stan... leave him alone." A voice struggled from behind.

"It'd serve this little creep well getting a few fists." The gorilla replied.

"You'll get kicked out; you can't risk it. Not now!" She'd stopped tugging at his arm.

He thought for a moment, her words had clearly had some effect on him. The world seemed to stop while they all waited for the verdict.

"You're lucky." He announced, back turned before he'd even finished speaking.

The troop walked away, revealing the familiar hero.

"Sorry about him, he's been in a mood since he lost the match last week." The happiness was drained from her face, but she tried to smile.

"I- It's okay. It's my fault... I..." He didn't really know what he wanted to say.

"It's okay, Adam. He's big and scary on the outside but he has his own issues. He's just not very good at dealing with them."

Adam mumbled back.

"What was that?" She asked, confused.

"It's Stephen. With a p h." He surprised himself as the words left his lips, leaving behind a slight smirk.

She shook her head. "That's a shame, maybe I should've let him pummel you then. I was trying to save Adam."

His eyes widened again.

"I'm just joking!" She noticed.

"Too soon." He bowed his head.

"Sorry, but you never called. You can't leave a girl hanging, I didn't have you as one of those guys."

Adam was just happy she remembered him, his face beaming. "S- Sorry, I... I got busy and... I... then I forgot."

"You often forget girls, Adam?" She grinned as she watched his brain panicking. "I'm not worth remembering?"

"I... Y-... No... That's..."

She burst out laughing. "It's okay, I'm just teasing you."

A huge wave of relief hit him. "I'll do it today. For sure."

"It's the least you could do for your hero." She smiled. "I'll be waiting." She walked away before he could think anything else.

Now was the real trouble. She hadn't forgotten him, and he'd just told her he would make sure to call her. How was he meant to gain the confidence to do that in a few hours?

The rest of his day was a blur, clouded by one thing. He was bombarded with every "what if" and struggling to keep up. He got home, pulled out his phone and typed the same message.

Hi, it's Stephen. With a p h

He stared at it, again. His mind kept racing. His heart was pounding. Was he sweating? He felt hot. What was going on?

Before he could talk himself out of it, he hit send and immediately dropped his arms, one dangling off his bed. The muted thud as his loosened grip gently dropped his phone on the floor. The phone no longer obstructing his view, he just stared at the ceiling and waited.

Everything went into overdrive as he waited. The short hit of adrenaline pumped through his veins as his heart thumped against his ribs. He painted his worries on the blank slate above him, waiting for the jury of sods to enact their justice.

Before he could get too carried away, a chime filled the room. Breaking him away from his demons, his hands patted the bed around him, until he remembered where it had ended up. He rolled over, letting himself fall to the floor.

The tiny dot of flashing light from his phone seemed larger when he was level with it. Almost like an emergency vehicle. He grabbed his phone and stared at the screen.

This must be SteVen, 'cos I'm pretty sure I asked StePHen to call me...

A lump in his throat as his body seemed to dry up immediately. He hadn't prepared for *this*. He'd spent so long thinking about that initial text, he didn't even consider the fact that he might have to reply. Everything became a blur as his mind calculated how the world would come to end now.

Before he could let this moment slip through his fingers and disappear forever, his hand shuddered. He wasn't cold. What was going on? And then the melody of his ringtone filled the room. He jolted at the noise, his phone jumping from his hand. The world faded to black as his eyes raced shut. His nose thrummed an ache.

"Fuuuuuuck..." he groaned, opening his eyes to a very obstructed ceiling.

"That's one way to say hi." A distant voice replied.

His eyes were wide open now, as he grabbed the phone and held it to his ear. "S-... Sorry. My phone fell on my face." He rubbed the bridge of his nose, deciding if he should nurse it or curse it.

Her laughter betrayed her words. "I'm sorry that happened to you!"

It was enough, though, to bring him calm. He was at ease once more. Maybe it was better this way. Don't allow his brain time to think and ruin everything. Let his mouth do the talking.

They talked for a while. About everything and nothing all at the same time. It was the start of their friendship. Adam forgave the world for wanting to self-destruct as he reassured it everything was okay.

The next few days were spent nurturing this new friend he'd made. He was picking up on her patterns. Frequency of texts, length of texts, her use of emotes. She would say something, he would try to think of a response as quickly as possible. He would reply, sometimes she would reply, sometimes it took a while. He definitely over-thought and over-analysed some things, but luckily he was self-aware enough to snap himself out of it... eventually.

He had such crazy thoughts about her, yet they'd only just met. He knew this too, but he allowed himself to dream. After all, how often does a queen befriend a cockroach?

It only took a few days for them to become good friends and she would quickly begin confiding in him. He didn't know why. The comfort of a stranger? Does that mean he had short-lived plans for him? Or maybe, probably, it was something to do with how conveniently around he was whenever she beckoned.

Whatever it was, he did his best to be there for her. It was all he could do really. He was in uncharted waters without a paddle or a sail, letting the waves take him where they pleased.

Chapter 2

She was still young and naïve, sheltered from the world.

"That's not how it went last time!" She protested.

"You're older than you were the last time you heard it, I figured you'd want the slightly more grown-up version." He retorted.

"Okay, just make sure there's a happy ever after." she demanded.

"Of course, I couldn't leave you upset." He bowed to her requests.

His phone rang one night. He checked who it was. It was her. Instantly, he picked up, only to be greeted by stifled sniffling.

"Are you okay? What happened?" He worried, grabbing his keys in case he was summoned.

"He dumped me." She barely managed to cry.

"Why?" He asked.

"I found out he was cheating on me." The faint noise of a cushioned punch into a pillow was heard.

"What? How?!" Adam fought back his anger.

"I saw them kissing in the park… He didn't try to hide it either. He said I wasn't giving him what he needed…"

"Kisses?" Adam's naivety would normally have been cute to her.

She shook her head as if he could see it. "A bit more than that… I just wanted to take it slow… Maybe I should've just…" She seemed hesitant.

"You never need to do anything you're not comfortable with, Eve. If he respected you, he would've given you the time you needed to be ready." Adam tried to reason with her.

"I don't know, I could've… been ready sooner."

"You're better than that, it's okay. How about we go out tomorrow so you can forget about all this?" He tried to cheer her up, desperately.

"Can you come over today?" She requested. "I need one of your hugs." She half-smiled through her tears, hopeful but knowing he'd say yes.

"I'll be there in ten minutes." He replied.

"But it's a twenty-minute walk." She replied, confused.

"I won't be walking." He smiled to himself.

"You're crazy." She sniffled out a laugh. "I'll be counting down starting… NOW!" She replied as she hung up, wiping away the tears.

He clambered to get his shoes on and sprinted out the door, making a beeline straight for her house. When he got there, out of breath, he held himself up by the rail as he walked up the short steps to her door. Lifting what felt like a cinderblock, his fist fell through the door as it opened before he could make contact.

"You're late."

He looked at his watch as he held himself up against the doorframe. "I…" He panted.

"…I…" He held up a finger to pause.

"…saved 8 minutes." He finally blurted out.

She shook her head smiling and then pulled him into the house. "You need to get into shape." She critiqued.

Adam waved to Eve's parents who'd overheard everything and were chuckling to themselves. They waved back as he crawled his way up the steps to Eve's room.

Adam collapsed on her bed, leaving no room for her, as she followed behind. She did not look pleased with his bed-hogging antics and jumped on top of him. He let out a groan but laughed through the subtle pain.

Eve made herself comfortable as she lay on Adam. She was smiling again, that's all he wanted. He gave her a tight hug, getting her prepared for the emotional outpour that was to come.

"Whenever you're ready, Eve, my ears are open and my shoulder is padded." He whispered to her.

She grabbed his shirt into a fist. "We got into another fight… But this time he said he was over me…" She choked on her words.

She hid her face in his shoulder, mumbling curses against his chest and letting the tears flow through, dampening his shirt and staining his skin. It was almost as if he could feel each drop, and they all stung. He wrapped his arms around her, rubbing her back slowly and gently, letting her empty out her heart.

Adam spent the night at Eve's house. Despite being their only child, Eve's parents didn't mind. They loved Adam. He had that courteous awkwardness to him, always asking to sleep on the sofa. Nobody knew if they would've minded if he slept in Eve's room, Eve definitely wouldn't have minded her teddy bear holding her back through the night, but he didn't want to step on anyone's toes, especially with Eve's family. He studied them for a bit initially, crafting the blueprint that made himself their perfect houseguest. They were so accustomed to having him over, it's as if he were part of the family.

Adam and Eve's parents had met through them two and became good friends just like their children. The parents could see Adam's love for Eve – who couldn't, really? – and they could only pray that she would feel the same. No-one knew though, and no-one asked. They didn't want to know the answer just in case it killed the dream. The only mention of it would be the inconsistent joke about the two getting married, a shared responsibility among the parents.

Adam woke up early the next day and made Eve's family breakfast. He knew everyone's favourites, but that knowledge didn't help him cook any better. A few burnt slices of toast, some overcooked eggs here and some strips of extra crispy bacon there. He tried, he would always try, for then nobody could say he didn't. He was improving with each attempt, but still not quite where he wanted to be.

They were all still sleeping, he knew they would be. He hoped it wouldn't take more than five minutes for them all to wake up but covered them up with whatever he could find to maintain the heat. Worst case scenario, they have to microwave an already okay breakfast and it's slightly worse. It wasn't hurting his chances at a Michelin star either way.

Sometimes he would make a small plate of extras and let the smell from it waft through the house. This time, though, he had used up all the necessary ingredients. No space for do-overs. They would taste his mistakes, but at least they were crafted with care.

He emptied his wallet onto a plate, definitely not enough to cover the damages. He quickly scribbled a little *"sorry for cleaning out your cupboards"* note and silently scurried out of the house. He had his own mother to screw breakfast up for, her own ingredients to waste.

Adam and Eve met up again the following night. He had offered to treat her, to make her forget her woes. They both walked, side-by-side, down the dimly lit trail towards the farm. Sometimes their conversations would just go on for hours, even entering completely nonsensical topics that they'd debate for way too long. Other times, they would just be completely silent, letting the dark night encompass them.

The silence made him a weird mix of comfortable and anxious. He would wonder what she was thinking. At the same time, though, he would just be happy she chose to spend her time with him. Everything revolved around her. *He* revolved around her. He was happy to take whatever he could get, almost to an unhealthy degree. But he was there for her, crafted to be hers.

"So, is this a date?" She broke the silence with a teasing smirk.

As nervous as she made him, even after all these years, he knew he had to fight back with confidence. He was prepared to fumble on his words and expose himself in his panic, but he would do so with a mask.

"No, definitely not. If it were a date, you wouldn't have to ask. It would be far more clad with cliché and the beauty wouldn't end at just you." He winked.

They both chuckled lightly and then silence befell him as he thought about it for a while, hoping she hadn't noticed. He kept a smile that wanted nothing more than to fade away to disguise his thought process.

"So, what would it be like if it were a date?" She asked, not giving him enough of a moment to get lost in his dream.

He bowed his head for a moment as he slowed his pace to allow Eve to step in front of him. "Well," he began, placing his palms on her shoulders and bringing her to a stop, closing in behind her.

After aligning himself, he let his hands fall all the way down her arms until his hands enveloped hers. He held her hands softly from behind and faintly rested his head on her left shoulder. All the while, Eve just watched his hands, unable to hide the smile caused by the blossoming caterpillars.

"We'd spend the morning during a glorious sunny day here." He waved their arms around, gesturing to the farm around them. "We'd feed some animals, stroke the really cute and fluffy ones, then trail off along the fields." He walked them forwards as he spoke. "Then we'd end up over there." He pointed to the silhouetted park across the lake.

"I'll have a picnic prepared for you, only the best for you, of course! Unevenly filled jam sandwiches *without* the crust and some sparkling water because we're so fancy. Pinkies up, of course. I'd definitely end up buying a cheese board but re-prepare it to make it look like I made it myself."

She broke a hand away to cover her mouth as she laughed, returning it to him when it subsided into a fixed smile. He was converting her to his dream.

"We'd lay in the sun for a little bit, talk some shit and I'd just get to admire how beautiful you are." He looked at the side of her face as he spoke, not letting her notice the pain in his eyes. "I'd tell you all the great things about you and make sure you recognised each one, even if you couldn't appreciate them."

"Yeah?" She broke him off, turning her head a little. "Like what, lover boy?"

"Like how your smile fills my world with colour, and how I would do anything to make sure it never left your face. I'd make myself a walking embarrassment if it meant I could hear you laugh every day." He nodded her back in the direction of the park, not wanting to lose himself in… her.

"We'd watch the sun set over the town on the top of the hill. And it would be okay 'cos you'd still be there to light up my world." He deflated against her cheek as he sighed. "And then we'd walk to that little rich-people area where those gorgeous ponds are."

"I love that place!" Eve exclaimed.

"We'd walk through there, greeting the stars in the reflection of the water. We'd struggle to see any fish, but maybe a swan or a duck. And then we'd walk over to that little sandy beach area by the river, and I'd paint the sky for you."

"Paint the sky?" She asked.

"Paint the sky." He answered. "The full moon would be there." Lifting her right hand slightly to the right of where they were now looking up into the sky. "Stars would be scattered everywhere. Not enough to make you feel insignificant, but enough to remind you of the limitless wonders the darkness hid. It would be like a child had been desperate to get the last bits of glitter out of the pot by violently shaking it; no real target for them, so long as the page sparkled that little bit more."

"You're crazy." She shook her head, the smile beginning to ache but the pain felt worth it.

"That's just the beginning. The sky would be so dark that you'd think it were black, but you'd stare longer and then realise that it wasn't quite there. It would be clear of clouds and markings, except one." He lifted her left hand to the far left of their view. "There would be a smudge of dark purple, as if an artist had run out of paint mid-stroke."

"Why purple?" She questioned.

"Why not?" He replied. "Purple is my favourite colour, and yours." He winked, realising that she couldn't see it. "We'll call it a parting gift from the sun as it faded into the darkness." He brought their hands to her belly, an excuse to give her a hug. "We would find ourselves lying in the sand, staring up at the sky. The purple is on the other side now. It's being pushed away by a hazy pink with some orange trailing just behind, as if it were a baby whale and the pink were its mother."

"What would the purple be?" She tried to throw him off.

"Uh... krill...?" He was semi-sure that made sense but hadn't planned for the intrusion.

He'd got a laugh out of her, and that was good enough for him. He had found himself in a moment of wonder, fuelled by hope and maybes. She just stared into the sky, trying to imagine it all. It wasn't awkward, somehow. They were both lost in their thoughts about the same thing from different lives, but he caught himself out and his mind was flooded with "what now?!"

He quickly let go of her hands and went back to her right side, clearing his throat as he did. Her hands momentarily rested where they were, remembering his touch and holding onto the warm imprints he'd left, and then gently fell to her side. He watched them fall as if they were snowflakes and it were his first snowfall. He smiled and then let gravity pull his head down. When he lifted it again, the smile had gone.

"Anyway, that's what would happen if it were a date, and I could play God for a night." He tried to laugh it off.

"That sounds like a pretty good date. You were right, I wouldn't have to ask." She smiled back at him, with a hollowness to it that only she could feel.

They both shook it out of their heads and carried on walking, dead straight. They'd found themselves on the trail that surrounded the farm. No matter what time, the farm was a hub of shortcuts, one with beautiful sights. Just as they were about to resume their walk through the trail, they noticed two figures.

At first, the figures seemed like normal pedestrians. They wouldn't have thought much of it until a blinding light had pierced Adam's eyes as it darted across his face. He squinted as the glare faded and he immediately noticed the strobing evil dancing up and down a slim line as its wielder's arms swayed casually.

The two figures turned around. Their faces were covered. Dark, sucking in any light that crossed them. The whites of their eyes seemed to float. They took a brief moment to figure out what to do and then swiftly ran up the path, like terrified mice. They were left, standing there, wondering whether to continue up the path or turn around.

"Let's just go b-." He began turning, only to be stopped by another two figures. "Oh, fuck..." He whispered to himself.

The two figures were slightly hunched, like primitive savages that had barely evolved. Adam noticed what they held in their hands. He found himself shielding Eve instinctively, although both were long enough to skewer them together. She tried to push him away but he just shook his head with very slight, stiff movements, daring not to look back.

The neanderthals walked slowly towards them. Were they calculating the risk or were they looking for a reward? One was obviously a leader but they both looked pretty similar. Were the guys they'd seen earlier on the same side or the guys these two were hoping to encounter?

"Seems like we've got a payday." The leader exclaimed.

He'd stopped in front of them as the other slowly circled around to make sure they had no escape. Eve watched the moving one, her back now against Adam's.

"She's a pretty nice one too." His buddy seemed a little too happy. "'Aven't 'ad a girl like this in a while."

"Just let her go and we can work something out." He gulped, determined not to show any fear.

The armed men stared at each other over the shoulders of their hostages. They took their time, almost as if to torture him with their silence.

Adam tried to control his breathing. He frantically patted Eve's sides as his hands blindly searched for hers. She clasped his hands with hers and they almost fused together.

"We don't even know what you look like." She tried to help with the negotiations.

The sidekick stepped right in front of Eve and pulled off his bandana, their noses separated by the safe barriers of a hair. "You do now."

"We won't say anything." Adam tried to plead.

The recessive goon slowly moved his head closer to Eve as she turned her lips away. He ran the back of his free hand across her cheek. Eve squirmed, causing Adam to jolt forwards, pulling her with him.

The leader had caught on to this and lifted his weapon. He placed it on Adam's cheek. It was cold. Adam closed his eyes and slightly bowed his head.

"Thanks to 'im, we've got a situation on our 'ands." He seemed to sigh. "Empty your pockets." The instructions were calm.

Eve freed herself from Adam's grip and began rummaging through her pockets. Adam was a little slower to comply, he just wanted to get Eve to safety.

"How do I know you guys will let us go?" He questioned, as the machete was pushed into his cheek by the movement of his jaw.

The leader shrugged. "Don't do anything stupid."

"Can I keep 'er?" A voice from behind Adam asked.

The anger in Adam's eyes quickly hit his face as the pair laughed at them. There's a very thin line between bravery and stupidity. Whether or not these two were serious about taking Eve was only known by themselves. Adam, however, was a little less keen to find out if they were just bad comedians or even bigger scumbags than he thought.

Eve shrieked and instantly suppressed herself as she felt a cold, bare hand running against her belly. It gripped her breast as she felt the pelvis of her captor thrust against her. They were finding out quickly.

Adam noticed this was off-script as the leader looked away for a second. He seemed off-guard. Adam thought this was his moment. He moved his head away from the machete quickly and reached for the handle. He'd managed to knock it free but it wasn't going to become a standoff.

He heard Eve cry aloud which was then followed by some rustling in the surrounding bushes. He couldn't see her though. His head fell forwards as his legs left the ground. He felt a body land on his, cushioning their fall but only adding to his pain.

This was quickly followed by a few hard kicks to the chest. Adam tried to curl up to protect his vitals but they didn't give him much space. He didn't care though. He was able to make out Eve running away in the distance. He smiled ever so slightly but this was quickly kicked away as more blows hit him.

Adam just closed his eyes. He was ready. He closed his eyes and let the numbness save him. Thankfully, the short five or so minutes of brutal, bloody kicks subsided. It had felt like hours. He could hear them breathing heavily as they took a moment. Adam couldn't feel much apart from the wind blowing cold against fresh blood leaving his body. Were they done?

No.

He could hear metal scraping against the hard concrete. He opened one eye and could see them coming towards him. He would've moved but it would've been pointless.

"We can't leave 'im here…"

"We can't take 'im! And if 'e survives this, you're screwed."

"Why me?!"

"You were the dumbass who showed 'is face. You keep thinkin' with your dick and it keeps causing problems for me. Your mess, you fix it."

"'E grabbed *your* knife. *I* saved *you*."

"And now you better get to saving yourself."

He heard the footsteps coming closer to him. He opened both eyes as he slowly turned his head to look up. He was blinded by that same light again. He was ready to go with it this time.

A ringing in his ears. A high-pitched scream. A familiar, annoying shriek. He covered his ears. How badly had they fucked him up?

And that was that. Or rather, almost that. Just before he gave up, he heard the heroes.

"POLICE, GET D-."

Chapter 3

She had taken it all as a warning, prepared but unaware.

"What happened to the criminals?" She asked.

"They got arrested, obviously." He pulled a face.

"Obviously, stupid. What happened after?" She replied, sighing.

"It's a story, use your imagination." He winked.

"I don't need to use my imagination if you're telling the story!" She shook her head, displeased.

"Everyone's a critic, eh?"

She rolled her eyes. "You'd get shutdown before you even opened."

"And you're going to get kicked out if you don't get a shift on." He hurried her to the door.

He squinted slightly as the bright lights bounced off her face. The infamous blue. He couldn't make out the look on her face, couldn't gauge how concerned to be. Her bottom lip was bleeding slightly from how much she'd bitten it.

He lost sight of her as two bodies stood in front of him. In his head, he was panicking to look around them. In actuality, he could barely move half the speed he wanted to catch her eyes again.

The two obstacles had parted like the Red Sea and there she was. Just standing there. Staring at him. Fidgeting with herself, unsure of what to do now.

She watched him struggle. She knew he wanted to be by her side. She knew he was willing any strength left in his body to break free of his shackles, to break free of his crumbling body, and to just reach her.

She took some steps towards him, watching as his expression changed. One from panic and desperation to one of confused hope. He was willing her closer. Closer. Please, closer. Just a few more steps, Eve. I'm right here, I'm not going anywhere.

She stood at his feet as they stared at each other. She just stayed still and said nothing. She wanted to grab him, but her hands were trembling. She wanted to speak to him, but her lips could barely manage a sound. He wanted to reach out and grab her but the straps on the gurney held him down. It's not like he could've managed anyway, his body had already given in.

He stared at her, shaking. His hands clenched into weak fists, through a pain that felt like his bones had turned to dust. But nothing hurt more than the aching his heart did. It thumped, begging for her. Pleading for her. It cried a deep, sad song, the pounding echoing through his body.

He watched her, unable to call out to her. His gaze was broken. She disappeared behind white. The doors closed and he was sped away, sirens screaming into the night. He closed his eyes, as he screamed with them. He closed his eyes and let the darkness take him.

He looked to his side and there she was, his guardian angel. "Hi, mum." He croaked to her.

She looked up, relieved. Letting out a sigh, she rushed towards him. She was halfway through throwing herself at him until she remembered his condition. He watched, smile not breaking. Her arms floated in the air as the hug she wanted to give was questioned.

"I get attacked and you won't even hug me, did you stop loving me?" He smiled at her, hoping she'd smile back.

He winced as she wrapped her arms around him. She tried to pull away but he rested his hand on her side to let her know it was okay, it was welcome and needed. The healing powers of his mother's hug.

She eventually let go and sat back, wiping a few tears as she did. She didn't know what to say. The one thing Adam hated was seeing his mother in tears; to him it was unjust and wrong. The only exception would be tears of happiness, of course.

"I'm okay, mum." He lay his hand flat as she rested her hand on his. "Tis but a scratch." He chuckled lightly and closed his eyes for a few seconds. "It hasn't been long, has it?"

"Only a day, doctors say you should be clear to go in a couple days." She tried to fight back more tears. "What happened?"

Before Adam could even think about answering, he felt a weight flung onto him. His eyes held shut as he groaned, but the weight didn't move. The light clanging of metal being hit let him know he was still awake at the very least. It was as if a large boa constrictor had starting to coil itself around him.

He opened his eyes and looked to his mum, hoping she had the answer he sought. She was somewhat smiling and mouthed the one name he was waiting to hear. Eve. She was here, she hadn't forgotten him.

He started coughing and she let go, arms still around him though. She pulled back a bit to check he was okay, only just realising what she had done.

"Holy shit, I'm so sorry. Are you okay?" She seemed mad at herself. "I'm so stupid, sorry Adam!"

Adam laughed. "I'm probably fine but I think you've just ruined the cleaner's day."

They all looked at the puddle of coffee on the floor that had only just trickled to the leg of Adam's bed. She had dropped the coffee she had gotten for Adam's mother as she speared herself into him, completely forgetting her hands were already occupied.

"Don't worry, I'll look for a mop." Adam's mother grinned.

Adam moved over slightly and let Eve accompany him in his temporary home. "What do you think?" He looked at her as he lifted an index finger and circled it. "Pretty sweet, eh?"

She laid her head on his shoulders and looked into his eyes. "It's nice but it could do with some decorating." She lay a hand on his belly as the other slid under him.

"Well, I guess you've had more of a chance to look at it than I have. Shall we take it?" He looked around, discovering the room for the first time.

"It's nice and cosy but I don't think there's enough space for the kids." She looked down at her hand that was drawling circles on his belly.

"I'm sure they'll be fine, this bed seems to be fitting us three now." He held her gaze as her eyes darted to his.

The world froze for a moment. Her finger just rest against his belly. It seemed as though they both had stopped breathing, neither of them even blinking. It all stopped. It was just them, in this moment, and the world was waiting for them.

"What did you say?" She asked.

"The three of us, why?"

"The thr-... How did you...?" She looked worried.

The smile dropped off his face. "Eve, you're not-." He looked at her belly and then back at her. "Are you?"

She stared at her feet. She didn't know what to say. It wasn't meant to happen yet, he wasn't meant to know. It was too soon, too early. She didn't even know properly herself.

"I might not be, I'm not sure. I haven't taken a test... I feel different though."

"Do you know who the father is?" He leaned a hand on her side.

She nodded. "He doesn't know though, and I won't say anything until I know."

"Do you think he'll want to keep it if you are? Will he step up?"

She shrugged, trying to avoid his concerned eyes. "I don't know, probably not..."

He moved his left hand under her chin and turned her head towards his face. "We'll figure it out."

"We?" She raised an eyebrow. "It's not yours... You know how babies are made, right?"

He grinned, holding back a laugh that would otherwise cause him injury. "We're a team. You're not alone in this, if you are pregnant. If he won't step up, someone has to. I've always had your back; I'm not going when you'll need it most."

A whole new world opened up in her head, one where Adam was the father of her child. Not one she had ever given much thought, but he had brought her into his dream and now the wave was carrying her too. Just like him, directionless and fuelled by nothing but the desire to not drown.

She nodded slowly, looking down again. She felt him pull her closer and then a warmth met her forehead. He kissed her softly and then pulled away.

"We'll figure it out." He said as he lay his head back and closed his eyes.

"Figure what out?" His mum had returned with Eve's parents, a cleaner and some more coffee.

"How to fight monkeys with jetpacks." Adam responded, eyes still closed.

Before anyone could begin that debate, he fell asleep. He rested. He didn't even notice Eve's parents walking behind his mother, but nobody wanted to disturb him now. He was a hero, her hero. He'd paid her back for one. Just one more to go... One more and his debt was paid. He'd be free. And yet, he knew he'd still be bound to her.

Chapter 4

She was hooked on these stories, using them as guidance as well as inspiration for her own dreams.

"Maybe I'm pregnant." She began. "I feel different too."

He looked at her. "You aren't getting out of school that easily; you can both learn in the same classes."

"I don't think they'd allow that." She fought back.

"Well, I'm not allowing you to be pregnant."

She shrugged. "Maybe I'll be the next Virgin Mary and we'll see what you're allowing."

"May He smite me now if that's the plan 'cos I won't let him get far." He laughed.

She watched his middle fingers dance in little rings as he pressed them into his temple. His thumbs help up his head, pressed deep into his cheekbone. His sigh opened his eyes.

"He's not worth it, Eve." Were the only words he could find.

He hadn't been long out of the hospital and Eve was already ready to return things to how they were. The equilibrium had to be restored. It wasn't going to be as easy as shedding blood and bones for her.

"He could be…" She began her defence. "He can change, I can see it."

He lifted his head away from his fingers to look her in the eyes. "You can't be with someone just to try to change them, Eve. You can't just try to think you can *fix* people. That's not how it works." This was the first time in a while he'd shocked her. "In trying to fix him, he will break you. And *maybe* you'll get to the point where he's the guy you want, but will you still be the girl he wants?"

He watched her closely, studying her. She avoided his gaze. They'd been through this spiel before and each time he believed he could get through to her. Her only response was a shrug.

"Eve." He summoned her eyes once more. "It's not about trying to put a square in a circle hole. You're trying to change the square *into* a circle. That takes time and effort, but you didn't pick the square because it was a circle, you picked it because it was a square. It's okay to want the square. Just don't try to fool yourself that it's something it isn't. You can angle the square a little differently and it might fit into the circle hole, or maybe it won't fit at all. But if you want the square, it's easier to just put it into a square-shaped hole." His voice was soft, a velvet knife cutting through her.

She nodded; she knew what he meant. He was probably right. Her ideas of love were always easy and free, but the reality seemed anything but.

He grabbed her hands with both of his. "You saved me twice when you barely knew me. Maybe it's time we save you, Eve." His voice was shaky, ready to beg her.

"It's not always that simple, Adam. If I don't give him a chance to be a circle…"

"You've given him plenty. He's shown you he's not a circle. Do you want a circle, or do you want a square?" He sighed. "All the chances you've given to people, but when are you going to give yourself a chance?"

"A chance for what?"

"A chance…" He closed his eyes for a moment, preparing his words. "A chance to be happy, Eve… Just let yourself even try to be happy." His head dropped.

"I'm not doing this to be miserable, Adam. I'm trying, I swear I am. It's just… way more complicated than that." She leaned in, her forehead resting on the top of his head.

"It's a simple situation made complicated. Why are you like this, Eve?" The question was innocent, but it seemed bitter.

She lifted her head. "I'm not like anything, Adam." She spoke, stern. "I'm not the only person who just wants to be loved. I'm not the only person who wants to be wanted, to be desired. I want somebody to smile when they wake up next to me, and for them to crave my touch before they go to sleep. I just want someone whose kiss will make the world around us stop existing. I want to love someone and for them to love me too. I don't wanna feel lonely. I just want to be happy, but there's no shortcuts to happiness, Adam. Everyone makes it look easy, so why is it anything but?!"

"I'm sorry… I didn't mean it like that, Eve." He lifted his head to look at her. "You've always been one of the most popular girls around. You could have any guy you wanted. Why are you going for the ones that don't deserve you? Why are you doing this to yourself? You don't need to find happiness in someone else!" He was pleading now.

Her shoulders answered for her again. "Maybe it's just something I have to do. It's the path I've chosen."

"Trial and error is fine, but you're meant to learn from your mistakes. You seem to have condemned yourself to them." He shook his head slowly.

"I know you love me." She whispered into his ear.

He stopped entirely. They had told each other those words before, but there was a venom behind what she had just said. It was different. It was fierce. It felt like his heart had stopped. His mind became vacant for the first time since he was a child. His body became an empty vessel with nothing but her words echoing through it.

"I know you're *in* love with me, Adam." She repeated. "But that doesn't give you the right to tell me who to love or how to love. I'm not yours, not how you want me to be, and you can't make me be yours. *I don't love you, Adam.*"

Her venom had struck, poisoning his body. His muscles tensed, freezing him in place. She could snap him right now if she wanted. He was ready to shatter, the cracks flowing through him like harsh rivers. He wasn't ready for the world to know, but now it lay bare before him. They all knew. And now he was forced to confront it.

Before he had a chance to reassemble himself, Eve got up and walked away. She just left him there, ready to crumble herself. She ran out the door, her body shivering.

Her steps quickly became echoes until they too were replaced by silence. A tear snaked its way down the side of his face. The rivulet revived him, as he pieced himself back together as quickly as he could.

She wandered aimlessly for a short while, reliving it in her head. How had it gone so wrong so quickly? She had just wanted him to console her how he normally would, the same way he'd done before. But she knew she'd gone too far.

Like a drunk, she found herself back home with no idea how she'd got there. She sought out her mother, throwing herself at her and giving her no time to catch her.

It all overwhelmed her now, as she blubbered to her mother. It hurt her now. She'd lost that coldness she didn't know she had. It felt like a superpower, but she hadn't yet learned how to control it.

"He didn't mean it, honey." She rocked with her child in her arms. "He was just trying to look after you. He wants the best for you, just like I do."

"Did I mess up?" Eve sniffled, worried about what might happen.

"Maybe, but the bigger mistake would be to not try to make amends. That's… if you want to make amends." Her mother was a little cautious.

She loved Adam. He was almost like another child to Eve's parents. They knew he cared greatly for their daughter. He seemed to be a good friend to her, and there were occasional whispers that he might even be a great husband to her one day. That made this a sensitive issue for them.

While they wanted the best for Eve, they also cared immensely for him too. They wanted the best for him. How could they navigate this without compromising either of them?

"I don't want to lose him." Her voice was almost a whisper.

"He's young, Eve. You're both so young. And you were right, nobody prepares you for love. There's no cheat sheet, no guide, not even a rulebook. It's the scariest thing you have to deal with in life." She rubbed Eve's head, soothing her sobs into sniffles. "Nobody knows what they're doing. I've been with your dad for twelve years and it seems like he doesn't know what he's doing half the time!" She managed to sneak a grin on Eve's face. "In trying to protect you, he hurt you. That was wrong. You both hurt each other. I know you love him, even if it is as friends, or even like a brother. Unfortunately, with love comes pain. But you strengthen the bond by dealing with the pain. If you want to keep him in your life, you guys need to talk. About everything."

Eve's mother seemed relieved. Children dating is always a nerve-wracking time for the parents, and she had no plan for navigating this. Where was her cheat sheet? She seemed pleased with what she'd said. It was only proving her point. She loved her daughter and still had no idea what she was doing.

"Mum, I need to tell you something that scares me." She looked up at her mother, her lips quivering.

The pat on the back her mother was giving herself was short-lived. Now, she was worried again.

"I think... I think I might take him for granted sometimes." Eve's voice was dry as the words scraped out, her realisation overcome with shame.

Her mother seemed to ease up at this, though, as she squeezed her daughter tightly. "Oh, my love! What are you going to do about it?" She asked.

"Huh?" Eve was stunned, not expecting that kind of a response, least of all with glee.

"If you think you've taken him for granted, it shows you do care. You value him and all he's done for you. You both really need to sit down and talk to each other about each other."

"What if he hates me?" Eve was concerned.

"If he hates you that easily, he never loved you." A deeper voice replied from behind.

Eve felt a hand on her shoulder. It squeezed gently, reassuringly. She turned to see her father, biting into an apple as he looked down at her.

"He doesn't hate you. He might be sad, or he might even be angry. He won't hate you though." He smiled down at her. "Your mum is right; I don't know what I'm doing half the time. All I know is that I love her. Sometimes I'll make mistakes, sometimes she'll make mista-... sometimes I'll make mistakes." He winked at Eve as he side-eyed her mother. "The important thing is to right the wrongs. And there have definitely been times where your mother has seemed like she hated me, but it's only because she loves me so much. The anger, frustration, and disappointment when you love someone sometimes comes across as hate, but it's just the other side of love."

"I make mistakes too." Her mother whispered into her ear. "Nobody's perfect. No relationship is perfect. But they require work. You will have to go through hardships in a relationship, and how you navigate those rough patches are what defines the bond you have. You are not defined by your good moments, but the ones you'd rather forget."

"I wish you'd forget some of them..." Her father mumbled, winning a smile from Eve.

Her mother gently flicked his arm, as he managed to get a slight grin from her too. He leaned over and hugged them both.

Eve broke away from them, wiping away the crusted tears from her face. She had a mission now and she was going to complete it. She ran to her room to prepare herself, wanting to get it done sooner rather than later.

Every second she thought she might lose Adam was daunting. She needed to know, needed him back before it was too late. He was worth it.

A rumble shook her bones. She peered out her window. Not now, not now! She closed her eyes to pray. Not now. The violent applause of rain hitting concrete let her know there was no god to answer her calls this time. The clouds barraged the city, but it felt personal. Why were they trying to keep her from him?

It didn't matter. She was determined. It had to be now. She was going now. She cut her preparation short, the rain would only ruin it. She threw on whatever barrier she could and sprinted out the door before her parents could try to delay her. It had to be now.

Chapter 5

She was learning more than ever about life, shielded from the realities of the world.

"You can't cut it off there! What did she do?!" She shouted, forgetting who the story was about.

"Tomorrow. Go to sleep, you've got an exam tomorrow." He replied as he turned off her light and closed the door.

"I bet this is the cliché ending where she shows up at his door drenched and it's the happy ever after." She shouted back.

He walked away without acknowledging her, not wanting to entertain her attempts to stay awake. Not every story has to have a happy ever after, right?

He was slow to the door. His mother had gone out and he wasn't expecting anyone – especially not in this weather. Anyone at his door right now was either crazy or really trying to get a sale. He dragged his feet to the door, peering through the peephole to determine if it was worth even opening the door.

He saw her standing there, head down, shivering. His eyes felt like they were trying to jump out from their sockets. His pace was the complete opposite now as he rushed to open the door and pull her in, not even waiting for her to acknowledge the door being open.

"Where's your jacket, it's raining?!" He exclaimed, a tinge of guilt sinking in for extending her stay with the rain.

He rushed to the bathroom, grabbing as many towels as he could. The only other person who lived in this house was his mother, would they even have enough towels? He stopped trying to keep count, grabbing as many as he could and then running back to her.

She was still at the door, head still down. The shivering felt like it had gotten worse. He started throwing towels all over her. One landed on her head, another draped over her shoulder. One fell to the floor as he threw it on the other shoulder, but she made no effort to keep it there. He tried to dry her as she just stood there. She didn't even try to help. She was just shivering, it was all she could do.

She went from embracing by the clouds to smothered by towels in seconds. The thorough pats were coming from a different side each second. Still, she just stood there, letting him dry off his guilt.

Her lips began trembling. As much as she was avoiding looking at anything, he was at her feet, trying to keep her warm and dry. Her body shook more, as if ready to explode.

His hands, masked by towels, took no notice as they slaved away. As if they were ants, they marched on and dried her off as quickly as he could. When he had done what he could, he dragged her into the living room.

"I'm getting you a change of clothes." He announced, not waiting for a response.

He ran upstairs and rummaged through cupboards, trying to find clothes he could give her. He grabbed a top of his and some shorts. He didn't fancy invading his mother's underwear drawer so he just grabbed some clean boxers and hoped that would suffice. As he headed back towards the living room, he grabbed a hoodie from the back of his door and hurried back to the queen.

"Here." He dropped the clothes on a chair and walked towards the windows. "I would offer a hand but this bit is on you." He laughed to himself as he closed the curtains and stepped out of the room.

She just stood there. She didn't want to move. Her mind was just lost. A million questions trying to cram themselves into her mind, fighting for attention. She had no answers for any of them.

"Eve, what are you doing?" He walked back into the room after not hearing anything for a couple minutes.

That was enough to break her. She wasn't shivering from the cold – she'd been numb to it. She was shaking because all she wanted to do was cry. And so she broke, with little effort, despite her attempts to hold herself together.

"Eve, it's okay." He ran over to her.

Without thinking, he wrapped his arms around her. She buried her head into his chest, the shaking seemingly stopping instantly. She held him tight, almost uncomfortably so, refusing to let him go as she sobbed against his chest.

"It's okay, Eve, it's okay." He whispered repeatedly, as if he were a parent consoling their child.

Her damp clothes seeped through to his, but her tears are what stained him. The warmth of her tears burned into his chest as he did his best to comfort her.

After a couple long minutes, Eve's rivers dried up, but she still cried into his chest a little longer. He could feel her easing up, and he was ready to leap back into action.

"I was going to step out into the rain but I'm thankful you brought it to me instead!" He joked, looking down at her.

She sniffled, trying to fight the grin that was taking over her face. It wasn't even a great joke; she had no idea why she gave away her smile so easily.

He snuck out from her grasp and moved his hands to her arms. "We need to get you out of those clothes, Eve." He paused a second. "Uhhh... respectfully, of course. And into those dry ones. You'll get sick otherwise."

She shook her head. He'd stolen another smile with his stupid awkwardness. She didn't move though. He may have painted a smile on her, but that's all it was: painted. The canvas was still smothered with sorrow.

Adam shadowed her, shaking his head as he stepped in front of her. "Don't take this the wrong way, but are you wearing a bra?" He asked her.

The slight motion of her head was enough to give away a nod. That was good enough for him. It was a race against time and she'd probably stop him one way or another if she wasn't okay with it, right?

He picked up a towel from before and threw it over his shoulder. He pinched the corners of her top and gently pulled them away from her. It was like he was peeling the casing away from a sausage, but it broke the hold the soaked clothes had on her.

He let go of one side and slid the towel in below the other. He pinched his way along the bottom of the top, sliding the towel in behind it. His hands worked cautiously around her body, doing his best to avoid touching her skin as if he'd leave a mark.

When the towel was sufficiently around her, he began to pull it up, the t-shirt trying its best to hold on. Like a parasite, it felt like it was fighting for its life. As if it hadn't taken enough from her. Eve began to cooperate, her hands holding up the towel as he pried the leech off her.

She managed to free both hands independently, her head the last to be rescued. It looked like she was being birthed again, the t-shirt shrinking around her neck, heavy with rain. Adam pulled, gently at first and then a little less so when it wouldn't give in. The top kissed her skin goodbye as he managed to rip it away from her, almost expecting a 'pop' as it did so. It plopped to the ground like an octopus as Adam watched his adversary drop.

He turned to face her again, something catching his eye. She had a tattoo on her right shoulder. When did she get that? He tried not to stare, with other pressing things to tend to, but he couldn't help but be curious. The splodge of black burned into his memory, no matter how much he tried to dispel it. He shook it out of his mind as he returned to his focus.

He chucked his slightly-too-large top over her head and pulled it down with one motion. Eve didn't even get her arms through the arm holes. Rushing to get her out of the drenched clothes, he pulled down her trousers, keeping his eyes down and hoping the towel would drop far enough to suffice.

"Eve. This is as far as I'll go." He avoided looking at her "Can you promise me you'll change this time?" He asked.

She nodded slowly. "Yes." She croaked.

He smiled and turned away from her. "I haven't got any bras and didn't fancy nicking my mum's. Hopefully the baggy clothes will do enough, else… we'll figure something out." He felt like he was speaking to himself.

Eve wanted to reply. She wanted to thank him, to let him know it was fine. Then she wanted to thank him again for not giving up on her. She opened her mouth but nothing came out, not so much as a raspy breath. Adam nodded to himself in the silence and left the room.

A few minutes passed and he was given the all-clear, although he'd probably seen enough already to make it redundant. He wanted to apologise for invading her privacy, he felt dirty for it. He walked back in and bundled up all the wet clothes that seemed to be nothing more than rags now. He threw them into the wash basket and returned to Eve.

She was sitting down, twiddling her thumbs nervously. She clearly had something on her mind. Adam watched her for a moment, not sure if she was going to break the silence or if she was waiting for him to do it.

He finally took a seat beside her. He scanned her body for any parts that might still be wet. He reached over for a towel and placed it over her hair, getting ready to be a cheap hairdryer.

"I'm" they both began at the same time. "sorry." They both finished together.

Eve looked at him confused, as he mirrored her confusion. "Why are you sorry?" Her voice a whisper.

"I just… With the clothes… I probably should've asked but…" His lips fumbling the sentences his brain was feeding them.

"Oh." She seemed taken aback by that. "It's okay. I-."

"You don't need to be sorry." He cut her off. "I'm not mad. You were right. Maybe I'm too one-sided to be giving you any sort of advice."

She didn't know what to say to that. He was conceding before she could take it back. She had planned a whole speech in her mind, one that had disappeared the moment he opened the door. It wasn't meant to be this easy.

"I need you to know, Adam, I do appreciate everything you've done for me." He tried to interject but she raised her hand to stop him. "All the time and energy you spend on me. The effort and care you've shown me. I know I've definitely taken you for granted. But I need you to know, I do appreciate you." Her hand fell back to her lap.

Now Adam was lost for words. His heart ached, those words hurt him for some reason. He couldn't explain why, but they jabbed at his soul. He just nodded. He didn't know what else to do, but he welcomed the apology.

The silence sat with them. Both had said something, although maybe not entirely what they thought would be spoken. Was this it?

He cleared his throat.

"I'm in love with you, Eve." He seemed ashamed to admit it. "I think I always have been…"

Eve sighed lightly. "I know, Adam." She placed a hand on his. "I just…"

"It doesn't change anything. I'm still here for you, as a friend. I'll get through this, don't worry." His voice trailed off a little.

"We'll get through this." She gave him a reassuring smile, grabbing both of his hands.

He nodded, smiling back at her. "We'll get through this."

They spoke of it as if it were a disease. Did it need to be cured? Was he broken? His love became a burden, but it was also his fuel. He needed it, he needed to keep burning for her. He'd been cursed.

Before his mind could run with the demons that taunted him, he afforded himself a mercy. One thing to break away from this before he dwelled on it too long.

"What's that tattoo? On your shoulder?" He asked.

"Oh, you saw it?" She thought for a moment. "It's easier if you just see it."

She pulled the clothes away from her left shoulder to reveal the splodge again. Adam got up and stood beside her, staring deep into it.

It was a butterfly, wings spread wide and proud, like it knew its beauty. It was a deep, dark black. One that pulled you in and threatened to capture you in an everlasting, ever-falling void. The darkness was disturbed in the middle. A sharp, bright white, the purest light the heavens could muster, cutting straight through it. His eyes chased it, all the way around, realising it was the shape of a heart separated right down the middle. Broken? Or never whole? He caught dabs of orange either side of the butterfly's body. And then he realised. The outlines were swans, the orange being the beaks kissing the butterfly's body. He traced the necks back down to the bottom wings, where the same shade of pure white met him with streaks of chasmic black. The swan's bodies. It was certainly a unique sight.

"I don't know why I got this, to be honest. But it means something to me. I don't know how that works... I don't know where it came from or why, but it's mine." She explained.

"Not everything needs to be justified, Eve. It's amazing. Perfect, even." He couldn't look away from it.

"It's a little fucked up, I need to get it finished properly." She shrugged.

"So it's perfuckt." He smiled down at her.

"Perfuckt. I'll take it." She smiled. "Are you done staring? You'd have thought you'd seen enough today!" She teased him.

He swiftly turned his attention to a wall, making Eve laugh a little. She let the clothes cover her shoulder again and pulled Adam onto her, hugging him tight.

"Thank you."

"For what?" He quizzed.

She shrugged. "Being you." She lay her head on his chest once more, taking in his warmth.

He tried to hide his blush, his years of learned vocabulary seeming to disappear from his mind. He tried to not let her words get to him.

"Why aren't the swans kissing?" He tried to distract her.

A mild sadness seemed to envelop her. "I think it's better that way..." She stopped to think a moment. "You know how swans mate for life?" She asked, as Adam nodded. "Imagine if you found your soulmate, your one true love, your swan... Imagine harbouring all the love you ever could love for someone, and then not being able to touch them. Being separated, prevented from being able to feel each other's affection physically. And all you desire... crave... yearn for... is their touch. You know they could make your life better just by touching you. Their hugs could hold you together, their kisses could glue you together again. Their touch could fix you, and you could feel it. You want nothing more to feel it... But you can't... There's a beauty to that sadness. Especially when they don't give up. They try anyway. Even though there's a barrier between them, they're still trying to reach each other. They can feel each other through that barrier, just through the other ways in which they can express their love. Through their words, through their dreams... Through their hope. Until, finally, there they are. Right in front of each other. Within each other's grasp... And it's so much more than they could've ever imagined. They never want to let go. They do everything to just hold on, to never ever ever let go... All their strength, all their power, all their energy just going into holding on. But they get separated again. They have to let go. For now, they have to let go... The only time they can touch is when their warden is resting... And they're hidden from the world. In their own little world. Going from being exposed to everything, where everyone can see the pain in their separation. The pain in their love. To suddenly being able to be together and nobody can see a damn thing. Can you imagine that? Counting down that timer... It would drive you crazy. The passion it builds, the intensity it invokes... Not even in a sexual way, either... Just how intimate that hug would feel... Knowing you'll have to let go eventually, be stuck behind that barrier again. It'll never feel like enough... but it's all they have, so it's enough for them. I think it's beautiful. It's sad, gut-wrenching, but it's beautiful. I want that kind of love..."

Eve seemed to get lost in her words. Adam seemed to vanish among them too. It was the first time he'd ever heard her speak like that, and she had captivated him. They were both hostages to the thought of that forbidden love. Two hopeless romantics, trapped in their hunger for love.

The lock on the main door clacked, announcing the return of his mother. They both turned their attention to the front door, Adam jumping up. His mother entered the house to the chorus of the clouds, hurrying away from the downpour.

She turned and noticed them both in the living room looking at her. "I'm not interrupting, am I?" She had just about noticed Eve seemed to be in Adam's clothes.

"It's your house, mum." Adam shook his head.

"Good, 'cos I've got food." She replied, lifting two bags that filled the house with the familiar smell of fish and chips. "Also brought a few guests along." She proclaimed as she walked into the kitchen.

Adam turned his attention to the door. Eve's parents straggled behind but eventually made it into the house. Adam and Eve watched her parents, as her parents watched them back. They noticed Eve was in different clothes, but nobody said anything.

"Adam," Eve's father stood by the door. "Can I have a quick word?" He asked, signalling Adam to follow him.

"Out there?" He looked disappointed to being asked to walk out into that.

"It won't be long, I promise. And I've got an umbrella!" He dangled the umbrella out the door.

Eve's father stepped outside as Adam looked around to see if anyone else had noticed. It was strange. Nobody seemed to pay it any attention, just him. And maybe it was just him who thought it was strange. He begrudgingly stepped out into the rain.

"Sure..." Adam seemed a bit surprised but left Eve and her mother as he followed.

Eve's father never really spoke to Adam alone. Not that there was any tension between them. They both cared for each other and admired one another. It was just one of those things that never happened. They were always with someone else. It led Adam to wonder what would happen. What was so important? What had he done? Was it about Eve?

Chapter 6

She was still trying to figure out what love and lust were, the distinction became a hushed secret from adults.

"I guess, you could say the difference between love and lust is one is physical, and the other is... everything. Lust is attraction, it's a desire to be with someone, to feel them. Love is engrossing. It will take over every part of you. It becomes your purpose, your addiction. When you fall in love, you'll know. It will be the scariest thing you'll ever go through, but also one of the best. When you fall in lust, there's a chance you could confuse it for love. But all it takes is something as small as someone simply opening their mouth to know which has you by the throat." He tried to explain.

"Judging by your story and your poetry, it sounds worse than that!" She half-giggled, bearing the truth in mind. "So, did Adam want Eve to be his girlfriend?"

"Yes and no." He smiled at the vagueness.

"That really cleared it up." She pouted.

He sighed. "All in good time."

She knocked on the door expectantly. It had only been a few days since their falling out, but things had seemingly returned to normal. Everything felt right about the world again. The equilibrium had been restored.

"Hey Eve!" Adam's mother opened the door. "How are you?"

Adam's mother welcomed her in. Eve seemed a little disappointed but managed to hide the most of it.

"I'm alright thanks, how are you?" She walked in, trying to look for Adam.

"Yeah, good thanks, little busy." Adam's mother answered, closing the door behind Eve.

Eve stared around the house, trying to look for clues on Adam's whereabouts. She couldn't hear any other footsteps in the house that would indicate he was home. Strange, he hadn't mentioned he was going out. Granted, she hadn't told him she would be visiting.

Then the waft caught her. Her nostril flared, hooked by the scent. She took a moment to study it, letting it swirl in the back of her throat like a sommelier with their wine.

She turned; the scent pulled her towards its source. That's when she noticed. Adam's mother was dressed up in a way she'd never seen before.

"Oh, I didn't realise you were going out. Sorry." Eve seemed stunned.

"It's okay, how do I look?" She giggled a little in response.

Eve took this as an opportunity to stare a little longer. Her eyes looked her up and down, as Adam's mother adjusted the fit in places. There was a new admiration for her. She'd always just seen her as a mother, but there was a whole other woman she had yet to meet.

"You… look amazing." Eve finally answered her.

"Really? It's not too much?" She seemed a little anxious.

"No, no. You look great. We might have to go clothes shopping sometime soon if you've got this hidden away! Are you..." Eve hesitated, but her curiosity got the better of her. "Are you going on a date?"

Adam's mother's gaze shot up to meet Eve's eyes. Eve jumped, as if her eyes had hit her with a physical weight. She wasn't sure what expression was on her face, but she was making Eve nervous. She was ready to trip on her words to try to make this right.

Eve tried to fumble a sentence, but she could only make noises. Her brain had abandoned her, her mouth had betrayed her, she was readying herself for the slaughter. She had never seen Adam's mother in any mood that wasn't happy. What was she like when she was angry? How bad could she get?

And before she could panic any more, the room filled with a hearty laughter. She just started laughing, uncontrollably, as Eve's nervousness turned into confusion.

"We're going to see Adam's grandmother." Adam's mother managed to collect herself to correct Eve. "Maybe this is too much."

The relief washed over Eve; her whole body deflated of tension. "You don't need to change, you do look amazing. She'll love it!"

Adam's mother thought on it a moment. "If I get in trouble, I'm dragging you with me!" She nodded and smiled. "Have you met his grandmother?" She asked, thinking on it as she did.

"Um... I don't think so...? No, I haven't."

"Do you want to come? Adam will be there, I'm assuming you came for him. Surprised he didn't mention we were going." Adam's mother nodded to herself.

"Uhhh… I…" Eve was caught off once more, she had never seen this coming.

"I'm sure he's told her a lot about you, and she'll be happy to meet you!" Adam's mother tried to reassure Eve.

"Sure, why not?" Eve finally relented.

"Great, we'll head over shortly. Adam left already."

Eve questioned how she'd managed to find herself in this position from just showing up unannounced to Adam's house. She had never made any plans to meet his extended family, despite how Adam had spoken about them on occasion. She was going to make the most of it though, see if she could get any juicy stories about Adam to tease him with later on.

They approached the house. It seemed small on the outside, small and quaint. She wondered what mysteries lay between the walls. Adam's mother stepped ahead to knock on the door as Eve hung back a little, still taking in the surroundings. She had no idea what to expect, but this wasn't it.

The door creaked open. The greetings between his mother and grandmother seemed faint as the nerves crept in. The sound of her name freed her from her thoughts.

"Hi." Eve smiled anxiously.

"Ah, so this is the infamous Eve." His grandmother beckoned her forwards with a welcoming grin. "Come, come, I've been waiting to meet you!"

His grandmother was just like the house. Small and quaint. Eve walked through the door of the antique house, between his grandmother and mother. Almost like she was being marched. Her eyes darted around the short hallway. There were pictures hung all over the walls, gateways into a distant past. The memories lingered in the house, you could almost feel them with each step.

"Take a seat, dear!" Adam's grandmother had led her into the living room.

Eve sat close to the door. She knew she was under no threat, but the worries creeping in made her feel like a hostage. This unsuspecting, frail woman somehow possessed the strength of a mountain with nothing but a smile.

"No Adam?" His mother quizzed.

"No, he called me though. He's just doing some shopping. Should be here shortly." Adam's grandmother sat across her.

Adam's mother sat beside Eve. She could tell Eve was tense and she wanted to offer her some comfort.

"Adam spoke about how beautiful you were, but I think he may have undersold you!" She chortled, a weak voice with a strong laugh.

Eve felt a smile take over her face. She didn't know if it was the compliment, or just the way she laughed, but something filled her with warmth. She could feel the stress alleviate itself.

"Thank you. Between you and his mother, I can see where he gets his good looks from." Eve tried to return the compliment.

His grandmother waved her hands, preventing the words from reaching her as she wafted them away. "No, no. He got his looks from his parents." She gave Adam's mother the full praise, causing her to blush. "I bet she worried about how she'd look today, right? But she's always been stunning!"

Eve wondered how she had ever been afraid of her. Within a couple minutes of meeting her, she was showering the room with joy, almost as if she enjoyed the challenge of trying to make them blush. How had a wrinkled, tiny, delicate woman seemed so intimidating?

"Tell me about yourself, dear. Adam's told me plenty but I think he might be biased." She grinned.

It seemed like an interview, but she didn't feel the pressure of an interrogation. She felt warm, as she talked a little about herself. His grandmother coaxing information out of her, listening intently and taking it all in.

"I knew Adam would pick great friends." She nodded.

Adam's mother looked at Eve, noticing how relaxed she was. "Speaking of, I'm going to find out where he is. He should've been here by now. I won't be a minute." She stood and left the room.

"Don't worry, dear, I won't bite." Adam's grandmother grinned. "I've got no teeth!" She chuckled to herself.

Eve choked on a laugh. She was definitely an interesting woman, and she had an opportunity now. She just wondered how best to take advantage of it.

"What's the most embarrassing thing Adam's ever done?" She grinned menacingly.

"I like how you think." Adam's grandmother closed her eyes with a smile. "Let's find a good one for you." She seemed to be searching the filing cabinet in her brain for an answer, talking to herself as she did. "He'd never forgive me if I told you this one. That one's not funny. Typical poop story... Ah!" Her eyes opened. "I've got one."

Eve leaned forwards, ready to file this all away herself. Before anything could begin, though, they were interrupted.

"He'll be here soon, he stopped by his grandfather's grave." Adam's mother returned.

Something about that felt off to Eve. There was something wrong there, but she couldn't figure out what it was.

"Does he still feel guilty?" His grandmother croaked.

Adam's mother shrugged. "He doesn't like talking about it. I don't want to push him."

His grandmother nodded. "Probably for the best... He knows we're here for him, hopefully he will come to us if he needs us." She rubbed her forearms, as if she were trying to comfort herself.

"When did he... pass?" Eve asked, putting it all together.

"Last year. Mid November." His mother and grandmother's heads dropped, their eyes falling to the carpet as his grandmother answered. "He had a heart attack." She quivered; her voice had become fragile.

"And he didn't go to the funeral?" Eve looked between them.

"No, something came up. Nobody knows what but he said it was important. Something he couldn't miss." Adam's mother answered. "He won't speak to me about it, but I think he regrets not being there." Her voice had softened too.

The pieces fell together in her head. She knew. But she couldn't let them know. She couldn't let them find out, not like this.

"I... I can try to speak to him." Her voice was faint.

She felt a hand cover hers. "I think we just let him process it how he needs to for now." Adam's mother looked at Eve. "I'm sure he'll tell us when he's ready." She rubbed the back of Eve's thumb with hers.

Eve nodded slowly. She knew. She cursed him in her head, an anger building inside her. Argh, why was he like this? What was wrong with him? She wanted to scream, but then it enveloped her. The guilt trapped her, smothering the enraged flames within her. She had gone from burning to freezing within mere moments.

It was her fault.

Adam arrived at the door. The house seemed quiet. The living room window was slightly ajar, but no sound escaped it. Not even a muffle. He knew they were in there, but he couldn't hear anything. Maybe they were further in the house.

He reached into his pocket, looking for the keys. No metal teeth greeted his hands like they normally would. He dropped the bags to free his other hand so he could search amongst himself.

He patted himself, looking through the most obvious places he may have put them. Not his front pockets. Not his back pockets. His hands fumbled over his body until he thumbed his ribs with something.

He stopped momentarily, unsure what it was. He buried his hand into the pocket, cautious of if it were a trap. It was, just not in the way he had expected.

He felt something hard. A small cube. He clawed it between his fingers and retrieved it. He looked down to be met by a small, black, velvet-covered box. He stared at long minute, the pitch matte black sucking in his stare. He ran his thumb over the soft finish, wanting to be sucked into its void. With a deep breath, he finally opened it.

It instantly smiled back at him, beaming with joy of having been blessed with sunlight. He was caught off guard, almost blinded by this trapped star, forgetting the sun was beating down behind him. He moved it into his shadow, mesmerised by its beauty.

He could feel it talking to him, whispering into his ear, entrancing him. He was being hypnotised by the ring. It was too easy, as it appeased his inner desires. He was being held hostage to its commands, as he grew an affection for his captor. The syndrome from Stockholm had him in its grasps.

And then it disappeared, as the black abyss welcomed him back. He had snapped the box shut, saving himself from his dreams. He tucked it back into his pocket, hoping a portal would open and make that box disappear. The world had betrayed him again, as he felt the light thump of it reaching the bottom.

He sighed to himself, shaking his head. "No." He uttered to himself, as if to silence all his demons. "Not like this."

He found his keys in one of the shopping bags. He took a deep breath to recollect himself. The key zipped into the lock and jangled as he twisted. He let himself in, picking up the bags behind him, leaving only imaginary ones at the door.

He poked his head into the living room with a painted smile. The three most important women in his life looked back at him with hollow eyes. Something had gone wrong.

Chapter 7

She was now experiencing her first true crush, not quite understanding the blurred lines that didn't allow it to be called love.

"This is definitely a different version to what I remember." She noted.

"You're a different person, maybe it's you who changed and not the story."

"No, it's definitely the story." She clarified. "This version is a lot gloomier, and a lot longer."

He shrugged in response, knowing she wasn't wrong. She was getting a different version; the one he had always wanted her to know.

"So, what did he do?" She asked.

"That's the funny thing about stories, the answers are usually right around the corner. Sometimes, right in front of you, no corner necessary!" He smirked.

She stuck out her tongue. "Smartass."

He held his tongue out in response, closing his eyes to rub it in. The pillow left parts of itself on his protruding tongue, taking with it its wetness as it fell to the floor. She smirked back at him and shook her head.

"Is everything okay?" He tried to swallow the lump in his throat.

"Y-... Yeah." His mum sniffled. "We were just talking about your grandad."

"Oh." He bowed his head.

He could feel their eyes on him. He could feel *her* eyes on him. And suddenly he felt guilty, ashamed, exhausted.

"I'm just going to..." He lifted a bag with a nervous smile. "... put these in the kitchen." He mumbled the rest of the sentence, letting it trail off without a care.

He made his way to the kitchen to unload the bags, his steps heavier now. Slower. There were walls between them now, but he still felt like he was being watched. The walk to the kitchen was short, but it felt like it took an age to pull his body there. The bags rustled alongside him, filling in the uneasy silence that befell the house.

He sat the bags on the counter, starting to slowly unload his haul. It all felt a little weightier than when he had bought them. Faint thuds littered with anger approached from behind. He turned to see Eve beelining towards him.

She stopped in front of him, huffing and pouting at him. She just stared at him as he looked back, confused by what was going on. She puffed at him as he answered with a confused frown. She was growing visibly frustrated, struggling to get the words out. He raised an inquisitive eyebrow.

"What?" He asked, perplexed by her nature.

She let out an annoyed growl. Angry at him, sad for him, and a lot of irritation at herself. All she wanted to do was ask him a question, but the slurry of emotions was intoxicating, and the words were fumbling over each other in her mouth. She could feel them tumbling from the back of her throat to the tip of her tongue, yet none of them made it out.

Without warning, and before he could ask what was going on, he fell back as a sharp pain met his cheek, followed with a thunderous clap.

Now hunched over, Adam held a hand over his cheek, mouth agape, and just stared befuddled at Eve, completely dazed. She holstered her hands, returning them to her hips, watching him fight the sting on his face. Once he'd finally composed himself, he straightened his back, still with a hand to his cheek.

"Is everything okay in there?" His mother yelled.

"Yeah, I... I just dropped something." Adam responded before she could interrupt, closing the door behind Eve.

He turned to her, nursing his reddened cheek. The confusion on his face had shifted to a mild anger.

"What was that for?!" He exclaimed hushed.

"Your grandad fucking died, and instead of telling me you just stopped talking about him altogether! You tell me what that was for..." She yelled, with no care for her volume.

Adam tried to get her to lower her voice, his hands reaching for her arms. "Eve, p-."

She shook him away from her. "And you skipped his funeral for me? For a stupid breakup?!" She growled at him. "I could've waited, Adam. I would've waited." Her voice had hushed now.

He held himself. "Maybe I just needed a distraction, Eve. Maybe I didn't want to think about losing him." He closed his eyes, his voice soft. "I'm not saying what I did was right, but it was my mistake to make. It's my regret to bear. And if you'd known about it, you would've just sunk me lower. Stupid breakup or not, it was an escape. Just for a day. For *the* day. The day when I'd needed it most." His eyelids retreated to look her in the eyes. "Do I regret it? Sure. Would I do it again? Probably, yeah. The grief is mine, Eve, and nobody gets to tell me how to deal with it."

He opened the kitchen door to see his mother and grandmother standing in the hallway. He hurried past them, avoiding any eye contact, as if they weren't even there. Without looking at anyone, without stopping at all, they were left with the goodbyes and well wishes of the door closing behind him.

Eve's anger had been gifted to Adam. Adam's guilt had infested Eve. Their parasitic emotions had found more appropriate hosts. They'd been hollowed out. They'd traded blows and both were on the verge of being knocked out.

Adam's mother ran over to Eve, blanketing her with her body. Eve broke down in his mother's arms. They both broke down, rocking in their embrace.

"It's okay, Eve." Adam's mother blubbered. "You didn't know, it's not your fault." She chanted it, repeatedly, secretly trying to console herself too.

Adam's grandmother welled up behind them. She had never seen Adam with that sort of temperament. He was calm, but his breath held fire.

"He'll be at the grave." She sniffed.

Adam's mother and Eve turned to look at her. Her words had stunned their sorrows for a moment.

"He'll be at the grave." She repeated, sterner now as she held her tongue. "We need to be there with him."

Adam's mother nodded, wiping away her tears and then attempting to wipe away Eve's, but hers were determined to keep flowing. Eve raised her hand to let her know she just needed a minute, as she turned away from the mothers and hushed herself.

She whispered a mantra to herself, as Adam's matriarchy collected itself. She cleaned herself up as best she could and turned back to face them. She nodded once in their direction and then walked through them, straight for the door.

She stopped and turned to them again. "Which graveyard is he buried at?"

Adam's mother smiled sadly. "They're buried at the one on the edge of town. I'll take you." She walked over to Eve.

"You're not leaving me!" Adam's grandmother beckoned, following in behind them. "I'll call a taxi, it'll be quicker."

They pulled up to the eerie field of headstones. Born from sorrow, watered by tears and nurtured by memories. There was a disturbing beauty in the land of the dead. The country of the past. They walked through quietly, not wanting to disturb the air, but their presence caused a ripple that seemed to bring this land of the dead back to life. The wind sighed into their necks, guiding them forwards. The leaves danced around them, crinkling against the concrete.

It didn't take long to creep up to Adam. He was knelt, defeated, between two towering concrete shrines. His mother approached him first, nervous, as if they were strangers.

"Adam, honey…" She bowed her head.

He didn't move and she didn't know what to say. They were at a stalemate, in this battle for redemption.

"Adam." Eve stepped forwards.

He moved his head the slightest bit to the left. She had elicited a response, but they were unsure if that was a good thing right now.

"Adam, I-."

"Eve." He sighed her name and let a pause freeze the world. "Can I talk to her alone, please?"

Adam's mother and grandmother looked at each other. His grandmother just shrugged and stepped away. His mother reluctantly followed, as they walked towards a nearby bench.

"Why did you come here?" Adam spoke gently.

"I…" She stopped and thought for a second. "I was worried about you."

Adam nodded to himself. "Come here." He summoned her forwards.

Eve stepped closer to him, as if breaking through a portal. The closer she got, the harder it seemed to want to move forwards. She managed to stop just behind him though.

"Grandad always wanted to meet you, although I'd assume not in these circumstances…" He looked to the ground.

Eve knelt beside Adam, shuffling closer. Their shoulders kissed, the wrinkled tongues of their jackets gluing them together. She glanced over the gravestones.

"I'm sorry." He almost whispered to her. "I'm sorry." He turned to look at her, making sure she heard it the second time. "I didn't mean to keep it from you... I just... needed to deal with it myself."

"Why?" She asked, looking back at him.

He shrugged. "Don't take this the wrong way but... I'm used to being the one that helps you. It's never been the other way around. And that's not on you, I know you'd help me if I asked... I just didn't want you to see me weak, to see me broken. I'm meant to be strong for you."

"Adam." She placed a hand on his shoulder. "I... I know what you mean. But I wouldn't have thought you were weak. And I don't need you to be strong. I just need you to be you." She turned herself to face him. "We're friends. Best friends. And best friends are meant to look after each other. I know I haven't always been the best friend to you, but I do care about you. I want to look after you too." She took his left hand in hers, squeezing it gently.

He nodded to himself. "I know... I know... I'm sorry."

"Don't be. If I had been there for you more often, you wouldn't have had to face it alone. It's gonna change though, Adam. I'm gonna be a better friend to you." She tried to catch his eyes from the side.

"For what it's worth, I don't think you're a bad friend." He turned to look at her.

She smiled back at him, both of her hands now holding his left. She rubbed his palms, unable to find the words to thank him. Unable to find the right way to apologise and...

Something felt cold. Wet. She looked up. The sky was clear. She felt her cheeks. They were dry. She retrieved the dampened hand and held it to her.

A crimson smudge. Adam's face dropped. He tried to pull his hand back but she gripped it tightly. She looked down. A trail of blood has slivered its way free from his sleeve.

She gently pulled the sleeve up his arm and turned his hand palm-up. There it was. There she was. There he was.

Eve.

Carved into his skin. Etched into his wrist. Tattooed in his blood.

Eve.

"Adam…"

He managed to reclaim his hand, freeing it from her loosened grip. He covered it back up, dabbing it with his sleeve to hide the slow red rivers. He shook his head in response and turned away from her. Her lips mouthed his name again.

"For what it's worth, I know it's not right. But sometimes pain is all I know how to feel, all I feel comfortable feeling. I can't deal with anger well, Eve. I would rather swap it for something much less… evil." Adam explained.

"Why?" She squeaked.

"You're my weakness, Eve. You know this. I just… I guess we're both dragging each other down." He shrugged.

She reached out to him, but something stopped her from touching him. Instead, her arm just floated there, hovering in despair. He was right in front of her, yet it felt like they were on different planets. She couldn't feel him anymore. She didn't recognise him.

"It's the last time, Eve. I promise. It ends with you. Just please don't tell anyone." He pleaded, turning to face her again.

She looked down at his wrist again. She held it in her hands once more, revealing it to the world again. Her thumb trembled as she slowly tiptoed it across her own name. It became a censored curse.

"Never again." Her voice was shaky, but her eyes were fierce as they pierced through his.

"Never again." He promised.

"Never again." She nodded.

Eve sighed, letting his hand drop. She shook her head and then closed her eyes. She took a few deep, slow breaths.

"What are we doing to each other, Adam? It's not meant to be this complicated." She half-laughed.

He shrugged. "I don't think you get quite how complicated it is, Eve."

There was a sureness about him that offset her. He knew something. She had a hunch she was about to find out what. Given the revelations she'd already had today, a trend had emerged that caused her to worry.

He reached inside his coat, rummaging about for a moment. He seemed to find something and then pause, contemplating his next move. He let the scenarios play out in his head, trying to find the optimal route. He quickly became overwhelmed, shrugging it off and revealing his clutched hand.

A small cube void sat in his palm, its fuzziness distorting its edges. He gestured for her to take it, as he held out his hand towards her.

She thought she knew what it was. The overall idea, at least. The intentions were inscribed all over it. She found it calling to her, as her shaky hands made towards it.

She held it low, amongst the shadows. It wasn't to see the light of day, that way she could try to banish it from existence. She flipped the lid open, staring it dead in its eye.

It stared back.

She closed the lid and made to hand it back to Adam.

"Adam... I-..."

"Your dad gave it to me." He corrected her before she had the chance to make the mistake. "I'm giving it to you, albeit probably not in the way he hoped. I don't want it. It belongs to you anyway, doesn't matter how you end up with it."

Her head swung from side to side like a pendulum. She couldn't believe it. It felt like a betrayal. It felt cruel and heavy. She felt sick. Her insides twisted, collapsing into a pile within her.

"Why would he...?" Was all she could manage.

"I think he had the right intentions, just didn't land the execution. In any case, it's found its way to you. It's all yours." Adam tried to make excuses for him.

He went to get up but Eve's stare held him. She allowed him to stand but froze him in place. She turned the box towards him and opened the lid.

"Adam..." She began, smiling up at him. "Will y-..."

"That's cheap, Eve." He shook his head with disappointment. "Not funny."

She stayed there for a moment, the smile melting away into a frown. She snapped the box shut and her whole body depressed as she exhaled.

"Sorry... You're right, it's not funny." She apologised, now avoiding his eyes.

Adam shrugged and walked past her, towards the bench behind them. She got herself to her feet. She looked down into her hand, losing herself to the cuboid abyss.

She considered hurling it in a random direction and being done with it. Then again, she was at a graveyard, where hopes and dreams came to die. It seemed fitting. She could rehome it here, let it be a distant memory and nothing more.

She squeezed her fist, trying to destroy the box. It dug its corners into her palm, letting her know it wasn't going to concede. She grew frustrated, ready to be done with it entirely. Instead, she found herself dropping it in her bag and walking back to Adam.

The black box seemed intent on claiming a victim, infecting both their minds with its poison. Its targets, though, were already sick. They'd already been claimed by a curse: the curse of their own love. That curse had a stronger grip on them, and its prey were guaranteed to fall.

Chapter 8

She was learning more about herself as life now moulded her for the future.

"You can always trust a heartless man to write a good love story." He spoke.

"Why? Surely he'd be the worst..." She replied, almost astonished as the plain stupidity.

"Everyone knows humans have hearts, and no-one can deny that they were human. So, if a human becomes heartless, the heart was...?" He prompted her for an answer with his open eyes.

"Lost?" She stared as he shook his head. "Broken?" Still seeking approval as he signalled she was getting closer. "Stolen!" He finally nodded.

"Stolen! The others can work too but that's beside the point." He applauded. "And someone who steals is a...?" He continued with the childish games.

"Thief." She looked almost proud until she realised how simple it was.

"And what does a thief do with whatever they've stolen?" He asked, one last time.

"...I don't know..." She seemed confused.

"Whatever they want, but they don't return it. A heartless human will have the best love stories because they are what they dream of. It's easier to write what you're passionate about than what you just think sounds good." He seemed pleased with himself.

"So, are you heartless? This is a good story." She tried to seem smart.

"No. I'm not heartless, I'm experienced. I know where my heart lies and it's there with consent." He winked, pleased he'd thwarted her attempts to outsmart him.

"Calling you 'my everything' is predictable. Calling you 'my nothing' is far more dangerous.

Your regular lover would claim nothing is perfect, but here lies much more.

A man with everything to lose is harmless, but a man with nothing to lose is your worst nightmare.

For now, I lay as a man with nothing to lose. Let me lay my soul down for you, my sweet and perfect nothing." He mumbled aloud to himself.

"What's that?" His mother asked as she walked past him, flicking his feet off the sofa so she could sit.

"Nothing. It's just stuff." He rushed to cover it up as he got up.

His mum gave him a confused stare but took a seat. Adam grabbed his stuff and moved over to the table, shielding his work from his mother. He placed the pieces of paper on the hard wood and began to scribble some more. He put the pen against his lips with his right hand and then lifted the paper slightly with his left.

"*A kind lie is much crueller than the brutal truth,*

Please spare me the trouble without being uncouth.

Won't you go ahead and tell me what's been troubling your mind?

Or do I have to steal your heart and hope the answers are there for me to find?

You torture me but won't kill me,

You want the guts but none of the glory." He mumbled to himself, quieter.

"Hey, Shakespeare, if you're trying to hide what you're doing, maybe don't speak it to the world." His mum chuckled, approaching him from behind.

He shrugged. "The words are stuck in my head, I need to get them out somehow."

"Eve?" She asked, now standing behind him, looking down at the table.

He lowered his head to put pen to paper once more, ignoring her towering presence casting a shadow over him, clearing his head with the harmonious words that pierced his heart.

"Eve?" His mother asked, once again.

She sat beside her distracted son, turning slightly to face him. She took his pen and paper and began scribbling with pace.

She paused a moment, reading over her writing, and then nodded to herself as she grabbed another sheet. Again, she let the pen dance its way over the blank sheet to the tune of her fingers. Soon, she was done with that one too, and she picked up one final blank piece. One last time, the pen did her bidding, quickly and assertively. When she had completed her task, she threw the pen behind her and walked away, leaving Adam with the three new pieces of paper and the ones he'd already worked on.

He looked at them for a moment, not sure how to react. His mother didn't wait to answer any questions, she was out of the room before he could say anything. His hand was shaky as he reached for the three sheets, as if they might bite him. His hand inched closer and closer, growing ever more wary of those tattooed sheets. With one quick motion, he threw his hand on top of the pile of paper and swiftly tamed it under his control. He ran to his room with his fresh kill, to digest it in peace.

"I watched my friends grow with their spouses, growing alongside them. I was content. They never understood my journey. I had experienced love, I knew what it was, but it wasn't for me. Then I met you and I learnt what pain was. Raw pain, fuelled by a careless heart that was dormant for so long. They say home is where the heart is, right? So, as long as I go where you go, I'll forever be home. You're unique, like no other I've ever met. You make me feel empty, cold, and hopeless. Hateful. But never hate for you. Hate for myself, for not being good enough. Never good enough to be your one and only, your forever and always. You fill me with a warmth I've never felt before. Like being hugged by fondness. I'd take all the pain my beings could endure forever just to get even one precious moment to call you mine. These dreams you inhabit are surrounded by nightmares. Give me visions of a future with you, only to snatch them away before I can make them so. I never stood a chance. I think I love you.

Your grandfather wrote this letter to your grandmother when they'd just met. She still turned him down." The first sheet read.

"Dearest, you use me and abuse me, tease me and haunt me. You've led me on, played with my dead heart and cursed my unstable mind. I love you and long to lose you, for you can't lose what was never yours. I wish you'd choose me, but you'll just never understand the love I nurture for you. Or maybe I'm just not making it clear enough? You are the foundations of my dreams, but with those my nightmares too. I want nothing more but to love you, yet you taint this heart with hatred. But I could never hate you and will continue to forgive you for all the pain you will always cause me. Even if you don't realise the effect you've had on my tortured soul. You give me faith, but you mercilessly take it away. You give me hope but your justice leaves me hopeless. I will continue to give you love to ensure you're not loveless. Maybe you can use it for the both of us.

Your father wrote this for me when we were in school. He was a desperate to date me. As advised by my father, he turned into a poet. I told him I'd give him a chance." The second sheet revealed.

"Finding love in all the wrong places; I didn't even want it. You were the one that crept in. You were the one I became weak for. You weren't meant to do this to me. Proved my usefulness and used me. Proved my loyalty and left me. Proved my love and hurt me. I'd always thought I was an annoyance, isolating myself from all. Yet, you gave the lonely wanderer an urge to seek more. Now, you've left him more alone than he ever was. You came and conquered, more fool me. You'd better not come crawling back else I'll make a fool of you. Although, your wicked tongue can cast its unforgiving spells and I'll be yours once more. Imprisoned within those eyes,

I will bend to your will. You are not mine and I'm refusing to be yours. I can't have you, but you've already got me. I am the worthless to your priceless. Your stains of abuse cause cracks in your armour. Cracks even I can see through, blinded as I've become. Wear down my charred soul but I will still burn fierce for you. Sing your Siren's song once more and set me free to my demise. I beg of you, let me die, for I no longer want to live if living is loving you.

They both wrote this together. When your father and I got married, your grandad took it as an opportunity to renew his vows with your gran. Talk about stealing the spotlight. It was meant to be a cruel joke. Your grandad began writing it as a revenge letter for all the rejections your gran pummelled him with. And then he stopped because, one day, she said yes. Your dad came across it and thought it would be funny to finish it off... My mother and I said we'd never leave them, and we didn't. They had us, they won. And then they left us."

Just as he pondered on those memorised words, the shuffling of his mother's clothes broke his focus. He looked up as she crossed his doorway.

"Is it worth waiting for someone you think is your true love or to find someone who will just love you?" He called out to her.

"You answer it." She replied, poking her head into his room. "Where has it gotten you so far?"

"Dad and grandad have stories of persistence. What if I just persist a little longer? Maybe I'll get a story like theirs." He sounded hopeless, even to himself.

"They lived through a different time to you. And, crucially, there was *some* interest in them to begin with. Their egos sensed it too, which is *why* they were persistent." She walked in and sat beside him. "So, Adam, is it worth waiting for someone you've convinced yourself is your true love, or should you try to find someone who will just love you?"

He sighed. "It's not that easy."

"I know, but you have to set your own path too, rather than just trying to forge your way into someone else's." She rubbed his back. "It's not like you only get one shot at love, what a cruel world that would be!"

"I never would've thought you'd be telling me to give up on Eve. I thought you guys were hoping we'd get married."

"I'm not telling you anything, Adam. Besides, as cute as it would've been if you did, I can see how much it's hurting you. You think I want my son getting hurt? It's okay to think about what you want too, you know? You're allowed to put yourself first. We're tricked into thinking being selfish is a bad thing, but it's not. It can be good too." She hugged him as he leaned against her.

"What would granddad say?" He sighed.

"If things aren't going right, just turn around and make them go left." She faintly laughed at the memory. "Don't worry, you've got your whole life to find love. Just focus on your future. Live your life the best you can. Only fear death when your legacy is just a mere reminder that you were once alive."

"I read the letter he left me before he died, finally." He informed his mother.

"Oh, what did it say?" He had piqued her interest.

"Most people have to die before you start quoting them." He laughed, wiping a tear.

"It's okay, we all miss him. He was one of the best men you could meet."

"He knew how to write a decent love letter too." He stared at the three pieces of paper his mother had previously given him.

"You might not want to refer to someone you're interested in as nothing, just a tip." She winked at him.

His mother took the pieces of paper from his hand and left the room before he could protest. Adam remained sitting on his bed, wondering what she was doing. When she returned, she jumped onto his bed and stuck some battered sheets on the ceiling, directly above his pillow. She then lay on Adam's bed, beside where he was sitting and smiled, patting the space beside her.

"Those aren't the ones you left with." He noticed as he lay beside her.

"They're the originals." She read them again, slowly, even though she knew what they said.

"I don't think Eve is the type for love letters." Adam sighed.

"No-one seems like the type, but everyone secretly loves them. Who *doesn't* want to be told they're desired? It's like poetry. Even the most ruthless of people will love a poem, as long as it speaks to them. Everything is situational. People are different but we all have emotions. We all feel things. We all live and become from our feelings." She lay her hand over his heart. "Just don't lose sense of the world chasing your feelings when the only thing you can feel is pain."

He placed his hand on top of his mother's. "Sometimes, I wish I didn't have to feel anything."

She smiled as she closed her eyes and just nodded. It was the easy way out, and a feeling she was familiar with. The words floated through her mind and the nodding faded into her shaking her head.

I no longer want to live, if living is loving you.

Chapter 9

She was now entering her teens, the troubles of life started to dawn upon her.

"That's not fair." She yelled.

"What's not?" He responded.

"His grandfather is gone, his dad is gone. Who taught him how to be a man?"

"What does it mean to be a man?" He asked her.

She thought for a moment, realising her prejudices were speaking for her. After a short while, she just shrugged.

"Exactly. Nobody needs to teach him *how to be a man*. All that is is an excuse for a lack of identity." He smiled back at her. "All he needed to learn was how to be a good person, and his mother was more than capable of teaching him that."

"But he deserved a father." She seemed to pout.

"Well, life's not fair." He shrugged, unintentionally callously. "While he may not have had a father, he was still raised with love. He had a mother that loved him enough for more than two parents. He had grandparents that loved him enough that he never had to worry. It sounds like he had what he deserved." He remained calm in the face of her anger. "He turned out okay, right? So, it's fine."

She sighed. "I guess you're right."

"It's okay. I know what you're thinking. But it's okay, you've got me, and I'm plenty enough as it is. Especially with this belly." He winked as she pushed him away gently to hide her smile. "And I've got you, and I couldn't have asked for anyone better."

He picked up his phone and read three crucial words. Three words to decide where they'd go, what they'd do and who they'd become.

I need you.

"What's wrong?" He was gasping for air as he reached her door.

She said nothing. She welcomed him in, not giving him any time to see if her parents were home and took him to her room. She sat him on her bed and turned away. She walked towards her door, closing it gently. She stood a few steps away from him, her hands on the door handle.

He watched her in silence, confused and hoping for answers. He saw her forearm move, as she moved a hand to her shoulder. She grabbed the left strap from of her dress and pushed it free from its post, her dress falling with it. The right one followed quickly after, her dress collapsing entirely, revealing her bare back to him.

"No, no. Stop." He leapt forwards, caught the dress and began pulling it up. "What's wrong? What are you doing?"

She stopped for a second as Adam ensured she remained covered, pulling the straps over her shoulders again. When he was done, he could see a tear flowing down her cheek. He pulled her towards him and stepped in front of her to see her eyes closed and a river forming as it trickled down the side of her face. She opened her eyes for a second and smiled. Not a smile of joy, but one that knew she had fucked up again. All she could do was shrug. He shrugged too, letting a shy smile take him.

She wrapped her arms around him, tight. Her cheek lay against his chest, quickly dampening his top. And then she broke. She just broke. Adam squeezed her tight. He rested his lips against the top of her head, mouthful of hair and the scent of coconut flooding his nose.

He rubbed her back and let her break apart in his arms, as he did his best to hold her together. She crumbled, and he questioned if the pieces of her would ever fit together again. This time it felt different. It was different.

He took her to her bed, refusing to let go of her for that short journey. He lay her down and rest beside her. Adam managed to catch her eyes for a couple of seconds and mouthed to her the question he had initially asked. She said nothing, turning away from him. She grabbed her phone from behind him and put it in his hands. She turned her back to him once more as she cried to herself.

Adam read what was on the screen. Disgusted, angry, but not surprised. His fist clenched behind her as he grit his teeth. He couldn't finish it. He simply closed the phone and placed it on the drawer behind them.

"Why?" Adam asked.

"We broke up..." She barely managed to get out. "He wanted to impress his mates. He used me."

"No. I mean, why send them to him?" He asked, slightly enraged but hidden.

"I don't know. I thought he had real feelings for me. He... he made it seem like I had to, a-as if it was a n-n-normal thing to do. He... He said... He said if he didn't get them from me, he would get them from somewhere... someone... else. I... I don't know." She answered, ashamed.

"It's okay, I understand." He dropped the phone behind him and wrapped an arm around her, pulling her tight against him. "It's not your fault."

She turned to look at him again. "He called me a worthless trophy." She sighed. "A... participation award."

"Worthless is on the borderline of priceless. He got the wrong side." He looked down at her to make sure she could see his eyes as he said it.

"I know you're just trying to make me smile. Stop. I don't deserve to. You should just judge me and leave me." She sighed again, moving his arms away from her.

"No matter what they say, everyone judges everyone they meet. They judge you every second they're with you. They have to. They judge what you're saying, how you're saying it, your mood. They judge why, then they compare it to what they know about you to judge the severity and how they should handle it. The difference lies upon how people react to the judgments they come to, and how they use them. Some people use their judgements as a tool, to build others up and patch the parts of them that were broken. Others wield their judgements as a weapon, seeking only to destroy everyone else – to feed on all their faults so as to disguise their own. I've already judged you. You're perfuckt." He watched her twiddling with her thumbs.

"Do I need to change? I feel like I don't fit in anymore. How are you so comfortable with being different?" She stared into his eyes to make sure he didn't lie.

"I don't change, I just change those around me." Lost in his thoughts for a second, he smiled back at her. "You'd be wise to do the same."

"I know, I know. I just... He seemed so-" She struggled to find the words.

"It's not your fault." He rubbed her arm. "Nobody introduces themselves with their ugly side. They want you to think they're a hero, but heroes need villains."

"Who's their villain?"

"Me." He answered.

"You? How are you the villain?" She wiped away her tears, letting him distract her.

"You know how sometimes you'll watch a film and realise the bad guy has a point? How they weren't so much *bad*, more so just *misguided*. Their heart was in the right place, their methodology wasn't." She nodded back at him. "I've got to be the one to bring you back to reality, I have to show you their true colours. I'm the one that has to remind you what happened, I've got to relive the pain with you. Sometimes, I don't always do it in the best way, and sometimes I'll nail it. I'm the one that keeps having the same argument with you, over and over again. I become *your* villain too."

"You're my *hero*." She smiled and kissed his jaw.

"How about I lock you in a burning building to prove it? I'll make sure to save you after!" He winked as she slapped his arm.

"You can't get rid of me that easily. Besides, you'd miss me if you failed." She grinned a little.

He didn't reply to that. He just grinned with her but was so distant in his head trying to imagine his life without her. He tried to imagine what he'd do and who he might end up with. He wondered if he could be happy without her.

"Adam." She stole him back from thoughts. "I'm ready."

He stared at her, confused. "For?"

"You." She smiled at him as the remnants of the tears crusted on her cheeks.

"I don't know what you're getting at but you most definitely are not ready for me." He laughed to himself.

She didn't know what to say to that. She knew Adam was the right one for her but was she there yet? Was she actually ready? Was Adam saving her from herself again? And then she wondered, with all the love Adam had for her, how could he say no? How could *he* be the one to reject *her*?

"Adam, stay the night please." She looked up to him. "I need my teddy bear with me."

Adam just nodded and held her for a few minutes. He cleared her face for her and just held her through the night. He watched her sleep. He guarded her. He shielded her. She was at peace, even though he was burning inside.

A teddy bear equates to all that emptiness. Holding on to nothing she ever had. Those feelings she was deprived of because she felt neglected, unsafe. The teddy bear is her last attempt at nurture – the nurturing she needed to give herself.

A teddy bear is reflecting the emotions she wished she'd received but never got. It's the empty Christmas list, the hopeless dreams. She kept holding on to her teddy bear, as he silently cried not to become a memory that faded away.

He didn't want to be forgotten and left in a box, only to be realised and remembered when it was too late to be rescued. He didn't want to be the reminiscing thought as she went over photos in later life. He didn't want to dissipate from her mind and be nothing more than particles lost to the wind.

He was scared, as he watched the dust circle him, waiting for their chance to consume him, to turn him. "*One of us, one of us.*" the dust would chant. He didn't want to fade away.

Chapter 10

She was experiencing the social dread that came with her age, looking for answers from her typical source of wisdom.

"Adam was an outcast in school, right?" She asked bluntly.

"What makes you think that?" He replied.

"Well, he was a geek..." She shrugged.

He laughed. "Yeah, he was somewhat of an outcast."

"How did he deal with it?" She waited intently.

After a brief thought, he readied himself for the words he would have to carefully curate. "A lot of the social pressures around that period come from other people. You care what everyone thinks about you, how you may be perceived and what your 'reputation' may be. Adam was aware that people judge you, no matter what you do. Maybe at one point he cared what they thought, but eventually you learn you can't please everyone. He also said that he doesn't change, he just changes those around him. He was comfortable in his own skin, proud of who he was. When you're proud of yourself, you tend not to care what the naysayers do or say. As long as you're comfortable with who you are, you'll be okay. It can be scary to stand out and be yourself when everyone else is trying to be like each other, but you'll have an easier time finding your crowd. Sometimes, that's more important than trying to please everyone." He paused for her reaction, to which there was none.

"When you're still figuring out who you are and trying to find your place in the world, it's easy to not want to stand out. If ten people wear the same outfit and an eleventh comes along wearing something different, even if it's only slight, they stick out. That can be uncomfortable for some. That discomfort can be intimidating. Some people react to that by using it as their opportunity to wear their own outfit. Others see it as a moment to shun that one person for being different. In reality, we're all the same. We just want to be accepted, but we're also scared of rejection. It's very vulnerable allowing yourself to stick out from the crowd, and if nobody else joins you then it's also very lonely. So, rather than being ourselves, we'll be someone else. We'll be everyone else. You can always be yourself though. You should always be yourself. Stay true to yourself and you'll have a much easier life. No matter what anyone else thinks." He tried to get something from her.

"What if you don't know who you are, how do you stay true to that?" She pondered.

"You'll never know if you're wearing someone else's skin."

"You should've asked her out." His mum yelled as Adam returned home.

"What?" He replied, befuddled.

"Eve's mother could hear you two talking and she told me everything." His mother clarified.

"Do you expect me to reply to that?" He stared, slightly agitated.

She turned to face him and shrugged. "What happened? Let me hear it from you."

"Well... I don't know. I'd do anything for her, but she was too vulnerable, I guess. I'll always be that guy who will be there for her, but I won't take advantage of her. If I do that, I just become another one of those arseholes that keep breaking her." He shrugged. "I will be there for as long as she needs me, but I can't let her think she loves me when she doesn't. She doesn't get hurt by that, I do."

"They'd be proud of you." She stated, to a raised eyebrow. "Your father and your grandfather. They'd be so proud of you." She sighed, walking up to him and cupping his face with her hands. "I'm proud of you, but I always have been." She smiled.

He smiled sadly back at her. "Thanks, mum."

She released his face and turned away from him. "Do you want to marry her, Adam?"

"What?" He seemed puzzled, this seemingly coming from nowhere.

His mother simply gestured towards the table with her head. There it sat, like a nightmare he couldn't escape. The little black box.

"Where...? How...?" He struggled.

"It fell out of your pocket as you sprinted away yesterday. I tried to tell you but you were already gone. I haven't opened it but it's... I don't think I need to."

Adam stepped towards the table, keeping his eyes on that mysterious black box the whole way there. He reached out towards its whispers, expecting it to jump at him. The velvet felt cold as he touched it. He lifted it slowly, gently rubbing the cold away. And then he flipped it open and stared at his nemesis once more. He barely gave it a second before he slammed it shut again.

Adam bowed his head. "It's not mine." He turned to his mother, lifting the box so she could see it. "Eve's dad gave it to me. He wanted me to propose. I couldn't do it, but he wouldn't take it back."

"And you've just held onto it ever since?" She questioned.

Adam shook his head. "I gave it to Eve; I told her what happened, about how her dad gave it to me. I think she was relieved it wasn't from me. I told her to keep it. She must've put it back in my pocket. Probably when we walked back from the graveyard, I gave her my jacket. I didn't even realise it was there."

His mother just stood there, taking it all in. Realising she was part of his problem, she looked away from the dark box. How had it gotten this far?

"I'm sorry, Adam. I sho-"

"It's okay." He shrugged. "I've gotten used to it." He turned to go to his room.

Those words stung his mother. It wasn't meant to be like this. This was never how they had dreamt of it. Not like this...

"What are you going to do with it?" She asked.

"Do what you want with it." He said, placing the box on the table. "It should never have been my problem."

"I really am sorry, Adam. I guess I got too caught up in everything, even though it was just the other day I was telling you to put yourself first. I'm sorry, I'll do better." She pleaded for forgiveness.

He stood at the bottom of the stairs for a minute and then just nodded. He made his way up the stairs and didn't say another word to her.

A few hours later he heard a knock on his door. He knew it was his mother, nobody else had come round. She peered through the door and looked at him. He didn't look up, just focused on his book.

"Can I come in?" She asked.

Adam let out a gentle sigh and closed the book. She walked in and closed the door behind her, even though they were the only two that occupied the house. She stepped nervously to his bed and sat beside him.

"I need you to know, I don't care if you end up with Eve or not. As your mum, all I've ever wanted is what's best for you. Sometimes I'll have my own version of what's good for you, but you might think otherwise. For a while, we all thought it would be Adam and Eve. We haven't been very fair on you or her, especially knowing how you two feel about each other." She stared at the ground, ashamed of herself. "But you're so much like your dad and grandad, I didn't know how far you'd go. There were times I thought you'd lost yourself. That you were so in over your head, you'd lost sight of reality. I thought I was losing you... And... And I can't lose you too, Adam." She brushed a tear and turned to him. "I can see you've got a good head on your shoulders, who knows where you got that from?" Adam's frown broke into a smirk. "You're not a little boy anymore, you're not a clueless teen. You can figure this out, and I'll do my best to support you." She seemed like a child trying to atone for her sins.

"It's okay, mum. You've always done right by me; I just need you to give me a bit more credit sometimes." He put a hand on her back.

She nodded. "That's true. I should know better. I did raise you, after all. I'd say I did a pretty good job too." She smiled.

"Thank you, mum." He wrapped himself around her, letting her know she was off the hook.

She was relieved. To think, she was pushing him into something he had been fighting for a while. Something that could've destroyed him. Something that *was* destroying him. She would never have forgiven herself, but he had pardoned her.

Eve went to visit him a few days later with some *important news*. She refused to tell him what it was over the phone, leaving him curious for days. She just wanted him to be ready. He prepared himself for the worst but kept the wishful thinking alive.

"Is he home?" She asked his mother when she opened the door.

"In his room." She moved aside to welcome her in.

Eve ran up the stairs, almost tripping. "Are you ready?" She asked, gasping for breath after that short run.

"How unfit are you? The stairs aren't that long." He smiled.

"I ran here, bus took too long." She threw herself onto his bed. "I don't know how you make that run."

"We didn't set a specific time, you know?" He stared at her.

"Oh. Oops." She replied, sitting upright, patting the space beside her.

"Well, what is it?" He asked, sitting beside her.

"Way to cut the bullshit." She grinned. "You and I are going to make a deal."

He stared at her, confused. "What type of deal?"

"You are going to approve of any guy before I date them. You are going to save me loads of time." She smiled at him, hoping he'd agree.

He stared at her in disbelief. *That* was what she had waited days for? The thing that couldn't be spoken over the phone? He had to hide his disappointment.

"You know I'll never approve of anyone. No-one is good enough for you." He looked down at her empty ring finger.

"That's why you are perfect to help me." She placed her hands on his shoulders and smiled at him.

"There's a guy, isn't there?" He asked, turning to face her.

She didn't respond. The way her smile faded said it all. She removed her hands from his shoulders and put them on her lap, watching them as she did.

"Tomorrow, at the café. Midday, I'll be there." He answered her.

She looked up, face beaming. She mouthed a thank you and made for his door. A few seconds after that, he heard his front door close. He watched her run away through his window, resting against the little ledge. He finally let out a massive sigh and planted his face in his hands. How did he keep letting her do this to him?

That whole evening, he prayed something would come up. Something, *anything*. Just an excuse to not be there. As the moonlight greeted him, he knew he was in for a rough time tomorrow. He let his thoughts carry him to a restless sleep with false hope.

He got to the café a little earlier than them. Choosing to sit outside although the sky didn't promise it would maintain its smile. He ran through scenarios in his head, giving himself a pep talk on how to approach it. What had Eve even told the guy? "I need my friend to approve of you?" Seems a bit intense...

His racing mind stopped as he saw them approaching. This was it. His eyes went from Eve to the guy beside her. He had his arm wrapped around her. The gross smirk on his face, the overconfident hold on her. This guy was just one in the same. He knew already his opinion would mean nothing. It only took him one look to see that he was just another mistake. *This* was a mistake.

She saw him and waved, still a few metres away. He ever-so-slightly shook his head to himself. He wanted to get up and leave. They were getting closer and closer. His time was running out.

"Hi Adam!" She exclaimed, grabbing the chair across him.

"Awright mate?" He tilted his head back as he took a seat.

Eve was a bit too excited. Her two guys sat quiet, as she rambled about each of them. Adam was leaning back, arms crossed, as those two held hands on the table.

He watched as the clone of her ex tried to lean into Eve. His hands were getting antsy around her as she gave the backstories of the pair. Adam watched, disgusted, knowing he was just trying to demonstrate control. Eve had trapped his hands between hers, trying not to lose her focus. Adam couldn't take anymore, his stomach had dropped and he could tolerate it no more.

"It was nice meeting you, I've got to go." Adam shot up and walked away, refusing to look back.

Eve called out his name but he didn't stop. She chased him, leaving the wannabe lover boy to just sit there. She eventually caught up, grabbing him and turning him to face her.

"Adam, what's going on? What was that?" She tried to catch her breath.

"No, Eve." He replied, shaking his head and looking away.

"You've barely even met him, give him a chance!"

"How long have you known him, Eve? I've seen him around, everyone has. We all know who he is." Adam sighed as he looked at her. "If you just want some fun, that's fine, but don't pretend like he is going to be the magical last piece to your puzzle. He is not the one and you already know that."

Eve looked at Adam for a few seconds and then looked over her shoulder to see the bewildered figure waiting for her. Between catching her breath and questioning if Adam was right, she had nothing to say.

"This was a bad idea from the start, I can't believe I agreed to it." He seemed disappointed in himself, beginning to turn away. "Eve, you do what you want. You already told me once,

I can't tell you who to love so I'm not going to. It's not fair on me. Whether you prove me wro-... You don't even need to prove me wrong. Whatever happens, do what you think is best for you. I'll be waiting if you need me. I'm not going to watch this." He freed himself of her loose grasp and walked away.

He didn't look back. He knew he would break if he did. He just walked. Eve stood there for a few seconds, caught between two worlds and two choices. Two choices that would change her life.

Chapter 11

Her popularity blossomed as her personality grew with the rest of her, her love for life blooming with it.

"Why did he leave? That was a shitty move." She shook her head.

"I've been waiting to use this." He propped himself up, excitedly. "Do you know the definition of insanity?" She shook her head as the glee spread all over his face. "Insanity is doing the same thing over and over, expecting a different result." He stared at her for a reaction to which he got none. "They both got trapped in a cycle. She would date the same type of people, have the same kind of heartbreak, and he would be there to pick up the pieces. He would console her, warn her, and then hope she'd learned her lesson. Only for that to not happen. They were going insane." He waited for a reaction again.

"Oh, I guess you're right..." Her mind trailed off into her own world. "It's not her fault though, right? She can't help who she falls for."

"She can't, but at some point you have to figure out why you're falling for the wrong people. How many times do you have to let something bite you before you stop trying to cuddle it?"

They hadn't talked for two weeks, the average lifespan of her relationships. He had wanted to reach out, but he couldn't bring himself to do it this time. Something held him back. He refused. He wouldn't be able to escape her though. Not that easily, not like this.

"Is he home?" Eve asked his mother at the door.

"No, he hasn't been for two weeks." She replied.

"Where is he?" She asked, shocked.

Adam's mother hesitated a moment. She had a suspicion his recent change in behaviour was due to her, but she also knew that Eve was probably the only person who could get anywhere with him. She just wanted her son back. Was she a bad mother for not caring about the cost?

"He's been camping at the cemetery. The police informed me on the first night, thinking he was some grave robber. He won't talk. I don't know what's going on with him." She immediately questioned releasing the information.

Eve had seen a ghost – the ghost of her past. Heartbreak after heartbreak, he was there for her. Every tear, he caught. All pains, he eased. Yet, she wasn't there for him. Her past sins encircling her, mocking her.

"I'm gonna go see him, thanks." Eve determined.

"Hold on a sec." His mother vanished into the kitchen and appeared a few long seconds later. "Can you take this bag to him?" She handed her a bag. "Thanks, dear." She half-smiled and waved her off.

Eve ran there as fast as she could. Just as he'd done for her so many times before, she ran without stopping. No matter how much her body called for a break. She didn't want anything to happen to him. He was her rock, her teddy, *hers*.

"You hate camping." She nervously tried to break the ice as she inched closer behind him. "Your mum sent this." She lowered the bag in front of him as she remained standing, looking down at him.

The sky was a dark blue, it was late and cold. Adam just sat at the graves from the door of his tent. He'd lost a lot of weight, evident from his lack of appetite.

She sat beside him, just outside his new home, and opened the bag. The smell of a homemade stew filled the air, stabbing his nostrils with temptation. He always loved his mother's cooking, never could resist it. A cheap trick, one he was determined to resist. Especially at *her* hands.

Eve removed the warm Tupperware from the bag and placed it in front of him. She fished through the rest of the bag, pulling out a few smaller containers. He had some bread and other sides to enjoy with his stew.

Eve had thought the bag to be empty, crumpling it up into a ball to pocket. The bag didn't ball, though. Instead, it revealed to have a solid heart. Her palm whacked against something hard, allowing each wrinkle of the bag to bite her skin.

"What did I miss?" She unscrambled the bag and dipped her hand in blindly.

She pulled it out, retrieving a small velvet box. It almost vanished against the night that surrounded them, save for the moon that was able to barely make it visible – most of its light seemingly unable to escape. Eve held it up, studying it a moment, before she realised what it was.

"How did she…?"

"You left it in my pocket." Adam's voice was shaky, dry.

He hadn't spoken for weeks and had to relearn that skill. He sighed, disappointed at himself for breaking his silence so easily, and reached for the container of stew.

Eve turned her head to him and then back at the box. "Why would she pack it here?"

"It's yours." He spooned some stew into his mouth, feeling the warmth light up his body as it flowed through him.

"I... I guess." Eve seemed lost now.

She lowered the boxed ring, not sure what to do now. She had planned it all out. She would get him some food, tempt him with the smells that had been crafted with love, make a few bad jokes about herself and he would reassure her. This wasn't how it was meant to go. She slipped the box into her pocket, not wanting to see it anymore. Out of sight, yet still on her mind.

"Why'd you come, Eve?" He bit into some stew-infused bread, now having found his voice again.

"For you." She turned to him. "I came fo-."

"He dumped you, didn't he?" He looked at her for the first time.

His eyes were hollow. Cold. Vicious. His eyes looked black, although she was only half-certain that was just an illusion from the night. His words bit through her, something the wind had been struggling to do. Now it had an opening, the chilling wind consumed her, taking a firm hold within.

She nodded, bowing her head. He nodded with her as he turned his head from her to the ground. She raised her head to the sky and closed her eyes as if it would ease the pain, taking in a deep, cold breath.

"I won't say it." He seemed to pardon her, but it was not mercy he was showing. "I don't need to say it. But it's not your fault. I think we've been misguided by our guardians, Eve. Or, rather, I definitely have. Your parents seem to want me to marry you. My mum was also on that train. My grandfather, my best friend, told me you'd want me one day. All it would take was one day." He turned to look at her with disgust. "Three one days later, he's dead."

"I didn't kill him, Adam." She bit back.

"I almost wish you had, Eve. That way, it would be easier to hate you. But instead, I have to sit here and watch you get fucked over. Time after time after time. You think you're the one getting your heart broken, think about how I feel having to watch that. Do you even know what heartbreak is, Eve? Because there's no fucking way you have enough time to fall in love with these freaks." He shook his head at the ground.

"You don't have to love someone for your heart to break." There was a flurry of anger and sorrow in her voice.

He nodded. "You're right. But your heart isn't breaking for them, Eve. There's no way it could be. You're smarter than that…" He thought for a moment. "Everyone's got it wrong. You don't need *my* love, Eve… You need your own." He chewed on a small piece of bread, nodding to himself. "If you loved yourself, Eve, you wouldn't put yourself through this. And everyone seems to think my love is somehow going to help you. It's not. As much as I would've tried, it's not going to help you."

"What do you want from me?" She hissed.

"*You* came to me. What do *you* want from me?" He barked.

"I just... I... I just want to go back to the way things used to be..." She seemed confused in her own desires.

"The way things used to be... before we met? I'd go back to those days."

"There's no need for this, Adam. You don't need to throw away our friendship."

"But I *want* to, Eve. I *need* to."

Her eyes darted to his. He looked into hers. His gaze did not falter, nor did it hesitate. Those dark eyes of his, they told no lies. They cut her a million different ways, but each with a truth she didn't want to know.

She stood there for a second, lips trembling and eyes watering. There was an unsettling calmness in his eyes, one that his voice didn't seem to hold. She had never regretted seeing him before, but she definitely regretted it now. She didn't even know if it was Adam anymore. There's no way Adam would be like this. *Her* Adam, like this? To *her*? No. Not her Adam.

The bag rustled as the wind whistled it away, flicking the air like a small flame. She turned on her heel and bolted away, almost slipping as her body wanted to collapse. She ran. Aimlessly. Away from him. Away. And then home. Where the heart is. Home.

He hadn't insulted her, but his words hurt worse than if he had. It was the worst thing she'd been faced with. The words rang far too true to be ignored this time. This was a side of him she hadn't seen before. Even when he plotted vengeance on her traitors, he had always seemed so gentle. There was a violence to him. A burning violence within him.

Slamming the door shut, she ran to her room and buried her face. She cried herself to sleep, for the first time in a long time. A damp pillow held her weary head rather than the damp shoulder she'd become accustomed to.

A single tear rolled down his cheek as he closed his eyes with regret. He felt freed, though, liberated. At what cost?

"I'm sorry you guys had to see that." He spoke to silent tombs.

Her parents tried to console her from her door to no avail. They had no idea what had happened, and they were unable to get anything from anyone. Ordinarily, the only person that could console her was him. In this case, though, there was no guarantee even he could.

Adam's mother went to see him after she got the worried call from Eve's parents. He said nothing. She sat beside him a while, letting the silence speak to him for her. He seemed to speak to her through the wind, though he didn't look at her once.

Her guts contorted themselves inside as she felt helpless. She couldn't help him navigate this sea. A mother, unable to protect her only child. A mother, unable to help her only legacy. A mother, unable to do anything. She was lost and there was no answer. There was no manual she could flick through. She could only try, as Adam ate away at himself. She could only try. But at what point does trying become pointless?

She looked at the graves in front of her. She closed her eyes and begged for their aid. She reached out her hand slightly as if it could be grasped. They'd know what to do, what to say. They could fix this. But they weren't here. They'd left her alone, with him.

Doubt. It's probably the cruellest thing someone can be left with. Doubt. She had plenty of it to infest her mind.

Chapter 12

She had opinions on everything now, wouldn't stop until she was right.

"She got what she deserved!" She yelled.

"Hm?" He replied.

"She was a bitch to him, pardon the truth. She didn't deserve him and he deserved better than her!" She waved her fists around.

"Maybe… He didn't deserve how she treated him, so he didn't deserve her. I don't know if she didn't deserve him. She definitely deserved him." He shrugged.

"She deserved nothing but what she gave out." She crossed her arms in anger.

"Everyone deserves to be loved. Everyone deserves to be cared for, to feel desired, to be wanted." He tried to negotiate.

"Not her." She scowled.

"Okay, okay. Maybe she didn't." He responded, hands up to surrender.

"There's no *maybe* about it." She slapped his hands.

Adam had returned home and festered in his guilt for a few days. Ashamed and embarrassed, he knew he'd done more damage than he'd ever hoped to. His mother fed him updates on Eve as she got them from her parents. Eve hadn't left the house in days, apparently.

The roles had reversed now. From him camping out at a graveyard, to her locking herself in her room. Except, he wasn't going to let her sit there for weeks. He tucked his tail between his legs and plucked up the courage to go and see her.

As he approached the front door, he saw her curtains flitter. She was watching. That made him even more anxious, as he began playing with his fingers. He stepped forwards to knock on the door, the pressure increasing as he got closer to her.

He was greeted by a relieved father. He wasn't angry, which almost surprised Adam. He had almost hoped for some sort of punishment from her parents. Just something to set him straight. Though, nobody except Adam and Eve knew what happened, so how could he expect them to hate him?

Adam greeted them, shyer than normal. It was like he was meeting them for the first time all over again. He was frantically waved into the house and almost ushered to the stairs.

He took slow steps to the bottom of the stairs. He held the banister and stopped for a second to gather himself. After a short break, he began his trek up the short staircase as if these were to be his last steps. A part of him wished they were, and he'd drop dead at her door, just so he didn't have to do this right now. He'd earn her forgiveness through grief, surely.

He opened her door slightly and stuck his head in to see what she was doing. It was the first time since that night that it was unlocked. She stood at the furthest corner of her room, back to the door. He coughed as if she didn't already know he was there. He walked into the room, closing the door behind him. A few small, nervous steps took him to her bed. He sat down.

"Do you hate me?" Her voice fainter than the wings of an owl.

"You know what they say, hate is too strong an emotion to waste on someone you don't like." She turned to him as he said that, hoping that wasn't the end of what he had to say. "Sorry. I don't hate you. I could never hate you, even if I tried. Even if you tried. I don't know where it came from, but I shouldn't have said what I said. I'm sorry."

She shook her head. "You've got nothing to be sorry for. You were right, as always, and I shouldn't have taken you for granted. I don't know what I'd do without you, you're the only thing in life I actually need. I've spent the last few days wondering what to do, how to approach you and I was just scared I'd lost you..."

"You shouldn't be scared of me or anything I do. I would never hurt you. I made you that promise and I stand by it. Even if I sometimes fuck up, I'll always do my best. I'll always be by your side, even if I'm told I should be somewhere else." He replied as she walked towards him.

"I love you." She leaned over and whispered into his ear.

The words struck his tiny beam of hope as they bounced their way into his ears, repeating in his head for the few seconds. He didn't reply. He had heard her say them before but it didn't sound the same. There was a different tone to it. He'd know, he had them each stored away in his mind. He was confused, happy, overjoyed but also disappointed. He didn't want it to be like this, not like this. She'd seen him lost in thought, clearly not knowing where to go from here.

"You love me too." She smiled to herself although secretly praying it was still true.

She sat beside him. He still hadn't said anything. She didn't know what to make of it, he clearly wasn't expecting that. Should she clarify what she meant? Or would he figure it out?

Adam looked at her. He was still obviously confused. Without saying anything, he put his arms around her and pulled her in close.

"Thank you." Is all he could say.

He didn't stay much longer after that. The rest of that stay was just one long hug. He needed to make sure she was okay, to know her teddy was back with her. It was silent. Eve didn't know what to do, Adam didn't know what to say. He just heard her words over and over again in his head, dissecting them too many times over.

On his way home, he was done over-analysing her words of three. Now, he moved on to the follow-up four. It was something that would irritate his sleep for ages, but he could do nothing about it. He knew this reality, but something was different about it.

They had spoken the sequence before. It wasn't new to him. Three into four. *I love you* into *I love you too*. It was easy, almost child's play. Dangerous. That's why it was dangerous. It was easy. And maybe they'd been meaning two different things every time they'd said those words. And maybe they were both changing their meanings.

When Adam got home that day, his mother awaited the news. Like a teen, gossip seemed to be all she lived for. It helped her feel young again.

"Well?" She asked, eager and hopeful for good news.

"Same old." He shrugged. "We're friends again."

"You could seem happier about it." She replied, concerned. "What's wrong?"

"Is it worth waiting for my perfect love, or finding someone who will love me perfectly?" He sat beside her with his head in his hands.

"If you are the one that always saying *I'll be here when you need me*, you are the one who'll be left behind. If you are the one that can spot someone's sorrows when no-one can spot yours, you are the one who will never be consoled. If your smile is someone else's pillar, you're the one who's going to fall apart. If you are the one who will always give, eventually you'll be left with nothing to take. If you are the one doing all the loving, you are the one who will be left loveless." She put her arms around him.

"That one was too on the nose, even for him." He lay his head on her shoulder as she comforted him. "I miss him."

"We all do, just don't let his wisdom go amiss." His mother reassured him.

"He didn't listen to his own wisdom, why should I?" He sighed.

"Murder is the body, torture is the mind. Behind it all, a broken heart you will find." She kissed his forehead.

"Murder, eh? That could make my life easier. Think I'd get away with it?" He grinned a little to himself.

"In order to leave no fingerprints, you must sacrifice at least one." She replied, side-eyeing him with a grin. "Besides, you're too caring to kill a soul."

"Can I ask you a cruel question?" Adam asked.

"Sure." She answered before she could process what he'd just asked, or even prepare herself for anything.

"What would they say if they were here? If they could see just how fu-... messy this had gotten." Adam censored himself.

"Honestly, Adam, with those two... I don't know. Your grandad was persistent. He just kept trying with your gran, but she never tortured him quite the w-..." She stopped herself. "And your dad. Well, my dad liked him so he had an unfair advantage. He cheated." She laughed. "He didn't give up though, ever. From when I first said no to all the times I pushed him away after. He never gave up on me." She sniffed. "Those two cared for you and loved you a lot, though. I don't know if they'd let you go on this much. It would hurt them to watch you fall apart more than it's hurting me."

"I'm sorry, mum." He placed a hand on her cheek. "I don't want to hurt you."

"I know." She replied, placing a hand over his. "I know."

"Why did you reject dad so many times?" He asked.

That question seemed to throw her off entirely. It took her back to days long gone, a past she had almost forgotten. The distant look in her eyes, he knew he'd sent her to a different world.

"I wasn't ready. He made it clear he was, but I wasn't ready." She eventually answered.

"How long did it take you to be ready? How did you know? What changed?" Adam had never asked, but he wondered how he had never thought to ask now the question hung in the air.

"I don't think I ever was ready. I just trusted him."

Adam nodded and wrapped himself in her arms. He knew she was going to be stuck in that thought for the rest of the night and it was his fault. He didn't know how often she thought of his father, but he didn't like seeing her sad. He just wanted her to be happy, but now they seemed to both be falling apart.

He lay in his mother's arms for the rest of that night. She tucked him in on the sofa and could only pray he'd be okay. Wondering what he was dreaming of, she watched him for a while.

She parsed her memories for the wisdom she sought to help him. For the answers she needed to help her. His two heroes, role models and best friends had left him. They'd left them both, and all she craved was their guiding light just one more time. But she was only left with one thought.

I no longer want to live, if living is loving you.

Chapter 13

She lived off these stories, dictating her own would-be mistakes.

"Humans, eh?" She sighed. "Can't live with 'em…"

"We are imperfect beings chasing the shadows of our dreams. It's our biggest weakness." He nodded.

"So, to be perfect, I should just not chase my dreams?" She asked.

"What *are* your dreams?" He quizzed her.

She pondered for a while. "I don't know yet…"

"That's okay, you know?" He put an arm on her shoulder. "It'll come to you one day, just make sure you're happy in the meantime."

"Maybe that's my dream, to be happy." She nodded to herself.

"You're not happy with me, hm?" He grinned a little.

She rolled her eyes. "Not anymore."

Eve's head was all over the place, but she knew she had one clear objective. The only way to ease her restless mind was to speak to him, so she wasted no time in heading over. Adam's mother was cautiously happy to see her, hoping she could ease his hidden pains.

"Hi Eve, happy today, are we?" She greeted her with a smile, letting her into the house.

Eve stepped forwards with her hands behind her back and nodded. "It's going to be a good day; I'll make sure of it."

"Yeah? So you're going to make all of Adam's dreams come true?" Adam's mother replied, a joking grin on her face.

"Something like that." She chuckled lightly.

Adam's mother dropped a suspicious brow. "I have no idea what that means but just remember that I know where you live!"

Adam's mother pointed to the stairs with her head, signalling to Eve that she was free to see him. She had been a barrier but decided to let her through. Eve hastily ran up the stairs and waited outside Adam's door, preparing herself for what would ensue.

She took a few deep breaths as she plucked up the courage to knock on the door. Two knocks and then a pause. A few anxious seconds later, she knocked once more. She heard the unmistakable metal clacking of a lock being opened and the groaning twists of the handle.

"Mum, I'm oka-." Adam stopped himself when he realised who it was. "Oh, hi. Come in." He opened the door.

"Are you busy?" She stood at his door, peering in.

Letters and photos covered his bed and parts of the floor surrounding it. Adam fell to his knees and picked them up, fumbling from letter to letter to photo, dropping more than he picked up. It was just like the day they'd met, and here she was to save him again.

"I- I wasn't expecting anyone. Sorry for the mess." He panicked, trying to hide the pieces of him that lay splayed across his room.

Eve knelt down to help him pick them up. Much slower than Adam, taking memorable glances at each photo and letter. She was more composed than him and he noticed her looking. When they'd all been cleared up, she handed him her neatened pile to his scrambled mess.

"Thanks." He nervously smiled, leaning over to receive it.

A single letter jumped from the pile and onto the floor. Adam noticed which one it was and dropped them all to grab it before she could. Eve saw it before he did, though, and caught it as it fluttered through the still air.

She saw the first two words, they were hard to ignore. She didn't mean to intrude, but those two words had given her no choice. She stared at it for a moment and then started to read it aloud. Adam had retreated back to the floor to clear up the new mess he'd made.

"*Dear Eve,*

You know I love you. Your parents know I love you. My whole family knows I love you. I know I love you. But"

The unfinished letter ended there.

Adam let the pieces lie on the floor. He gave up. He remained on all fours, head down and trying to avoid her. He didn't know whether to cry or laugh. He just sighed and knelt there, waiting for her to break the silence.

She looked down and stared at him, surprisingly... surprised. He didn't look up but he knew she was looking at him, her eyes etching their acknowledgement into the back of his head. She lay on the floor and dragged herself under his eyes, smiling up at him.

"Why are you hiding?" She asked, softly.

He sighed, still defeated on all fours. "I don't know."

"You realise I can see you, right?" She reached out towards him and placed both hands on his cheeks.

"If I can't see you, you shouldn't be able to see me." He tried to console himself a little with a jab at humour.

"I wanted to ask you something, but I can't ask you when you're like this." She began.

He stopped trying to avoid her eyes. He had to bring himself to look into her eyes, it had never been such a struggle to do so. She smiled up at him, welcomingly, and rubbed his cheek with a thumb. She could see the loss in his eyes.

He was bruised, yet no punches had been thrown. He was crippled, yet no kicks had flown. He was damaged, yet he remained untouched. Nothing, that is, except the reality of his own situation. Or, at least, the reality his mind was trying to convince him of.

"Adam," she began, as his eyes sighed and lowered their guard. "Will you be my boyfriend?"

His eyes bulged and her smile faded into a look of concern. He couldn't look any more down than he already was, so he turned his head to look towards his chest. He didn't know what was happening anymore. He didn't know whether to panic. He froze, mind racing all over the place, his heart pumping faster than ever. Adam's breathing got quicker, heavier, more desperate.

He didn't know what to do, how to react. This was what he'd been waiting for, right? This made it all worth it, surely?

He lowered his head as he let his hands close in on his temple, palms flat, just beside Eve. He wasn't trying to drown out any noise, he was trying to shut out the world without losing the light. His hands panicked, covering his eyes, he didn't want the light anymore.

Eve, no longer smiling, saw his distress. She rushed up and knelt in front of him, rubbing his back. She didn't know how to comfort him, how to help him. Was this her fault?

He went limp, eyes slowly shut as his body collapsed into a puddle of his former self. Eve tried to catch him but he fell to his side and caught her arm, pulling her down a little with him. She freed herself, but her hands remained on him.

"Adam?" She held him, concerned.

Her face was overrun with worry and fear. Eve didn't know what to do. Her eyes watered as she screamed his name, hoping for a response to a sick and twisted prank.

All he could see were doors. He ran through one but found no exit. Just more doors. He ran through another. More doors. So many doors. He was trapped in a continual maze of doors. The light died, his world was blackening and all he could do was run. Run through the doors, run from the collapsing darkness.

"Adam! Adam, stop now! Adam, talk to me, please! Adam, not now!" She yelled repeatedly.

She kept trying to shake him awake. Her hands went from his body to his face, to just trying to grab any remnant of him before it would seemingly disappear. She could feel him in her clutches, but it was just a shell. It wasn't him. Eve screamed, wailed, and howled his name.

Heavy footsteps raced up the stairs, blind in distress. Adam's mother burst through the door to see Eve enveloping a husk of her son. She was rocking and crying, body wrapped around him, pleading for Adam to wake up.

Adam's mother slid to the floor, reaching for her son. Had her fears come true? Had he left her? Just like his father and hers?

She pulled him away from Eve, cradling him in her arms. She brushed his hair aside and started patting his cheeks, trying to wake him. She was doing her best to stay calm, she knew panic would only make things worse.

Eve had fallen to the floor, taking Adam's spot. It was warm. It had his warmth but lacked his comfort. She held herself, as if she could pretend her arms were his, as if it would make him come back to them, come back to her.

Regretfully accepting he wasn't waking up; she knew there was only one option. Scanning the floor, her eyes managed to find his phone. She placed her son gently on the floor and threw herself over to it, dialling only three numbers.

As confirmation of dispatch reached her ears, she dropped the phone and wrapped him tighter in her arms. They both rocked, pleas being thrown without pause. Adam didn't respond. The seconds felt like hours, with every plea and each heavy tear.

The sirens grew closer. This was her notice. Adam's mother had to compose herself. Eve had sat upright, hugging Adam and his mother. She released Adam back to Eve's grasp, entrusting Eve to never let him go. She raced down the stairs and opened the doors as the blue lights faded behind two men in fluorescent coats. She pointed them up the stairs and everything disappeared behind them.

All she could do was pray to a God she'd lost faith in. The same God that had taken her husband and her father. All she could do was hope, as she watched her baby being taken. She watched her son being carried away, bringing back the memories she'd buried deep down inside her, memories she'd never wanted to relive. Her eyes blurred as she followed them into the back of the truck.

Eve didn't move from Adam's room. She just lay there, cradling the space Adam had left between her arms as if he were still there. She had lost sight of everything. Her eyes were dried up but she cried. She wanted to cry tears of blood. She wanted to drain herself, to be with Adam. She threw vicious words at herself, tugging at all her insecurities and doubts. She was punishing herself. She did this. He was hers, and she had destroyed him. She tore at every seam that desperately clung to hold her together, as she frantically tore herself apart. This wasn't how it was meant to happen. It wasn't meant to happen like this. Not like this.

Eve's parents got the news from Adam's mother an hour or so later. Nobody knew where Eve was, but they'd managed to retrace her back to Adam's room. She lay asleep on his floor. She was carried away as if she were a drunk who'd just been beaten. Her face was stained with makeup. The skin on her palms had been broken from nails that were just trying to cling on. Her body was weak and limp. She was one step closer to him, at least.

All they could do now was wait. Wait for Adam. Wait for Eve. Wait. And they all hoped that neither the silence nor the time would consume them.

Chapter 14

She was preparing to become a young adult, the world raring to be unleashed upon her.

"Did he die? Don't tell me he died." She pleaded.

"It's just a story, we can rewrite it whenever we want." He smiled at her.

She composed herself. "Does he die in your version?"

He just shrugged at her. "Would you want him to die?"

There was no delay to her head shaking. "Of course not."

"I guess we'll have to find out." He bowed his head.

"If he dies, I want a version where he doesn't." She bargained.

"Deal. Are we keeping in all the stuff that's happened prior?" He asked.

"Maybe try to make it a bit less… how it is right now." She scrunched her nose.

"That's harsh, I didn't think it was that bad." He shook his head.

"Fix it then." She smirked back at him.

Eve was asleep, using Adam's mother's shoulder as a pillow. Adam's mother stared blankly at the wall opposite her, eyes reddened. Eve's parents didn't dare say anything. What would they say? What could they say? The pain was too raw, too easy to turn into chaos. Their words would only ring hollow when their child was right there, resting peacefully, against a woman whose world was crashing down around her.

"Thank you." Adam's mother broke the weary silence with a croak. "For staying here with me, thank you." Her gaze didn't break from the wall, her eyes remained hollow.

"We're here for you, we're practically family. He's like a son to me." Eve's father replied.

Adam's mother almost scoffed, those words enough to break her trance. Her gaze fell to her hands, as she nervously twiddled with her fingers. She rested her head on Eve's gently but refused to fall asleep.

"No, Adam!" Eve jumped, screaming desperately.

"Nightmare?" Adam's mother asked, rubbing her head from where she'd been headbutted.

"Sorry." Eve nodded, rubbing her own head now too, as the adrenaline quickly faded.

"Have we had any news?" Eve asked, looking down at everyone.

"No, dear. Not yet." Adam's mother answered, bowing her head again.

"Oh." Eve was disappointed, sitting back down beside Adam's mother. "Sorry… for your head." She tried to help soothe her wound, but it wasn't where the pain was. "And… for everything else."

"It's okay." Adam's mother answered, though it felt shallow.

Eve placed her head back on her shoulder, as Adam's mother rest hers against Eve. Her motherly instincts desperate to nurture, she accepted Eve's request for a shoulder.

Many thoughts ran through Eve's head. She kept blaming herself. She didn't know what to do. She felt responsible. She had tormented him for so long, and this new world of opportunity for him may have been the greatest torture he could imagine. And then she remembered the *but*. He loves her *but*... Maybe... maybe it wasn't his dream after all. It wasn't his dream anymore. Maybe, this had become his nightmare... *She* was one of his demons.

"What happened, I never asked?" Adam's mother spoke aloud, her voice seemed empty.

"It was my fault." Eve closed her eyes. "I did this to him."

"What?" Adam's mother lifted her head whilst trying to hide her concern, almost filling with anger. "What happened?" Her voice was still soft, but there was a heat behind it.

"I walked in on Adam. Well, he let me in, but only because he thought I was you." Eve raised her head, looking at his mother. "He was looking at photos and letters. Love letters and happy photos. Of his grandfather, and his dad. I'm guessing they were love letters they'd written because they didn't match his handwriting. I think Adam was trying to write me a letter. I don't know what it was going to say, but he had started it... I still remember what it said." She paused.

"What did it say?" Adam's mother seemed worried.

"*Dear Eve,*

You know I love you. Your parents know I love you. My whole family knows I love you." She paused, biting her quivering lip. "*I know I love you. But...*" The words had replayed in her mind ever since they entered it.

"And then what?" Adam's mother interrogated.

"I read it aloud, I don't think he wanted me to see it. He didn't look at me, I think he cried. Then I..." She hesitated.

"You what?" Eve's parents asked.

"I asked him to be my boyfriend." She revealed, distraught at her crime.

Just then, a nurse walked to them to update them on Adam's condition. The parents, however, didn't notice. They all stared at Eve, amazed. The widest of eyes, and jaws digging their way to the Earth's core. Emotions ran amok, with thoughts tugging and teasing. They didn't know how to respond. No one spoke. They just stared at Eve. Eve stared at the ground. Their hearts were racing, their minds were pacing.

"You can see him now." The nurse broke the awkward silence, feeling like they had spoken to nobody.

Everyone remembered where they were and turned their attention to the nurse. They all got up and waited for them to signal the way. Eve hid at the back of the line, wanting to stay hidden. She felt their eyes clawing at her, even from behind them all.

The reality had become a foggy mess of confusion and shock, completely overwhelming them. Between the three parents, they must've covered every possible outcome from this revelation, borrowing scenarios from every universe imaginable. They were saved from themselves, though, as the walk to the ward was a short one.

Adam's mother immediately rushed to his side and ran his hair through her fingers, finally being able to smile properly. "Adam... My son..." She'd lost her words.

Eve's parents just watched from the foot of his bed. He smiled at his mother before waving to Eve's parents. They broke a smile as they waved back. He looked around the room a bit, as if something were missing.

"How are you?" Eve peered out from behind her parents.

She watched the best thing that had ever happened to her lay there in a clinical white, almost unholy with innocence. Tubes and machines surrounding him, beeping away their discontent. He barely moved; no-one knew what to do. He just lay there as he caught sight of her. It's as if he'd given up and just wanted to rip off the monitors and let whatever would happen, happen. You could see it in his eyes.

"Look at me and answer it yourself." He grinned.

"Shut up, Adam." His mother placed her head against the side of his.

"Did they tell you what the deal was?" Adam asked.

"It was a stress-induced attack of... some sort." Eve's father answered.

Adam bit his lip nervously, hoping they hadn't found out. They all watched him, waiting for something to happen.

Even in this moment, they looked to him to ease their concerns. All he could do was shrug.

"Happens." Was the only answer he could give, accompanied by a blasé shrug.

Nobody had a response to that, not even his mother. Minutes passed in silence. Noone knew how to support him. There were too many questions, but it all seemed to tense to ask any of them. Everyone just sat in silence, waiting for something. Anything. Something.

"Could I-..." Eve started, as everyone swiftly turned to look at her. "Could we have a moment... alone?"

The parents were confused at first and then remembered. Eve's parents looked at Adam's mother. She seemed flabbergasted at the request, almost sizing up Eve. The cat was well and truly out of the bag, and it had its claws out.

She felt a warmth envelop her wrist. She looked down. It was his hand. She traced it back to him, just to make sure. He nodded slowly with a wink. Eve's parents hastily got up and crept out the room, almost as if they couldn't wait for the excuse. Adam's mother kissed his hand and then his head, and begrudgingly followed them.

Other than the silent hums and alarming beeps, there was a silence. They'd learned to drown out the other sounds. He watched her as she watched anything else but him. She slowly made her way over to his side, grabbing the handles on the bed. She was starting to regret her request, but she'd got herself into it now.

"I'm sorry I did this to you." She started.

He closed his eyes for a moment, then opened them to catch hers. "I'm probably more responsible for this than anyone else." He put his hand beside hers, the cold metal a light relief. "It was stress, Eve. Anything was enough to push me over." He tried to shrug it off.

She looked down. It didn't stop her feeling guilty. It wasn't *anything* though, it was *her*. Of course it would've been her. What else would've done it?

"Adam." She lifted her head to look into his eyes, hers were broken with regret. "I meant what I said, what I asked."

He sighed. "Eve." He slid his hand over hers. "You have to understand it from my perspective. It's a pipe dream. You don't love me like that, and I don't know if I'm strong enough to be okay with that." He fought through his tired body. "I'm needy, obsessively clingy even. I'm annoying and incredibly smothering. I'm constantly a mess with how my mind will run with *anything*. I get sick of myself when I'm in love, I can't imagine how the recipient of all that emotion would feel! I can't manage all of that whilst holding onto something... someone... that won't understand how crazy I am for them. You need to feel *just a little bit* of that too. I don't think you do. Not in the way you might want to."

"I mean it, Adam. I love you. I really do." She replied, teary-eyed.

"I know you love me, but not like that..." His voice was soft, but there was a drowning weight to it.

"I prom-."

"You can't promise that. You can't promise that, Eve. I couldn't hold you to that one... Besides, promises on your half, I can only hope you keep. But..." He paused a second to grit his teeth. "But I can't promise I'll have the energy or the strength to keep my love as strong for you as it has been all these years. I don't know why, but I can't promise I'll be there." He blinked away the film of tears that was building up over his eyes.

"You're being silly and scaring me. Don't cry. You don't cry in front of me. I can't be the only person to make you cry, it's too much. It's the biggest sin I'll have committed." She grabbed his right hand with both of hers and hid her face with it.

He watched her breaking in front of him. It was just how he felt. They were finally the same. Maybe it was different this time. There was definitely something gnawing in the back of his mind, but he'd finally have a chance at happiness. Or what he thought was happiness. But his gut... he was fighting his gut.

"Yes." It sounded like a whisper, but that's just how quiet his voice had faded to.

"What?" Her head shooting up.

"I'll try, for you. I'll be your boyfriend." He smiled at her, but the words seemed to sting him.

She threw herself on top of him and hugged him tightly. He winced a little but was still smiling. His dreams could come true. His dreams were becoming true. But... The dreams had become a little dated. Could he still close his eyes and dream those same dreams with the same burning passion he'd created them with?

"You can come in now!" Eve yelled. "Come meet my boyfriend."

Her parents ran in and joined the hug, yelling congratulations all over them. Adam's mother followed swiftly too, but her smile seemed cautiously drawn. She ran over to Adam's side and made herself part of the group hug.

Amongst the pile of bodies, Adam caught his mother's eyes. She could see there was something in them, something other than the light that was always there when he'd dream about Eve. It's like it had faded.

She tilted her head forwards a little, asking a question with no words. After a long blink, Adam nodded with the smallest movements. His mother leaned over, their heads now together. They both closed their eyes.

Eve was normally the wildcard, but Adam had taken her place. He had set the deck on fire, but maybe it was the only way to relight the flame within him. Eve had asked one question, but there were many more to be answered. The only thing missing was someone to do the asking.

Chapter 15

She was a critic of the world, taking it in her stride.

"They're finally dating? And *she* asked *him*?!" She celebrated.

"Yeah. Every tale needs a happy ever after." He responded.

"...Something tells me this isn't it, is it?" Her scepticism kicked in.

"You were shouting at me to fix the story, now you're doubting the ending I've given you? There's just no pleasing some people..." He mimicked her rolling her eyes.

"You're horrible at lying." She shook her head.

He shrugged back at her with a smile. "That's a good thing."

Adam was out of hospital a few days later, rejuvenated and renewed. The extended camping trip had accelerated his destruction, but his new purpose seemed to be the focus he needed to recover. Eve visited him every day, more so than his own mother. She'd spent her days wasting light with him. She'd spent many heart beats and many breaths without him, and now she was investing them in him. It was her chance for a new beginning.

"Thank you." She had a smile on her face, one purposed with genuine happiness.

"For what, pray tell?" He asked, bemused but distracted by her newfound smile.

"Giving me a chance. Me and all my baggage. Me and my *perfucktion*." She chuckled.

"You don't need to thank me." He tried to shrug her off.

"I do, though. I'm damaged... I was going to say *goods*, but that doesn't seem right." She erased her own smile, a new truth surfacing.

"You're not damaged anything, you just weren't appreciated. You weren't given the respect and care you deserve. You may not feel you deserve it, but that's only because you were never given it to begin with. Your past is your past, we will leave it behind you. Behind us. We'll give you a new future, and we'll reshape how you see yourself." He leant into her.

"Thank you, Adam." She rested her head on his chest. "That's a future I can look forward to." She didn't know if she could believe everything he said, but the comfort he'd given her filled her with trust.

"Well, there's still time to regret it." He began to chuckle as she jolted her head up.

"Shut up!" She gasped, pushing him and pouting. "You had to ruin it."

He stayed in his new position, laying back, and pulled her down with him. He wrapped an arm around her and guided her head back to his chest, rubbing her shoulder softly.

"I've had plenty of time to regret you. Maybe there were times I did. Right now is not one of them. You're perfuckt." He kissed her head.

"What is '*perfucktion*' anyway." She asked, tilting her head up at him.

"You really wanna know?" He looked down to her.

She nodded against him, placing her hand beside her face, right over his heart. "Tell me your pretty lies, *lover boy*."

He chuckled, causing her to smile. "Okay." He took a deep breath and placed his hand over hers.

"Perfucktion is... Well, I don't know what it is really. It's hard to... put into words. It's every time I look into your eyes and I see you smile. You look happy, and very pretty.

But deep down, behind those beautiful eyes of yours, there's a sadness that sits there. There's just that little bit of sadness, surrounded by all the other parts of you. And it's that lonely nugget of sadness that drives you. It's your motivation, your desperation, to... be happy. To destroy itself and be replaced by something kinder. It's suicidal because it cares for you.

That sadness is all your innocence. It's all your hope, your dreams. It's you, in the purest form. It's that tiny ray of sunshine that sacrifices itself to the darkness, just so someone else has a little bit of light.

There was a time when you looked broken when you smiled. I knew that there were so many tears that were shed just so you could smile for a moment. Your happiness was broken. It was tainted. Because it was misdefined. You weren't happy, you were content. Content with not being alone, even though you still felt lonely. Content with being someone's, even though they just saw you as something. They had claimed you, but they didn't *desire* you. And you knew. But you were okay with it, just because you could pretend for a moment that you were happy.

Perfuckt is... trying. Trying when you know, deep down, you don't believe in it. You know it won't work, but you're going to destroy yourself trying. You're going to lose so many pieces of yourself just trying to stop the cracks. And when you're left to shatter alone, you try to put yourself back together again. But you'll never be the same again. You know you'll never be the same again. Even if you can perfect the act, you will never be the same again.

You're perfuckt, Eve. Your painted smile became a permanent stain, but hopefully we can help you find the real one again. Hopefully, one day, that little bead of sadness within you can be put to rest."

She nestled against him, lost in his words. He'd been preaching to the sky and she was floating on every word. Happy, but also sad. He was speaking from experience. She didn't say anything, though, she knew he was already in his own head.

As they lay in the park, the sun as happy as their days and the clouds dancing like their souls, Adam noticed something on the lower part of Eve's arm. She had started wearing long sleeves for some time, he couldn't quite remember when though. He thought nothing of it at first, until he caught sight of a faint red enveloping a slightly deeper red near her wrist.

"You're perfuckt too." She whispered.

He didn't say anything. He just held her hand a little bit tighter. He closed his eyes and just let his dreams play out for a moment.

"I love you, Adam." She broke his thoughts.

The words hit his ears with a ring. His eyes shot open. She had her eyes closed against his chest, not realising his moment of panic.

"I love you too, Eve." He replied, trying to convince himself if it was true.

"I love you more!" She teased back, a smile on her face.

He was overwhelmed with guilt. He had doubted Eve's ability to love him. He had questioned his own love for her. He almost let her slip right through his fingers, even as they were clutching onto her. He let her words float in the air, as if he'd never heard them, not wanting to touch them at all.

The sun beamed down on him. He felt warm, he felt... happy. Not content. *Happy*. The true dream. A gentle breeze caressed his exposed skin, teasing him with its gentle touch.

And then the cold didn't disappear. On his chest. It had somehow crept under his clothes. He slid his hand from above Eve's to below hers. He felt the dampness of his t-shirt.

"What's that?" He inquired.

"What's what? Eve replied, blissfully unaware, her eyes closed against him.

He looked down at his fingers. When he saw them, they started shaking. He pulled his top away from his body, giving him a better view. The small dark patch confirmed a truth he had wanted to deny.

Adam gently grabbed her arm and pulled her sleeve up. Eve realised what had happened and tried to retreat, but Adam swiftly tightened his grip around her wrist.

Her skin betrayed the secrets her eyes held. It revealed a small tally of deep red strips. A sleeping army. She'd been through a battle, and these were her soldiers. And right where the patch had been, a recently fallen unit. Some were older than others, telling their age through their different shades of red. The youngest ones, the traitors of this secret, were as fresh as the Sun's joy on the day. He gently ran his thumb along them, smudging her pale skin as he dragged the ink of her arm down it. She winced, a sting shooting through her, but he didn't stop.

He finally relented, releasing her arm, but it was a short-lived decoy. As she used her other arm to cover herself up again, he pounced on it. And just like before, he inspected it the same. It was a work in progress, one that had just begun, but there was definitely intention for it to mirror the other.

The whole time, she watched him with worry. She said nothing, just waiting for him to play his hand. She tried to think of how to explain this away. She knew he would ask. There was no way he wouldn't ask. She had to come up with something. Who did this to her? How did they do it? When? But as she watched him, she knew she couldn't lie. The pain in his face, the sorrow that spilled from his eyes. She couldn't lie.

Adam eventually let her other arm go, but only to trap her into a worse fate; he looked into her eyes and ensnared her. She stared back, locked in his gaze. She didn't know what to do or say. She didn't know what was worse: the sting from the sun or the burn from his eyes.

"There's one for every day you were in the hospital." She answered before he could ask, trying to take control of the situation. "It was my fault you were in there. And everybody just seemed to forget... They... they let me get away with it."

"I wasn't in the hospital for that long, Eve." He shook his head slowly. "And nobody let you get away with anything.

You weren't excused, you weren't pardoned, you weren't forgiven. You didn't *escape*, Eve. The easy way out would've been if I'd said no. The yes was where the punishment lay."

"Being with you isn't a punishment, Adam."

"Yes, it is. You've got to put up with me and all of *my* baggage. You've got to deal with me, my love, my sorrow, my desires, my needs. You have to *keep* me, Eve. That's your punishment. Everyone knows it." He was gentle but firm.

"I deserve this, Adam. I can't say if I deserve you, but I deserve *this*." She spoke with determination.

"Explain, please." He began, gently.

"You opened my eyes to how wrong I was. I was bad. I was so, so bad. I didn't deserve you. I deserved those guys, but I never deserved you." She grabbed his arm and revealed her name bruised into his skin. "That day. I realised on that day. I don't know why it took me so long to realise. I'd been hurt so many times, I was becoming numb to it. Yet, there was always one person I'd hurt over and over, without even realising because he never let me see it. Always one person. The only person to treat me right. I counted my sins and I won't let myself forget how much I've fucked up. I won't be blind again." She let his arm go. "You risked your wrist for my name. I'm paying for that crime with my body."

"That's not okay, Eve... It wasn't okay when I did it, and it's not okay when you do it." He held her wrists softly. "This is all my fault." He traced it back to that day at the graveyard. "You would've never done this if you hadn't seen..."

She shook her head so quickly, she felt a little light-headed. "No, Adam, no. The blame is mine. Please. Don't. It's not you, it's me." She begged him to regain the life that once dwindled in his eyes.

"Then why are some still fresh?" He asked bluntly.

"Because I deserve to feel the pain you have. No amount of hurt I inflict on myself will ever be enough though, because I can't imagine the agony I put you through." Her voice quivered.

"You *chose* the pain... You chose pain over happiness…" His voice trembled, soft and aching. "You wanted the guts, but none of the glory." He whispered to himself. "We can't do this, Eve. We're not gonna be like this."

"I-…" She wanted to argue, but she didn't know what to say.

He wrapped her in his arms and squeezed her tightly against him. She broke on his chest, as he rocked her. He let himself fall apart in her arms too. Whispering words of comfort to her. He would protect her from the world. He had to.

"It's okay. Eve, it's okay. Just stop, okay? I felt the pain I felt, but I would never wish it on you. Never. You've already felt too much. This isn't the way, Eve. We're gonna leave the past where it should be – it's not gonna hurt our future. We're giving ourselves a fresh start. We deserve that." He felt her nod against him. "Just promise me, you'll stop."

"I promise." She responded through her cries.

"Promise me you'll never hide anything from me again, no matter how bad." He kissed her head repeatedly.

She hesitated for a few seconds, realising what was going on. She'd realised even more but could no longer punish herself.

The hesitation was only brief, short enough for Adam to not notice, but to her it felt like a whole extra year.

"I promise." Her voice no longer shaky, a purpose behind it.

He picked her up and walked her home, her hand never leaving his heart as she counted every beat. The continuity of his beating heart was in sync with the bad thoughts running through Eve's mind, a new one with every new thump. The pounding of his chest healthier than her mind. He was oblivious to Eve's guilty conscience. He was oblivious once more.

Chapter 16

She had grown an impatience during her learnings, desperate to get all the cheats to life.

"WHAT DID SHE DO?!" She bellowed in rage.

"I don't know." He shrugged.

She jumped on his back and got him in a loose chokehold. He stayed the same, denying he knew anything else. He smiled as she gritted her teeth.

"It's a story, calm down. I could change it any second." He defended himself.

"But you already know what happens, I see it in your twisted eyes. TELL ME." She slapped his chest.

He stood up with her wrapped around him and walked up the stairs. He laughed as she screamed with fear. He dipped and dived to make her regret her choices, reasserting his control.

"You make a nice blanket." He joked. "Now sit in your room and, when you behave, I'll tell you the rest." He ripped her off him as he left her to sulk alone.

"I'm almost an adult, you can't do this to me!"

"Then behave like one." He yelled back.

Adam was cautious at first. He wanted Eve to prove something to him. Whether it was her love, or her commitment. He didn't say anything though, he just let her take the lead. And lead she did.

Eve would come to Adam more often than before. He was usually at her beck and call. He could probably get to her room from his with his eyes closed. But now, she would make the trek. Now she could make the walk with her eyes closed. Initially, he was surprised, but he grew to expect her. He was following her lead, after all, letting her show her dedication.

As much as Eve was their shepherd, Adam was still determined to go at his own pace. He didn't want to rush, didn't want to risk ruining everything. He had to prioritise his comfort, and Eve seemed to be okay with it. He was seeing a different side of her, one he never thought he would see. One he was pleasantly surprised by.

They'd been dating for a couple of months, with the same routine. He would wake up and wait for her. They'd either have plans and he'd be waiting at the door, or he'd send her a text and be on call. They'd spend days together, be wrapped in each other's arms, potentially make some memories, and then he'd drop her off and look forward to their next date.

Their most recent date had ended at her house. He was laying in her bed as they watched whatever parts of the sun setting from her window they could. The night sky swallowed the fading, restless sun, and with it, Eve flopped into her bed.

Adam watched her land, looking back at him with a grin. He tilted his head, admiring her from that short distance away. She propped her head up with an arm and winked at him. He laughed a little and shook his head with a smile. She beckoned him to her with a curling finger. He shrugged, resisting her tempting ways. She scooched over and patted the space beside her. He bowed his head with a chuckle, hiding his face from her.

She pouted but he couldn't see. And before she could complain any more, he pounced onto the bed, collapsing into her, and granting her the wish she'd asked for, just not in the way she'd asked for it.

She groaned, a part of his flying weight knocking into her. She could see the worry in his eyes at her pained moans as he tried to comfort her. She just laughed at him and leapt on him instead.

They hadn't spoken for minutes, but they were having a whole conversation. Between their noises and their gestures, they had told a tale. She settled against his chest, letting his blanketing arms swallow her.

He looked down into her eyes and wondered for a moment. He wondered how he had ended up here. How he'd ended up dating the girl he'd been in love with for years, but she was the one who asked to be his. How this woman he had elevated in his head for so long was actually closer to him than he realised. They weren't too dissimilar, they just had different means.

She watched him watching her, wondering what was going through his mind. She watched his eyes change, from curious, to content, to sad, to happy. They finished on happy. A smile confirmed it. He was happy.

She felt herself moving. He pulled her up to him and rolled them over. Now, he looked down at her, as he tried not to crush her under him. She raised a brow in response, questioning him. He just shrugged.

Everything went dark. And then it was half-light again. She felt a gentle, warm touch against her. Soft. Delicate. Precious. She smiled against him, closing her eyes. The warmth flowed through her now. He'd taken his first kiss. Their first kiss.

He pulled away and looked down at her. She had a wide grin on her face. It had a smugness to it as she bit her lip. Now he raised the eyebrow at her, asking her a question. She just shook her head and with no further warning he found himself below her again. She had wondered how this moment would go. It was nothing like she'd imagined, but better in every way. And now it was her turn to show him what he'd been missing out on.

The night ended shortly after. As much as Eve wanted him to spend the night, Adam was adamant he had to go home. He had *something to tend to*. She begrudgingly let him go, but she made sure to let him know she wasn't happy about it.

"I'll make it up to you." He blew her a kiss from her door.

He watched her catch it and put it in her pocket and then flip him off. He chuckled and left, chasing the sun to where it shone, for his world was bright right now.

And now it was his turn to surprise her. He had chosen a specific day to make an important decision. This day, of all days, was Valentine's Day. A good day to be in love. A great time to surprise her. The perfect day to let Eve know that he was ready to fully realise his years of dreaming about her.

"Is she home?" Adam asked, handing her mother some flowers.

"We just got home but I think I heard her upstairs." Her mother replied, stepping to the side whilst graciously accepting the flowers.

He danced up the stairs joyous and gleefully. He was unbreakable today, determined to make his first real Valentine's a good one. He'd planned this day out in his head so many times, and he finally got to see those dreams come to life.

As he neared her door, he could hear her scurrying around and talking to someone. Maybe she was on the phone or had a guest round. After all, he came unannounced.

He didn't think much of it. Eve has friends. Everyone has friends. He has friends. He was friendlier with voices than people, but he has friends. His mother has friends. His hopeful in-laws have friends. Everyone has friends.

He stood at her door, and realised there was another voice in that room. He decided to let them finish their conversation, or at least take a pause, before he intruded. He listened for their sounds but trying not to listen to what those sounds were.

"I'm the only one who wants you. It's Valentine's Day, and you were here all alone until I came by. It's not like you have a queue of guys waiting outside." A male voice pleaded.

"I can't. I ju- Wait, Valentine's?" Eve's familiar voice of confusion and realisation. "Oh shit."

"Don't tell me you forgot. I thought that was the day all women in relationships looked forward to. Especially when their boyfriends visit with gifts." The voice replied.

"Fine. Quickly. I need to go, just keep everything on and get it done with. But this is the last time. I can't do this anymore." She replied hastily.

"Yeah, yeah, I've heard that before. You'll be back. You can't resist me. I know how to make yo-."

Adam couldn't hear the rest of their conversation. Not because they spoke quieter, but because he couldn't hear them speak anymore. She was meant to be his. He was ready. He was really ready for her. She was his...

The unmistakable screaming of fabric tearing. It broke him away from his anger. As much as he tried to drown them out, he was brought back to them now.

"What the fuck?! I liked that top!" She yelled.

"And I like your body... and those tits!" He grunted. "Come here, I'll take care of you."

It was swiftly followed by hushed moans. He knew it was her. The noise of lips meeting flesh came quickly after. He tried to mute them out, but the sadistic games his mind played forced him to listen. He managed to make out the fumbled clattering of a belt buckle and the dull thuds of falling clothes. The blanketed landing of a body landing on a bed, and the mixed orchestral groans. He could hear when their bodies met. Each and every time.

Adam kicked the door. It was locked. He kicked again. Still locked. And again. And again. And again, until it swung open. Eve's parents ran to the bottom of the stairs to see what was going on. They only managed to catch the back of Adam bursting into the room.

Eve got up from the bed as she and her *friend* stared at Adam. He was desperately trying to do up his trousers and put his belt back on as Eve covered herself with her duvet. Adam just stood there.

"This isn't..." She had nothing to say.

"Who's he?!" The guy yelled loudly. "I knew you were a slag but even he's a bit low for you." He replied.

Adam dropped the gifts that filled his fists and lunged forwards, pushing the guy into the bookshelf that contained no books, only memories. He was not expecting Adam to do that, the shock on his face gave him away. Adam locked eyes with him.

He didn't know what to do, he'd never been in this situation before. He just held him against the now collapsing bookshelf which no longer held anything but his hatred, his arm across this demon's neck. Eve's friend could see Adam's hesitation. That caused him to make the mistake. He had misjudged Adam. He had mistaken him for something he was not. He thought him to be a man of peace. But Adam's mind was far from peaceful. And that misplaced assumption sold his soul. With an arrogant confidence, he smirked.

He was moaning and groaning in a different way now, as the heavy blows kept landing against his gut. Each one was intentional and powerful. There was a pause, giving him the opening he needed to huddle over and shelter his bruising body.

CRACK. His face flew back, body falling with it, as Adam's knee impacted his head. There were a few spatters of blood, but there was no pause now.

He felt the cool air brushing past him. It felt relieving. It soothed his pains. The world seemed to be slower, he found some peace. But he'd been fed false hope. He came crashing into Eve's desk, wood and body crumbling together.

He had found a strength no-one knew he was capable of. A destructive, raging burst of energy that even Adam couldn't comprehend. He was throwing kicks and punches, channelling his new power. He wanted to feel it, each hit fuelling him to keep going. It was addictive, the brutality he was able to cause with his own body. He relished in its awe. This was the other side of love: hatred.

He clutched his hair and lifted his head, almost like a cheap trophy. Adam's eyes would be pure black if you stared into them now. He could see the fear in this pathetic being's eyes. He looked just like her past. Disgusting, disgraceful, diabolical. With all the force he could muster, he slammed his head into the floor.

He was out for bloody murder. He wasn't going to stop. There was no tiredness wearing him down. There was no guilt holding him back. He was okay with going down with this burning ship. Their relationship. Smouldering in front of her, as she watched the man she loved trying to kill the man she lusted.

Eve's father ran in and tackled Adam. He held him against a wall. Adam was ready to attack him too until he realised who it was. He tried to quickly compose himself, biting his own teeth but refusing to unfurl his fists. Eve's mother hurried in afterwards, escorting the bloody body out of her house and returning to Eve's room for further investigation.

"Please don't let it be what it looks like, Eve." Eve's mother begged her to lie. "Anything but that." She pleaded, watching her poorly covered daughter trying to melt away into the corner.

Eve's father turned to Adam. "Can I let you go now, son?" He asked calmly.

Adam nodded. He didn't even look at Eve, he just stood where he was, between the wall and her father. Eve's mother tried to check Adam's wounds, but he denied her access to his body, shaking his head.

Everyone stood where they were, her parents between the pair of them, watching Adam for his next move. He had been working on calming his breathing, slowing himself down in the process. He had barely managed to unball his fists, stretching out his fingers to ease the aching that was settling into them now.

When he'd finally felt normal again, he shook Eve's father's hand, pulling him into a hug and apologising into his ear. He then hugged her mother, apologising to her too for what she had seen. He then hastily limped towards the door, refusing to face his other demon. He was so caught up in causing pain, he hadn't noticed he was taking any. It was catching up to him now.

"You won't even let me explain?!" Eve yelled, her hands waving angrily and releasing the garments that covered her.

Adam stopped at the door. He refused to look back. He just stopped.

"You hadn't even kissed me until yesterday, Adam." Her tone was calmer now, but her voice was breaking. "We've been together for months, and we've kissed *once*. I have needs. You made no indication you were going to tend to those needs. If you weren't going to... I needed to find someone who would." She had managed to stop the shakiness in her voice.

His head gently dropped. He sighed and just shook his head. It was a sluggish shake, the consequences of his actions materialising quickly through his body. But it was obvious.

"Look at me, Adam." She demanded.

He just stood there, observing the trail of blood that left her room. He took no pride in it, but he also felt no shame in what he'd done.

"We can talk this through. Adam, please. Talk to me." Her voice was soft now.

Eve's mother stepped towards her, obstructing her view towards him. She tried to cover her up, but Eve had little care for her parents' presence. She stepped around her mother with anger.

"You really want nothing to do with me? You're going to throw what we had away?! You could hate me that easily?" Eve screamed at him, lips like two colliding tectonic plates. "This is your fault. Why couldn't you just give me what I wanted? I guess you didn't want me as much as I thought."

Adam turned his head slightly so she could see his lips, but he still refused to look at her. "Fuck. You." He spat those words with pure anger.

"Maybe if you had, we wouldn't be in this mess!" She screeched back.

She took a moment to breathe. She rubbed her hands over her face, trying to calm herself down. It was a sensitive moment, but surely he wasn't going to leave her. He was hers. Adam and Eve. She was his.

"Adam, please. I was leaving him. I was all yours. We can start again. We can be happy. Don't throw this away, Adam. We were good together! You've waited forever to be with me." She begged.

He shook his head subtly. She felt like a negotiator, she just had to get him talking. As soon as he was talking, she could fix this. She could fix this. He just had to talk…

She ran over to him and grabbed his hands. "Adam, look at me." She tried to run into his view but he just closed his eyes. "Adam, please. It's me, Eve. *Your* Eve. I'm your future. I'm your first love. I'm your first kiss. I can be so many more firsts too. I want to be so much more with you!"

Adam shook her off and stepped away from her. Eve's mother gently held Eve, walking her away from him. But Eve wasn't going to let it end there. He hadn't walked away yet, there was still…

"Fine, maybe you didn't love me as much as everyone thought you did. Go spend the night at that fucking graveyard and maybe you'll realise what you're doing. Or maybe you can dig yourself a grave and lay in it!"

That had done it. She had done it. She got what she wanted. Adam turned to look at her. He ignored her bare body and looked straight into her exposed eyes. The anger in her throat turned to a fear trickling down her spine. Her eyes had lost their fire, her flames extinguished by the ice-cold stare he stabbed her with.

"I give you my word, Eve, I will dig myself a grave." He spoke softly. "I'll only lay in it once you've filled it with the blood from your wrists, though." He wasted no more of their time and headed out after that.

Eve dropped to her mother's feet, crying for forgiveness. Eve's mother crouched beside her, holding her and trying to comfort her. She noticed Eve's arms, each mark slashing itself into her heart.

Her father, however, just stood there. The words dug a little deeper for him. It's as if Eve had murdered the son he never had. The son he could've had. He didn't even mean to call him "son", but he wasn't going to apologise for it. It just reminded him of the time Adam had called him "dad". He was happy and sad at the same time.

He felt a weight on his calf that snapped him back to the room. His wife was nudging him as his daughter tightened her grip on his ankles. He looked down to see his daughter weeping at his feet. He crouched beside her and lifted her up.

They took her to their room; she was in too much of a state to be by herself. Eve's mother helped her get dressed. Her mother tended to her arms, cleaning them up and ensuring they'd be okay. She couldn't help but count them, each one cutting through her, wondering how Eve could've committed so many sins. How nobody noticed them either. And then, the question that broke her even more: what sins had she committed that were so bad that she had to engrave them into her flesh?

Eve curled up against her father, crying herself to pieces in his arms. As she lay with him, drifting in and out of sleep, he thought about all the dreams that had shattered right before him.

Adam was laying too. He was on the ground, eyes wide open but fading ever so quickly. He was falling asleep in the arms of a darkness he'd felt before.

The boy Eve had cheated on him with had returned with friends. He was in no state to do anything, and he definitely couldn't go to any authorities for the sake of his pride. This had to be a different sort of justice. They waited for him nearby, armed and vengeful.

Their ears perked up when they heard the door close. They counted the footsteps, letting them get louder, closer. They stalked him, making sure the trap they had set would lead him right where they wanted him.

Like rabid dogs on an injured deer, they pounced and ferociously attacked, their only goal to rip him apart. They'd take him from his emotional death to a physical one. They'd make sure he wouldn't have to feel this pain for too much longer.

Adam lay just around the corner from Eve's house.

Eve lay with her parents.

Adam was losing blood. Eve was losing tears.

Adam was fighting for life. Eve was mourning his love.

Adam wanted to let go. Eve held on with all she could.

Adam was fading. Eve was being given a new light.

Adam had been ripped apart. Eve was being pieced back together again.

The ring of lost memories. The circle of forgotten souls. The dust had finally consumed him. The teddy bear was engulfed. He didn't have to deal with her breaking his heart. He was being set free. Free from the evil clutches of love. Free from the never-ending pain. Adam welcomed the end of his tale.

Chapter 17

She had a vested interest in the stories, they helped shape her into who she wanted to be.

"Didhedie?!" She asked with speed.

He shrugged in response.

"Soooooooo he doesn't die. Got it." She was still prodding for clues.

He just shrugged again.

"There's no way she threw it all away! For what?!" She yelled.

He shrugged once more.

"She asked him to be her boyfriend, right?" She replied.

He nodded.

"But she cheated on him?" She grew ever more impatient.

He nodded.

"Why?!" She asked.

"He couldn't provide what she needed, apparently." He shrugged again.

"But did he know she... wanted that?" She seemed confused.

He shrugged again. "Probably not."

"He could've said so much more. He should've!" She blurted out, annoyed.

"He said a lot with his actions, he didn't need words. Besides, the words he did say…"

"They were cruel… Dangerous, almost. He wanted to hurt her." She seemed to have switched sides.

"She brought out the worst in him, and she showed him the worst part of her. He chose to use his words differently to how he had before. He didn't need volume because volume is what you use when you lack substance. It's easy to wave away screaming and shouting, excusing them as being an emotional reaction. But when you speak softly, you can't make that excuse. When someone speaks calmly, you assume they have put thought into their words. You have no choice but to listen. And that's what makes the words hurt more. They're intentional. Maybe that was reckless of him, but I'm sure he had his reasons." He left her to dwell on that.

Adam's mother had finally found the hospital Adam had wound up in. It was some specialist one that had a name she felt she should know but it kept slipping her mind. She had other things to worry about, so it wasn't a concern for her right now. She ran frantically to the reception, asking where he was. Though words were flying out of her mouth, a proper sentence was unlikely to be pieced together. Just words, noises and sniffling.

A few short moments later, Eve's parents ran to her aid. Eve's mother dealt with her whilst her husband requested information on Adam. There'd been no updates on him, all they knew was that he was in an operating theatre. There was no sign of Eve.

The waiting was the worst part. Again. It's always the waiting. Just the silence that allows you to think too much. The lack of answers that would only be flooded out with more questions. Patience is a virtue but this waiting was just torture. The last time Adam was in hospital, the unknown entity that caused his collapse was eating at their minds. This time they knew, and it felt much worse.

A few long hours later, a nurse approached them to break the news. They couldn't see him; it was too late. All that waiting, for what felt like nothing in a single moment. They were sent home but were somewhat optimistic with what they were told. Better it be time-related than him-related. Adam's mother remained pale, unable to see any silver lining.

Eve's parents took Adam's mother to their house. They wanted to keep an eye on her, make sure she was okay. It's moments like these where it's for the best she wasn't left alone. The choice was short-sighted, though.

They approached the house, following the trails of blood that pointed the way. Adam's mother watched it, not sure whose blood she was looking at. It stared back, she could feel it. Cold, brutal. It watched her follow.

"Sorry about the mess…" Eve's mother regretfully apologised, realising that maybe this was not the best place for her to be at this moment.

"…Is it… his?" Adam's mother asked, unable to look away from the crimson streaks on the floor.

They knew what she was asking about. They didn't know the answer though, which was probably not reassuring. They tried to lead her to a part of the house that wasn't so chaotic, that wasn't a constant reminder of her son's current fate.

After some silence, they told her the story. They knew she had to know. After all, it's why he ended up like this. They'd want to know too. She was speechless. Her gaze was hollow. They felt guilty, as if they'd taken the last remaining part of her that made her human and destroyed it. She'd become a zombie, just staring emptily into nothing. She was completely blank, a living ghost.

"She didn't even have the guts to come here and explain to me herself, I see." She sighed. "Thank you, though, for letting me stay here. Don't take this the wrong way but I think I'm just gonna go home. I need some time to myself. I don't think it's a good idea for me to be here either." She seemed calm as she placed the cup on the coffee table.

Eve's parents nodded, they couldn't imagine what she was going through but they understood. As much as they thought she needed to be anything but alone, they would never really understand the pain she was feeling. She had to know what was best for herself, in some capacity. If not for herself, then for Adam.

They guided her to the door. Eve's father repeatedly asked if she wanted a ride home, knowing the streets outside had yet to be cleaned up. He was rejected each time.

Eve stood at the top of the stairs as Adam's mother reached for the door, trying to hide herself as she watched. Adam's mother caught her, though. They both locked eyes for a few long seconds. Neither said anything, they didn't have to. Their spoke through their eyes. It was a brief conversation, very one-sided.

The cold glare of a mother who couldn't protect her child. The scorned lover who'd set her house on fire. Eve's eyes didn't have any fire behind them, though. She'd burnt out. She'd been extinguished. Adam's mother had only just been set alight, roaring to go.

Before her lips could part uncontrollably, Adam's mother walked out the door. Her tongue wanted to be wicked, but her heart showed mercy. It wasn't the time, she needed to save her energy for her son. And, ultimately, she had deemed Eve unworthy. Unworthy of her time, unworthy of her words, unworthy of her son. Eve was weak, she was hurt, and she knew Adam wouldn't forgive her. That was more wicked than anything she could've said.

He hadn't woken up in days, but Adam's mother stayed with him every second she could. She'd often talk to herself, hoping he'd wake up and tell her to shut up. She hoped he could hear her. She hoped at any moment he would answer a question he'd asked days ago, and she'd sit there confused until she eventually remembered. She wouldn't leave. She couldn't let go, not for a third time. No parent wants to outlive their child. Either they both left the hospital, or neither of them did. She had no intention of losing him. She no longer wanted to live, if living was losing him.

"I was hoping something would happen to me. I was praying. I can't deal with this. You're all I have left and even now I have to loosen the reigns. I'm losing my little boy, sooner than I'd like." Adam's mother rambled as Adam slept.

The nights were long for her. The world seemed darker, crueller. She was awake and at the hospital doors a few minutes before visitors were allowed. She'd wait to be the first in the door. Even though she knew she wouldn't be the first to see him, in her head she was. She had to be.

Adam hadn't woken up. She spoke to him as if he had, hoping he'd reply. He didn't move. His heart was slow, but at least it kept going. Her eyes had a tiny spark of hope, but they remained heavy and void of anything else. She was losing herself, driving herself mad with her grief.

But she reminded herself that he was her son. He was his father's son. He was his grandfather's grandson. He had their blood in him. And their hearts kept going for as long as they could. His heart would keep going. It had to keep going. It had so much love left to give, it had to keep going.

"They say the slower your heartbeat, the longer you live. You'll live long, eh? Apparently, you only get a certain amount of heartbeats in a lifetime. A certain number of breaths. You should live forever then, you lazy git!" She attempted to mimic his humour to cheer herself up, but it only hurt her more. "Wake up, please, Adam. I'll let you be as lazy as you want."

"Mum?" Adam groaned as she jumped up, rushing to his side.

"I'm here, I'm here. Is there anything you need? Are you in pain? Where does it hurt? What do you need? I'll get you anything. Tell me what's wrong, Adam." She was a mess.

"Shut up." His voice was slow as he struggled to speak but it was worth it to see her grin.

"How are you feeling?" She blurted, wanting to slap herself for such a question.

"Like a spring buck, ready to gallop through the forest." His arm crept up like a rusted machine as he held up his thumb.

"Shut up." She rolled her eyes. "Are you okay, though?" She asked.

"If you're worried about me, you should see the other guy." He choked on a laugh.

Adam looked into his mother's eyes for a minute, feeling all her sadness and guilt. It hurt him more than anything that gang could've done. She got caught in the crossfire and she wasn't even there. It's not fair. Not her.

He tried to sit up, aching and groaning as he did so. Adam's mother quickly stopped him and shook her head. She put her hand on his head and stroked his hair to comfort him.

"Dad had a recipe for wooing women, didn't he?" Adam tried to reminisce with his mum.

"He called it his *'Formula for Love'*." She laughed. "It was pretty good, I won't lie."

"Tell me it." Adam smiled back at her.

She looked to the ceiling as she tried to remember it and then locked eyes with Adam once again. "Ask her out, subtly, once a day. Don't make it an official date, just act like you were going somewhere and see if she wants to tag along. She knows what you're doing, though, you're not very good at being subtle. But that's okay, the lack of subtlety plays in your favour if she accepts. Take her to a place you know well and hope she will enjoy. You don't have to wine and dine, don't try to impress. If you try to impress, she won't get to know you. Focus on fun. You can learn a lot about a person by how they have fun. More importantly, it only takes a single moment for you to make a memory, and then you've imprinted yourself into her mind. Make sure she remembers you for the good times. See every bad choice as a good opportunity to redeem yourself. Bad memories can become good ones. She'll know you won't give up on her. And if all else fails, you can move on knowing you tried." They'd both closed their eyes as she recited the formula, but only he opened his when she'd finished.

"Did it work?" He asked her.

"Nope, it was terrible. He would just say it to annoy your gran." She laughed, opening her eyes, and freeing herself from that bittersweet memory.

"It did sound pretty bad." Adam grinned.

"The real advice was great though. Let me see…" Her mouth opened as her mind drifted once more.

"You're a friend first. Always be a friend before you're anything else. You see someone gorgeous and you wanna make sure they're yours forever? Be their friend. Don't go into it with the intention of falling in love. Be their friend. Start pure, with an open mind, else you'll become tunnel-visioned and stupid. Get to know them while they get to know you. Be open. Share and be happy 'cos, no matter what, your partner always ends up being your best friend. So, be their friend before you become their lover. If you find out that maybe you're not quite the right fit for each other, at least you gained a friend. You can't lose.

Once you're their friend, make sure you're always there for them. Make sure you're always their friend. No matter what. No matter how much they annoy you or hurt you, no matter how much they push you away and kick you. You're always there to make sure they're okay. Make sure they know it too. And let them know. Advise them, console them, make them laugh, be honest. Just make sure they know that you value them as a friend.

And this is the difficult part. The part of showing them you value them that people often shy away from. Be vulnerable around them. Let them in. Don't be afraid to let them see the parts of you that you like to hide. Let yourself feel weak. It's what makes you strong. Open the door for them and they will have an easier time letting you in. It also proves to you that they care for you. So, you can't really lose here either. Start off small and slow but let them see the parts of you that nobody else does.

Sometimes, you may even have to hurt them, if it's for the best. And that don't mean punch 'em in the face; it means sometimes you gotta be the one to tell them a truth that ain't so pretty but it's gotta be done. They'll respect you for it, and it will build your trust.

But sometimes, you'll just end up hurting them. You didn't mean to. Or maybe you knew it would, but it was something you just managed to justify for a different opportunity. Don't see it as a failure. It's still an opportunity to make it right, to learn and grow together. You just have to make sure it's on their terms – especially if you've hurt them on yours. Their forgiveness is theirs to give, not yours to take.

Never forget to remind them how beautiful they are, how happy they make you and how much you love them, no matter how hard it is to get the words out. Just make sure they never lose sight of all the great things about them. Always lift them up, hold them high, celebrate them.

If they don't love you back, it's fine. You can still be a friend. You can still have a friend. Sure, it might hurt to begin with, but sometimes the hurting is worth it.

That's the thing about love. It's both a blessing and a curse. It can be the most amazing thing in the world. It can bring you joy like nothing else. Or it can be a purely destructive force that destroys you and everything you touch. Just make sure you don't lose sight of what love really is and make sure, regardless of how they feel for you, you give them the best of your love at all times. Love them till you can't love no more and you'll sleep a little easier knowing you gave them your all. Doubt is such a powerful thing, and if it has *any* room, it will find its way in. Don't live doubting your time with them.

Sometimes people can't realise what they have and what they feel until it's gone but that's not your fault. Don't abuse that though. Don't disappear just to make them realise. *They* have to realise. *They* have to accept their own love for you before they can give it to you. You don't want to be with someone who could only love you when you left. All you gotta do is just make sure they get the best of you at all times.

And when you can't love any more, if you can't endure it any longer, it's okay to walk away. It's okay to save yourself, it's okay to put yourself first. It's okay. As long as you don't have any regrets, as long as you know you did everything you could. Not everything is gonna work out, not every love story is gonna last forever. Your heart will be completed one day, but don't let anyone give you any reason to say you couldn't love them enough. It's draining, it's painful and it's stupidly difficult at times. But it's worth doing. You'll get someone who will love you the same way you love them as long as you don't sell yourself short. Just always make sure to spread your love.

Make as many happy memories as you can. You will leave your print on their soul no matter what, so make sure it's a good one. You can either reminisce with them a few years later or they can be left wondering where you ended up. Just do your best to leave good thoughts, sincere smiles and warm hearts, even when you're nowhere to be seen." He told her younger self.

She sat there for a moment. It felt good to hear his voice, but she knew she couldn't reach out and grab him like she so craved to do. He blew her a kiss, waved her goodbye and disappeared into the darkness of her mind.

"How do I know when to walk away?" He asked.

"Only you'll know. It's your relationship. You have to be the judge and the jury. Love is complicated, it can get really messy. You shouldn't give up on it, but don't let it kill you. It's walking on ice that's paper thin. Love changes your life. You will change yourself for someone, both unconsciously and willingly. You will change to make yourself more accommodating, more compromising, and maybe even more forgiving. But don't let it be a one-way road. It's give *and* take. It's love and be loved. It's two, not one. Sometimes listening to outside voices can help, which is why it's important to make good friends. Sometimes you just have to trust yourself. You know your situation better than anyone, no matter how much you try to explain it. I could tell you one thing now and something else next week if you asked me. Take note but draw your own conclusions."

"Perfection is an ideal and obtaining an ideal is an ideal." He whispered to himself.

"Amen to that." She grinned at him.

"You dad would say he didn't *just* love me. He never just loved me with his heart. He loved me with his entire being. His heart would ache for me, it would call out to me and beg for me. His lungs would breathe for me, desperate to feel the air I walked in. His hands would feel my phantom body when I wasn't around. He could feel my hands in his, he could feel my hair dripping through his fingers. He could feel me, without me being near. And all it did was make him desire me more. He'd say how I infested his mind. He'd see me everywhere. He'd see me in everything. He just wanted me all the time. He said his soul would sing for me. He could feel his soul dying with every kiss goodbye. And then it would be reborn as soon as he saw me again.

He said I was his battery. His source of energy. He didn't need food anymore, he just needed me. I almost believed him too. Whenever we were together, he'd have so much energy. He was like a coked-up puppy. Just boundless energy. But whenever I left, he said he just deflated. He felt drained. He was slow, sluggish. I told him he was crazy, and the fool agreed. He admitted to me he was. He was crazy for me. He said if he could let me see inside his mind, he would never let me, because then I'd realise that he was *actually* crazy. He was such an idiot sometimes...

But he knew how to make me smile. He knew how to turn me to jelly, make me all mushy inside. He filled me with butterflies with those careful words of his. And I know there were times he would've thought of a line and just sat on it all day, just waiting for the moment to steer the conversation into it. You definitely remind me of him, and that's why you can't leave me."

She could see him waving to her in a far corner of her mind. She kept running towards him, but he never got closer. She kept running, but he only seemed to drift further away. Back into the blackness that surrounded him. Back into the past.

"Am I a bad person, mum?" Adam asked.

"No. Never. You're an angel, why would you even say that?" The smile disappeared from her face and was replaced with shock.

"Even the devil was once an angel." He shrugged. "When I was... there... I felt so much relief. I was happy. I wanted to hurt him. I thought such violent, cruel things."

She winced, his words stinging her. "You're not a bad person, my sweet sweet child. You've been through a lot. And… there's probably a part of you that didn't just do it for yourself. You did it for her too. He wasn't just the guy that ruined your relationship, he was a representation of all the guys that she had chased before. All those years of watching her get hurt, never being able to do anything. Feeling helpless, weak, scared. As much as you may not want to have, I think a part of you did it for her too."

He let her words sink in. He didn't want to care for Eve, but he couldn't deny that a part of him still did. He could feel the truth in her words. There was a part of him that did it for her. But it was probably too late to have any desirable effect.

"Why do bad things have to happen to good people?" He sighed.

"Bad people prefer to let good people suffer the consequences of their actions. Since they're good people, they'll take it. It's okay, though, I won't let any more bad things happen to you. It's all over now, honey." She resumed stroking his hair, as she kissed his head a few times.

"I'm tired." He announced, closing his eyes.

The door clicked. Adam's mother turned to see who it was, hoping it wasn't an unwanted guest. She had no idea what was to come.

At the door stood a woman she'd never seen before. Adam's age. She wasn't a nurse, or at least she didn't look to be one. She was smiling. She wanted to growl, to charge. She wanted to protect her son. This stranger was too close.

"Mum, meet Rose." Adam introduced the figure as she closed the door behind her.

"Pleasure to finally meet you." Rose smiled as she put her hand out.

"Before I shake your hand..." Her face flipped back to her son, concerned. "Adam, explain. Now."

"Rose is a good friend. She knows everything, mum." Adam explained. "If you want to hate her, though, she was my first kiss." He winked at Rose.

Adam's mother's eyes darted back to Rose, ready to fire. She'd let her son get hurt once, she couldn't let it happen again.

"We're just friends now." Rose stared daggers back at Adam. "We met at school, then we went to different schools... I happened to bump into him a few months ago and we've been friends like no time had passed." She explained.

Adam's mother seemed relieved, her shoulders dropping. "Well come here, you!" Adam's mother ignored the handshake and went straight for the hug. "He never told me about you."

"He's told me plenty about you." Rose welcomed the hug.

"Rose i-." Adam tried to jump in.

"Shut up, Adam." Rose cut him off. "You rest, I'll introduce myself to your mum since you couldn't be bothered."

Adam's mother nodded. "I'd listen to her if I were you." She smirked at him, mockingly.

Adam raised his arms in surrender, although he couldn't lift them too high. It was enough for them to notice and laugh. Rose sat across his mother, sandwiching Adam between them in his bed.

They spent a few hours talking about how they'd met, how life had interrupted and how they rekindled. Rose shared her dreams, her visions. Adam's mother shared hers. Adam just lay between them both, a smile painting across his face as he just listened, whilst drifting in and out of sleep.

None of them noticed, though. During the hours that passed as they talked, they had been watched. Through the glass of the ward, there were jealous eyes. Eve had arrived. She stood outside, watching them through the glass. She could see the three of them laughing. She saw *her* hand on Adam's. She could see everything she had finally lost. She watched for too long, every second inflicting its own painful wound. The seconds were like metal snowflakes, caressing her skin as they drifted by, their sharp edges cutting her with their kisses.

Eve just watched until she could watch no longer, she had tortured herself enough for one day. The memories would play out in her mind to punish her further. She would be able to create new memories too to castigate herself later on. She dragged her weary body back to her bed. Who would nurse her back to health? Whose hand would she hold? Who'd distract her with laughter?

She was left with nothing but her regret and someone else's dream. She could sleep on her apologies, but they wouldn't turn back time. She had become her past and tainted her future with it. She had turned back time on herself, but she'd forgotten who she was.

Eve lay in her casket. It was cosy, moulded to the shape of her body. It hugged her like it remembered her. She closed her eyes and welcomed the end of her tale.

Chapter 18

She was growing wiser, borrowing from his bank to fill her own.

"She deserved that!" She screamed. "Thank all the gods and everything else, holy and unholy."

"Someone's happy. Is that the end of the story for you then?" He replied, grinning.

"There's more?!" She was stopped in her celebration.

"There's always more." He smiled.

"Just don't ruin it…" She sighed and rolled her eyes.

As Adam began to heal, he was moved to a different ward. One that was less intense, where the air was less harsh. To his mother's joy, they were permitted to stay overnight with him. Rose volunteered to stay the first night. It was a risky play, given how she was coming between mother and son, but she knew his mother needed a break.

It took some convincing, but she had finally convinced his mother to go home and have some rest. She'd protect Adam for her, he would be safe with her. She needed the rest more than she allowed anyone to know, despite how much it showed.

Visiting hours were finishing up. Rose left the room to get a drink, she was allowed some breaks after all. Adam sat alone, enjoying the peace. He lay back on his bed and closed his eyes.

"You're back qu-." He opened his eyes as he heard the door close.

He lifted his head with a smile. When he saw her, his smile had been stolen, along with his voice. He struggled to speak, scrambling to the other side of his bed, risking falling out of it if it meant being away from *her*.

"No... Not you... No." He rasped.

"Adam, please." She responded, almost begging already.

"No, you've said enough. You've done enough." His voice was hoarse, but he was determined to not let her win this.

"I'm sorry, Adam. I love you, I still need you. I'm lost-." She pleaded.

"I think there's a map outside... It'll show you the way out." His voice had found its sternness.

"Adam, there's no need for this." Her voice began to break. "I just came to talk."

"You've talked enough. I listened to you for years. Spare me this one time, please." He bowed his head, disgraced, but at himself.

"Adam, please." She lunged to his bedside, falling to her knees as she did.

Adam jumped off the bed from the other side. "I gave you so much of my life, of my love. I gave you *all* of it. All I could, why do you still demand more from me?"

"How can you expect me to think you love me when you never even *made* love to me?!" She yelled back.

Even through all they'd been through, she still managed to surprise him. His jaw hung with shock. The sheer disgust on his face, the vitriol that bubbled at the tip of his tongue.

"Really? You think I didn't love you because I didn't *fuck* you? But for years you never questioned it? *That's* your excuse?"

"I-... That's not-... I have needs too, Adam. You hadn't even kissed me until the night before Valentine's!" She cried out and tried to grab his hand.

He pulled away and turned his back to her. "I was going to turn my life around, Eve. I was finally loosening the chains you had on me, I was this close to being free from the stranglehold you had on me. And then you asked me to be your boyfriend and I crashed. I wanted to say no. I should've said no. WHY did I say yes?"

The rain from the clouds that were her eyes started opening up, but he wasn't done. And he had to make sure she understood what he was about to say. With all the strength he had left, he convinced his body to kneel beside her and looked right into her eyes.

"The reason I didn't have sex with you, Eve, is because I stopped loving you." He'd lost the anger in his voice. "That's why I was so passive in our relationship. I needed you to prove to me that you loved me before I could be ready to love you again. And, to your credit, you did manage to do that... That's why I kissed you. I was ready to give you everything, Eve. And you threw it all away. Even though I'd fallen out of love with you, it didn't make you cheating on me hurt less. It did help me get over you quicker, though, so I guess I have to thank you for that. I just want to be happy, Eve, and I don't think I can do that, *be that*, with you."

He stood up and walked away from her as she fell to the ground. She begged, pleaded. She didn't want it to be true. She prayed he was lying, but the softness in which he spoke betrayed her hopes.

"Eve, if you ever really loved me, please just give me a chance to be happy. I did my best to do that for you, watching you with guys I knew would only break your heart, all the while I just wanted a moment to show you how much better you could have it. But you didn't want it, not enough. You didn't want *me* enough. Don't hold me back anymore, please. Let me go." His voice was shaky, he was desperate.

"I think you should listen to him." A firm voice from the door agreed.

They both turned. Rose stood there. They had no idea how long she'd been there, or how much she had heard. This was the first time they'd seen each other though. Rose stared at her on the ground, pity in her eyes. Eve's cries paused as she stared back, trying to see if she could figure out who this person was.

"Who's she?" Eve asked with a repulsed tone.

Rose stepped forwards before Adam could answer. "I'm Rose, I'm looking after Adam. He has told me way too much about you." She seemed bitter. "I wish we could've met on better terms, but it is what it is." She sighed.

"Just go, please." Adam requested, his voice close to a whisper. "Go."

Eve pulled herself up and headed for the door. As she passed Rose, they locked eyes. Rose's were red-hot, Eve's were pitch black. Neither backed down. Eve brushed Rose's shoulder as she walked out the door. A warning? A threat.

"I'm sorry about that, Rose." Adam turned to her.

"Never mind me, are you okay?" She guided him back to his bed.

"Yeah, I'm fine, thanks." It was all replaying in his head, he seemed flustered.

"Did you mean it, what you said to her?" Rose asked quietly as she sat by his legs.

"You wanna know the truth?" He asked her.

She nodded. She didn't know what side of Adam was about to come out, and she wasn't even entirely sure she wanted to know. But she'd asked, she couldn't back away now. She looked into his eyes, trying to gauge what was about to exit his mouth.

Poker face.

"I didn't know. When I was saying it to her, I didn't know. But it makes sense. Something didn't feel right for a while, even before we got together. It didn't feel entirely wrong, though, it just wasn't the normal I'd known. I felt different." He bowed his head. "And when she asked me to be her boyfriend, I froze. I panicked. She was so certain I still loved her. Everyone thought I still loved her. I didn't, though, not like that anyway.

And I knew she wanted an answer right there… But now that I've said it, I can't really say I disagree with it. I still care for her, that doesn't just go away. And yeah, I probably do still love her in some capacity, just not how everyone thinks I do." He lifted his head again to look at Rose. "I'm ready for a new chapter in my life. I wish it would've happened differently, but I can say that I tried. At least I tried."

Rose nodded with him. "You did your best, that's all anyone could ever ask of you. It's all you could ever ask of yourself."

"Do you think there's hope for me?" He asked her bluntly.

"How'd you mean?"

"Well… I don't know how to love like a normal person. I'm either too much, or too little. I'll never be *just* right. I'll never be just right. Does that mean I don't deserve love… or shouldn't love… at all?" He seemed lost in himself.

She placed a hand over his. "No, it just means you haven't found the person that's the same level of broken as you. You haven't found someone who just understands you. That doesn't mean you don't *deserve* love, it means you haven't *found* love." She smiled at him.

"Are you calling me *broken*? Do I need to be *fixed*?" He seemed concerned.

She shook her head, stifling a chuckle. "No, no… That's my bad. What I mean is… we're all different shades of broken… Well, except for kids who still get to be kids. Kids that still get to be innocent and naïve. Other than them, we're all broken in one way or another. And there is no fix. Once we've been broken, we will never return to what we once were. We can't be fixed. But it doesn't mean we can't try to put ourselves back together again. And we don't have to do it alone. The beautiful thing about being destroyed is you can choose how you rebuild yourself. You don't have to be an outline of your former self, you don't have to live in your own shadow. You can be whatever you want to be and bathe in your own light. You can still be you, just a new you. Maybe that you will *feel* fixed. And that's all we can really hope for." She placed her other hand in his.

"What kind of broken are you, Rose?" He rubbed her knuckles with his thumbs.

"The kind that's ready to be rebuilt."

Chapter 19

She had become a dreamer, expecting life to let her fly.

"What's the new chapter?!" She interrogated.

He just shrugged. "Maybe it hasn't been written yet."

She squinted her eyes at him. "Then write it."

"And make it good?" He asked.

"Are you even capable of that?"

"Life is a cruel thread of blood and tears. It ain't me." He shrugged in response.

A cautionary week later, Adam was allowed to leave the hospital. He was given the usual warnings: don't overdo it; if anything feels wrong, blah blah blah. He did his best to listen to the advice being hammered into him, but he was just happy to be out. He was happy he had his freedom again.

"Thanks, Rose, for everything you've done for me." He smiled at her.

"Just know that if I ever end up in hospital, I expect you to be there!" She smiled back.

"That sounds like terrible time, let's hope you never end up in hospital." He chuckled as she frowned.

He stared at her, she wore that frown for all it was worth, even though she knew he was joking. It only made him laugh a little harder.

"I'll give you one chance to fix that, else you'll be sorry, mister!" She pouted.

"I'll get the smallest, tightest nurse outfit I can, on standby, just for you." He stifled a laugh. "I'll make sure to wear it under everything, just so I'm always ready to be there for you."

She shook her head, each sway wiping the frown away and replacing it with a smile she was fighting. Her emerging smile sent a shiver that rippled through his body, momentarily stunning him. He pulled her against him and wrapped his arms tightly around her.

"I'll be wherever you want me to be, whenever you want me. Just say the word." He squeezed her tight and made sure she could feel the truth in his words.

She couldn't help but test the limits of her facial muscles as it pulled an even bigger smile onto her face. As if life had never gotten between them, as if time were only a façade.

"What's on your agenda now that you have your body back?" She asked as their hug finally broke.

"You were here for me, now I'm here for you. What do you wanna do?" He asked her.

"I want an actual meal for the first time in weeks!" She exclaimed, excited.

"Pick anything you want, it's my treat!" He joined her in her glee.

"Be careful what you say, Adam, I'll happily break your bank after the week I've had!" She laughed.

"Try me." He bowed for her.

She began walking forwards, ready to test his limits on his offer. He didn't hesitate, he just followed behind her. He was adamant to let her know he meant what he said.

She stopped in front of the fanciest restaurant in town and turned to look at him. She tilted her head towards the door. He tilted his the same way.

"You ready to put your money where your mouth is, Mr Money Man?"

He reached his arms out to his side, indicating her towards the door. "After you, milady." He bowed.

She looked at him. He kept his head down, holding his bow. She inched closer to the door, waiting for him to react. He stayed bowing. She walked a step past his arms, waiting for him to get up. Still, the muppet was bowed.

She rolled her eyes and sighed, grabbing his hand and pulled him as she walked away from the restaurant. He almost fell, face-first, into the floor, unprepared to be dragged away like a disobedient child. She let go after they were a few steps away.

Adam jogged to catch up beside her and smiled. She turned her head as he caught up to her and saw the smile on his face. She faced forwards again.

"You're an idiot." She couldn't help but grin a little.

"I was looking for an excuse to eat there and you just took it away from me."

"Shut up, it's not our style and you know it."

"What is *our* style, Rose?" He leaned in a little closer to her.

"Okay, maybe I shouldn't have lumped myself in with you." She nudged him away, smirking.

He stumbled a little as he laughed. He jumped beside her again, eager to see where she'd take him. For the first time in a while, he was just able to enjoy himself. He really had been freed.

She stopped in front of a building. Adam bumped into her, not expecting the suddenness in her pause. She began to fall forwards, but Adam lunged ahead and grabbed her. He slowly unwound his legs, helping her upright as he did so.

"Alright Prince Charming, we haven't got all day." She broke free of his grasp as she headed inside.

It was the diner that had been there since they were kids. It used to be a popular spot, favoured by the locals. While its popularity may have waned over the years, it still had a loyal following who managed to keep it happily afloat.

"I haven't been here in years." Adam seemed amazed it still existed.

While Adam hadn't left his hometown his whole life, he couldn't be completely blamed for forgetting its existence. It was tucked away in a quiet part of town. A hidden gem among locals. He had only ever come here with Rose when they were younger. Without her in his life, he had no reason to go back.

"Good thing you're paying then 'cos they've bumped up the prices." She scooted into a booth.

"Is it as good as I remember?" He slid in across her.

"Depends on your memory, old man." She teased, even though neither of them were even close to old.

Adam kept looking around, reliving memories as his eyes scanned the interior. He'd been here enough times that each booth had its own set of memories. It was truly surprising he hadn't been back in so long.

"That's the booth where I threw up from eating too much and then trying to force down an ice cream." He pointed to a booth across from them.

"There's the one I banged my head on when I tripped over my laces because *you* undid them." She pointed in the other direction as he blushed. "You must really want me to fall for you, eh?" She laughed.

A waiter came over before they could reminisce any further and placed some menus in front of them. Adam's eyes interrogated the words, checking how much had changed over the years. While there had been some additions and some cuts, some of his historied favourites remained.

"I'll have the classic double cheeseburger please." Adam pointed to it on the menu. "And a vanilla shake too."

"Vanilla?" She scrunched her face. "*How daring!*" She teased.

"You can always tell how good a place is by their vanilla milkshake!" He defended himself. "Let's see how good your taste is."

"I'll have what he's having." She passed her menu back to the waiter. "Because I know it won't disappoint." She squinted her eyes at him as if it had somehow become a competition.

They shared a few more memories before their food arrived, laughing together and almost crying at one point. For the first time in a while, reliving the past didn't hurt him. It wasn't eating at him, consuming him, fighting him. Everything just seemed... happy.

"What do you want from life, Rose?" He asked, carefully watching her smile.

"Is this a job interview now?" She scoffed, but saw he was waiting for an answer. "I don't know, I just want to be content." She shrugged it off.

"Not happy?"

"Nah, I'm okay with just being content. Happiness is an ideal only the rich can afford." She seemed so blasé about that concept. "Content is good enough for me." She nodded to herself.

They saw the waiter heading towards them with their food, ending the interview. They both fell silent. A tension filled the air. Now was do or die. Would the food be good? Could Rose's food recommendations be trusted?

They watched the plates floating through the air on the magic tray, forgetting there was a whole human carrying them. Like snakes being charmed, their eyes followed the plates from the kitchen entrance all the way to their table. Neither of them said anything.

The waiter laid the tray on the table and placed their food in front of them, both locked on each other's plate. The waiter looked at them, weirded out, but said nothing. He placed their drinks with a quiet thud. His eyes jumped between both of them. He contemplated saying something but knew they probably wouldn't hear him. He just walked away, definitely ready to mock them in the back.

Adam lifted a stick of fried potato to the air, inspecting it as if he were valuing a diamond. He pulled it slightly below his nose and inhaled slowly but dee-. He began coughing. Pepper. Rose went from watching him intently to breaking down in laughter.

Adam laughed with her after he cleared his throat. He threw the chip in his mouth and began crunching. He tilted his head and raised his eyebrows. So far, so good. But he didn't say anything.

She had a smile on her face now, the tension had gone. From the chip threatening to kill Adam to him enjoying it, she knew she would win this competition they'd made up.

He lifted the burger with both hands and stopped at his mouth. He looked at her and then back at the burger. She rolled her eyes, no longer admiring his intensity. He bit into it and then placed the burger back on the table.

He chewed for a couple seconds. Then chewed some more as he changed thinking poses. Then he kept chewing. He was definitely over-chewing. She shook her head.

"It's hard to mess up a burger though." He had finally swallowed that poor bite.

He pushed his plate a little and then slid the heavy glass in front of him. He lifted the straw, the movement releasing a small waft of vanilla into the air.

"This is the real test." He announced, placing his lips against the straw.

Rose counted the seconds and watched as his throat pulsated. He was definitely drinking it, and if he hadn't spat it out by now then that was surely good news, right? He broke away from the straw. He bowed his head. After a moment of deliberation, he cleared his throat and looked at her.

"Rose, I don't know how to say this, so I'm just gonna say it." He sat upright. "That is quite possibly the best milkshake I've ever had. Better than I remembered it somehow…"

Rose jumped up and cheered way too loudly. Some scattered customers look at her. She instantly sat back down; the embarrassment had silenced her cheers but it had not shunned her.

"Told you, bitch!" She stuck her tongue out.

Adam pretended to be offended but he couldn't hide it. He definitely owed her for this, more than the price of the meal. She brought back a piece of his childhood that he loved, and he was still able to love it as a young adult.

Halfway through their meal, Adam got up to use the bathroom. He took his time walking to it, letting more memories seep back in through his pores and give him a tight hug. He couldn't help but smile.

On his way back, it was the same. He'd remembered most by now, but there were still some out there waiting to be rediscovered. It was when he saw her there, in that corner booth she'd claimed, that he stopped to really think about one.

The one. It was this one. And all this time he wasn't able to see it because he was sitting in it. This is the booth he had his first kiss. And it was with her. Did she know that?

He just watched her in the corner, the smile fading. She was still eating slowly. He just watched her eat, staring at the side of her face. More memories came back, different ones. Not of the diner. Of her.

She turned, breaking his thought. She looked at him confused. He snapped away from memory lane and sat across her once more. He didn't say anything, he just smiled.

He went back to eating his food, but this time he spent a little more time looking at her. As she talked, as she ate. He looked a little closer. And he couldn't help but smile.

He was ready to be rebuilt too.

Chapter 20

She was ready to write her own story but was still adamant about borrowing his pen.

"There is no fucking way." She shook her head.

"No fucking way what?" He faked confusion.

"Don't play dumb, I know what you're doing." Her eyes turned to daggers. "He falls in love with her, doesn't he?"

He shrugged his shoulders. "Would you?"

"Is this the happy ever after?"

"Do you want it to be?" He looked back at her, not sure if he needed a shield.

"You're definitely going to ruin it…" She sighed.

Adam knew what was happening. The longer he was around her, the deeper he fell. He didn't know if he needed to panic or embrace it. He knew one thing though; walking away was not one of the options.

"Rose." He cut her off from whatever she was saying.

"Adam…" The smile on her face seemed to fade.

"Do you remember this booth?" He asked.

"What?" She replied, hesitant about if she should even enquire.

"I mean, do you remember what happened in this booth?"

She didn't say anything. Adam watched her, trying to figure out what was going on in her head. He got out from his side and scooted in beside her.

She stared at him, not sure what was going on. He looked deeper into her eyes and he could practically see the memory playing out in them.

He nudged closer, right against her, just like that night. He leant in towards her, their noses crossed, almost touching.

"Jogging your memory yet?" He asked again.

She could feel the warmth of his words on her lips. She nodded slowly, coyly. She felt tingles all over her body. He felt them too. He just didn't know if he should react to them. Or if she even wanted to…

He leaned a little closer, their lips practically touching. He held himself there, letting her make the choice.

She didn't know what to do. She wanted to, with every fibre of her being she wanted to. She knew, though, if she did this, there was no going back.

"You know I'm single, right?" She whispered back at him.

"I do now." They both grinned.

"Are you gonna change that?" She completely opened herself up to him with that simple question, nervous about his response.

"I'm ready to be rebuilt too, and I'd like to rebuild with you. If you'll let me, that is…" His chest felt heavy, the anxiousness building in him.

She placed her palm on the back of his neck and pulled him closer, their lips no longer teetering on Schrödinger's choice. She smiled against him, returning the kiss she'd been waiting for. They locked into each other, reliving their memory once more.

The clanging of metal and ceramic broke them apart. The waiter had come to clear up their table. They'd finished eating a while ago, moving onto their own dessert. They both looked at each other, slightly embarrassed. The blushing turned into smiling, which turned into laughter.

Adam put some money on the table and slid out the booth, pulling Rose with him as he held her hand. They both giggled like kids, as they ran out the diner.

They stood outside. He grabbed both of her hands and stood right in front of her, not knowing where to go from here. He leaned in for another kiss and she practically leapt up to meet him halfway, jumping into his arms.

As their tongues danced, their minds drifted into a new world. One to make up for lost time. One to make up for lost love. One to make up for all that lost joy.

Their eyes opened as she broke the kiss, placing both of her palms on the sides of his head. She pressed her forehead against his. The tips of their noses finally kissed. She locked eyes with him, smiling through his soul.

Without a second thought, she turned away, grabbing his hand and skipping down the road, pulling him with her.

He had no idea where she was taking him, but he'd follow her to the ends of the Earth right now. He hadn't been able to smile like this in a while, so he was just living in this moment.

She didn't live that far. I don't think either of them had a plan for the day, but they definitely didn't plan for this. Her hand jumped around in her bag, desperately searching for her keys. She could hear them clattering around, but her hand didn't have ears.

Adam slid his hand in under hers which stopped her. His head brushed into her hair as he leaned in over her shoulder. He'd found a confidence he never knew he had.

His warmth swallowed her as he closed in behind her. She closed her eyes, letting her body remember this feeling. A second later, she feet the cold touch of metal against her fingers as he handed her her own keys. He could feel her hand shaking in the safety of that bag.

Her hand closed around them. She didn't want to move. She leant her head back against his shoulder, revealing her neck to him. He wrapped his hand around hers, ceasing the shakiness that was creeping its way around her body.

He pressed his head into the new space she'd granted him. He could feel how hot she was. He pressed his lips against her and brought them together on her skin.

Stomp, stomp, stomp.

Her eyes shot open. He pulled back. Shit, they're still outside.

She rushed to open the door, her hands no longer trembling. She didn't need to encourage him in. He kicked the door closed behind him and tackled her onto her sofa.

He didn't want to be separated from her anymore. She had been yearning for his lips since he gave her a reminder of how they tasted. *Of him.*

Their bodies intertwined as they locked together on the sofa. This was a side of Adam he hadn't known existed, one that she wanted more of.

He held himself up over her, staring into her soul. They'd been making out for the past half an hour, and he just wanted to stare at her smiling eyes again before he went back for more.

She wanted a different kind of more.

He felt her hands slither down his back and make their way around him. A faint metal tapping. A silent pop in his head. He felt a pressure disappear from his waist. She'd loosened his belt, ready to rip it from its rungs.

She smiled up at him inquisitively, not moving an inch more. Was he ready for this? Another first with his first of firsts?

He lowered himself against her and started kissing her again. Wrapping himself around her again, he rolled them over.

A bit too much.

They made the short trip to the floor with a loud thud, Adam's back cushioning the blow. She landed on top of him. That's one way to achieve what he wanted. They laughed against each other, but it didn't stop them.

He trusted her, so he let her take control. And this was the side of Rose he never thought he'd see.

A methodical chaos. She knew how to skirt along all the lines, even blurring some of them in the process. He craved her in a way he never thought he would. He began to beg for more and more of her as she teased and toyed, knowing she was just as desperate, knowing she was only aching for more of him.

He learned a lot about her that night, and even more about himself, but he definitely wouldn't have traded it for anything in the world. Or anyone. This was the kind of knowledge you never go back from. The kind of learning you revisit, a fond memory ready to be replayed. He sought more of her teachings, yearned for all of her wisdom.

They lay on the floor, her head resting on his bare chest. He ran his fingers through her hair gently, playing with it with one hand as he rubbed her back with the other. He could feel her grinning against him.

He closed his eyes and grinned with her. It all just seemed to be perfect. Finally, he could be happy. Finally, he was happy.

She had only aimed for content. She had lowered the bar for life, having struggled through its trials and tribulations. Content was a second-place prize she had learned to be okay with. But now, now she had a taste of happiness. It was addictive. She wanted more. She wanted to drown in it. For the first time since she was a child, she wanted to be happy, and he was her shot at it.

Chapter 21

She had crossed the harsh threshold into adulthood, her preparations being put to the test.

"You ruined it in a different way. T-M-I dude." She groaned.

"You say you want it to go one way and then complain when you get what you want. There's just no winning with some people." He scoffed.

"That's *not* what I wanted. Most people just let it be implied with kids or something."

"Kids, huh?" He pretended to think on it.

"Shut up." She scoffed.

Their schedules didn't allow them to meet every day, but they met whenever they could. Whether it was the puppy love, or the fact that he had two waves of love flooding him, he just wanted to spend every moment he could with her. To make up for lost time, whilst falling in love all over again.

The love he had for her all those years ago, that young and pure love, had come back in tremendous waves. Simultaneously, he was filled with a new kind of love. A matured one, a seasoned one. One that was rough, filled with impurities. The impurities were all the pieces of him that were too small to rebuild with. This was a matured loved, one that had been tested, but one that just wanted a good home. The two mixed in places creating an unholy concoction, one that was melded to be the best for her.

It had been a few weeks since they slept together. Their first time and, to date, their last. They'd slowed down a bit since that night, but the passion still lingered. He was letting her go at her pace. For the first time ever, he was ready to do anything. She just had that pull on him. His first of firsts, always finding new firsts.

He hadn't seen her for a few days. He knocked on her door, knowing she had the day off. The smell of roast duck climbed out the bag and crept under her door. It snaked its way along the carpet and climbed up her legs. It only stopped once it had snuck its way into her nostrils.

She opened the door to see him standing there. She didn't reflexively smile like she normally would, but she managed to paint one on before he could see her blankness. She invited him in, although it had a hesitance about it.

Adam placed the bags on the coffee table and sat in his usual seat. She closed the door and followed him to the sofa, stopping at the end of furthest from him. She took a seat, facing towards him and using her knee as a stand for her arm.

He started taking the food out of the bag. "How's your day been?" He asked.

She shrugged. "Just had a lie in and did some stuff around the house."

She had a different air about her. If she was trying to hide something, she wasn't doing a good job going about it. He turned towards her and placed a hand on the part of her arm that lay across her knee.

He smiled at her reassuringly. He wanted her to know she could talk to him. She forced a smile back, but he could see the absence in her eyes.

He decided not to press it, she was obviously withdrawing from him, and he didn't want to push her too far. He pushed himself away a little bit and turned to face the TV. He put on a film they'd both wanted to watch and helped himself to a plate of food.

She lowered her leg from the sofa, she didn't need the wall anymore. She made herself a plate of food, appreciating the space Adam had given her. They both sat at opposite ends, watching the film they both wanted to watch, with the person they wanted to watch it with, without each other.

Adam had left his body open. His arm lay on the back of the sofa with the other on the armrest. Her sofa was comfy, but she knew his arms were comfier. Over the course of the film, she had crept her way closer to him and snuggled up against him. As much as she had wanted to resist, he had a hold on her too. He tried not to give it too much attention, but he couldn't hide his smile.

She started to comment on the film. Adam would chuck in a few short responses here or there, still testing the waters. She made jokes, he made some too. She yelled, he laughed. She was becoming herself again.

Towards the end, Adam had stopped watching the film and just watched her. As she enjoyed it, as she hated it, as she went back to liking it again. He preferred watching her.

The credits rolled as did her eyes. They finally broke from the screen, and she caught a glimpse of him staring at her. She did a double take, looking back at him. Her eyes asked questions, his just smiled back.

He leaned in, gently brushing her nose with his and held himself over her for a second. He waited for her. She felt the same tingles sprinkling themselves across her body. He felt a cold thread rip down his spine.

She moved in closer. She could feel the warm tip of his lip against hers. She missed it more than she knew.

And then she turned away.

Adam didn't move. His shoulders dropped, disheartened, and confused. What happened? He leaned back a little and looked down at her.

"I'm sorry." He whispered. "I shouldn't have…"

She shook her head to let him know it was okay. She pressed her head against his chest and wrapped her arms around him. As much as she had stopped it, she still wanted him. She just couldn't surrender herself to him right now.

He put his arms around her, resting his cheek on her head. He felt a familiar dampness on his shirt seeping into his chest. She was sobbing against him, silently, he hadn't even realised. He wanted to join in with the waterworks. He held back, though. It was her moment now.

She'd been there for him for the past few weeks. Hell, even the past few months. He couldn't steal this from her after all she'd done for him.

She looked up at him. "I know I've been distant, Adam. I didn't want to be, I'm sorry."

"You don't need to apologise, it's okay. I could tell something was wrong. I should've used my lips for words, not for anything else." He rubbed the sides of her arms.

"I've just been... confused. I thought I knew what I wanted, but now there's this..." She paused for a moment to look at him.

"A while ago, I met a guy. He was great, he was everything I thought I wanted. We seemed to just be on the same page with everything. We both valued our careers and were really driven to succeed. We both shared similar political beliefs. We both wanted to get married, have kids... But then one of those things happened too soon." She swallowed the lump in her throat. "I found out I was pregnant. I was excited too. I thought *wow, I can settle down with this guy! I can make him mine!*. And I thought that's what he would want too, or some variation of it. I was so happy when I was telling him, but when I looked into his eyes, all I saw was regret, disdain, shame. He wasn't ready, he said. He hadn't made his millions yet. He practically threw money at me to terminate. He didn't want this *burden* holding him back... He became everything I thought he wasn't." She hesitated to carry on.

Adam placed his palms on her cheeks and wiped her tears with his thumbs. He lowered his head to make eye contact, letting her know she was safe. She could let it out.

"He... If I tried to fight for our child, fight for us... He'd get angry and violent. He never hurt me, but he'd throw things, hit things, and he just kept getting closer and closer. He thought I was trying to steal his world. I thought I was giving him his world... As you can see, there's no baby here. I got the abortion, but not for him. I did it for that kid. I did it for me. I knew he wouldn't have been a good dad, or a good partner after that. I left that night without saying anything."

"He didn't deserve you. Either of you." Adam kissed her forehead softly.

"Do you want to get married someday, Adam?" She asked him.

Adam nodded. "Yeah. I've spent enough days daydreaming about it." He smiled.

"Do you want kids?" She asked.

He hesitated for a second. "I've changed my mind about this so many times, but I know in my heart of hearts I do." He replied. "The only time I ever *didn't* want kids was because I thought I'd be a horrible father. I never had mine to teach me. I had my grandad, but that's a different kind of love… I just never believed I could be a good dad. But I have so much love to give. And I know, deep down, I would do anything for my kids. I would strive to do right by them every day."

"I think you'd be a good dad." She pictured it in her head. "I think you'd be a great dad."

"Thank you, I'm glad you think that. I think you'd be a great mum." He smiled at her. "And I'm not just returning the compliment. I know you'd do right by your kids."

She nodded with him. They had both planted a dream in each other's heads, and they were both stuck for a moment just letting it play out. They would be a great team, they had no doubts about that. And they both wanted that with each other, for each other.

She took his hands in hers, sniffled a few times and looked him dead in the eyes. "How about in a little over 8 months, Adam?"

His eyes widened.

She stared at him, waiting for a reaction. He didn't say anything. His eyes just darted from her belly to her eyes. Belly. Eyes. Belly. Eyes. Her head dropped, breaking him out of it.

"Do *you* want kids, Rose?" He brushed her thumb with his.

She kept her head down but nodded.

"With me?" There was apprehension in the question, as if he expected her to say no.

She nodded ever so slightly against him. "I did think it was a bit too soon to be thinking about it, but I do…"

He shrugged. "How about in a little over 8 months?" He whispered to her.

Her head bounced up and she caught his gaze. "Really?"

"Whatever you choose, I'll stand by you." He brought her hand to his lips and kissed it.

Her eyes had an uneasy smile. "I think I might need some time to figure some shit out. That means… Can we put a pause on *us* for now?"

He nodded. "Just being your friend is a blessing enough, Rose, if you'll allow me that. If not, I get that too."

"You're still mine." She frowned at him. "I just need to get myself together…"

"You've always had me. I was only ever not yours when you left, but I'll be yours for as long as you'll have me."

She smiled at him, her eyes flooding again. She threw herself into him, wrapping herself around him again as she used him as a tissue once more. He could feel tears flowing down his cheeks too. He had thrown himself in at the deep end with this one, but he felt ready for it. He was ready for anything, with her. More than he realised.

Chapter 22

She was exposed to reality, yet all she wanted to do was stay in her dreams.

"Were they ready to be parents?" She asked.

"Nobody is ready to be a parent, and it's not for lack of preparing." He replied, cutting into an apple.

"Why didn't she just accept him then and there if he was so willing though?" She thought.

He placed the knife on the cutting board and looked at her. "She'd been burned before. Just because it wasn't his fault doesn't mean the scar isn't there or has just healed itself. Some things require a bit more time."

She shrugged. "I don't envy her position. I think I-." She saw him raise an eyebrow. "I would like to think I'd deal with that kind of trauma before risking getting pregnant again."

"It's easy to react to someone else's mistake, especially when it's not a situation you've found yourself in. I could say I'd handle it differently too, but I will never be in that situation." He resumed cutting apple slices. "The only thing we can ever do is make the most of our situation."

Rose spent the next week trying to figure out what she wanted to do. She knew she was ready to love again, but was she ready to take that kind of plunge so soon? Could she trust someone that much again? Was she okay with settling down sooner than she'd expected? Was she prepared to be a single mother and share a child with a friend? Or would she go the *other* way *again*?

She'd never forgiven her ex for that, and she never would. The insurmountable pain she felt having to say goodbye. Not just to a child she was ready to accept, cherish and love, but to her hopes and dreams. The cruel hand of fate had grabbed her and grinded her down between its fingers, its vice grip clutching her soul and forcing it to watch her crumble.

It's crazy to think how one unplanned moment, a single lapse in judgement, can interfere with your life so much. You either have to spend the rest of your life preparing, or you end up with more heartbreak than you ever thought you could feel. There's no instruction manual for it either, just the same old advice that you get sick of. Everyone's an expert, it seems, yet they all have different answers.

Adam had given Rose some space. He knew she needed some time to just evaluate everything. He had no intention of leaving. He was going to be there, one way or another. He just had to let her run through her process, as much as he wanted to jump in and prove he was ready for whatever came his way. It wasn't him who needed to prove they were ready, it was Rose. To herself.

Can we meet?

He stared at the text. He didn't know how to respond. He wanted to immediately say yes, but he also didn't know if he was completely ready to hear her verdict.

I just wanna take my mind off this week

He exhaled, relieved. She just wanted to hang out and relax. He immediately replied.

Just say when and where.

She sent him a shopping list. Snacks, a couple toiletries she'd forgotten to grab herself, and a film they could watch. She wanted a film night. The last time they had a film night, he found out she was pregnant with his child. Was this really her way of forgetting about everything?

Adam kicked her door a few times. His hands were filled with the groceries and he didn't want to put some stuff down only to pick them up again. The balancing act had been perfected, he just wanted to let them lay where they would remain.

He peered over the bags to greet her with a smile as she finally opened the door. He caught a glimpse of her eyes. They seemed tired.

She let out a laugh, unsure if she wanted to help him by taking some of the bags or just watch what happened as he tried to relieve himself. She opted for the latter. Adam took it as a challenge.

His feet felt their way to her kitchen. He had a rough idea of the layout of her house but had to make sure she hadn't changed anything to obstruct him. She closed the door behind him and leaned back against it as she crossed her arms and observed him carefully fumble around.

Adam managed to get to the counter as he slowly tilted his body forwards. He didn't really have a plan, other than to hopefully slide the bags onto the counter and carefully step away. It seemed foolproof, surely it would turn out okay.

Rose stalked behind him, stopping at the kitchen door, eager to get a closer look. She watched him making the smallest of movements, progressing the bags away from him and onto a more even surface. She would've been impressed if it didn't look so dumb.

When all seemed to be steady, he slowly unclasped his hands and cautiously moved them away from the bags. He nodded ever so slightly, impressed with himself. Then, just as he'd planned, he began to step back. Slower still. Just a few steps. Three... Two...

The room flashed in front of him, everything a blur. He caught a long glimpse of her ceiling – it was white, and she had small round lights built into it. Fancy, he thought. He closed his eyes, preparing himself for the pain.

Silence.

Darkness.

He opened one eye.

White.

Oh, it was her ceiling. He opened the other eye, there she was, holding back her laughter but her quivering smile was giving it away.

"What's the view like from down there?" She was making it harder for herself to contain the laughter.

He turned his head, making her take up more of his view. "Beautiful now."

"Okay Casanova, we haven't got all day." She mocked him.

She pulled him towards her, back onto his feet properly. Finally knowing he was okay, she could hold it back no more as she burst out laughing. Adam couldn't help himself, her joy was too infectious. He laughed with her, just happy to see her still smiling.

"That was definitely one way to do it." She noted, composing herself.

"Still did it." He seemed proud of himself.

They unpacked the bags and made their way to the living room, finally ready to start their film night. Adam had picked a comedy, hoping it would help distract her from the world, even if only for an hour or so. He turned off the lights as she got the film ready, snacks laid out in front of them. They both sat on the sofa, a gap between them.

Adam felt a nudge. He turned; her head was on his shoulder. She didn't look at him though, she was still watching the film. He looked back, acting as if he'd not noticed.

Over time, the gap between them closed. He could tell, the cool air that sat between them was replaced with a warm glow. He crept his arm around her and she welcomed it, wanting to be held by him again. It didn't take long after that for her to wrap her arms around him and rest her tired head on his chest. This felt familiar. It felt right.

The film ended, credits darkening the room, but she didn't move like she normally did. He peered around her. She'd fallen asleep. He smiled to himself, not sure how trapped he was but he didn't seem to mind.

He held her head up with the side she was leaning against as he carefully turned. He slid his free arm below her thigh and lifted her slowly.

Either she was heavier than she looked, or he was weaker than he thought. Whatever the case was, he somehow mustered the strength to carry her to her bed – one of the perks of her living alone was that it meant it wasn't a far trip. He tucked her in, covered her up and kissed the side of her head.

He knelt beside her and just watched her sleep for a moment. She looked like she was at peace, happy. The distraction worked. He sat beside her on the floor, back against her bedside drawer. He tilted his head to look at her.

"You know, whenever someone used to ask me *"do you want kids?"*, I used to always answer *"with the right person"*. I stopped when I realised how stupid it was. *"With the right person?"*" He scoffed, looking to the ground. "I'm never going to intentionally have kids with the wrong person. Sure, life happens sometimes, and things turn out differently, but it was a cheap answer. I just never knew if I could be a good dad. I didn't have someone to show me how to be one, or even how not to be one. I didn't really understand why I would say that." He looked back at her. "Until a week ago, when you told me. And then I thought *"with the right person, it makes sense now"*. You're everything I've been looking for, Rose. Everything I wanted and everything I didn't know I wanted. You've shown me a side of me I didn't know I had. I feel like a different person around you. I feel loved, cared for. I feel strong, confident. I feel like I can actually be happy." He gulped and exhaled deeply. "You're my right person, although I think someone as amazing as you could be anyone's right person. I just wish I could be yours." His eyes had drifted back to the floor.

He didn't realise. While he'd gotten lost in his hopelessness and self-pity, she'd woken up. She looked at him, as he lasered a hole into the ground.

"I never said you weren't."

His eyes jumped back to her, shocked. She grinned, seeing how confused and panicked he was. She grabbed his shirt by the collar and pulled him onto the bed.

Their lips fused, their tongues tangoed. He was beaming against her. She *had* made up her mind, she just didn't know how to have the conversation. She feared being that vulnerable again. She was scared she might be abandoned once more. Luckily, he had the conversation for her.

Chapter 23

She felt she'd learned all she could about love, yet it still left her feeling unprepared.

"And they lived happily ever after!" She smiled.

"Yup, that's the end." He nodded.

"Really?"

"It's a story, you can end it wherever you want." He replied.

"I would've ended it ages ago, but you're clearly not done yet..."

He shrugged. "Maybe *they're* not done yet, but they could be. Happily ever after?"

She shook her head, disappointed but intrigued.

Rose had begun to show, which meant they couldn't hide it for much longer. Adam had told his mother, instantly leapfrogging her approval rating from a warm like to a strong love. She was getting there anyway. They got along well but, more importantly, she could see she treated Adam how he deserved. He seemed truly happy for the first time in a while. Getting pregnant was definitely one way to accelerate the process though.

Once the initial glee from being a grandmother had temporarily subsided, she then began to question if she was old enough to be a grandmother. The realisation hitting her, aware that the title came with assumptions.

"You're definitely old, so grandmother suits you just fine." Adam laughed.

His mother pouted in response.

"Ignore him, you don't look a day over 20." Rose white-lied.

"She's my favourite person now, Adam. You've been demoted to second place." His mother hugged Rose.

"Well, she's *my* favourite person so you're demoted to second place too!" Adam retorted.

After the laughs had subsided, he took a second to take this all in. This was it. It was what he'd dreamt of for ages. Happiness. He just stood there with a smile watching his mother and Rose bonding. Happy.

He felt a buzzing against his thigh. He put his hand over it, his phone. He retrieved it from his pocket and looked at the screen.

Pain.

It was *her*. His smile faded as he thought about his choices. If he answered, he'd have to deal with her. If he didn't, she might try more drastic measures. But she hadn't spoken to him for a while. So, maybe this isn't a casual conversation. Maybe something...

"Hello?" He asked cautiously as he stepped outside.

He heard sniffling. Panting. Stuttering. Something had happened, and she was struggling.

"I... He... H... He's dead..."

"Who, who Eve? Who's dead?" Adam began to worry.

"The... Th... Guy..."

"Where are you, Eve? Tell me where you are." The panic took over in his voice.

"...F... Fa... rm..."

"Stay there, I'm coming." Adam hung up and stuck his head through the door.

"I have to head out for something, I'll be back soon." And with that, he ran.

It had been a while since he'd run for her. Run to her. He had become dead set on running away from her, he never thought he'd be racing back.

He made it to the farm quicker than he ever had before. Even now, he was still breaking records for her. The sky was dark, making it hard to see anything. He had no idea where she could be though. He looked around, trying to sleuth her location out.

Why was she even at the farm this late? All the animals are herded back inside so you can't interact with them. It's too dark to be wandering about the fields, lest you get caught on something and trip over. There's nothing to see. Literally. Unless... Unless she never made it to the farm...

There was a footpath in a corner of the farm that was surrounded by nature at its core. It was poorly lit, but it was calm. The trees were friendly in the day, waving gentle greetings to passersby. During the night, however... They became sinister in the night, providing cover to the demons and giving shadows an easy time to stalk.

He began walking along the path, remembering what had happened the last time he was here. The last time with Eve. He knew it wasn't a good time to be here.

Inching his way forward, slowly, cautiously, slightly paranoid. He had *some* light from the moon, but it wasn't as guiding as the Sun's was. Until...

He saw a glimmering on the floor. Something shone. He edged his way closer and looked down. A dot. A dot? He knelt down to see if he could figure out what it was. It gave him no clues. It was just a dark, round, empty coin with the moon waving in its reflection.

He found a short branch nearby and poked at its centre. He felt the resistance of the ground, not the coin. He lifted the branch up to the sky, holding it over the moon. It had carried something with it, a piece of the coin.

Red.

Blood.

He threw the branch to the side and moved forwards, faster this time. More bloody dots. More frequent. Larger.

The last couple of drops were disturbed. Their edges smeared. He followed them off to the side, hoping the grass would lead him to her. Hoping she was still alive.

He thought he could hear a distant sob. He tried to follow it, aware it could be something worse than a sob. It was too dark to follow any tracks. He didn't want to use his phone as a torch, just in case. He didn't want to telegraph his position so easily.

He darted among the trees, between the ghosts that gloomed in the darkness. He tried his best to keep quiet, mostly so he could try to hear who he hoped was Eve, but also just in case he needed to maintain the element of surprise.

The search quickly seemed hopeless, at least how he was doing it. He looked around but saw nothing. He couldn't even hear her anymore. Had he taken so long she'd stopped crying? Or… taken so long she'd stopped…

"Eve?" He called out. "I'm here, Eve, it's Adam."

He'd just thrown his own safety out the window. Instinctively. He didn't mean to do it… He looked all around, hoping she'd respond, hoping she'd make it worth it. She didn't.

Rustling. Adam jumped to face the sound. He stood still, waiting for whatever evil to show itself. He had given himself up, he was at its mercy, but he wouldn't go down easy. He had a family he had to live for.

A primal, guttural scream burst through the air. It echoed a short distance away. Without hesitation, he sprinted straight towards it. Eve was in trouble. Eve was in trouble… He was too slow.

He slid across a bloody patch of grass as the roar got louder. He managed to stay on his feet, creeping forward at pace. A new sound rang through his ears. A soft, wet squelching. Fast, repeated. Someone was getting carved.

"Eve!" He yelled, running straight towards the noise.

He saw the silhouette of one body sitting atop the other. Mounted victoriously, as it made to defile its enemy. He bolted towards the demon, tackling it off Eve. He couldn't protect her, but he could try to preserve her.

A new scream yelled in response. He grunted, flailing with the panicked limbs that had been kept from their purpose. He tried to pin the arms down as he smothered this monster.

"Let go!" She yelled.

He stopped. He didn't ease his pressure, but he stopped fighting. It was her. She was the beast. He didn't know she was capable of such a sound.

"Eve, it's me." He spoke gently.

She stopped trying to fight him. His voice seemed to sedate her. She went limp.

"I'm going to let you go now. Just… don't do anything." He almost begged her.

She nodded, letting the knife fall beside them. He nodded back to her as he loosened his grip and retreated off her. Before he could completely separate his body from hers, she jumped at his chest and wrapped herself around him, tight. She began crying into his chest as she had done so many times before.

There was a reluctance to touch her. He didn't know if touch felt poisonous to her right now, if it would burn into her skin and cause her pain. He didn't know if he could touch her. He hesitantly placed one hand on her back, letting it fall softly, as if it were barely even there. It was her bare back. He hadn't been able to tell if she were still... clothed... in the darkness. She hugged him tighter as she felt the slightest warmth against her. She knew the shape of his hand, the tenderness of his touch.

"What happened, Eve?" He whispered to her as her cries reduced to sniffles.

"Men..." She took a deep breath. "...are so fucking stupid." She sighed a heavy sigh, her voice cold and emotionless. "I just came out here..."

He pulled off his jacket and wrapped it around her. He wanted her to feel some sort of comfort, some barrier of security, before he could see what had been done. And just like that, it seemed to flick a switch in her. She went from not being able to feel anything, to feeling everything all at once.

"I just... I just wanted to relive our better days... I've been so lonely without you, Adam... I've been so lost... I've been so numb... I didn't mind the numbness, I actually loved it. It was a relief... But when I could feel again, it just felt... worse... I just came out here to remember the good times... I just wanted one more of those... I just wanted to be happy again... And he was here. He got out, Adam. How did he get out? It... It was like he was waiting. Like he knew I'd be here... He was so happy to see me, but his smile was not human. He's not human, Adam. It was evil. He's evil!" Eve cried. "He grabbed me, said he was... making up for lost time... Revenge..." Eve stopped.

He retrieved his phone from his pocket, no longer worried about who'd see its beacon. He turned on the flashlight and watched as its light exploded on the ground, revealing all the secrets the darkness had hidden.

He started with the further out areas, panning across the scene, aware that the true horror was only a few steps away from him. There were drops of blood everywhere, as if there'd been a geyser of it somewhere. He saw shredded parts of her clothes lying around. Amongst a pool of blood, whose he didn't know, sat Eve's panties, soaking up the sins of the darkness.

He followed the blood trail as it approached him. He wanted nothing more than to close his eyes and turn away, but a part of him felt compelled to see. He had to see. He had to feel… He had to know the terrors she'd been subjected to.

His light caught the head. Face up. It was him. The guy from that night. The expression on his face was one of remorse, but he deserved none. He scanned across his body.

So many slits. So many slits… He tried counting but it was hard to know where one individual slit stopped and another started. There were so many overlaps, and so many chunks missing that hid the true count. So many slits. He deserved it. He had this coming. He deserved it. Every. Single. One.

Adam noticed his fist curling and his foot twitching. He really wanted to make this body unrecognisable, the anger flooding through his veins like a superpower he never wanted.

Eve watched Adam's reaction. She could see his desire to destroy again. His fists were shaking. His body seemed tense, firm. The sweet boy she once knew, now a tool for chaos…

"I don't want to be scared anymore, Adam." Her voice was dry.

She broke him away from his thoughts. The sound of her voice seemed to scare away his anger. His fist instantly softened as he turned to look at her.

She looked up at him. "I'm done being scared. They don't get to ruin my life anymore. I'm no longer afraid."

A shiver scurried across his spine. Her words filled him with fear. Fear and worry. She was already a victim of her past, but the stillness in her voice... She was rebuilding herself. Each stab with the knife had cut away a layer of her. Each drop of blood that sprayed her face was to water a new seed that had been planted in her. Now she was going to make the future her victim.

"Eve, I'm going to call the police." He knelt beside her.

She shrugged in response. She didn't care. It didn't matter. Nothing mattered. She just wanted to relive some memories. She just wanted to feel the comfort of the good days. Instead, she would be subjected to numbness. Just numbness. She wouldn't have to feel ever again.

"It was self-defence, Eve, you won't get in trouble." He tried to reassure her as he dialled.

She looked into his eyes. They were warm, worried, caring. But beneath them, he could see the fear. She didn't want him to be scared of her. She didn't want him to be scared for her. She didn't want to be his nightmare. She just wanted to be his...

He stood up and took a step away as he spoke to a voice in his phone. He tried to avoid saying anything that might upset her, as much as she was already traumatised. He paced around the grass, trying to calm himself as he had to relive it all. He wasn't even the target.

When he was done with the call, he sat beside her. Her head fell onto his shoulder, as it had done so many times before. Neither of them said another word. He waited beside her, counting the stars in the empty sky. He waited to hear the sirens. He waited to be blinded by their lights. He waited so she could be safe again.

Chapter 24

She was self-proclaimed, determined to write her own prophecy.

"Poor Eve…" Was all she could say.

He nodded in response, not sure what to say.

"Why did Adam get involved?" She asked, trying to dispel the sorrow thoughts.

"She called him." He responded.

"After all she'd done to him?"

"Just because someone hurts you, it doesn't mean you stop caring about them. And it's a good thing he did. No matter what she may have done to him, she didn't deserve that." He answered.

"Nobody deserves that, he got what he deserved for sure." She agreed, bitterness in her voice.

"The world is filled with terrible people; we just have to make sure we don't become one of them." He put an arm around her. "And you're definitely not one of them."

"I've got you to protect me, right?" She didn't look at him as she said that.

"Always." He reassured her.

She scrubbed and scrubbed and scrubbed but her hands were stained. Even if the blood washed away, her hands would forever be stained. She couldn't see them as clean ever again. *She* couldn't feel clean ever again. Try as she might, without peeling away her skin, she would always be stained.

The desire to no longer be afraid had worn off. Everything was terrifying now. It's like she'd been woken up. Nothing felt safe. She had gone from having no fear, to having all of it.

Knock knock. She turned to the bathroom door, panicking. They were coming for her. She couldn't run. She couldn't hide. Her breathing got faster, shorter, desperate.

"It's me, Eve." Adam called out, hearing her panting.

She stepped forward and clumsily opened the door, her hands trembling with each movement. When she'd managed to unlatch it, she peeked it open a little. She had to make sure.

She caught his eyes. Those familiar, safe, comforting eyes. She stepped back to open the door. Adam didn't enter the cramped bathroom, he just wanted to make sure she was okay. She had been in there a while.

"I've just given my statement to the police, they've told me I'm okay to go. Do you want me to call anyone?" He asked her.

She looked down and shook her head, hiding her hands amongst themselves. Adam noticed she was picking at her palm. He took a step forward and reached a hand out. He made sure not to touch her, he just reached his hand out, palm up. She saw it and hesitated, but she eventually placed her hand within it, palm down.

Any hope she had of keeping her palms hidden lay in his hands. He turned it over. As much as she may want to conceal her work, he knew she had to confront it eventually, before she did any further damage to herself. She didn't watch him, ashamed of herself. She felt disgusting, gross, deformed. Her palm had been scrubbed brutally, as if she were trying to erase the markings of her palm. She couldn't read those lines, but she knew whatever future they held was one she didn't want anymore. There were small pockets of blood spooling where she'd been picking at her skin, the rest of her hand an aching, sore, pale redness.

"You're gonna end up with no skin, Eve." He shook his head a little. "Let's get you to a first aider."

He let go of her hand and stepped aside, signalling for her to walk with him. She brought her hands back to her chest and walked forwards.

The halls of the police station were unnerving. Even though she knew she was safe, the looming threat of criminals being in the same building shook her to her core. She couldn't trust the walls, the corners, the doors and especially not the windows.

Adam walked slightly ahead of her, at her pace, clearing the way for her. He was letting her know it was safe, or as safe as it could be. He would be her shield, for now. If anything came to hurt her, Adam would be there.

He led her to the main lobby where he asked the officer at the reception for someone to look at Eve's hands. Eve scanned the room, memorising all the faces, just in case. She couldn't afford to relax. She couldn't afford to be comfortable.

A lady approached Eve with a hopefully-reassuring smile. She placed a small box beside them and asked Eve if she could look at her hands. The lady spoke softly, trying to calm Eve's nerves and let her know she was there to help. Eve slowly settled, her tremoring hands steadying as they sank into the lady's, so they could be cleaned and bandaged.

Adam sat beside Eve as she now picked and poked at her bandages. They'd have to bandage her whole body before she left, else she'd only redirect the scars to somewhere else. He tried to comfort her, offering to hold her hand. As much as she wanted to, she couldn't accept. Not right now.

The report had been filed, she'd been looked over and the police were waiting for some results from the hospital. There was nothing more to be done for now. His eyes stumbled to a clock, realising how late it was. Or early, depending on your point of view.

"Do your parents know, Eve?" He asked her, staring at the wall in front of them.

"No." The first time she'd spoken to him since they were at the scene of her horror.

"Do you w-." He began.

"No." She cut him off, short and assertive.

Adam didn't know what to do. He hadn't seen this coming. He should've been at his mother's, celebrating with her and Rose. He was never meant to be here. Eve should never have been here. They were meant to be moving on…

"Would you guys like a ride home?" A police officer approached them.

Adam looked at Eve, waiting for her to answer. She thought on it for a moment, not sure what the best choice was.

She knew she had to go back eventually, and she knew she'd have to tell her parents. Was she ready for it?

She turned to Adam, an anxiousness on her lips. "Will you come with me?" She asked shyly.

A lump in his throat caught his words. "Sure, if that's what you want." He managed to get out.

"I'll get a car ready for you outside." The officer replied, turning away from them.

"They offered to tell them." She told Adam. "I told them not to call my parents, not yet."

"Do you know what you're gonna say?" He asked.

She shook her head slowly.

"Do you want me to tell them?" He asked.

She shook her head again. "It needs to come from me."

Adam nodded. She was right, but it would rip her parents apart. It would tear them up and shower the pieces all over the place. This was going to break them all. They'd be reduced to sprinkles of their former selves. The parts of them that once held them together would be indistinguishable, nothing more than a pile of dust. And from that, they'd all have to rebuild themselves. Together. For doing it alone would be succumbing them to a long and painful death. Their existence would become torture. They needed to do it together.

His phone pinged.

"*Where are you?*"

He noticed there were a few missed calls and rattled texts. Amongst the chaos, he had forgotten to tell Rose where he was. He took this brief moment of respite to quell their nerves, though it may be a bit late for that.

"*At the police station. I'm safe, wasn't for me. I'll be home soon, will explain then.*" He replied.

They heard the rumbling of an engine pull up outside. The same officer from before approached them again, with a colleague behind him.

She approached Eve and asked her if she was ready to leave. Eve nodded, but she didn't look like she believed it. She slowly stood up, knowing she couldn't turn back now. She walked towards the car slowly, a million different thoughts racing through her mind.

Adam thanked the officer and then followed behind her. He had no idea what to expect when they got to her house, but he was part of this now, part of her turmoil. Somehow. Just like he had been so many times before.

The drive to Eve's house felt like it took days. The silence definitely made it feel longer. He didn't know what to say. She didn't know what to say. Aside from some initial advice and comforting words initially, the police officers read the silence and didn't say anything more. The air in that car just felt like it had slowed time.

And then it all sped up ten times faster when they pulled up in front of Eve's house. As she turned to see the front door, everything flashed in front of her eyes. Things that had happened years ago. Things that happened today. Things that hadn't even happened yet. She played out all the scenarios in her head, stuck in a loop.

She felt the cold air bite her face as the door on her side opened. His familiar face leaned over to greet her, followed by the hand she'd missed holding. She grabbed it and let him help her out of the car.

"Would you like us to come with you, Eve?" The police officer asked.

Eve shook her head.

"Okay then. If you need anything, just give us a call." She reached out a card.

Eve looked at it but didn't move. After noticing she wasn't going to move, Adam leaned over and accepted it.

"Thank you. Thanks for everything you've done tonight." Adam thanked them with a joyless grin.

He waved the police officers off as they drove away into the fading darkness and then turned to see Eve just staring at her front door.

The last time he had been at her doorstep, he nearly died. He was ready to die too. He almost hoped to die. He looked over at the spot where he could still see himself bleeding out. He had almost died for her, because of her, and here he was trying to save her. Now he was even from all those years back when they were kids in school. His debt had been repaid.

He stepped beside her, letting her know he was there. He could see her bracing herself for what would happen when those doors open. For all the unknowns that would fall into place and make themselves a cruel reality.

"You ready?" He asked.

She shook her head but stepped forwards. It couldn't get any worse than it already was, she could no longer avoid it. Might as well make it hurt while she was still numb.

Her keys chattered and jingled as she moved her hand closer to the keyhole. Her hands were shaking again. Not from the cold, from the fear. Not the fear of what had happened, but the fear of what was about to take place. She knew she was about to wreck her parents' world.

He gently placed his hand on hers. He guided her to the keyhole and just stood with her there. She turned to him. Her eyes were filled with horror and dread.

His eyes told her it was okay, they had hope. The corners of his mouth twitched as he grinned at her. She was safe now. It was all going to be okay. They just had to get through this, and he was there with her. As much as everything was going to come crashing down, she would be rebuilt. She wasn't alone, she didn't have to be alone. They were a team again.

He bowed his head once to nod. She managed to smile a little as she nodded too. He released her hand and stepped back. She pushed the key in and turned.

Clack.

She unlocked the door.

She pushed it open. It revealed her parents, anxiously watching the door. They knew Eve was the only other person with the key, but they still didn't expect to see her there. They didn't know who to expect. They both rushed to her as soon as they saw her. They pulled her in and held her tight, worried sick about where she'd been.

Eve's father caught Adam standing outside and smiled at him. Through worried eyes, he smiled at Adam. He sent Adam his thanks with a nod, unable to find any words for the moment. Adam shook his head. Not yet. He followed them into the house and closed the door behind him. He sat them down in the living room. The curtains were closed, they were hidden from the prying eyes of a sinking moon. The uneasy gaze of her parents' stares weighed him down. With a heavy sigh, Adam sat across from them.

He turned to Eve and nodded, ready to pick up the pieces of a family that was about to be destroyed.

Chapter 25

She grew more intuitive, skirting a dangerous balance with being right and accepting wrong.

"Should Adam have given her parents a heads up?" She asked.

"If she asked him not to, definitely not." He replied, seeing the look of confusion on her face. "She had just had her autonomy stripped from her. She was seeing the world in a different way. A darker way. If he went against her wishes, he was pulling her further into that darkness. I wouldn't say it would necessarily be on the same level, but it would still be damaging to her. Especially in that state."

"Wouldn't it have made her life a little bit easier?"

"Maybe, but either way she's going to end up in the same place. If she let someone else tell her parents, she is entrusting them with her future. Maybe not entirely, but enough of it. She can't control what they say, how they say it. Maybe they say too much, maybe they say too little. She has to deal with the fallout *and* fill in any blanks. It's a lot of trust to put in someone, especially for such a sensitive issue. Whereas if she speaks for herself, it's completely in her control. In a time where she probably feels she's lost all control of her life, of herself, it can be enough just to have control over that moment." He answered.

She thought about it for a second and shrugged, but also nodded. She didn't know what to make of it, but she could understand.

The nervousness on their faces revealed they were waiting anxiously for the bad news, they knew something was wrong. She sat between them, preparing herself to be enveloped by them once more.

She hesitated at first, she didn't know how to start the conversation. She started playing with her fingers, drawing attention to her hands. It was then that her parents realised they were bandaged up.

Her mother instantly leant over and grabbed her hands, gently brushing over them with her fingers. She brought her hands to her lips and kissed them repeatedly, as if she were a child who'd fallen over. She didn't utter a single word as she did so, scared of what would be revealed. The bandages were the least scary revelation of the night, and they knew it.

Eve reclaimed her hands and turned to Adam. She put her fingers together in the form of a rectangle. He seemed confused for a second, until he realised what she meant.

He leaned forwards slightly as he reached into his back pocket, retrieving a small card. He stepped forwards and handed it to Eve and then retreated back to the wall.

Eve studied the card for a moment, covering it from the sides so her parents couldn't gain an early peek. She closed her eyes and she clasped her hands together, the card now stuck between them. She inhaled slow, deep, long. She held it for a second. Then she exhaled slow, deep, long.

She opened her eyes and revealed the card to her parents, laying her palms flat with the card resting across them. They both leaned forwards to get a closer look.

The crest was familiar, but it took them a second to realise what it was. They managed to make out the words that circled the emblem. The local police station. Uh oh... the worry began to seep into their pores.

They looked at the letters below it. The name of the police officer who'd offered the card and her department. The department, they paid no attention to. It was the officer. It was a small town, they knew what she did. They knew of her work. She was admired around the town, but every parent dreaded the day she might come knocking.

Her parents looked at each other, mouths open, eyes astonished. They turned to Eve. Her eyes were closed, she couldn't bear seeing their faces. The tears had already begun trailing down her cheeks.

Everything became blurry. They held each other so tight they became a bundle of limbs. The silent sobs as they all cried. They cried by themselves and together at the same time.

"I'm sorry." A voice muffled, over and over and over again.

It wasn't his fault, but he felt he'd failed her. He didn't protect her. He didn't know she needed protecting. He would've been there if only he were omniscient, if only she'd called for him. His trembling voice faded as the tears took his body hostage. He never wanted to let her go again.

They cried together for an hour. Adam stood there the whole time, watching over them. He tried to comfort them where he could in silence. He wished he could've protected them all. None of them deserved this fate. His heart was heavy, his soul had sunk to his socks, his mind had grown weary. The only reason they stopped was because they had nothing left to shed, they were recharging.

They all composed themselves for the moment. They knew there were going to be some difficult conversations to come, and even more difficult days, but for now they would do their best to stay together.

Adam watched them, biting his lip the whole time. His body felt tired, but his mind wasn't ready to rest. He couldn't leave them yet, could he? How would he live with himself if he abandoned them in their time of need? After all they'd done for him.

Eve's father saw the heaviness in Adam's eyes. The tiredness, the shock, the misery. He approached Adam, each step slow and dragging. He nodded his head towards the kitchen. Adam's head bowed back as he followed.

He tried to speak, but no sound left his mouth. He coughed into his upper arm and tried again. Nothing. The defeat was written across his face. He couldn't protect his daughter, and now he couldn't speak. What *could* he do? What was he good for? Why did he even exist?

He began to break down again, but before he allowed himself to collapse, he grabbed Adam's hand and pulled him into him. Adam embraced him, giving him the hug he needed. He could feel the trembling that rocked his entire body. Adam hugged him tighter, trying to stop the shaking at his core, trying his best to hold him together.

"Thank you." He squeaked into his ear. "Thank you. Thank you. Thank you." Repeatedly, weakly, faintly, into his ear.

Adam shook his head against his shoulder. He didn't want the thanks. Not for this. He didn't want them. Adam wasn't there to protect her either. He wasn't there in time to save her. Not before she had saved herself. Not before she'd rewritten her story.

"Thank you." Eve's father broke the hug and just held Adam's hand as he looked him in his tired eyes. "You must be tired, you've had a long night. Your mother called, asking for you earlier. I can't thank you enough." He placed a hand on his cheek. "And congratulations on your new family." He managed to bring on a genuine smile.

Adam looked at him in disbelief. Through all he was going through, he was still able to offer what was probably the only shred of happiness left in him to Adam. He was stunned by the grace of the man before him. And it all got washed away by pure, unfiltered, unadulterated guilt. He didn't deserve this. He didn't do anything…

All Adam could do was nod in response. He gave Eve's father another hug. Words had failed him. He let the silence hang as he turned quietly towards the back door. He opened it as slowly and noiselessly as he could.

Adam looked back at her father. He just watched Adam, seemingly unbothered by the tears streaking down his face. Adam could feel a cold, sour rivulet sliding down his cheek. As much as he wanted to wipe it away, he let it stay there. He thought it disrespectful to try to hide it, to shun it. Eve's father nodded towards him again, letting Adam know he was free to go. Adam nodded back and turned away into the darkness.

He closed the door behind him and stopped. He sat on the steps, head in his hands. He didn't know how to react to it all. He just sat in the cold. He didn't know if he wanted to fall apart and let his pieces float away with the wind or if he wanted to let himself freeze, to be stuck feeling this pain forever.

He was so close to being happy, but his past just kept holding on. He couldn't escape, no matter how hard he tried. But he was determined to have a future. One that wasn't drawn by his past. It was his turn to take the pen for the remaining chapters. He was going to have his happy ever after, by pen or by sword.

Chapter 26

She was still understanding how to navigate her emotions, although she'd hidden the precious ones away.

"It's a dangerous world out there…" She sighed.

He noticed the concern on her face. "There are more good people than bad." He tried to reassure her.

She shrugged, somewhat discontent with that answer.

"Not everyone out there wants to hurt you. Sometimes, people want the complete and utter opposite. If you assume everyone is there to hurt you, you're going to end up shutting yourself off and getting hurt in a different way."

"What way?" She quizzed.

"Loneliness. You'll be hurting yourself, but all the while you'll be wondering why there's nobody you can fall back on. You'll completely ignore the fact that you pushed everyone away. Sometimes, we have to let ourselves be vulnerable in order to be secure." He placed his hand on her arm.

"I get it." She smiled at him. "It's scary, but not all scary things are bad. Sometimes the scary things are necessary."

"If you always assume the worst of everyone, the only thing they'll have to offer you is their worst."

He nodded, proud of her. She was definitely her own woman, one he was proud to have shared his life with.

He really got to admire the handiwork of her top as he laid his head on her chest. He drew little circles on her belly. Her lips lost among his freshly washed hair, pressed against his head. Her fingers weaved their way through the strands of his hair, gently caressing his skull. He wasn't used to being on the receiving end of this kind of care.

He had just gotten out of the shower and she could see the heaviness weighing him down. His whole body drooped as he fought himself in silence. She didn't say anything, she just let him get himself together and then pulled him into her.

His mind drifted back to the police station. The calmest time of his night. He was in the bathroom. They had just given him a change of clothes. He hadn't realised, amongst it all, how much blood he had ended up being covered in. He felt some of Eve's pain. Every time he looked at his hands, all he could see were blood-stained reminders of that horrific scene.

The tattered corpse didn't bother him one bit, surprisingly. He understood why it had to be like that. If anything, it looked too preserved for his liking. And that disturbed him. The fact that he would've relished in making it worse. As much as he wanted to be a pacifist, there was too much violence in his mind for him to have that kind of luxury.

"Eve was attacked." He broke the eerie silence, wanting to break free of himself.

Rose stopped moving entirely as those words haunted her body, shaking her all the way from her ears to her toes. Adam placed his hands flat on her belly as if they would somehow cover their child's ears. He didn't want their child to know the world they were bringing it into. They'd somehow protect their baby, they'd find a way. They'd make them a new world where such things couldn't exist.

"It was one of the guys that tried to attack her the last time we were at the farm at night, from a while ago. He... got out. And he found her..." His throat seemed clogged, the words difficult to get out. "She killed the guy. He definitely deserved it, but she really messed up his body." He spoke softly. "A part of me feels guilty, like I could've done more... It was the same guy... I could've done more back then. Or, if I'd never walked her down that trail, she would've never been there. I knew it wasn't safe at night..." His agitation stiffened his body.

"Hey, it wasn't your fault." She leaned over to look at his face. "You couldn't have known Eve would've gone down there alone, or even that that guy would be there. You went when she called and you did all you could when you were there. You did your best, Adam. You're not the villain here."

Adam's body deflated as he loosened up. Her words had snuck through his body and soothed him, despite his efforts to remain angry at himself. There was a part of him that wanted to fight back, let the thoughts in his head win out and free his demons. But he knew it was a losing battle, Rose wasn't going to let him blame himself. There was only one guy to blame, and he didn't deserve anyone's sympathy.

Rose kissed his temple a few times as she felt him getting lighter, rubbing her hands from his head to his back. He kept playing with his fingers on her belly, letting himself get distracted by their future.

"Thank you." He stared at her belly. "For more than you realise."

He leaned over, uncovered her bump, and smothered it in soft, frantic kisses, rubbing all the spots he couldn't get his lips over. Rose giggled, letting his lips tickle her. She enjoyed watching this side of him, it made her excited for what the next chapter in their story looked like.

Without warning, he jumped up and covered her smile with his own, leaning her back and laying her on the bed. He pressed his lips against hers as he wrapped his arms around her. She was happy to reciprocate, the passion in his soul making her giddy.

He broke away from her and stared into her eyes, smiling more than he'd ever smiled before. He kissed the corner of her mouth and then began kissing all the way around her face, smothering her with his affection and a little saliva. She laughed as he did so, just enjoying every moment. When he'd completed the circle, he pressed his lips over hers again and let his tongue meet hers.

She placed her hands over his shoulders, connecting them behind his neck. She grinned as he pulled away again.

"What's gotten into you?" She chuckled.

"I just love you so much." He answered without hesitation.

The smile on her face faded. When he saw that, the smile on his face faded. The butterflies were pounding at the walls of his stomach, begging to break free.

"You what?" She asked, her voice was softer than before.

This time he hesitated, thinking on it a bit more before replying. He didn't want to put a foot wrong; he didn't want to ruin this.

"I love you." His eyes fell to the bedding.

"Hey," She got his eyes back to hers. "I love you too." Her eyes beamed as she smiled from ear to ear.

He squeezed her tight against him, his head buried in her neck. They just lay together for a while, enjoying each other's warmth, each other's joy, each other's love. He didn't want to move; he could've stayed there tangled in her arms for the rest of his life.

"I'm not losing you again. If you decide you want out of this place again, I'm coming with. You're stuck with me." His voice was quiet, but stern.

She nodded. "I think I can live with that." She teased. "But you're coming with me *everywhere*. You're not allowed to leave my side."

"Deal." He answered, with no hesitation.

"Deal." She grinned, kissing his neck.

That was all they had to say. They allowed the silence to carry them away into a future far away. They shared their dreams, as they began to plan out the smallest details of their lives in their minds. They let their imaginations run wild and free, with no care for the world or anyone else in it.

His phone rang, breaking his concentration on her cheek. He let it ring for a moment, hoping it would go away. It didn't. He begrudgingly reached to the side to retrieve it from the table, huffing and puffing as he pulled it to his ear.

"Hello?" He hadn't checked who was calling.

"Can you come over?" Her voice stunned him.

He looked over at Rose. She was just as stunned as him, overhearing the voice. He looked to her for an answer but she didn't have one for him.

"Adam?" The voice broke the blanket of silence that had covered them.

He looked at Rose again. This time, it wasn't asking what he should do. He wasn't looking for an answer, he was looking for permission. She could see it in his concern. She nodded, knowing Adam only ever wanted to help.

"I'll be there soon." His voice cracked; his throat had dried up.

He hung up the phone and just stared at it in his hand. He had no idea if he'd made the right choice there, but he couldn't deny he still cared about her. You can't spend years loving someone, caring for them, and just turn that off overnight. He had always been her friend before he was ever her boyfriend, and he was always determined to be a good friend.

"I'm sorry." He turned to Rose.

She shook her head and leaned in closer to him. "You've got nothing to apologise for. You're a good friend, Adam." She placed her hand on his cheek. "You being so caring is one of the many things that make you so great. Just make sure you take care of yourself too, okay?" She smiled at him approvingly.

He leaned in and kissed her. "Thank you. I'll be back as soon as I can."

He got ready at his own pace. Only a few months ago, he would've been trying to beat a record to race to her house. He wasn't slow, but he didn't rush. Rose just sat on her bed and watched him the whole time, admiring his movements.

He was ready to leave. He did one last pat down of his pockets to make sure he had everything and then stood by the bedroom door. She could feel the weight on his shoulders, the sluggishness setting in to his joints. He made to leave when he heard a forced cough behind him.

"You're forgetting something." She tapped her cheek with a finger.

He smiled, scurrying over to her and giving her a kiss on the-. She turned her head just in time to get a kiss on the lips. That got a chuckle out of him.

"Love you." She smiled at him.

"I love you too." He smiled back.

His short walk back to the door had more energy in it now. She'd refreshed his battery with a simple kiss. It's often the simple things, the small things… The things that seem insignificant are the ones that leave the longest impression.

"Miss you already." He blew her a kiss.

She motioned to catch it and pocket it. "I'll hold onto this one for later, just hurry back and give me the real thing."

He chuckled as he walked out the door. As he began walking towards Eve's house, he could only think about how much he enjoyed spending time with Rose.

Her place was comfy. He loved spending time with her there. He admired the way she'd decorated it, and how he'd slowly begun sneaking his way into her space. He had a toothbrush there, that was a big step. It was *her* idea. Maybe he needed his own bright idea…

And then thoughts trailed to their little family. How much he was looking forward to being a father, despite having no idea what he was in for. No first-time parent does. The unknown is terrifying, but he was determined to conquer this demon.

Before he knew it, he found himself rounding the corner to see Eve's house. The smile that had danced its way to his face and kept residency there had been evicted. The house looked sad. The curtained windows its droopy, tired eyes. He felt the sadness envelope him. It was a familiar hug, but one he no longer wanted to know.

He took the last few steps to her door. He closed his eyes, mentally preparing himself for... whatever may happen. He had no idea what he was preparing himself for. He opened his eyes, cleared his throat and lifted a fist to knock on the door. He swung the pendulum forwards.

It fell all the way forwards, more forwards than it had ever been swung, and almost took him with it. She'd been watching for him and had opened the door before his fist could knock. She let out a stifled giggle, as he readjusted himself and cleared his throat.

"Hey." She greeted him.

"Hey." He half-nodded back.

He didn't really know what to say. She didn't seem like she did either. Until she realised she was just standing at the door and he was out in the cold. She stepped to the side and let him in.

He saw her parents in the living room. They looked wrecked, completely shattered, but they were all processing and healing together. They smiled a greeting to Adam. He pulled his lips in and half-smiled back, not really knowing how to respond to them. To anything, really.

Eve coughed behind him, prompting him to turn around. She pointed her eyes towards the stairs as he nodded. He let her lead the way, still not sure how to compose himself.

She sat on her bed and patted a spot beside her. He hesitantly stepped into her room and sat near her, but not as close as he once might have.

He looked around her room. It had been a while since he'd been here. She'd gotten some new furniture to replace the ones he'd… It looked like she'd redecorated some parts of her room too.

"I-" They both started at the same time, unable to take the tension anymore.

"Ladies first." Adam bowed his head.

"Ever the gentleman." She seemed nervous. "I know you're wondering why I asked to see you. I just wanted to say thanks, in person. After everything I put you through, you still came to help me in the lowest point of my life. And it feels like I've said that so many times, but-."

"It's okay." He stopped her, not wanting to know where that was going to go. "I still care about you, Eve, I still want you to be happy. We were great friends, once upon a time, that doesn't have to go away."

She exhaled, seemingly of relief. "I'm glad you said that. I thought you hated me… And I wouldn't blame you if you did."

He shook his head. "Hate is too strong an emotion to spend on someone you don't like. I'm just focused on the future, we can't change the past."

She looked into his eyes. They were reassuring, comforting. How she'd always known them to be. She was glad the pain wasn't there anymore. She noticed, as time went by, there was more and more pain in his eyes. He seemed... happy. She wanted to be happy too.

She leaned forwards, closing her eyes. She tilted her head slightly as she got closer and closer to his face. Her lips parted a little, allowing a little gap for...

She fell forwards onto her bed. She opened her eyes. He wasn't there. She turned to her side. He was standing, heartbreak on his face as he watched her. The pain had come back to his eyes. He knew she was in a bad place right now, he didn't want to do this. Not like this. Not ever again.

"I'm sorry, Eve. I-." He tried to explain.

"It's okay Adam, you're not taking advantage of me. I want this." She tried to reassure him as she stood up.

"Eve."

That was the first time she'd ever dreaded hearing him say her name. It was stern, cold. It had reason behind it. No feeling.

"I've got a girlfriend." He finished damning her.

She turned on her heel as soon as he said that, hiding her tears. She had tried to find her own way out of this, and her last door had just closed. Or, rather, it was never open. She just thought it was. A mirage. She couldn't drink from this pool, lest she want the sand to consume her.

"...I-... I-." She tried to fight herself. "Is it *her*?" She sputtered, almost with disdain.

Adam knew who she was referring to. There was only one suspect. His silence was the answer she was hoping not to hear.

"I'm going... to go..."

He began walking to her bedroom door. Eve didn't move, she just huddled her face away from him. As he turned to face the stairs, he looked at her one last time. He didn't want it to end like this.

Goddamnit Eve, why'd you have to do that? We were so close to being able to be normal. Maybe even be friends. Maybe even happy... Not like this, Eve, not like this...

Chapter 27

She was learning the lessons of the world, trying to become her own beacon.

"He was stupid." She yelled.

"How?" He paused her to cover his ears and then prompted her to begin.

She slapped his hands from his ears and began. "That was something he could've done over the phone, avoid all that… awkwardness…"

"Some things are better done in person. Some things you just feel you *have* to do in person." He shrugged. "She asked him over, so he probably felt it was important for her to do it face-to-face."

"I wouldn't have risked it, and I would've been right. There are just too many things you can't control." She crossed her arms.

"Some risks are worth taking. The problem is, you never know which ones are until you take them." He smiled.

"How are you meant to make that call after all she put him through?" She sought wisdom.

"Experience. Trust." He replied.

"Trust in what?" She inquired.

"Himself. He went with his gut. He knew what she was like, he knew he could handle her in probably any situation. He just had to trust himself to follow his judgement. Assessing risk is a calculation, and he had the experience to make that call. They were best friends for years, it's not like she was a stranger to him." He tried to fill her appetite.

She shrugged. "Still a waste of time if you ask me."

"Good thing nobody is asking then." He chuckled.

When he closed her front door, he heard the fumbling groans of wood and screaming scatters of glass. She was redecorating again, it seemed. He got to the end of the street when her roar reverberated through her window and echoed through his torso. He had to walk away though, going back there would be too dangerous.

"She did *what*?!" Rose seemed angry, a side of her he'd never seen before.

He shrugged. "She tried to kiss me."

Rose lifted her hands to her temple, not sure what she wanted to do with them. One wanted to lash out, the other wanted to cover her face. She was overwhelmed. He watched her for a moment as she paced around the space behind her.

He stepped forwards, slowly and cautiously, arms spread out at hip level. As she completed the latest circuit, Adam caught her gently, locking his fingers between hers.

She looked to the ground, not wanting to look at him. She wasn't angry at him; she was just angry. She didn't know how to process it, not sure if she'd felt betrayed or not.

"I didn't kiss her. I didn't even let her lips touch me. I didn't even let *her* touch me. I promise." He tried to chase her eyes as she avoided his. "She fell on her bed 'cos I moved away from her as she leaned in."

"She what?" Rose finally looked at him.

"I was sitting next to her. She started off by thanking me, so I thought nothing of it. Then she moved a bit closer and closed her eyes. And she started moving her face towards me. So, I got up and she fell forwards."

Rose couldn't help herself. The frustration on her face broke away and was replaced by a raucous laughter. Adam laughed lightly with her, relieved she hadn't jumped into the gun and off the ship.

"She knows we're together. And so does all her furniture, or whatever is left of it."

She lay her head on his chest. "I'm sorry, I should've let you explain properly before I got worked up."

He lay the bottom of his head against the top of hers. "It's okay. I don't blame you for getting upset. At least it's one way to show you care about me, eh? I just didn't want you to find out about it from anyone but me. I'm gonna do right by you. I want you to know that. I'm gonna do everything I can to prove to you that you made a good choice in being with me. I'm going to do right by you. I'm all yours. Always have been."

She looked up at him with a grin. "Yeah?"

He nodded. The grin turned to a smirk. She pushed him onto the bed and jumped on top of him. He chuckled, placing his hands on the back of her hips as she began smothering him in kisses.

She scooted back and lowered her head above his belt, looking up at him with a wicked grin. He watched her tease him, frozen in her gaze. She placed her thumbs on the sides of his jeans and winked at him. He was struggling to hold back his eagerness, but she wasn't done playing.

She moved her thumbs up until they slid below his top and hooked it from the sides. She slithered her way up his body, revealing it as she did so. Her tongue dried quickly as it slid up his body. She kissed the remaining way up to his neck as he lifted his arms for her.

She began rolling his shirt up his arms. She threw the top off him and kissed her way down one of his arms. He enjoyed the soft pecks, each one imprinting itself against his skin, forever trapped there in his mind. He would be able to feel them later on, whenever he wanted.

And then she got to his wrist. She paused a moment; something had caught her eye as she began kissing closer towards it. She rubbed a thumb over it, wondering if it was just some residual dirt. It wasn't. It was a stain of a different kind.

Her palm covered her mouth as she pulled his hand closer to her face. Her face instantly dropped. She knew. She'd found it. She was astonished she hadn't noticed it before.

"When did this happen, Adam?" The playfulness had dissipated from her voice, now softened and filled with worry.

At first, he was confused. When did what happen? He hadn't hurt himself in a while... And nothing had happened to that wrist since...

He felt her finger run over it, drawing the letters in his mind. She turned to look at him after investigating it for a while, the panic written all over his face.

"It's not recent, I can tell. I'm not angry, I promise." She reassured him.

He thought for a moment. She allowed him to collect himself. She knew there was probably a lot going through his mind right now, and she didn't want to add any pressure on him. She did want to know, though, for her own sanity. She wanted to protect him, even during a time when she wasn't there.

"I did it a while ago. When I was still crazy for her. I... I used to self-harm when I was younger. It was one of the ways I'd learnt to control my emotions. I stopped as I grew up. My mum found out. She was so upset, so angry. She thought she'd failed me. I had never been so heartbroken to see her blame herself for that... She helped me manage myself better. And I owed it to her to never do it again. I hadn't done it for years... And I haven't done it since, I swear." Now he reassured her. "But there was this one time I was just so angry at Eve for this... this cycle she put herself in. This cycle she trapped us both in. I was angry that I couldn't be enough for her, why couldn't I be enough for her? What i-... What was wrong with me? I was angry I couldn't break either of us out of it, and I didn't know how to stop loving her. Even after all the times she'd hurt us... I didn't know how to deal with all that anger. I just had to get it out. So, I ended up hurting myself. Relief through pain... It was stupid, I know that, but I was desperate. It's working its way off my body. One day, it'll be gone entirely. She's a wound that will probably never heal. I will probably always care for her in some capacity, but I don't need this reminder."

Rose went quiet. She didn't know what to say and was now regretting ever finding this. She was caught in the middle of his past. The past he had after her. The past she wished she could erase. The past that kept creeping back. Adam only saw her as his future.

"If this is too much, I get it." He caught her lost in thought.

She turned to look at him with hopeful eyes. "Are you really all mine, Adam?"

He pulled her closer to him. "If you still want me."

"I need to know… This is going to seem unfair… Do you still love her?" The question seemed genuine, concerned.

The hope in her eyes had disappeared, only to be replaced by regret. Regret for ever asking. Regret for ever leaving. Regret for ever returning.

"I do." He sighed.

Rose's head dropped instantly, and she made to leave. Adam stopped her, he wasn't done yet. If he was going to be honest with her, he was going to be really honest.

"But…" He added, before the pain could really seep into her. "Not like that. I was in love with her for so long, so I can't just pretend I hate her. The only reason her cheating on me hurt is *because* I loved her. But I don't love her like that. I don't love her like I love you. And maybe that answer is disappointing to you, maybe it hurts you and you're starting to question our relationship. Before you do that, though, I need you to know this: they're very different kinds of love…

The love I had for Eve was very one-sided. It was me giving and her taking. It was her breaking and me fixing, but then me breaking and nobody to fix me. It was exhausting for me, but it was the boost she needed. When she asked me to be her boyfriend, I knew I was falling out of love with her. To this day, the only reason I can think of for saying yes was desperation. Loneliness. I was scared. Without Eve, what was

I? *Who* was I? She had become part of my identity, in a purely unhealthy way. I was losing myself. I gave her the chance to prove to me that she could be the partner I so desperately wanted. And she was doing a good job. I told myself I could learn to love her again, but deep down I knew I would never love her the same way ever again. My love for her had changed. I love her like a friend, a really, really close friend.

But I tried to lie to myself. After all we'd been through, *me* being the one to walk away? Not even I could believe that. So, I kissed her before Valentine's. Just to see what would happen. Just to see if I could give it a better try. And I did feel like I was being unfair to her. Through that kiss, I felt... like I had let her down, but she was still trying. For me. *She was trying for me.* So, I was going to try, for her. But you know how that ended up..."

Her eyes no longer held the pain that had covered them so swiftly. She understood. She nodded. But he wasn't done yet.

"The love I have for you is different. The love I had for you all those years ago, that was different too. We need to start there, really. Way back when, in a time simpler than this, you saw something in me. You were the reason I became addicted to... love. To being in love, to being loved. You were the reason I just wanted to love. And then you left. I know it wasn't your fault, you had to go with your family, and I couldn't follow. I felt betrayed, but ultimately, I knew you had no real choice over it. But thinking you chose to leave me did make it a bit easier to get over you, so you'll have to forgive me for that. I cursed you out *a lot* but only ever to myself. I would never speak ill of you to anyone else. But yeah, I had to get over you somehow... And I did. Eventually.

But then you came back into my life, during my lowest time, and all those feelings came flushing right back through my body. You made me feel the same as when we were just silly teens who didn't know anything but hopes and dreams. You make me feel like a teenager again, going through his first love all over again, in all the best ways. And I've been so grateful for the patience and time you have shown me, all the effort you've put into us – from our friendship to our relationship.

I get that you were scared and hesitant, but even through that you showed me how love *can* be. How it *should* be. You showed it to me all those years ago and I forgot it. I let someone else taint it, purely because I wanted nothing more than to be loved. I didn't care what that love was like, I just wanted to feel something. But you've shown me how I *can* be loved, how I *should* be loved. And I am forever grateful to you. That's why I've always been yours. You never lost me, you just forgot me for a little bit. And then you remembered how great I was and came running back." He smiled as she chuckled.

"I want you to know how much I appreciate you. For everything you do, and for all the other things you do that you don't realise you're doing. Like how you will tease me, but you'll also make sure that I'm okay too. I love everything about you. I could speak for days and days about all the things I love about you and how great you are, but I think you'd get sick of me. That's just because you're humble, which is another reason why I love you. There's not a single part of you I don't want. I want all of you, Rose, thorns 'n' all. If I could go back and never do *this*," He shook his wrist, whilst she still held it. "I would, I swear it. Even if I wasn't with you right now, I just wouldn't want this on my body. But I can't change it. The wound Eve caused on my soul has already healed, my body just hasn't quite caught up. She doesn't come close to you, Rose, she never will. You're all I've ever wanted and a lot more I had no idea I wanted. You're all I'll ever need ever again. I'm not letting you escape twice. I've felt the pain of you leaving before and I do not wish to relive it." He ran a thumb over her cheek. "So, yeah. I do still love Eve. But it's a different kind of love to the love I have for you. One of them, I had to get over. The other, I had to learn to let go of. If there is truly even the tiniest part of you that thinks I would rather have Eve over you, I won't stop you from leaving. But, just know, it won't stop me from trying to prove it wrong."

"That's a little creepy, Adam." She teased.

"How does that one song go...? *I'm aaaaa creeeeeeeeeeeeeee eeeeep, I'm aaaaa weeeeeeeeeiiiiiiiiiiiiiirdoooooooooooooo oooooo...*" He poorly sang with a smile.

"You really don't know when to stop, do you?" She seemed to smile.

"The heart wants what it wants, and you're definitely not worth giving up without a fight." He smiled back at her.

She looked at him for a minute, from his smiling lips to his hopeful eyes. She could see a future with him and that's what scared her so much. The thought of losing all these dreams before she ever got to have them. Their love had the potential and the passion to get there, and she didn't want to lose any of it.

She placed a hand on his cheek and rubbed it with her thumb a few times. Adam held his hand over hers. She leaned in and kissed him, giving in to her craving mind.

"I'll make your life easier for you, but only in this moment." His smile had infected her face too. "But you won't have it easy for long." They both looked at her bump and then back at each other. "You better pray you don't regret those words 'cos I'll make your life Hell if you do." She let her dreams take over.

He shook his head. "There's nothing you could do to make me regret those words."

He pulled her right against him, making sure there was no air between them, and cradled her against him. He felt her place her hand back on the scar. He closed his eyes as she crossed out what was there and rewrote his sins.

"I want you to know, Adam, there's nothing wrong with you. There never was anything wrong with you. Just because she couldn't see it, doesn't mean it's not true. I would know. I never forgot you. I had to get over you too, and I lived with that knowing that I had left you behind. You had it easy."

"It's okay. None of that matters now. We got here in the end." He kissed her head.

She closed her eyes, doing her best to forget the past she could've prevented. She couldn't help but feel guilty for the mistakes of her parents. But he was right. They got there in the end. They were here, together. Nobody could get in their way anymore.

This time, they had nothing to break them from this moment. They just lay there together, until Rose had drifted off in his arms. Her peaceful snores sang him to sleep. Their puzzle was falling together, piece by piece. They were rebuilding.

Eve had woken up from her enraged slumber. She looked at all the broken pieces on the floor, almost confused as to what had happened until it all came flooding back to her.

He was hers. He was always hers. How could he be with someone else? She made one mistake. There's no way it all came apart from one dumb mistake. That's not the love she knew from him.

She looked down at her hands. The bandages were frayed and dirtied. The stiff brown dots had made brighter, fresher red friends. The hands that had killed had now destroyed. They held a new power within them.

Chapter 28

She grew more insightful, learning to let go of her judgements.

"Why is love so complicated?" She sighed.

"Because it's something we all want, but not all of us know how to give." He sat across from her. "Love is like language. There are so many ways of expressing your love, communicating it, and even just basking in it. We all have our own love language. If someone doesn't speak your language, then…"

"You don't get very far. What's your love language?" That question seemed to perk her up.

"Grandeur." He took a bite of his food. "I like to plan elaborate, crazy things to express my love in a way my words fail to." He took a sip of water. "But it's not sustainable, so I mostly do small things more regularly. Just the simple, cute, vomit-inducing stuff that makes you smile. At the end of the day, I like to create memories. What's yours?" He seemed to regret asking that as soon as the words left his lips.

"If I told you, you'd definitely vomit. Sooooo… let's not go down that road." Her lips fell back into her mouth as she hid a smirk.

He nodded quickly as he turned his attention back to his food, eager not to travel down that road.

Rose had been extremely cautious during the first few months of her pregnancy, skirting the lines of paranoia. She didn't want to set herself up for another gut-wrenching devastation if anything went wrong. It was a morbid thought, thinking about death before life could begin, but her past had built up a shield she hated. One she felt shame for having, clouded with tremendous guilt but reinforced with understanding. That was the worst part; she understood why it was there.

She still allowed the small celebrations, like sharing the *good* news. Only a special select few got to know. Adam, his mother, and today, her parents. There was an uneasiness in her gut, nervous and anxious about everything. This was the first time they'd meet Adam as an adult, and it was to announce he'd be the father of their grandchild.

"It'll be fine." He shielded her shaking hands with his calm palms.

"My dad is pretty protective… Especially after what happened the last time…" Her voice trailed off, as did her gaze.

She faded away into past memories, nightmares that lingered on the horizon. She got caught in the grip of her past. She felt trapped by it, but she was so desperate to escape it. Wriggling and writhing within its clutches, trying to fight back with whatever strength she could find.

"Good, he should be protective. I'm the same way. I wouldn't let anybody hurt you." He bent his knees as he lowered himself into her sightline. "Proving myself to you extends to proving myself to them too. I want the whole world to know how much I love you." His eyes smiled up at her.

She nodded, letting a grin take over her face. She broke her hands free from his, no longer shaking, placing them on his cheeks and pulling him in for a grateful kiss.

She hadn't visited them in a while, and this was definitely one way to remind them of her existence. She wrapped herself in one of Adam's coats, tactically masking the bump until she was ready to make her announcement. Well, that was partially the reason. His scent also soothed her. She felt safe, protected. Even though he was right there, willing to do all of that anyway, it was an added layer of comfort.

He stood at the door and watched her prepare herself. When she could avoid it no longer, she walked towards him and stopped in front of him. He tilted his head towards the door, an eyebrow raised in question.

She closed her eyes, took a deep breath, and exhaled slowly. When she opened her eyes, she allowed hope to envelope her face as she nodded. He let her lead the way, now becoming a barrier to prevent her from retreating as he followed in close behind.

Rose didn't say anything for a majority of the walk there. Adam contemplated saying something, but he let her run with her thoughts. He didn't have much room to console her since he hadn't seen her parents in so many years – he barely remembered them, and this was a different context for introductions. He was no longer the innocent child who had befriended their daughter. He was the damned lover who'd entrapped her way too soon into their relationship. He spoke to her through his hand, as it wrapped around hers and rubbed her knuckles for the entire walk. A feigned confidence, one he hoped would calm her whilst he tried to build up the real thing.

"I don't think they'll hate you." She finally spoke.

"Thanks, I think." Adam laughed back.

"Just don't…" She started but then lost herself.

"Be myself? Say something dumb? Break anything?" He teased her.

"Shut up, Adam." She scoffed.

"You should've given me a cheat sheet so I could study two hours before the exam." He gently nudged her.

She shook her head. "You seem pretty confident you'll win them over. What's gotten you so perked up?"

He shrugged. "I don't know, but this all just feels right. And I'm ready for it. And I want it. They could hate me, but it wouldn't stop me loving you, wouldn't keep me from you." His face glowed, the actual confidence shining through.

"It would make it a lot easier if they didn't, though." She sighed.

"Yeah, you're right. But even if it's difficult, you're worth all of it." He had managed to break the concern from her face.

"Let's hope they don't make you regret those words. Being stuck with me means you're stuck with them too." She laughed.

"I'll just send my mum on a peacekeeping run." He chuckled.

"Ah, so there's your secret. That's devious." She smirked.

"There's no rulebook!" He winked at her. "Besides, I'm pretty sure I've got her charm. Worked for you, right? Should be fine."

She shook her head, this time with a smile. Despite the unwavering chaos and unpreparedness with which he spoke, he'd somehow managed to ease her nerves. Maybe he really did inherit his mother's charm.

She felt a tug on her arm. He'd stopped walking without any notice and jolted her back accidentally. It caught her off-guard, but she was able to catch herself.

"Sorry, I just…" He made sure she was okay, realising what he'd just caused.

"What the hell, Adam?" She wasn't angry, just agitated.

"What do you think of this house?" He seemed unbothered by her agitation, returning to a place where hopes ran free.

They stood in front of a medium-sized detached house. The front had a small garden that could be beautiful with enough sweat. There was a driveway to the side that led to a single-car garage. From what they could see, it looked to be a three, maybe four, bedroom house. The size of those rooms was debatable from the outside, but it looked like it was enough. The kitchen overlooked the front garden, and it looked like it connected to the garage. The windows across it revealed what looked like a dining room, with a spacious living room in the background. He'd noticed it from a short distance away and had been analysing it as they approached it. The analysis didn't take long, though. He could already see his future running rampant between those walls.

"I don't know, Adam, I've only just seen it." She replied confused.

He tilted his head towards the sign by the picketed fence that kept them at bay. Her eyes followed the direction, quickly landing on what he'd noticed.

"You wanna have this conversation right now?" She asked.

"I just asked what you thought of the house, nothing else." He shrugged.

"You're sweet," she stepped towards him and placed her free hand on his cheek. "And stupid." She smiled up at him. "Can we not do this right now, though? One step at a time, hon."

He nodded, a slight sadness enveloping his face, but he understood. He knew she wanted to go at her own pace, but there was an unexpected bump that sped some things up. He'd lost sight of it, but he couldn't disagree with her completely. Especially not today. One step at a time, hon.

They walked past the house. Adam took one look back to wave away his future with his eyes before turning his attention back to his present, the gift that was currently attached to him stressing away in her own mind. Maybe if he aced this interview, it would be the next step.

"It did look like a nice house though." She added before shutting down that conversation, smirking back at him.

It was all she needed for the smile to dance back onto his face. He walked with a bit more purpose now. He was looking forward to this next potential step, but he had to get over this hurdle first.

She was adamant to deal with one stress at a time, not wanting to risk pushing her limits. One problem at any moment. Just one, please. And he understood. He didn't want to cause more headaches for her. But it was her fault, really.

If it wasn't for her, he wouldn't be having those hopes, those dreams. If it wasn't for her, he wouldn't be filled with this love, this unwavering love that sought only to grant her every wish she could think of. This infectious love that filled his entire being, down to the spaces between the atoms that made him. This unfaltering love that saw her everywhere with him, doing the mundane but somehow making it a memory. She was the blessing he'd been cursed with, and he wanted nothing but to devote himself to her.

But amongst it all, he had to remember to not push her. He had to pace himself, had to manage himself. He had to make sure he didn't overdo it. He couldn't release all his love for her, it would be too much. It would be suffocating, she'd drown before he could save her from himself. He had to temper it. If he could, he would give her the world, but she barely even wanted an address right now. For now, he would just devote a pathway to her.

One step at a time, hon.

Chapter 29

She had an unruly spirit, one she wrestled with to regain control.

"Was he still living with his mum?" She realised she had no idea.

"He was unofficially living with Rose, but still had most of his stuff at his mum's place." He clarified.

"And now he wants to go from that to just buying a house for her?"

"*With*." He corrected her. "If they were having a kid together, is it not easier to be under the same roof?"

"I suppose, just seems like something they should've figured out sooner." She shrugged.

"They still had time; she wasn't due for a couple months."

"Buying a house can take ages though, and then there's the stress of moving... Seems like something you wanna get sorted as soon as, no?"

He shrugged, unable to answer her questions. "One step at a time, hon."

They stood outside the intimidating doors. Adam looked all around them, feeling like he was being watched. He had lost the confidence he'd managed to discover for Rose earlier, but he wasn't going to back down. He could fake it again, surely.

Rose was by his side but completely in her own mind. She was preparing herself for what was about to happen. All the things that could go wrong, the few things that needed to go right. Every possible thing he could be asked, all the things he would be asked and all the things they definitely shouldn't ask.

She jerked his hand to get his attention. He turned to her. She could see the slight worry setting into him, which somehow eased her. At least it wasn't just her, and at least she could now trust he'd take it more seriously than his words had suggested previously.

"Are you r-."

The door squealed open, telling on itself. They both immediately turned their heads. There she stood.

They had the same eyes, the same hair. They shared the same smile but different lips. Hers were smaller, shyer. She was a little shorter too, whether that was always the case or something time had taken from her, he'd never know.

"Hi, mum." Rose interrupted Adam's thoughts. "This is Adam."

"Are you ready, Adam?" Rose's mother asked, teasing Rose.

Adam chuckled nervously and stepped forwards to shake her hand. He froze. Is he meant to shake her hand? Or is he meant to bow? He definitely couldn't kiss her hand, that would be playing with fire. The rules of etiquette had completely abandoned his mind.

The cold was stolen from his palm, replaced with a delicate warmth. Rose's mother had met him halfway, noting his worry, and then pulling him in for a hug. She had relieved his troubled mind, for now.

"Your hand is so cold, let's get you inside." She suggested.

Her words were warm, but they just made him colder. He had talked the talk, but the walk wasn't walking. *He* wasn't walking. He'd frozen. Rose nudged him from behind, almost pushing him into the house. He wasn't going to escape now.

He followed Rose's mother into the living room, his head twisting and turning as he took in the sights. He felt a little disoriented, the memories of this house flooding back to him all at once. They were hitting him hard, making sure he recalled it all with no time to fully appreciate any of them. And amongst the madness of reminiscing, he was taking in the evolution of the house too. Noting all the slight changes here and there, and the not-so-slight ones too.

There were memories on the walls that were once bare. The furnishing had been updated as the layout of the rooms had changed. The house was no longer a work in progress, but closer to complete. Almost complete, the last part of that left to their daughter.

Adam caught sight of Rose's father, sitting in his chair, eagerly waiting for them. Rose shot out from behind Adam and into his spreading arms as he noticed her. That seemed to ease him up more, good job Rose.

Her mother sat on the sofa beside him. Adam watched them hug and share greetings before they broke apart. Rose turned her body slightly to turn their attention back to Adam.

"This is-."

"Adam." Her father finished. "It's been a while; you've definitely grown since we last saw you." He stretched out a hand.

Adam didn't hesitate this time, but he began to overthink about how tight the handshake was meant to be. You can supposedly tell a lot about someone from their handshake, apparently. He never could, but he also didn't go around shaking hands. How good was her father at reading palms? Could his hands trace his secrets? Would he be able to feel his nerves?

"Hi, it's been too long. I'll blame Rose for that." Adam smiled back.

"You can blame me, I moved away for work and Rose wanted to explore the world a little." He turned and smiled at her. "I moved back with her mother a few years ago. We missed this little town. Rose took a bit longer to come back. Maybe she didn't miss it quite as much, or us." He laughed.

Rose sat beside her mother. Adam took a seat beside her. The introductions had gone down smoothly enough, but he supposed this was the easy part. The worst was yet to come.

"I never thought you two would end up together, but it makes sense. You were such good friends." Her mother turned towards them. "I'm guessing that's the news you were going to break to us, right dear?"

Rose nervously nodded. She wasn't lying per se, but she didn't know what she was getting into. Her mother pulled no punches, but her aim was a little low for the real prize.

"How did you reunite?" Her father asked.

The interrogation was beginning under the guise of a fairly innocent, curious question. How did they meet? Straightforward enough, right?

Rose was sitting with her back against the sofa, but her eyes were focused on Adam. He was sitting slightly in front of her, as she hid behind him. They knew they wanted to answer to come from him. He turned his head a little to look at her. She nodded.

"I was running to a friend's house and tripped on a loose paving slab. Rose was across the street; she saw me and ran over. She seemed to know who I was straightaway and started laughing. I didn't recognise her at first, she looked so different from when I last saw her. She helped me to my feet, reintroduced herself, rejogged my memory, laughed at me a little bit more and then we kinda just got to talking again."

"He's missing out the part where he walked into a lamppost." She added.

The shame took over his face as he lowered his head, using a hand to cover his embarrassment. He shook his shielded head and sighed. Why did she have to add that bit?

"Oh?" His mother perked up a bit, intrigued.

"We had a little chat, a sort of speedy catchup session and then he had to go. As he was walking away, he turned to look at how gorgeous I am and, when he turned back around, he got greeted by the lamppost." Rose burst out laughing.

Rose saw his blushing cheeks and placed a hand on his thigh. As much as she may have been exposing him, she was trying to lighten the mood for them all. And what better way with the antics of her obsessed lover?

Her parents laughed a little lighter than she did, but they were amused. Adam couldn't help it and joined in with them. It *was* a pretty funny story.

"What can I say? She *is* beautiful. I just had to get another look, just in case I never saw her again. In case she *disappeared* again." He shrugged off the embarrassment, jokingly nudging Rose.

"When did you start dating?" Her father asked once they'd settled from Adam's mild humiliation.

"A couple months ago." Adam answered. "We were friends for a while. I was in the hospital for a bit and Rose visited a lot. That's when I got a reminder of how caring she is." He placed his hand over hers. "Just like I remembered."

"Why were you in the hospital?" Her father sat up, more attentive now.

Adam looked at Rose. She didn't know what to suggest in that moment, she hadn't foreseen this coming up. Her eyes shrugged at him, her shoulders confirming, this was his disaster to create or avoid.

"I got into a fight with... the guy my ex was cheating on me with. I went to visit her on Valentine's Day and caught them... I lost myself and attacked him, and then I got jumped when I left her house by him and his friends. It's a day I'm not proud of. But if it hadn't happened, who knows where I'd be today, where we'd be." He had opted for honesty, hoping it to be the path of least resistance.

The room was quiet for a moment. Her parents took in what had just been said. He didn't seem like a violent man, but he had just admitted to being hospitalised from a fight. There was some concern in their eyes as their brows furrowed.

"I'm not a violent guy." He turned to her father. "I was just in a relationship I probably shouldn't have been in, with someone who wasn't good for me, and it all came to a head when I caught her cheating on me. I'm not proud of it, but I can't change the past. We can only change our future, and I'm building a pretty good one right now." He spoke with a newfound stoicism.

Her father's expression changed. The worry had dispersed, it had been replaced by curiosity. Intrigue. Anticipation.

"What's this future you're building towards, Adam? What does it look like?" He leaned forwards, ready to critique Adam's response.

Adam knew *this* was the moment. It was make or break, right here, right now. Whatever he said now would decide if he won their approval or would have to grovel for it for years to come. This was the moment he dreaded, but it was the one he was ready for.

"I'm a daydreamer, I like to get lost in playing out scenarios of a perfect world where we could have everything. Realistically, not everything is gonna work out like that." He turned to look at Rose. "But I'm determined to give Rose everything she wants and everything she deserves, with a little extra sprinkled on top." She broke his stare, looking down to blush. "She'll want to kill me for admitting this, but on the way here I saw a house that was up for sale. It looked perfect. For us. For all of us."

Rose's eyes darted back to Adam's, widened and ready to burst. Her parents were puzzled. Was he inviting them to live with them? Adam just smiled back at her, taking both of her hands in his. She knew she couldn't avoid it and he had masterfully deflected the attention to her.

Although, there was a brief moment of doubt. Announcing she was pregnant with his child before they had been able to get to know him properly. Before they'd cast judgement on whether they'd accept him or have him crawling behind them, though they didn't seem the kind of people to do that. It didn't seem quite so masterful in hindsight.

Rose cleared her throat. She turned to her parents, who had a sense of what was about to happen. It was obvious at this point. She turned to face them both, Adam peering over her shoulder.

"Mum. Dad. He's not inviting you to move in with us…" She stood up, letting Adam's jacket fall off her arms to reveal her body. "We're having a baby." She placed one hand on top of the small bump and one below.

Adam stood behind her and put a hand on her waist. He watched a flurry of emotions wash over her parents' faces. It was quite the slideshow to see, their eyes popping and darting in a flurry of confused transitions.

Rose's mother was the first to jump up and wrap her arms around Rose. She smiled at Adam behind her and pulled him into the bundle too. He wrapped his arm around them both, a smile masking his concern. He was waiting for her father.

His eyes bulged. A vein in his forehead seems to be close to bursting. There was a frustration building within him. They separated from each other and watched him. They could all see it. They could all feel it. They were just waiting for him to release it.

"H-… How?" Is all he could stutter.

Their expressions dropped from worried to concerned. Surely he knew how babies were made, and they doubted he wanted details. He could see their puzzlement, the air of judgement that blanketed him.

"I mean... What? Since when? How long?" His voice grew more irate.

"I'm a few months in..." Rose's voice was faint.

Adam closed the gap to Rose, wanting to protect her from this fury. He knew it would never be aimed at her, though, but she would need protecting from it nonetheless. He placed his hands on her shoulders, trying to ease her.

"You can't, Rose. No. No. You barely know him. You can't go through this again. No. I don't care how sweet he is, he can't be trusted." The anger seemed to twist into sorrow. "No. I won't allow it. Not again..."

"I am, dad. And I will." She could feel a fire light in her. "You don't get to make that choice for me."

"I..." He was tripping over himself now, realising what he'd just done.

"Stop." Rose's mother cut in.

She noticed Rose's temper flaring up. She wasn't going to go down without a fight. And rightly so. Rose's mother pulled him to his feet and dragged him to the hallway, her face filled with disappointment. She closed the door behind them, trying to mask the berating she was about to do.

Adam could feel Rose sink as soon as the door closed. The words had stung him too, but she's the one that was holding the grief. The burden lay heavier on her than it ever would on him. He turned her around and pulled her into him, rubbing her back and whispering into her ear.

"It's okay, it'll be okay." He repeated.

She wanted to cry but there was still a rage that refused to let her do so. How dare he try to say she couldn't. He had no place, no right. No matter how much he was trying to protect her, it was not his place.

He knew it too. He knew those words were wrong as soon as they left his mouth. He had been left with nothing but the mutterings of a lunatic as he failed to find the right words to fix this. He felt that everything he wanted to say would just be wrong, he would just make it worse. Noise was all he could muster, empty noise. Hollow, desperate noise.

The door opened. Adam looked up to see Rose's mother. Rose didn't move, letting his arms shield her from this cruel world. She didn't want to be there anymore. She should've let him distract her with the house. She would've been happier getting lost in that fantasy, rather than reliving her nightmare.

"I'm sorry about that. I'm sorry about him… He's… He's not great at controlling his emotions. When he gets like that, he doesn't think. He just speaks. I would say he doesn't mean it, but there's probably a part of him that does." Rose's mother explained, a sadness in her voice.

"It's okay." Adam answered, only really caring about Rose. "Thank you."

"Rose, honey, he'll be a minute, but he needs to speak with you. With both of you." Her mother announced.

Rose nodded amongst Adam. She gently patted his arms, letting him know she could let him go now. As much as she wanted to melt into those arms and be stuck against him forever, she had to face this head-on. She collected herself and turned to face the door, ready and waiting.

Her father hesitantly, shamefully, stepped into the doorway. His head was bowed, he knew she would be looking and he couldn't face her immediately. But she wasn't going to let him get away that easy. As if their roles were reversed, Rose prepared herself to discipline him.

"Look at me, dad." She demanded.

His neck fumbled, bobbing his head up and down as it tried and faltered. There was fear running through him. He couldn't protect her anymore. He wasn't hers to protect right now. Instead, in his attempts to save her, he was the one who had hurt her. And that was the toughest thing to accept. No matter how much he wanted to shield her, to save her, to make sure she would never be hurt, he had to accept that he had, and he most probably would again. There's no pain like having to accept that.

He was finally able to find the strength to look his daughter in the eyes. He was the child who had misbehaved now, and she was the parent who had to correct his mistake. He had to learn.

"I know you're just trying to look after me. I know it broke your heart, what happened last time. I know you just want me to be happy and safe... But you don't get to choose how I do that. You don't get to decide who I want in my life." There was a heated focus in her voice. "All I need you to do is be there for me. That's it. Let me make the mistakes if they end up being mistakes. I'm not a kid anymore. I'm the opposite. I'm going to be a mum..."

Her father stood there nodding the whole time. He agreed with her entirely, he knew he was in the wrong. But that last sentence... All the weight of his failure hadn't been enough to break him. But her statement did. She was going to be a mum.

She wasn't his baby anymore; she was having her own. She was going to be a mother... And it reduced him to nothing but tears.

Rose's mother went to comfort him, but he stopped her. He had to do this alone. He had to let this happen, else he wouldn't be able to forgive himself. He allowed himself a moment to cry before he packaged it away and saved it for later.

"I'm sorry, Rose." He managed to get out. "I'm sorry."

He cleared his throat, allowing himself another chance to gather himself. He stepped towards them, no longer wanting to feel isolated from the family. He wanted to be a part of it. He wanted this too. He just worried too much, even though he knew she would have been worrying about it too.

"I thought I was just meeting my daughter's boyfriend, but it appears I'm meeting my grandchild's father." His words hung in the air, everyone watching them flitter there. "You better buy that house; her apartment isn't fit for a family."

He reached his arm out, letting a sad smile welcome Adam in a way he wasn't expecting. Adam met him halfway but wasn't prepared to get pulled in closer. He felt her father's arms surround him, patting him on the back, smiling against him. Adam returned the hug, grateful for this moment.

Rose stepped towards them. They both looked at her, some happy tears dripping off her jaw. Adam brushed one cheek clear as her father brushed the other. Rose brushed both of their cheeks in return. She threw herself between them and hugged them both. Adam waved her mother over and they all surrounded Rose with their love, swallowing her up in their arms, filling her with a warmth she hadn't planned for from today.

Adam was right, it was all going to be okay. It was all going to be okay after all...

They shared some congratulations and thanks as they made their way to the dining table. Rose's mother had prepared some dinner, but nobody had much of an appetite. They were still digesting the news that had changed their world.

"I'm sorry, Adam..." Her father looked at him. "I know Rose is a smart girl. She wouldn't have chosen you if you weren't good for her. I-."

"It's okay." Adam shook off the apology. "I don't blame you. Rose told me about what happened before she told me she was pregnant. I probably would've reacted the same way in your shoes. But I was ready for anything with Rose. I will always be ready for anything with her. I just want to love her until I've no love left to give, and that's going to take a while."

Her father nodded. He felt worse now, but also somehow soothed. He'd thought Adam to be Lucifer himself. Instead, he just seemed to be a guy who loved his daughter. A guy who had loved his daughter and lost her once. A guy who'd been given another chance to love her and wasn't going to let it go to waste. After all, *he* was the reason Adam lost Rose in the first place. He nodded it all away, letting his terrors be banished into the darkness from which they came from.

As the food arrived, they shared some stories of love, of life and everything in between. He felt like he was home with them, finally. The awkwardness of the earlier events drifted away. They felt like a family. This was a family. This felt right.

All it took was a second and they went from being terrifying to sweethearts. He was surprised at how much fear he held within him until he realised how much lighter he felt. Her father wasn't as tall as he'd seemed from the chair either. Her mother, how he was ever terrified of her he'll never know.

Rose seemed to glow brighter now too, the worries of the world no longer weighing her down. Everything was going to be okay. It all worked out. They had crossed what they thought would be the biggest hurdle.

They could be a family now. They could live, laugh, and love all they wanted. They could be happy.

Chapter 30

She grew older still, but none the wiser.

"Was it that easy to win them over?" She seemed displeased.

"Probably not, but sometimes you have to compromise for someone else's happiness." He leaned over the counter. "Besides, the rules went without saying."

"What rules?" She asked.

"You ever make her cry, you die. You ever hurt her, you die. You ever abandon her, you die. You know, the standard stuff." He gave her a nod.

"Maybe he should've clarified them, just to make sure." She seemed to relish in that thought.

"Not everyone wants to look like the big, bad, tough guy. Sometimes... sometimes you can just express something with just a look, or an expression. A handshake, maybe. A handshake that gets turned into a hug, maybe. A hug that has a little whispering sprinkled into it. Maybe."

They waved her parents goodbye and began the walk back to Rose's place. They took their time now, the worst the day could offer was behind them. He hadn't quite asked her if he was living with her officially. He was just mostly sleeping at her place. It played on his mind on the walk back, though.

Especially when he saw that house with the sign still sitting there. How fast was too fast when you were expecting a child? And what was considered too slow?

"Told you, I had it. In. The. Bag." The smugness pranced around his face.

"If you're gonna keep this up, I'll put you in a bag." She smirked back, shaking her head.

Behind that lovingly evil grin, she was happy for him. She was happy for herself too. She was happy for *them*. There was potential for that all to come crashing down, for the ship to sink to its own cannons, but they had managed to keep sailing. The clouds had cleared, the waves had calmed, and the sun shone down on them.

"Thank you." He leaned into her.

"For what?"

He shrugged. "It was at the tip of my tongue, bashing at my lips to throw itself out there. Just, thank you. For everything, I guess."

"Thank you too." She leaned her head against him as they walked.

"Okay, I already did that bit." He chuckled.

"Shut up, I mean it. You did good today and I really appreciate it." She gently patted his forearm.

"Okay, so... that's that step done. Check box ticked; item crossed off the list." He felt Rose nod on his arm. "What about this one?"

He had calculated that perfectly. He knew when they were approaching the house, waiting to time his words until just the right moment. They stood in front of it, and she couldn't avoid it. He was eager for this step. At least eager for an answer. He knew he would go to sleep and dream about it, and he wanted to know if those dreams were going to be happy or hollow.

"Really? Right now, Adam?" She lifted her head from him.

He shrugged. "Why not?"

She let out a small, hesitant sigh. "I don't know, Adam. It seems…"

"I get it, it seems fast." His voice disheartened.

He walked Rose over to the wall in front of the house. He helped her take a seat on it, giving her a chance to rest her feet. He placed his hand on her thighs as he gently moved them apart and moved between them. He looked at her, his hands running up to her waist, and prepared himself for his next battle.

"I know you want to keep a steady pace, Rose. I understand it. But we have a clock we're up against. And I just… I really want everything to be the best it can be. I'm ready for you." He kissed her nose. "I'm ready for them." He rubbed her belly. "I'm ready for us." He placed his forehead against hers. "Your place is great, but I still think of it as *your* place. And that's because it is, there's nothing wrong with that either. I just want a tiny corner of the world that's *ours*. But I get it, I do. I don't want you to feel pressured or forced into anything, despite the huge emotional weight I just dropped on you." He somehow managed to smile, as did she.

She placed a hand on his cheek and shook her head gently. "It's not so much that I *wanted* a line between us. I just didn't want everything to change so quick. But you're right, we have a baby we're gonna welcome in a few months. I can't really avoid my life changing."

She turned herself on the wall as he held her, leaning back against him. She stared at the silhouetted house. In her head, she saw the lights. She pictured herself walking through the door and discovering a new world, their new world. Walking through the doors to kiss her Adam and their child. Walking through the doors and smelling a dinner that he might have ruined or might have pulled off – it remained to be seen, he was still a practicing chef. Going up those stairs and tucking their child into bed. Then walking those few steps down the hall and cuddling up with the love of her life. It wasn't a dream he held alone. This dream had potential, and it lingered right in front of them, reaching out, calling to them.

It would need a bit of work, from what she could see from the wall. A lick of paint, at least. She wanted it to be theirs, so they had to do it their way. She didn't know how much work it would be either, so the sooner they started really...

"Let's do it." She nodded.

Adam grabbed her by the shoulders and leaned over to look at her, a smile wanting to rip through his cheeks greeting her. "Really?"

She nodded. "We can't really afford to wait; this baby isn't going to."

He threw himself around her, squeezing her so tight she thought he'd tried to suffocate her. Her squeal alarmed him to loosen up. He pasted her skin with kisses, implanting his lips wherever he could.

"I'll call them tomorrow. Thank you so much, Rose, you're a dream that just keeps getting better. I never want to wake up." His eyes were teary.

She pinched him, making him flinch. "You're already awake, don't try to fly!"

They walked back, already planning for the house. They hadn't even called the seller, let alone bought it yet. But something was telling them it was going to be theirs, no matter the cost. They were going to have a house, all to themselves. A little corner of the world they claimed all to themselves. It was going to be their paradise, their safe haven, theirs.

"I can see this being a nursery and eventually being the baby's bedroom." Rose's voice echoed in the empty room.

"We could paint it yellow." Adam added.

"Yellow..." Rose thought on it, looking around the barren room again. "Yellow. I like it."

The estate agent stood by the door. They were selling the house to themselves, doing her job for her. She just sat back and admired themselves falling in love with the house with each step they took within it.

"I-... We want it." Adam turned to the estate agent, making her entire week in three words.

"Great, I can get the paperwork started. Let me just grab my bag." She hopped and skipped away.

Rose placed a hand on Adam's shoulder. He turned to see her, not expecting to see that look on her face. Her eyes looked heartbroken, like someone had just taken a hammer to a heart made of glass.

"Can we afford it, Adam? It's so nice... We probably should've discussed that part first." Her voice was quiet, both in sorrow and to hide from the estate agent.

"I already had a plan for that, but I didn't know if you'd agree..." He tried to avoid looking at her, but he could feel her burning a hole in his jaw. "When my dad passed, he left me some money. I never touched it, mostly because for a lot of my life I couldn't, and I ended up forgetting about it. But, when my grandad passed, he... He did the same. I never wanted to touch the money. I didn't know what to do with it, but it can cover a decent chunk of the price. It would pretty much guarantee us the house unless someone else just bought it outright for more." He leaned over and tapped the wooden floor twice. "But nobody will, because it's ours."

"I don't know if I can let you do that, Adam. This is meant to be *our* place, we should split the cost." She seemed uneasy, more so than before.

"It *is* our place. It's *our* baby, but you're doing all the work. I just want to give us a little head start with this place. Both of our names are gonna be on that paperwork, regardless of whose money goes into it. Both of our time, our energy and our love are going to go into this place. You'll get your chance to put some money into it, but the money isn't what makes it ours. It's what *we* do with it. It's how we do it. Besides," He pulled her against him. "I'm going to marry you one day, and then you'll have no choice but to take what's mine."

"I don't know if you're crazy or stupid." She seemed happier now, a massive smile on her face giving her away.

"Both. And I'm pretty sure I'm doing this, even if you decide to be mad at me for the rest of our lives. It's our moment to buy some happiness." He grinned at her, pleading for permission for a decision he'd already made. "That money is meant to secure my future, and my future is right in front of me."

"Okay, but when our baby grows up and can't go to a fancy university, I'm gonna tell them you blew their uni fund on a fancy house."

"It is a pretty fancy house, eh? Maybe not our style?" He poked her nose with his.

"Nah, we're more cardboard-box-under-the-bridge kinda people." She chortled.

"Not anymore, I'm gonna give you the world." He kissed the top of her head. "I'm gonna spoil you both."

"You're about to spend all of your money, Adam. Good luck with that." She teased him.

"There are other ways to spoil someone. I can't wait to live, laugh, love with you."

She scrunched her face at that. Somehow, he'd managed to find the line for "too cheesy" and leapt right over it. He couldn't help but laugh.

The crashing waves of flustered paper disrupted their joy but added to it in a different way. The estate agent walked back in, papers and pen in-hand. It was happening. They were securing their future, buying their own chance of happiness.

Chapter 31

She was hopeful, letting her dreams inspire the actions she took.

"I see your story took my advice." The smugness on her face was palpable.

"If that's the ego boost you need, sure." He smirked back at her.

"When are you gonna say *"and they lived happily ever after"* then?" She rested her head on her palm. "Or do you need me to write that in for you too?"

"And they lived." He smiled back at her.

She waited. She just stared at him and waited. He just kept smiling back at her, unwilling to break first.

"This is all ours!" She shrieked; arms outstretched as she spun around a couple times.

"This place is beautiful." Adam's mother placed a hand on his shoulder.

He placed his hand on hers, turning his head to smile back at her. They watched Rose giddily skip around the empty room, their heads already filled with ideas on how they'd fill it. It was theirs. They could touch their future. They could feel it below their feet.

"I didn't think you'd actually buy a house, I'll be honest, but I'm glad I told you to." Rose's father walked into the room.

"Oh, stop it. Don't try to take credit for his idea." Her mother followed in behind. "I'm so proud of you two! I can't wait to see how this place looks in a month or two." She walked between the couple and pulled them to her.

Rose's father and Adam's mother completed a triangle around them. They all just stared at them, basking in their glory. They relived their younger days through their eyes, seeing parts of themselves in them.

"So, when's the wedding?" Adam's mother tossed it into the air.

Adam turned to her as everyone else spun their heads to her. Rose's parents didn't want to say it, but they were thinking it too. Rose hadn't even thought about it. Adam had definitely contemplated it.

"One step at a time, mum." Adam gracefully blew away any tension the air held.

"You're right, you're right. My bad." She held up her hands, surrendering.

Rose giggled behind him. Adam turned on a heel to catch her, stepping towards her as the giggle faded to a smile. She tilted her head to the side, innocently observing him.

He cleared his throat, looking down at the space between her feet. Then the world slowed, as he moved his right foot back and slowly lowered himself. As if his knee were mechanical, they watched the gears turning the belts that lowered him slower still. Until the clap of his right knee hitting the floor echoed through the room.

Rose had lost her smile. Their parents had lost their bottom jaws. Adam kept his head down, leaning forwards, saying nothing.

The room froze, as if they'd become a photograph of the moment and nothing more. The air squeezed their throats dry, nobody able to utter a word or thrum a breath.

"Adam." Rose squeaked quietly, her hand reaching for the top of his head.

He looked up. "Why do you all look so pale?" He got up lightyears faster than he'd knelt down. "I was just tying my laces."

Rose started flapping her palms at his chest, both annoyed and relieved at the same time. He laughed as their parents finally exhaled.

Adam grabbed her hands by her fingers, just as they were winding up to whack him again. He pulled her against him and quickly locked his fingers around her lower waist.

"I would propose, I'd be more than happy to marry you right here, right now." He grinned.

"But...?" She seemed a little heartbroken.

"We just spent all our money on this house, I don't think we could afford a wedding."

She shook her head, each shake turning the frown upside-down. "I hate you."

"I love you more." He nuzzled his nose against hers.

"You're playing with fire there, boy." Rose's father laughed with his belly, reminding them they weren't alone.

"If she doesn't kill you, I will!" His mother chimed in, fanning away the wickedness in the air. "Almost had me going there."

Rose started the official house tour, sharing her vision for the house. They all threw in their own ideas, Rose choosing the best to claim as her own. Adam threw in a few thoughts here and there, some more serious than others. Truly, he didn't really care how the house ended up, just as long as she was in it with him.

Once Rose had concluded the tour, she let her parents wander freely. She needed a break. Adam swooped in behind her and pulled her away from ogling ears. He wanted her to himself, even if only for a moment.

"What's gotten into you, Adam?" She looked at his expressionless face.

He was close to her. Incredibly close. She could feel his slow, warm breath against her. She looked up at him with confused eyes. He had something on his mind, he was just struggling to get it out. She tried to rub his arm to help him. She dreaded any bad news, but she was ready to fight with him.

She felt his arm moving. It was fidgeting out of eyeshot. And then it slithered between them and began to lift towards her head. He stopped his hand between their chins and held it there a moment.

His fist slowly unfurled, as he turned his palm to look to the ceiling. It all moved so slowly, but the sun helped give it away before it was completely revealed. The glint that hit her eye, she knew what it was. There, in his palm, sat a ring.

"It's beautiful, Adam…" She was caught in its spell. "How? When? What?!" A hushed exclaim.

"My grandma's." He whispered back. "She gave it to me recently. Said I might have some use for it. That bit is up to you…" He held it with his thumb and his index now. "I chickened out in front of our parents. Well, I didn't… I just wanted this to be between us, where there's no pressure, there's no audience. Just you and me." He looked down at her belly. "Cover your ears, baby." He smiled, looking back to her. "I meant it. I do want to marry you. It doesn't have to be now, it doesn't have to be a week from now, a month from now or any time soon. But I do want to marry you. One day. The money was to secure my future. This is to secure my love. There's no future without my love. Will you, Rose? Will you marry me?"

Rose gasped. She covered her mouth with both hands, trying to smother any sound she made. He was really doing it. He was proposing. He wasn't on one knee, but it didn't change anything.

This wasn't how she'd imagined it, although she didn't really know how she'd thought it would happen. She didn't even know if she really thought it would *ever* happen. But her eyes did not deceive her, her ears were not lying to her. He stood in front of her, holding a ring, asking for her hand.

She found herself nodding. Without really thinking. She just nodded. She threw her arms around him and nodded even more.

"Yes." She let out a muffled cry into his neck.

Adam tightened his grip around her hips as he lifted her and began to spin them in an overwhelmed celebration. She said yes. He didn't know why, but he couldn't believe she'd say yes. Even now, after getting her pregnant and buying a house with her, he didn't expect her to say yes.

She still made him feel that anxiousness of the first love. The constant butterflies, the trembling knees, the insides turning to jelly. Even after all they'd been through, she still made him shy, made him nervous. He just couldn't believe he was hers. She was his future. She was his. He just wanted to scream, to yell it to the world. She was his.

Even with all he thought he knew about love, she was still teaching him there was more to experience, more to feel. He was learning it all over again, feeling ways he had never felt before. The world could end right now and he'd die the happiest he'd ever been. But his life had more purpose now. He wasn't trying to lose out on all that time loving her.

He lowered her and kissed her multiple times. And then he remembered the ring, not wanting to lose it. He held her hand and slid it onto her ring finger. They both watched it slide on and almost click into place, planting itself on its new home. She spread her fingers and twiddled them. She couldn't help but smile.

"I've lost my breath, Adam. What are you doing to me?!"

"I'll do the breathing for you, come here."

He pulled her into him, placing his mouth over hers. He shared his breath with her, as she shared herself in response.

The sky was closing out their day, ready to beckon them back to their homes. Funny thing about that was Adam *was* home. He had finally claimed his home. If it wasn't for a lack of a bed, he would've happily stayed in it. He didn't mind the alternative though, cuddling up with Rose, his *fiancée*, at her place for another night.

He had begun counting down the nights. The countdown for the move. The timer on their new start. Any spare time he had now was spent at their home, getting it ready to move everything in, getting it ready for their next chapter. Rose was eager to help out while she still could too, knowing her days were numbered until she'd become a waddling incubator.

The sky was on the verge of becoming a dark blue. He was heading back to Rose, ready to settle in for the night. It had been another productive day, so he treated himself to a little diversion through the park. The world felt beautiful to him, so he wanted to experience the beauty it had to offer.

It was a friendly park during the day, filled with charms and glee in every direction your eyes could see. The little lake in the middle was the spot for the local duck populus to gather and be overfed by everyone. The flowering bushes that lined the gravel paths. The hairy, waving arms of the trees that provided refuge from the cheerful sun. It was a happy park.

The night seemed to lose a lot of that charm, masking it with darkness. The dispersed light from the lamps only made things more ominous. Like you were being watched, followed. The park's eyes knew where you were, you couldn't hide.

But the calmness was always there. You couldn't fake the calmness. It was still safe. It was everyone's park, so it had to be safe.

"Adam!" A voice called out.

He stopped in his tracks, no longer admiring what he could barely see. His attention turned to the voice, his ears twitching and tingling warm, but not in a good way. It's like they were warning him. Don't listen. Run. Don't stop.

The gravel groaned away, as the pats of her feet dug their mark into it. The noise became less severe, less violent. She had slowed down as she got closer, realising he'd stopped. She was greeted by his back and nothing more.

"Thanks for stopping." She panted. "I needed to talk to you."

He turned his head so she could see barely more than the tip of his lips and nose peering out from his hood. The same lips she had tried to capture not long ago. The same lips that had been at her side so many times. The same lips she still yearned for.

"I'm sorry for cheating on you, I… I don't have any way I can justify it, but I'm sorry. I'm sorry I pushed you away when I needed you the most. But you don't have to do this." Her words seemed rehearsed, but there was a messiness in the delivery that had revealed she hadn't quite committed it to memory.

"Do what?" He asked, completely mesmerised.

"I can be better for you now. I can be the Eve you dreamt about for so many years. I'm ready, this time, properly. You don't have to be with her."

Adam turned to face her, eyebrows raised. "Eve, you need to understand this. I don't *have* to be with her, I *want* to be with her. I do *not* want to be with you. I want to be with my fiancée, the mother of my child."

Eve stood there, stunned. It was obvious she had no idea just how far Adam was in his relationship. She just thought it was a temporary thing, a small thing. It was bigger than she had ever thought. She was losing him. She had lost him. Adam wasn't Eve's anymore.

"I... Don't... A-..." She hadn't planned for this outcome; she didn't think it was possible. "I need you more than she does."

This could've been true. It most probably was true. She was desperate, clutching at whatever straws she could get between her fingers. Whatever would get through to him, make him see sense. He was meant to be hers.

"You've been through a lot, Eve. Go home, get some rest, focus on yourself for a while." He tried to prescribe her the space she needed. "I don't think we should be friends anymore, not for now anyway. You need time to heal. I'm not going to get in the way of that, I won't let you get lost in something you don't need."

He didn't wait to see what else she had to say, he just turned his back and left as quickly as he could. He listened attentively for the gravel to give way again, assuming she might try to follow him. He didn't want her near him, for both their sakes. For all their sakes.

He scurried back to Rose, comforted by her presence. She patted the empty dent in the mattress beside her, beckoning him into the him-sized hole. She could see there was something wrong; he may have tried to hide it with his face, but his eyes were terrible at hide and seek.

She pulled his head to her chest, resting her cheek on him and rubbed his shoulder. "What's troubling you?"

"Eve was at the park." Adam cut straight to the chase; Rose slowed but didn't stop.

"Did she try anything?" She was ready to be angry but had to confirm.

"She told me to leave you for her, that she needs me more. As if I'm just meant to bow to her feet now she wants me." He seemed to be getting worked up but steadied himself. "I told her I don't want to be with her, I just want you. And then I told her we shouldn't be friends anymore. I walked away before she could try to say anything else."

Rose dismissed her anger, she didn't need it anymore. There was a giddiness inside of her; knowing Adam had chosen her and that he was willing to cut her out filled her with a teenage glee. She didn't say anything else; she just used her lips to patter the top of his head with thankful kisses.

Adam fell asleep in her arms, massaged by her hands and her lips. She silently cried to herself while holding him. There was a part of her that doubted it. As soon as he had said her name, there was a part of her that thought he was going to cave in. After all, Eve had years of Adam's love whereas Rose only had a few months and an immature childhood love that never managed to bubble into anything more.

She cried from shame, from insecurity. She cried from happiness, from gratefulness. She cried herself to sleep, holding him as tightly as she could, knowing she never wanted to let him go.

Each step he took had broken her down more and more. He had crept in, and she had given him the keys. She felt a hostage in her own body. He had her for ransom with every breath he took. She had allowed herself to fall, and now she felt like she was plummeting.

If he were awake, she knew he would've caught her. She knew he would've washed away those fears that sat in the back of her mind. She felt evil for even having them there. But she had him, and she kept reminding herself of that.

In her thoughts, in her tears, in her dreams. She had him, and that's all she needed.

Maybe she did need him more than Eve.

Chapter 32

She was drawing her own lines, finally feeling ready to take on the world.

"How is Eve that blind? He's not even hinting; he's been straight up telling her." She seemed annoyed.

He shrugged. "Some people don't want to accept the truth; some people just don't believe it."

"Isn't that the same thing?" She contested him.

He shook his head. "If I don't believe something, I can plead ignorance. If I just don't want to accept it, that's arrogance."

"I guess. I just don't get why she won't leave them alone."

"You could say the same for him for all those years he was swooning for her. He knew she didn't love him back, yet he stuck around."

"But he was never trying to make her be with him. She seems to be forcing the issue, even when he's stated he has someone else." She snapped back.

"And that's why she's arrogant, not ignorant. She knows he's with someone else, she just doesn't want to accept it. You can't fight arrogance."

"Then how is he supposed to make it clearer to her?"

He didn't have an answer for that. He just stood there as she watched him think but nothing came to him.

He kissed Rose goodbye as he headed for the door, their moving date was closing in and he was anxious to get everything done as soon as possible. The summer sun had come out with a vengeance, eager to cook the hearts and souls of all the little ants below it.

"Can you open that window before you go?" Rose called out.

Adam slid over and cranked it open, letting the hot, stale air get pushed around by the warm, stale air. He stood at the window as a gentle breeze tickled his chin, enjoying the momentary relief from the beautiful torture.

"Anything else, my love?" He asked, heading for the door again.

She hobbled over in a hurry and grabbed his cheeks. She tiptoed to his lips and planted herself against him, making sure she'd be on his mind for the rest of the day.

"Hurry back, miss you already." She finally released him.

"Love you more!" Adam yelled, closing the door behind him and running out of sight.

"What a cheat." Rose huffed. "We'll make sure he doesn't get away with that one later." She cradled her bump, smiling to it.

She felt her hand jump, startling her. She rubbed her hand over the same spot to see if it would happen again. Nothing.

"We're gonna get your daddy back!" She cooed.

The same spot bounced. She squealed with excitement, only wishing Adam were here to experience it. She immediately reached for her phone.

BABY KICKED!!

Before she could turn her attention back to their child, he responded.

I missed the first kick?!?!?! I'm coming back before you tire them out

If you come back, you cant leave again!

She waited for his response. She'd given him a tough choice. He had to choose between his future plans and his present memories.

I'll be back for lunch, setting a world record for painting

She giggled at her screen, feeling youthful again. He had a way of bringing her back to younger years, as if they were their first and only loves. An innocent kind of love, shielded from the world because it didn't know any better.

She put the phone away, ready to get on with her day. Ready to stare at the clock every few minutes and wonder why time was so slow, so cruel. The door clacked open and he barged through it.

"I MISSED IT?!" He yelled, kicking the door shut behind him.

She nodded with a smirk. "Guess you should've never left, lover boy."

She reached out to him, beckoning him over. He didn't need the invitation, running over to her, placing his hands within hers.

"If I had the choice, I'd never leave your side again." He sighed.

She guided their hands to her belly. Right to the spot where their little kicker made themselves known.

"Right here. Say something, they seemed to respond to you being a little meanie to us." She taunted.

"Hey, little one. My little love. I'm here." He lowered himself, his head level with his hand. "Come say hi, pleeeaaaaseeeeee?" He pleaded.

Nothing.

He looked up at Rose, a heartbreaking disappointment painted across his face. She shrugged, she couldn't control their child. Not yet, anyway.

"Why won't you say hi to me?" He turned back to the bump.

"Maybe you're trying too hard." Rose laughed.

Adam frowned at her. "You told me to!"

She just shrugged again. He tried to rub her belly, coaxing their child to kick again. He tried gently poking, inviting a response. He tried to sing, he tried to talk, he begged and pleaded. Nothing worked.

"Okay, I give up." He placed his forehead against her belly in defeat.

His head knocked back. He looked up at Rose, who was already watching him, her mouth agape. He looked back to the large bump, then back at Rose, then back to the bump. Their baby just kicked *him*.

"Little…" Eve looked down at him with a stern look. "…*bugger* just kicked me." Adam took the warning.

"Seems like you're going to have a difficult relationship." Rose snorted.

"Why won't you love me? I have so much love to give you." He asked.

"Probably shouldn't be abandoning your pregnant *fiancée* and unborn child every day." She knew she was twisting his heart, but she had to feel the pain of missing him too.

"That's unfair. You know I'd rather be with you. If paint wasn't so evil, I'd have you come with me!" There was a real sadness in his voice.

She pulled him up. "I know, I know. I'm sorry, my love." She placed a hand on his cheek. "I just miss you. *We* miss you."

Her belly kicked again.

"Okay, I miss you." She laughed.

Adam somehow laughed too. This child either loved him a lot or really held a grudge against him for something. He wouldn't be deterred though. He was going to love their child to the ends of the earth, even if it killed him.

"I just need one more day to finish with all the harmful stuff. And then it'll be safe for you again. Maybe I'll even take a day off, just to be with my loving and caring family." He kissed her forehead, pulling her against him.

As their bellies touched, he felt a quick nudge against him.

"Maybe they're just kissing you back?" Rose shrugged.

He knelt down to the bump, keeping his head away from it. "I get it, you want me to go finish that house so it's ready for you." He looked up at Rose. "The boss has given me my orders, guess I've got no choice." He shrugged, standing back up.

"Well, if the *boss* has said it, guess I've no choice but to let you go. But you better come right back here for lunch." She gave him a stern look, letting him know she wasn't playing.

He nodded. "May the gods try to stop me, I'll be here."

She wrapped her arms around his neck and gave him a big, sad kiss. He felt the same sadness, knowing the day would be a drag but he had to do commit the necessary evils for her. For them.

She let go and turned away. "You have ten seconds to get out that door before I tie you up."

He kissed the back of her neck and scurried out the door. It slammed shut, with barely a second to spare. She could feel his lips against her neck. She let them sink in, letting herself think he was still there. It staved off that draining feeling of missing him.

And so began the timer that counted down the hours. He normally spent the weekends as if he were doing a work shift. He'd spend a little time with Rose in the morning, get ready and then head on over to their new house. He'd spend a couple hours doing some work before getting some lunch.

Sometimes he'd come back to eat with Rose, sometimes he took food with him so he could spend more time there. The days he did come back, Rose loved and hated. She got to spend more time with him, but she also had to say goodbye to him again. Knowing he'd be back in a few hours filled her with butterflies. Knowing he was staying made her feel like she could fly.

She had wanted to go out to help, but Adam was worried about the fumes from the paint. He didn't trust it, wanted to make sure they took no chances. No matter what the labels said. He wanted to make sure she was completely safe and well, so he asked her to just let him get that portion of the house done. He'd made good headway, with only two rooms left to paint – something he should've been able to get done on this day.

The few hours passed by agonisingly for both of them. Adam had created a bit more of a mess than he usually would've, but he felt it added character, a story to the room. That was his excuse anyway for when she'd come to inspect it. Rose wasn't there to make him fix it, so he let himself off the hook.

Rose, meanwhile, did her best to keep occupied. She had a few more attempts at baiting kicks at Adam's expense, but it's like their child knew he was coming and wanted to savour some energy for him. Seems they both held a grudge against him. She decided to read to the baby, now aware she was being listened to, taking a seat by the window to let the breeze brush her neck.

Whether it was the book or the warmth, or most likely a combination of them both, Rose had fallen asleep. Adam was finishing up the painting, tidying up before trying to make himself semi-presentable.

Ding dong.

Not the alarm she had set, but the one that woke her nonetheless. She jumped up, her eyes fell to the clock. It was lunchtime. She shuffled to the door eagerly, waiting to throw herself at Adam.

Ding dong. Ding dong.

"Okay, hon, I'm coming. I thought you took your keys!" She yelled back.

She'd barely managed to unlock the door as it violently swung into her.

"You're e-."

She lost her voice. She could only hold herself. She felt warm and cold at the same time. She began to feel weaker than she already was. Everything became a blur.

Thud.

Silence.

Heavy footsteps vanished into the distance.

"I'm... sorry..." She surrendered herself to the pitch-black darkness that circled her.

Chapter 33

She had a tetchiness to her, no longer letting him control her time.

"No, carry on. I'm not letting it end there." She demanded.

"Okay, you're the boss." He surrendered.

Adam crept up on the door, not realising it was wide open until he was only a few steps away. He thought nothing of it at first, maybe Rose had just gotten back from shopping. He approached slowly, not wanting to scare her.

He tried to peek around the doorway, noticing how quiet it was. Rose wasn't home? But why would she leave the door open? As he reached the point where he could see clearer into the building, the silence had made itself understood.

He stumbled into the door, scrambling on the floor to pass that cruel threshold. His vision was already completely blurry by the time he saw her laying there.

"No." He croaked; it was the only thing he could get out.

He ignored the pool of blood staining his clothes, his skin. He slid his arm below her neck and lifted her. Her limp head just fell around the curve of his arm. He shifted his arm a little to get it behind her head, still hoping there was *something*. He tried to support her neck, as he was dreaming of doing for their…

He saw the bump. It was the source of the crimson lake. He shook his head. He tried to speak but all he could do was cry. No... No... Not like this... No...

His free hand smudged her face with her own blood as he brushed her hair away. He tried to shake her awake. He tried to shake her awake.

He tried to shake her awake.

He ran his hand all over her body, feeling all the indentations across her skin. He counted each and every one he could find as his blood boiled a degree higher for each cruel discovery.

He closed his eyes and tilted his head back, not wanting to see her like this. Not wanting to remember her like this. He let out a tortured cry that reverberated through the neighbourhood.

A passerby ran to the door, unwillingly walking into the mess that now stained them too. The wailing of sirens waned in the distance. Closer and closer. Louder and louder. But it was too late.

Two figures blocked the sun from the room. Adam still held her in his arms, not making a sound as he pressed his cheek against hers. They tried to pry him off, but he refused to let go. They begged and pleaded, but they couldn't undo his hold. They couldn't reason with him, for in his eyes, reason had died too.

Two more beings entered the doorway, each of them grabbing an arm and ripping him from her. As he felt his grip break, he let out a scream that left him unable to speak for days. He tried to fight them away, to get back to his family, but they threw him to the ground in a desperate act of self-preservation.

He could see her face, mere meters away from him. His arms were held behind him. He could do nothing. He watched her get carried away. He knew they were there to help, but they were too late. They were all too late. And he had to watch her lifeless body get ripped away from him. It felt nothing less than pure evil. Cruelty for the sake of being cruel.

He felt their grip loosen as they'd heard the doors of the van close. There was no point now. He melted into the floor, limp and lifeless, no longer able to hold himself. He just lay there as more and more bodies approached the house that was no longer anyone's home.

"We can't let anyone in, ma'am." A voice barked.

"I'm his fucking mum, let me in!" She screamed back.

The violent thudding bounced in his ears. She shook the floor with purpose as she made her way to him. A gasp, she had seen the floor. A yelp, she had seen him. A sigh, she was upon him.

"Adam, I'm here, it's me, your mum. Talk to me." She placed a hand on his head, trying to coax him to turn it away from the puddle of blood. "Adam, please." Her voice was shaky.

Adam couldn't speak, his voice body began to fail him entirely. He did the next worst thing. He turned his head to his mother and made sure she looked deep into his eyes. He looked at her, the blackness in his eyes taking over. It was an empty stare, devoid of anything. No anger, no hate. No sadness, no distraught. Empty, and hollow. He had died multiple deaths in that moment. For her, for their child, for their future. He no longer felt.

That was all she needed, bowing her head so she didn't have to stare into those eyes anymore. Eyes she had possessed twice before. Eyes she knew too well. Eyes she'd never expected to see in someone else, least of all him. That's what hurt the most. The fact that she knew those eyes and it was *him*.

She had managed to coax Adam into the back of a van, having to drag his droopy body into it. She knew the only place he'd want to go was also the only place he'd be at his true worst: at the hospital. She fell apart beside him in the back of the police van, cursing everything she could that this had happened to them. If there was a god, she'd definitely have secured her place in their bad book for eternity.

Adam managed to pull himself out of the van, ready to limp his living corpse to whatever room she was in. His mother thanked the officers for the ride, knowing they weren't done with him yet. There was an unjustly acceptable fury in his eyes when he realised his mother had taken him to her house. She could see he felt betrayed.

"Adam, you're…" She choked on her words. "Your clothes are soaked in blood; your body is stained with… it too. Please, let's just get cleaned up. I promise we'll go straight over there. Just not like this." It took every fibre of strength she could find to not break down.

The flames that flicked in his eyes were suffocated out of existence. His eyes went back to being empty, a vacuum where nothing survived. He knew she was right, though nothing felt *right* anymore. He carried his animate carcass to his old bedroom that still had some parts of him tucked away.

His stripped himself with a greater effort than it had ever been before, dumping the discoloured clothes into an empty box. He hauled his weighted cadaver into the shower, holding a hand against the wall to hold himself upright.

He just stood there, knowing what was about to happen. He looked over his blemished skin, gritting his teeth as he noticed just how much of him had been tainted.

He turned the handle, the hot water trickling over his head and dripping down to the rest of him. He watched as it went from a peaceful clarity at his hair to a reddened muddiness at his feet. And mixed within the water and the blood, his salty tears helped wash her off him too.

That felt worse than anything for him. It was bad enough that he had to wash her off of him, but that his own tears that begged for her were doing their microscopic part in carrying her away too. As he got cleaner, he felt dirtier. As the pool below him got clearer, his thoughts got muddier. He couldn't hold onto her anymore. He'd washed her away. He'd cleansed himself of her... For this, he would never forgive himself.

The ride to the hospital was the quietest the day had been. You could hear a pin prick the skin with how quiet it was. His thoughts had turned from anger and confusion to blame, and he blamed nobody but himself.

He could've let her come with him and just sit outside, basking in the sunlight while he worked. Or, better yet, he could've stayed with her. He would've been there when his child had made its first formal introduction to Rose. He could've been there to share that with her. They could be at home right now making memories. He could've been there to save her. He should've been there to protect her. Instead, he left her alone. Helpless and alone. He made her a sitting target.

The slight jolt as they pulled up outside the hospital. He tugged his skeleton out the car and lumbered towards the entrance. His mother followed slowly, closely behind him.

Rose's parents were already there, having been given the heads up from Adam's mother. They'd been waiting for what felt like days, but it had only been an hour or so.

Rose's mother saw him, her maternal instincts kicking in, as she rushed to him, all while her own daughter was probably waiting to be confirmed dead. All while her own grandchild was waiting to be confirmed dead.

She wrapped herself around him with the comforting blanket of shared grief. Adam broke down again, crying into the dent in her neck. She tried to hush him through her own tears, knowing it was pointless. She still wanted to believe there was hope, but that felt worse.

He caught sight of her father, sitting there watching them, trying to keep himself together. Adam clambered his arms away from Rose's mother and towards him. As he got closer, his legs felt weaker.

Closer. Weaker.

He fell at her father's feet, wrapping his arms around her father's shins. His head resting against his knee as he bawled. He felt a hand slide gently onto his head, patting him gently. He let Adam cry against him, not having the strength to let him cry beside him. He didn't let himself break, though, he felt he had to stay strong for everyone else.

The crust on Adam's face had hushed his woes for now. The streaks of the brittle, white salt from the dried rivers that had flowed marked their history in the banks that were his cheeks. He could feel them there any time he moved his face, their stabbing reminders of his failures.

"I'm sorry." His voice was hoarse and faint. "I could've saved her." He rasped. "I should've saved her. I should've been there." His larynx was like a pen that had just run out of ink.

His mother straightened like an arrow; the first time she'd heard him speak since she found him. Rose's mother turned to him, noting his gravelly voice.

"If I had stayed with her, she'd have stayed with us. We wouldn't be here right now!"

That was what did it. That's the one that crossed the line. He couldn't be strong anymore. He broke. Rose's father wept, shaking his head.

He folded his body so he could sit on the floor beside Adam, knowing he wouldn't have the strength to get back up. He sobbed to himself, knowing they were all watching.

"You can't blame yourself. If you start doing that, I'll start too. We'll both lose ourselves down that hole. It wasn't your fault." He whispered his cries to Adam.

Adam watched him, astonished at the forgiveness he'd been granted. He watched her father weep on the floor to him, all to relieve him of the guilt he felt. But it was a guilt they both shared. A mercy bestowed upon him, but one with selfish remorse fuelling it.

They'd both failed in protecting her. They'd both let her down. Neither was there to save her. That was their sole job. And they had both failed it in the worst of ways. Right at her doorstep. Where she was meant to be safest. They'd let everyone down, and it was something that would haunt them forever.

Adam reached out, offering himself as the blanket this time. They both needed it. He felt the warmth being stolen as her father's tears ran down his neck, accepting his offer to share the burden of pain.

A doctor came out a few minutes later, but their gait revealed everything before their lips could. They needn't say anything for the four of them to break down together, a heaping mess of loss.

His happiness had been stolen. His love had been killed. His life had been ended. He'd learned the hard way what those words meant.

I no longer want to live, if living is loving you.

Chapter 34

She had never considered the end, intentionally avoidant but remaining hopeful.

"I need to know now, does the murderer get caught?" Her hushed tones conveying her severity.

"No." He allowed her the relief of knowledge, though it didn't seem reassuring.

"Do you think there's anything... after?" She fidgeted with her fingers.

"Do you want me to be honest?" He asked earnestly.

She nodded, but there was a hesitance to it. He didn't know if he should even entertain the conversation, but he wanted to respect her request.

"No. I think you get one shot, no do-overs."

She seemed disheartened by his honesty, her shoulders sinking a little. She wasn't a child, but he hoped he'd lie to her, sell her a false dream she could hold onto for hope.

"Then what's the point?"

"That *is* the point. You get one chance. There would be no point to life if you lived forever. You'd get infinite chances. Life would get boring; it would become a chore. You'd be begging for a merciful break at some point." He observed her reaction, cautious to not worsen her mood. "Getting one chance is what gives it meaning, gives it purpose. It's why it's special, and why we have to value the time we have while we still have it. That's what I think, anyway."

"I get what you're saying, and there's a large part of me that agrees." She sighed. "It's just scary, thinking that one day I'll just fade away forever."

"Yeah, but you can't run from it. Not this. So there's no point trying to escape it. Rather than give up, go the exact opposite. Do what you want while you can. Make sure you're living while you're alive, else then it *really is* pointless."

She nodded, knowing he was right. He could see the heaviness weighing her down still. He sat beside her and pulled her into his chest. She felt his heart drum against her ears. His fear comforted her, knowing she wasn't alone in this existential terror.

He shook his head in disappointment, anger, sadness. He said nothing, maintaining his vow of silence. Adam's mother thanked the officers and escorted them to the door.

A couple of days had passed. He'd moved back in with his mother. It was more her request, wanting to look after him, but he also knew he would be unable to be in either of the other two homes. The police still had no leads, no suspects. It would've been less agitating to arrest Adam and try to pin it on him. He'd probably take it too, no prison worse than living.

"They're trying, Adam. At least they're trying." His mother walked back in and sat beside him.

He could feel himself getting warmer, hotter. His fists curled; his teeth gritted. He wanted to lash out. He wanted to scream. He wanted to just release it all. He missed the numbness he felt the second day. It was so serene. Nothing could hurt him. He just wanted to be numb again.

What good is *trying* when an expectant mother was murdered at her doorstep? What good is *trying* when his daughter never even got to take her first breath? What good is *trying* when he only found out her gender through a coroner's report?

He bit his tongue. He turned his cheek. He lay down his fists. It was of no use.

She watched him fight with himself. His heart and his mind had never been so conflicted. One wanted to set the world alight, but the other knew it wouldn't be enough. Nothing would be enough anymore. It just wanted to give up and let the world consume him, at least he could be with her again.

He stomped his way out the door, needing to escape the walls that seemed to get smaller and tighter with each blink. It was dark, just how he preferred it. The cold air nipped at his unprepared skin. It carried with him the waft of his own scent, something he'd wallowed in for a few days and never had to notice until now.

He hadn't showered since returning from the hospital. He hadn't done much really. He didn't smell dirty or unclean, but he reeked of grief. The tones of earthy, warm numbness accented by the salty tears he could no longer cry.

He thought to turn back in. He knew his mother would be worrying about him now, even though he was right at the door. He couldn't bring himself to turn around, though. Nothing felt right anymore, nothing felt safe, nothing felt like home. He was in a world of familiar strangers. A world where he felt he knew what surrounded him but couldn't place it. The tip-of-the-tongue curse.

He took a few steps forwards and peeked out the edges of his hood, checking either side was clear. He didn't really have a plan on where he wanted to go or what he wanted to do. He turned left and just began walking, the mantra hushing him in his head. When things aren't going right, just turn around and make them go left.

He walked towards the darkness that never seemed to come, always being broken by a dim light. He'd never wanted the power to cut out so bad. He didn't want to be reminded he was still able to walk, able to talk, able to think. He just wanted the darkness to consume him and let it be over.

The town he'd lived in all his life, the one he knew like the back of his hand, seemed different now. It seemed like it was taunting him, poking, and prodding, trying to get him to strike back at it. And he wanted to strike back, he was just looking for an excuse. He just needed someone to give him a reason. As much as he tried to talk down his anger, as much as he could hear Rose trying to comfort him, he sought no such luxury. If he was to feel, it would be all the worst parts of himself. Pain, anger, grief. Love.

He noticed a couple of strangers in the distance. They ignored the world around them as they got lost in each other. He just stood to the side, watching them as they got closer and closer. They weren't too far from his age. He was a little taller than her. She wanted no space between them, pressing herself into him. They were too busy in the bubble they'd created to protect the little world they were building to notice him. He envied them, hated them, and then pitied them. As they disappeared into the distance, he closed his eyes and prayed for them. As much as he wanted to hurt the world, it seemed to disarm him with ease.

He continued walking, away from the couple that had just passed him. He noticed an old man sitting on a bench across the road, alone and unbothered. He was wanly lit from the nearest streetlight, casting down on him like a dying angel.

Adam watched him. He seemed like he was in his own head, just like Adam was. It did make him wonder why he was out so late and all alone. He looked both ways. No floating lights either side, no distant hums of impending trouble. He crossed the road, not sure what he was going to do next.

As he got nearer, he could see a comforting emptiness in the man's eyes. He wanted to reach out to this stranger, to give him the hug he'd been yearning for.

He sat on the other end of the bench, saying nothing. He watched the small plumes of white splay out from the man's mouth and vanish into the air. He turned his head forwards, thinking about what his next move would be.

"You'll get sick being out here like that." The old man croaked slowly.

His words made Adam flinch. Or was it his voice? He couldn't quite tell yet. They turned to face each other, a slight hesitation on Adam even though he'd instigated this meeting.

"Whatever you're going through, torturing yourself won't make it feel any better." He could see the surprise on Adam's face. "Your eyes give you away." He smiled at Adam.

"I don't know…" Adam's voice was still a little scratchy. "I don't know how to make it feel better."

The old man nodded his head back to looking forwards again. "Not like this."

Adam's head drooped. "My girlfr-... fiancée was murdered. My unborn daughter died with her." He still wasn't completely used to them being engaged.

As he spoke, correcting himself, he didn't feel himself get angry. For the first time he'd spoken on her fate, he didn't feel anger. Just sorrow. Raw, painful, sadness.

The old man gently shook his head to the ground. "I heard about that." He leaned over and placed a hand on Adam's thigh. "I'm sorry for your loss."

Adam didn't say anything. He just sniffled from the coldness, not from the sadness. A part of him wanted to lash out, what would his sorry do? It meant nothing. It was just a customary thing you were meant to do, meant to say. But, at the same time, he didn't want to fight. Not this man. Not like this. He felt lost, no longer having a purpose to live for. He couldn't manage himself anymore.

"It's funny to think how much we can love someone we never even met." The old man retrieved his hand from Adam's thigh. "You fall in love with this person who you only held the highest hopes and unfulfilled dreams for. So much love, so quickly. I understand why you're wandering this dark, cold night. Alone."

Adam turned to look at the old man. He was staring off into the sky, looking at a distant something that only he could see.

"Are you religious?" He turned to Adam.

"If there is a god, I wouldn't bow to one who'd let that happen." The bitterness found its way to his tongue.

"And nobody would blame you for it. I'm not religious either, but sometimes there can be comfort in those scriptures. That's why religion is so tricky – there's so many ways to interpret the holy writings, people end up creating their own beliefs. And people just follow the version they want to hear, or the one that's most convenient for them at that moment of their life."

"You're not doing a good job at recruiting me to your faith." Adam watched the man.

He laughed, bowing his head to enjoy the joke before turning to him. "It's a good thing I'm just rambling then."

"Why are you out here?" Adam asked.

"My wife passed away a few years ago. We would go on walks down this road with our dog. She passed away a few months ago too. Now it's just me, but I'm walking for them. I just have to take more breaks than I used to." A sad grin scribbled itself onto his face.

"I'm sorry for your loss." Adam felt a lump in his throat.

"You may want to be angry, and nobody would hold it against you. But is that an anger they would've accepted? Would they want you to lash out in their name? Is it worth trying to satiate a revenge that will never be quenched?" He slid closer to Adam. "It's tough now, I know, and it doesn't seem like it will ever get easier. But you have to live on, for them. Let the world feel the love you gave to them. You can't bring them back, but you can take them forwards."

Adam stared at the old man for a moment. He traced the wrinkles that cracked his skin, like an endless network of caverns. He followed them from his weary eyes to his tired grin.

Adam leant over and wrapped his arms around this kind stranger and held him tightly. He borrowed his warmth as the old man patted Adam on the back a few times, letting him have the time he needed. Neither of them had anywhere to be, time was meaningless to them.

"You remind me of my grandad." Adam muffled against his shoulder.

"Hopefully that's a good thing." He replied, hoping to get a smile out of Adam.

"The best." Adam grinned against him.

Adam eventually let go, stealing back all the hugs he had wished his grandad would've given him. He thanked the old man and shook his hand a few times before continuing his way through the night.

He knew he wasn't expected to just get over it all, that's not what he was saying. He just wanted Adam to not lose himself in seeking something that would never fulfil him. He needed Adam to remain himself, if not for himself then for the memories of those he mourned. He couldn't sour their lives by living in hatred.

He turned his way between the stone walls and into the familiar park. He could feel the cold biting at him now, the numbness of his pain having surpassed for now. He used the park as a shortcut, eager to get back to his mother, not wanting to cause her any more worry than he already had.

As he walked through the park, his mind drifted to all the moments he would've loved to have with his new family here. Feeding the ducks by the pond, having picnics on the grass, playing in the playground. It was a cruel reminder of what he had lost, and what he could never have again.

He stared at the pond, knowing he could just jump in and let the cold claim him. It wouldn't be quick, it wouldn't be painless, but it would eventually be over. He felt himself gravitating towards it, being tempted by the night's tricks. It would be so easy. He could be with them again. He wouldn't have to suffer this existence anymore. He found himself at the edge, his toes hanging over nothing.

No.

He caught himself, stepping back towards the path.

Not like this.

As desirable as it seemed, he begrudgingly trudged back down the path. He couldn't let it end like that. Rose would never have let him do this to himself. She'd be so disappointed in him right now. She'd know how to break him out of this, but it was only her who could put him in this state.

"Adam." A familiar voice.

He jumped, turning towards it. Hope. Joy.

No.

He shook his head as soon as he saw her. Not right now, not here, not like this. Was she following him? Or was she just here more than he knew? He turned to walk away, but she wasn't letting him go.

"I heard what happened. I'm sorry for your loss." She walked towards him, having frozen him where he stood. "If there's any way I can help, if there's anything I can do."

She'd managed to creep her way right behind him. He felt her hand on his arm, looking down to confirm it was there. He didn't know how to respond; he hadn't expected to see her. Not so soon, not ever again really.

"Thanks. I think. I've got to go." He seemed uncomfortable.

She held his arm, tighter. She stopped him again and stepped in front of him, placing her other hand on his cheek. Her hand was warm, his cheek was frozen.

"I'm still here for you, Adam. I'll always be here for you. Whenever you're ready, you know where I am."

He pulled away from her, slapping away her hand, a look of disgust on his face. "Are you trying to make a move on me, Eve? You're sick."

He shook his head, taking a few steps back. She threw her arms in the air in defeat, disturbed by his rejection. He began to turn to hurry away from her, not wanting to give her any more of his time. Of all the people in the world, why must he be cursed with her? Why? Why couldn't it have been her instead?

"Why the fuck won't you love me anymore, Adam? You wanted me to love you for so long, so many fucking years, and it all just went where? Sure, it took me a while, but I'm here. I'm ready. I love you, Adam, I need you. I would do anything for you. I would kill f- *I HAVE KILLED* for you." She fell silent.

His eyes widened, as he slowly turned back to look at her. He observed her. The bulging eyes, the chewing on her lip, her whole body stiff. It all made sense now.

"It was you." He was quiet. "It was you. There were so many stab wounds, just like that guy at the farm. It was you." His voice got louder as he spoke.

Eve panicked, worried someone might hear him. She fanned her hands through the air, trying to tell him to keep it down.

"You killed Rose, you killed my daughter. And you thought I'd come running back to you? You're unbelievable." He turned again and began walking, feeling the adrenaline pumping through his veins.

"Where are you going?" Eve chased him.

"No sentence they give you will ever be enough, but at least I'll never have to see you again." The venom dripping from his fangs.

"Adam, please, no. I did it for us." She tried to reason with him, following behind him.

She tried her best to make him stop. She jumped on him; he just pushed her off. She tried to plead with him; he just ignored her. She tried crying, threatening, bargaining. Whatever she could, just anything to make him stop. But he had never walked with so much purpose before. She had to stop him.

She jumped on him again, wrapping her arms around his throat. Tight. Like an anaconda, seeking to subdue her prey.

He reached behind and grabbed her jumper. Leaning forwards, he began to pull her. As he tilted forwards, he began to yank her with unprecedented force. She fell to the ground in front of him with a thud, the gravel track not much for cushioning her landing.

She yelped in pain, arching her back as she squirmed. "Adam, please…" She cried.

He walked over to her and knelt over her body. He pulled her towards him by the scruff of her neck. There was fear in her eyes. There was nothing in his.

"You touch me again, I will put you in the ground. And I'll enjoy it too." He threw her back down.

He got up and just looked down at her in disgust. He shook his head. He wanted to hurt her so much, but he couldn't bring himself to do it. He spat down at her and began walking away. He was done with her. That was it. She was dead to him, lest she pushed him to his word.

His body thudded to the ground. She gasped, throwing the boulder to the side, almost astounded that she'd managed to lift it. It grunted a loud thud as it hit the hard earth, denting it as it rolled a little. It looked bigger on the ground. She took a moment to marvel at how she'd managed to lift something that heavy, how she was able to wield it so quickly and efficiently.

She watched as a dark pool started to form around his head, the panic kicking in again. Had she killed him too? She leant over his body and felt for a pulse. His skin was cold, making it hard to feel for anything, but she felt that faint beating through his neck.

Now she had to move his body. What would she do with it? She hadn't had to think this far for her previous victims. How would she deal with him?

She had vowed to no longer be scared. And this is what it did. She was taking control of her life, whilst rewriting the stories of everyone else. She had no ink though, writing fate the only way she knew how: blood.

Chapter 35

She was chasing after demons, eager to be free of any.

"She could've killed him too…" She commented.

He didn't respond, not really knowing how to.

"If she wanted him so bad, why would she risk killing him?" Her puzzled expression looking at him for answers.

He just shrugged and said nothing.

"That makes no sense, is she stupid?" She scowled.

"Not everything we do makes sense, especially those guided by emotion." He finally found something tangible to give her.

"I guess if she can't have him then nobody can, eh?" She raised a brow.

There was a mighty throbbing pulsating from the back of his head demanding his attention. He groaned a little as he raised a hand to feel it. There was a stickiness to his head, one he didn't expect. Had he fallen in something?

He pulled his hand back and held it in front of his face as he tried to open his eyes. They seemed heavier; it was a struggle for him to lift his own eyelids. Through the shaking blinds that were fighting to close, he could tell there was no blood on his fingers. That was good. Right? Probably.

He looked around the room hazily, trying to gather his whereabouts. He thought he knew where he was, but there was something off about it. He turned his head to where the window should be. He met its gaze, the dimming light peeking back into him.

His last memory was of the nighttime, but the sky seemed to have painted itself a new time. The deep black of the night was no longer, just a fading orange being chased by a deep, dark blue. It was now the dawn of a new eve.

He tried to move but his body wouldn't let him. His upper torso jolted as he tried desperately to build the momentum he needed to swing against gravity.

"Hey, relax, you're still healing." She hurriedly knelt beside him from out of nowhere.

"Wh-… W… What h-… ha…" He was fighting himself just to do basic functions.

"I asked you to be my boyfriend and you fainted. You hit your head on my desk." She started brushing his hair with her palm.

He remembered her asking, but not much before or after that. He could hear her saying those words, stuck in a loop in his mind, holding onto the only memory that made him feel like he knew who he was. She had gifted him a part of himself.

His lips parted, wanting to say something. His mind went blank, failing him like his body was. He closed his mouth again and just gave in to it all, closing his eyes and hoping it would all figure itself out by the time he woke again. *If* he woke again.

Eve sat beside him a while, watching him sleep, nursing his unconscious body. She lay against him, her head resting on his chest, smiling up at him. She finally had him. She was ready for him, and he was all hers for the taking.

He woke again a few hours later. Maybe it was a few days, he had no concept of time. Her room was dimly lit, the curtains drawn. The throbbing had mostly settled by now, allowing him to regain more control of his body. He leaned his head up and looked around. He was still in Eve's room. It took him a minute to notice, but Eve was still draped across him.

He was completely lost. It seemed like the world had left him behind, as if he were someone from the past in a familiar future. He just wanted to go back to his time where the air was less uncertain.

"Hey, sleepyhead." She yawned; his movements having shaken her awake. "Rise and shine!"

She sat up, helping Adam sit up too. The smile on her face was one he recognised, but it had something to it, something that made him uneasy. He knew it was Eve, he could tell she was happy, but why did it seem disturbing? Why did this feel wrong?

"I'm gonna get you some food, you stay right there." She instructed, as if he had a choice in the matter.

She giddily skipped out of her room and ran down the stairs. He counted the steps as she rushed herself down. Ten steps, just like he remembered. He was definitely in her house.

He studied the room a bit closer. That dresser wasn't the same as the one she had before. The desk wasn't there last time, and it was a different type of wood. Had she redecorated?

While he had passed out, she changed her room around? It wasn't making sense.

"Brunch is served for dinner!" Eve exclaimed as she carefully made her way through the door.

There was a tray between her arms. He could smell fried eggs and French toast. As she placed the tray on the bedside table, he noticed some beans and sausages that his nose somehow missed.

She sat on the edge of the bed, turning herself towards him. He watched her grab a knife and fork as she started cutting a slice of toast. She was feeding herself and leaving him starving, dangling the food in front of him? That didn't seem right.

That's because it wasn't right. It was somehow more awkward than that. She moved the fork from the plate towards him, a piece of toast held hostage at the end, its last delicious wafts of breath reminding his stomach how empty it was.

He leaned forwards cautiously, nervously, awkwardly. She smiled brighter as she pushed the fork between his teeth, watching as he gently closed his mouth around it. She retrieved the fork. He only began chewing once her arms had fully retreated to her own body.

That was one weird bite, but maybe she was just being endearing. Surely, she'd let him feed himself. It was frankly inefficient and ridiculous for her to feed him the whole me-. He watched as she began preparing more bite-sized pieces while he chewed. Something told him she wasn't quite done.

He regretfully swallowed and was instantly greeted with another forkful of food knocking at his teeth. He grinned awkwardly at her, but she wasn't taking the hint.

"Can I... feed myself?" He asked, trailing it with a nervous laugh.

He watched as she just smiled back at him. She didn't say anything. She didn't move. She didn't even blink. She just stared at him, his concern growing more and more into a frown.

"Of course, silly." The fork clattered on the plate. "I'll get a little bell and you can just give it a shake when you need me." She stood up and bowed. "I'm sorry for trying to look after you." She spouted with a bitterness as she walked away before he could say anything.

He was confused but didn't know what to say or do. He didn't have to think hard to make a choice, though. Eve's storming off was quickly forgotten as his stomach pleaded for more food. Adam didn't hesitate to get the rest of it portered over to his belly.

Eve sheepishly returned to her room after an hour, her head tucked between her tails. She seemed saddened for the first time since he woke up.

"I'm sorry for that outburst, Adam." She played with her fingers. "I wasn't trying to be weird."

"I-... It's okay. I appreciate it. I'm sorry if I came across ungrateful." He instantly regretted those words, fearing she'd try to feed him again.

"It's okay, it was my fault." She paused, her frown becoming a smile. "You're mine now and I'm gonna make this right. Wait here." She ran out the room with a mischievous hop.

Adam heard the main door close; someone had left. He heard the light patter of her footsteps making their way round the house, like dripping raindrops. Eve was still here... Adam had no idea what was happening, but she had piqued his interest as he sat up to wonder what she was doing.

After what felt like an eternity, the footsteps grew louder and louder until they stopped.

"Close your eyes!" A muffled voice called.

"They're closed." He responded.

He heard the door close. "You can open them now." She finally announced.

Her back was turned to him as she stood by the door. He stared at her, not quite sure what was going on. She'd changed her clothes, and he was taking it all in.

She looked back at him with a cheeky grin and then swiftly turned her whole body to face him, keeping her hands behind her.

Her right hand peeked out from behind and waved to him, then quickly retreated. He just watched her.

His eyed darted from her head to her toes as her right leg moved forwards. Covered in criss-crosses, the stitching of the black stockings did the absolute bare minimum to conceal legs that seemed to be endless, as Adam ran his eyes all along them.

Her left leg flicked its way ahead. His eyes followed, realising she was wearing a skirt that her swiftness had gently lifted. He managed to steal a glimpse of her bare skin below the skirt, before it flittered back against her thighs. Her foot graciously and slowly sank back to the ground. He kept following her movements, stuck in a hypnotic trance, from the quick flicks from her feet to the gentle sways of her skirt, slowly getting higher as each step grew into a stride and the skirt's limits were tested. Bouncing higher and higher as she closed the distance, revealing more and more, closer and closer to... Was she trying to seduce him? Trying to reveal... It played on his mind. She was definitely tempting him. But he wanted no part of this game.

Her door was not far from her bedroom, but her lack of pace made it feel like she'd been walking for miles, all while testing him. She stopped a step away from him.

"Hold this." She smiled at him as her hands finally came out from behind her to reveal a small, white box, neatly sealed with a red bow.

Enchanted and dazed, he followed her instruction and lifted his palm. He watched her hands as they moved towards his. He barely even felt the box resting on his palm - had it not been for the corners prodding his palm, he wouldn't have noticed it at all.

She lifted her left leg and placed it on his right knee, the overlap revealing the bare right thigh under her covered left. The tips of her index and middle finger of her left-hand rest against the top of her left knee. She waited for his eyes to finally notice them and then began making them stroll backwards.

Adam's eyes were bulging, watching her fingers kick back her skirt, revealing more of herself. Her eyes stayed focused on his, as his stayed focused on the skirt as it was dragged across her thigh.

Just before her fingers ended up giving away the surprise, her other hand pulled the bow on the box. She motioned with her eyes for him to open it. He lifted the lid off it. There was a mess of black lace. He didn't know what to do, didn't know what to make of it. She plucked it out between two fingers and let it reveal itself. Her lace underwear. She noticed the shock on his face, winking back at him. With a little flick, he found himself draped by them. She giggled to herself, he froze, unable to give her the reaction she wanted. He shook them off him, not wanting to touch them with any other part of him.

But she wasn't done, she would get what she desired. She moved her hands over to the top of her stocking. With no effort at all, she ripped them free from her skin and threw them behind her, revealing legs that were barely concealed in the first place. Somehow, though, it had some sort of effect.

With one less layer to worry about, she began to unbutton her shirt, drawing his attention away from the fallen garment and back to her. She started from the bottom, right in Adam's sight line.

Each undone button threw her shirt back a little bit more. Was this shirt even big enough for her? Why would she have worn a shirt that was slightly too small? Mesmerised, stunned, he couldn't look away. All the way up, until both sides of the shirt had parted like the Red Sea.

His eyes traced it as it gently flew to the floor. He stared at it, watching it collapse, not quite sure what to do.

"I'm over here, Adam." She tilted her head to appear in the corner of his sight.

That was all he needed to break the spell. He blinked a few times, then his eyes went back to Eve. Her sour face sweetened again when she realised she'd got his attention again. Why was he staring at a shirt when she was giving him the show?

"Eve, I-." He began.

"It's okay Adam, I know it's your first time." Her hand hugged his chin. "I'll take care of you." She leaned over and placed her lips over his.

Something was banging at his mind, begging to be let in as he heard those words. He could see pieces of wood splattered across the floor, drops of blood on a floor. He couldn't make it all out, it was so blurry, so distorted, but so familiar.

He kept his lips shut tight as hers started to separate. He felt a warmth that was followed by a coldness. She couldn't break through. As much as she tried, he wouldn't let her in.

Adam moved back in her bed, breaking them apart. "Not like this, Eve."

He was on the other edge of her bed; he'd risk falling off if he weren't trapped against the wall. She stood and watched him, bewildered.

"What do you mean?" She seemed annoyed.

"I-... I'm... I'm not ready." He bowed his head.

She lunged forwards onto the bed, towering Adam as she leaned over him. He felt a blunt force grabbing him as she locked eyes with him again. His body had betrayed him, and she knew about it.

"You seem ready." She replied, emotionless.

The force got tighter. Her eyes had lost their playfulness. She could see his discomfort, but she enjoyed the feeling of control. And then she let go, as if teasing herself. He wanted to sigh in relief, but he wasn't out of the woods yet.

Her hand made a short trip up and, without breaking eye contact once, she started breaking the walls down. That's when he realised he'd lost his belt. How had he lost his belt? She had an easy time tearing away at the barriers that remained. He tried to meet her hand with his, but she swatted it away. In no time at all, he felt her palm against him. Skin on skin, no hiding anymore.

She squeezed, taking control of him again. She was testing his limits, and maybe even her own. Eventually, mercifully, she pulled away and brought her hand beside her face. She held it between them, as if showing off a trophy. He just shook his head, his face twisting and contorting in ways it hadn't before.

"You definitely seem ready, Adam. You already started, you cute little pervert." She smiled at him, but there was something off about it.

"Eve... please..." He pleaded, his voice waning.

"You're gonna give me everything I want so I don't have to get it from anywhere else, then we can be happy again." She growled.

She looked at her palm as she simultaneously turned it to meet her eyes. Without any hesitation, she ran her tongue from the very bottom of her palm to the very tip of her middle finger. She chuckled to herself and looked down for a moment.

Her words rang in his ear, like an alarm. Why would she need to get anything from anywhere else? Something kept pounding at him, trying to break in. Something needed to be known, desperate to be heard. It was door without a handle, he didn't know how to open it.

His head bounced off the wall and eventually came to rest on her bed as the crackle of her skin meeting his enveloped the room. She was displeased by his lack of participation in all she'd done for him, all the ungratefulness he was showing.

"I did all this for you. I've done so much for you. I would kill for you. Why can't you love me like I know you do?" She began to sob, the tears resting on his lower chest.

He saw her sitting in a forest, covered in blood. A part of her was screaming in pain, the other with joy. She seemed hauntingly comfortable with the blood running down her body. Someone else's blood. She wore it like a new skin, a trophy.

He closed his eyes and began praying to all the gods he didn't believe in. He prayed to as many of them as he could remember. He didn't want to move. He took as few breaths as he could, hoping maybe she'd leave him alone if he seemed dead.

She stared down at him. A sinister glint in her eyes had taken over. She wasn't evil, she was Eve. She was just naïve. She made mistakes. But she had a good heart. Good intentions. She wouldn't hurt him. She didn't mean to hurt him.

"Let me love you. Properly this time. Maybe you'll understand." She sniffled, makeup running down her face.

Adam's breathing got heavier. He felt Eve's hand meet his cheek. She leaned in for another kiss. His lips stayed stiff as hers softly met his. She used one hand to grip him across the jaw and force his mouth open, to let her in. Her other hand started dancing down his face, slowly. She ran them over his top and stopped at his waist. She snuck a hand under his t-shirt and let her fingers dance circles on his belly.

She tried to lift his t-shirt off him. He didn't move, he didn't oblige, trying to hold it down. She just shook her head and laughed to herself. It wouldn't stop her. She grabbed it by the collar with both hands and pulled in separate directions. The screeching of the fabric made it clear to Adam what she'd done. Her nails clawed into his upper chest, leaving bright red streaks. She had marked him, branded him. She tore the rest of the t-shirt to shreds and threw it in the air, confetti to mark their special occasion.

Adam tried to stop her. He tried to get up. She noticed. She felt heavier than she ever had before. He couldn't break out. She held him down with an arm across his throat, beginning to kiss her way down from his lips to his neck. From his neck to his shoulders. His shoulders to his chest.

Adam tried to push her off him once more. All the adrenaline he'd allowed to build up, his superpower. It was his last shot, and he knew it. He felt lighter, watching her stumble back onto the floor. She stood up. He sat up and observed her, waiting to see how she'd react. He began to get up from the bed, trying to make himself harder to contain. She shook her head and jumped on him, kneeing him in his already damaged ribs as she did. Punches and slaps followed to which Adam could only cower. His broken body couldn't fight back. He just fell onto the bed and tried to protect himself. He set her free. He let her loose. He did this.

"This is how you love a cheap, easy whore, Adam. This is what they did to me." She growled; her pupils dilated.

She was like a tiger that had just brought down a deer, ripping into it. As its heartbeat faded and its breaths grew more distant, it was closer to feeding time. It was almost feeding time. Ravenous and brutal, she made sure he had no hope of escape anymore.

"I'm sorry that had to happen, Adam." She spoke softly, brushing his cheek again. "I just want to take care of you and you're making it difficult. Just sit back, let me help you." She stroked his hair.

She lay on him, running her fingers through his hair. She stared into his eyes. Hers were wide. His were empty. She sat up on top of his chest, her other hand running up and down his side slowly. Something felt different to him, but he couldn't make out what. Until he remembered that she was bare. Before he could do anything else, she decided to waste no more time.

"Why are you trying to resist when you're clearly so happy to see me?" She tutted; the smile had come back. "You didn't even fully appreciate the present I got for you."

She leaned over to Adam's side and grabbed it, dangling it above his face again. With nothing but chaos in her veins, she released her fingers, letting her gift fall onto his lips. Never had lace felt so heavy. She giggled to herself, letting her eyes lie to her. In her mind, he enjoyed them. That's why she had to follow it with a hand, making sure he couldn't throw them off him again. He just enjoyed them so much, she made sure they wouldn't fall again.

"I put a lot of thought into this gift Adam, I hope you like it." She seemed almost nervous. "Who am I kidding? Of course you like it, I can feel it right now!" She started rubbing her gift into his lips with one hand, letting her body work its way down him.

She retreated her hands back to herself. She giggled as if she had no idea what she was doing, as if this was *her* first time. But every passing second was becoming more and more expensive as her expertise kicked back in.

Her bra seemed to fall off her and she aimed it towards his face. Unfortunately for Adam, it didn't block his sight. Even if it did, sight was only one misery he had to endure. He could still feel everything.

He felt her lift herself slightly as her hands played around below her against the remains of his barriers. The ruffling of clothes being dragged away from him. The last shelter he had being destroyed, as he felt the cooler air of the room welcome him. His eyes closed and the muffled scratching of his skin against his jeans became the exasperated chorus to his fading song.

He was running out of time. He needed to get out. Now. Her moments of playfulness and methodical pace had allowed him some time to recharge. Would it be enough though? He shot up, face to face with Eve. She wrapped her arms around him as his arms went around her. He kissed her once, letting her know she'd won.

"I knew you'd come around." She grinned.

She closed her eyes and began kissing him. Adam's remained open, each moment she was against him feeling like it was corrupting him. He felt gross, withered, disgusting.

Their lips danced the dangerous tango as Adam's hands caressed her back. Eve was giving in to him, letting him take control. She wrapped her legs around him as he stood with her, holding her by the thighs. Gravity betrayed him, pulling his jeans away from him. He stepped out of them, letting her enjoy herself, teasing her with the faintest of touches of himself just below her. He let her believe what he needed her to.

He pinned her to her wall. She let out an excited gasp. She hadn't seen this side of him, didn't think it existed.

"Oh, Adam…" She squealed.

He said nothing, kissing her neck as he removed his hands from her thighs. She held onto him, letting him stroke his way up her body, right to her shoulders. Her hands were carving into his back, marking her territory. His hands crept their way to her neck as he distracted her with a kiss. He wrapped around her and started to squeeze. Gently at first, trying to gauge her reaction. Her hands fell to his waist as she gently moaned against his mouth. It was his chance.

He pulled back and put all of his force into his arms. Every inch of strength he could find rerouted to his hands. He squeezed. He went for it. He squeezed so hard he thought his forearms would burst. Eve froze, her eyes shot open. She gasped for air. The kiss that had given her life was taking it from her. She flailed against the wall, dangling in the air, each struggle strengthening his noose. He was saving himself. He was in the cl-.

As he froze in that moment, he remembered this wasn't the first time he had tried to escape from her. It most probably wouldn't be the last. But something in her grew more and more dangerous with each step he tried to take away from her. It was all starting to come back to him. If he was to be rid of her, he would have to make sure she would never be able to bother him again. He had to keep his word. But it was too late.

His arms fell to the side, he fell to the floor. In his head, it was all in slow motion. He could watch parts of his life again. To her, it took mere seconds. She had fashioned a makeshift club with her intertwined hands and pounded into his chest, stealing any hidden breaths he may have held onto. He was numbed to the pain, the drumming of his body ticking away his time, as he could feel her hammering away at him. He coughed, he wheezed, he panted. When he could move no more, she took a moment to rush the air back into her lungs before she would carry on like nothing happened.

"Next time, we're using safe words. You got a bit carried away there!" She exclaimed, still panting.

He watched her hold herself in the air for a second. And then she lowered, slowly. Her head tilted back as her eyes closed. A smile painted her face once more. His eyes were blurry now. He blinked. She was raised. He blinked again, bringing back parts of him he thought he'd lost. She was lowered. His blink was slower now, as he allowed himself to remember. She was lowered, his eyes no longer keeping her pace. His blink was slowed still, the short breaks felt like different lifetimes. She was raised. He blinked one last time. She lowered heavier and his eyes just closed. They closed for a while. Eve had won.

Chapter 36

She was lost in a world he'd just flipped upside-down, her instincts unable to navigate her through it.

"Sh-Sh...?" She seemed bewildered.

"These things happen. We all have the potential to do bad things. Sometimes, we can even try to justify them." He seemed unfazed.

"Did he die?" She seemed lost in herself.

"It seems like, no matter what she threw at him, he wouldn't die. That's not for lack of wanting, mind." He tried to comfort her poorly. "It'll all be okay." He turned and walked towards her, open arms welcoming a hug she so desperately needed.

His eyes opened to a sunlight that stabbed his eyes. He knew where he was, but he wondered how the sun had managed to break in. It was then he noticed that it had slid in under the curtains. He was still on the floor. He could feel a weight on him. He looked down to see an arm draped across him. He looked to the left and there lay a sleeping Eve.

He was sore. He tried to get up but everything ached. He carefully plucked Eve off him, limb by limb. When he was comfortable with the space between them, he tried to roll himself upwards. The momentum failed him. The best he could manage was a crawl. On all fours, he scoured the bedroom floor for his clothes.

Not far from him, he saw the base of a statue covered in blood. How…? And then it came back to him. He reached for the side of his face, it stung. It confirmed what he already knew. The blood was his. He gulped. She was more treacherous than he knew. He was desperate to escape and now was the best opportunity he'd get.

He found his jeans, the denim not so easy to tear, thankfully. He crawled his way over to them, grabbing them and scanning for more. He found his boxers as he scurried over to them. He sat upright and began frantically pulling them on, wary of falling back. He knew he wouldn't be able to muster the strength to get up again. It was then that he saw.

"What are you doing, Adam?" She had been watching him, her chin resting on her palm.

"I-I… I need to go." Adam had stopped moving.

"There are easier ways to get dressed, silly." She smiled and got up, neglecting to cover herself.

She walked over to him. He tried to shield himself, make himself as small as possible. She knelt down beside him. He was petrified, watching her close in on the parts of him that she had exposed.

She freed his tangled boxers from his ankles and slid them up his legs. He knew how tall he was, and roughly how much of that height was his legs. That didn't stop him feeling like his legs had stretched out for a mile as he waited for the comforting hug from the elastic securing him.

She seemed to stop three quarters up his thigh. He closed his eyes shut tight, his teeth trying to bite each other, as he prayed she'd carry on. She laughed playfully as she poked him and finally let him return to his tainted sanctuary.

"Gotta leave you wanting more!" She giggled. "We need to get you a new top too, yours got ruined during the fun last night."

Luckily, Adam had spared her enough clothes over the years that she had some of his older ones. She pulled him up and helped him put a top on, pushing it over his head. He noticed there were two distinct handprints on her neck. He looked down at his hands as she began pulling his top down his shoulders.

"You need to help me help you here." She laughed.

He rushed his arms through the sleeves, breaking away from any potential guilt, and looked at the door. Still locked. Would he be allowed to leave? Would she grant him this mercy?

He picked up his shoes from two different places and made his way over to the door. Eve blocked him off. She looked cross. Adam started biting his lips. His eyes darted around hers, doing his best to avoid eye contact.

"Leaving without a kiss goodbye?" She crossed her arms. "You really know how to keep a girl wanting."

Adam was slightly relieved. The thought of kissing her sickened him but it was something he was willing to do. Between kissing her and staying her prisoner, he could stomach her lips and pay the price for it later.

His eyes closed. He leaned down at a snail's pace. He barely opened his right eye just to see how much further he had to go, how much longer this had to last. He inched closer and closer. And then finally it was done. She had tiptoed up and met him halfway. He'd never been so pleased to kiss her, never been so relieved to have her lips against his.

When they broke, she smiled and moved out of the way. He could escape, the exit was right there. He was free. The clack of the latch had never sounded so angelic. The squeak of the hinges like the harps at the gates.

"You'll stay for breakfast, won't you?" Her words practically pushing his eyes from their sockets.

He could feel the twitching in his legs as he tried to run, but he froze. He knew she wanted an answer, and it would decide what would happen in the next few seconds. Even when he had the exit right in front of him, she still had a grip over him, clasping him against her.

He turned to her slowly, she stood there in nothing but her skirt. Why wouldn't she just go get dressed? Why was she still following him, so close to the door? What if her parents saw?

"Sure." He couldn't believe he'd just said that.

She jumped gleefully, turning to get clothed. Adam lunged out the room and closed the door. At least he wasn't stuck in that prison with her anymore, he was closer to freedom.

He was interrupted by the smell of freshly fried eggs and bacon. Eve was in her room, so she wasn't cooking that. That realisation filled him with reassurance. He might be in the same house as her, but he didn't have to be alone with her. He'd managed to catch a break.

He worked his way prudently down the stairs, leaning forward slightly to get a peek into the kitchen. He caught her father wielding the pan, a wave of solace splashing over him. He took a seat on the penultimate step, letting his feet rest on the floor as he placed his shoes between them.

He slid his socks on and slipped his feet into his shoes, ready for a quick escape. He made his way over to the door, it was right there waiting for him. He was so close. So close and yet it felt like the most difficult leg of the escape.

He heard the familiar creak of the third step from the top. His head darted to the stairs, anxiously waiting to see who'd come down. He relaxed as he saw Eve's mother's hands gliding down the banister.

"Morning Adam." There was a pleasant surprise in her voice as she made her way over to the table.

He smiled back, not wanting to say anything. He just watched her as she took a seat at the table. He began thinking about where he could sit now that one of the six seats had been taken, but there wasn't a guaranteed safe chair right now.

"Is that Adam? I thought it was Eve!" Her father laughed to himself. "Morning Adam. If I'd known you were still here, I'd have put a plate out for you. Help yourself, I'll grab another on my way in." He called out.

"What happened to you?" She asked, as she got closer to him.

His body was a mess, especially his head. It was apparent he'd been through something.

"I... Uhh..." He tried to think.

"He got jumped by some guys last night." Eve answered. "I found him nearby, so I brought him to my room."

"We should take him to the hospital, some of those injuries look terrible." Eve's mother had a concern amongst her.

"Let him eat first." Eve fought back.

"I'll head over after some breakfast, if that's okay." Adam didn't want to anger Eve again.

Eve's mother shrugged. She felt something was wrong but she couldn't argue with him.

Adam took a seat beside her mother. At least he'd have some comfort being close to her, knowing Eve wouldn't risk hurting him right now.

And then she galloped down the stairs without any warning, and teleported herself to the empty seat beside him, kissing him on the head as she did so. Her mother watched with a smile, completely unaware of Adam's panic.

"Morning!" Eve called out; her voice brighter than it had ever been as it rippled through his chest.

"You're cheery this morning." Her father replied, making his appearance with a platter of food.

Eve just grinned, letting her father's words float in the air. She was, indeed, very cheery this morning. She leaned her head against Adam's shoulder. The adrenaline that was fuelling his morning helped hide his discomfort behind a smile, giving him a fake strength that was depleting rapidly.

Adam helped himself to one plate of food to be polite, his stomach not ready for that load let alone any more. He ate quickly but kept a pace that disguised panic with eagerness. Hunger instead of fear, let them take it as a compliment.

He fought back the need to vomit. He had to let them think everything was okay.

"I've got to go, thanks for breakfast." He excused himself from the table, feeling like he would explode at any minute.

He stood up before anyone could stop him. He began tucking his chair in as she leapt up from hers.

"I will see you very soon." She yelled, gleefully.

Those words haunted him. As he stood there, the words just played over and over again in his head. He was scared. He had never felt this terror before. Why was he this fearful? This was Eve, the girl he fell in love with for so many years. Why? Eve... She had given him the fear she had removed from herself. A harsh gift.

He was awoken by a kiss on his cheek, freeing him from the curse she'd cast on him, but not from her chains. He nervously smiled as her parents watched. He turned swiftly and headed towards the door, waving to them before opening it and closing it shut behind him.

He ran to the edge of the pavement and just stood there, leaning against a lamppost, regaining himself. The adrenaline had worn off, he'd lost the strength he never had, the aches and pains of his body hitting him at once. He had to hold himself up, letting his body recover enough for him to trek back home.

"Adam." A voice called from behind him.

He turned around as the door slammed shut. He saw her father walking towards him. He couldn't make out the expression on his face, but it looked distracted.

"I'm glad I caught you, Adam." Either Adam was doing a good job of hiding it or he really failed to notice Adam nearing collapse. "I just wanted to say thanks, I've never seen Eve so happy. Especially not after..." He choked on his words, clearing his throat. "Thank you. I want you to have this."

He looked down as her father held out his hand. In it, the small, black box sat innocently. Adam gagged at the sight of it, as if that was the final straw. He just shook his head and turned his body away from it.

"No thanks." Adam responded.

Confusion swept over Eve's father's face. Adam really had led them on, better than he'd thought he had. Better than he'd hoped he had, silently wishing one of them would spot his distress.

"I thought you two were..." He tried to explain himself.

"She attacked me. I don't know how she got me back to her room, but I wasn't using my legs when she did." Adam grunted; her chains were breaking.

Her father shook his head in disbelief. There's no way his little princess would hurt anyone. She couldn't hurt anyone. Especially not Adam.

Adam could see his reluctance to believe it. He stood himself against the lamppost, using it as a temporary spine, as he lifted his top to reveal the damage she'd done to it.

"Your daughter did this to me. I know you don't want to believe it, but I promise you it was her. Go up to her room right now, all the proof will be there. My blood is on her floor." Adam paused, watching her father's reaction. "Just think about it... I didn't do this to myself. But if someone else did this to me, why wouldn't I be in a hospital right now?" He stretched out his arms and almost collapsed, managing to catch himself against the lamppost again.

Her father couldn't argue with it. He knew Adam wouldn't lie like this. But Adam wasn't done... He was getting ready for the final blow that would exhaust him as much as it would destroy her father.

"She killed Rose too. On her own doorstep. My girlfr-... My fiancée. My *pregnant* fiancée. And my *unborn* daughter. They were both innocent. They didn't do anything to her. They were innocent in all this. She didn't leave me anything. Why couldn't she have killed me too?!" His voice broke, crackling at the reminder. "I just need to be away from her, away from here. I'm not safe. And you need to pretend like you don't know anything. If you ever cared about me, you need to pretend like you know nothing." Adam pleaded.

He watched as her father wrestled with it all. Confusion. Anger. Sadness. Frustration. Remorse. Guilt. He mourned his daughter for all of twenty seconds, no longer recognising what she was now. After those seconds had passed, he composed himself and shook his head. He didn't want to believe it, but there was a part of him that did. He began to nod as he came to terms with the revelation. He would protect Adam against his own daughter.

Adam mouthed the words "thank you", his voice too weak to croak them out. He began limping away towards his safety net, the one place he knew he could turn to no matter what.

He collapsed at the door, his shoulder knocking against it loud enough for her to hear. He had no more strength to knock with his fists. He tried to hold himself up against the door, but he could feel himself slipping down it.

The door opened swiftly and he fell into the house. A gasping shriek as she fell beside him, screaming for her son to wake up.

"Wake up, Adam. Wake up. Not again, please…"

Chapter 37

Her brain slowly melted, hating the revelations that were being thrust upon her.

"She's fucking evil." She remarked. "How could she be so oblivious?!"

"We've definitely had this conversation before." He smirked at her.

"I just-… I don't get it. It doesn't make sense." Her frustration boiling over.

"I don't know what you want me to say. Sometimes there are things we'll just never understand."

"She keeps pushing him closer and closer to death, it's barbaric." She shook her head.

His shoulders did the familiar bounce they were used to doing. "Whatever she is, at least he's alive."

"Just because he's alive doesn't mean he is grateful to be." There was a bitterness to her tone.

"Maybe not right then, but that doesn't mean it has to stay that way forever."

"Are you hinting at something?"

He just shrugged again with a slight grin.

A bright white flowed into his eyes. It was eerily quiet, and seemingly endless. Pure white. Calm, and still. This wasn't how he'd thought the end would look, but it was unnervingly comforting.

He waited for something to happen. Was someone meant to appear, to greet him? Was Rose here? Was Rose here? He jolted, trying to rush into the vast expanse of whiteness, hoping he might find her somewhere. Even though he could see nothing for miles, surely-.

"Adam." A voice echoed through his ears.

He turned to the direction of the sound. He wasn't dead, he'd just wound up in hospital. Again. He struggled to hide his disappointment, knowing he'd have to trudge along for her sake, as he stared into her relieved eyes. Eyes that looked like they'd been grieving.

"How are you feeling?" She loomed over him.

"Right as rain, mum." He groaned.

She shook her head, hating his humour more and more with each hospital visit. He never seemed to quit though, whether out of pity or mockery she'd never know. Or maybe it was just hope. If he kept at it, she'd know he was okay. Maybe it wasn't cruel at all.

"Have I been out long?" He spoke slowly and quietly.

"A couple days. You seemed to daze in and out of consciousness the first day. I didn't know if that was good or bad. But then you didn't wake up for two days and I'd wished you'd go back to the dazing."

"Have you tried switching it off and on again?" He achingly grinned.

"One of these days, your jokes are gonna bite you back." She snapped at him, wiping the grin off his face.

"What's the damage?" He didn't try moving, not yet.

"You lost a rib. It snapped but somehow didn't do any damage any of your organs." She sniffled. "It's a lower one." She gestured on her own body to demonstrate. "Some of the others were damaged, but they did some stuff, I don't know… My mind drifted when the doctors were telling me."

Adam nodded with his eyelids. He could feel something broken somewhere; he just couldn't confirm it from where he was. He could feel it now though, making him wonder if she could've told him anything and he'd have felt that too.

"You had two nasty cuts on your head too. Sorry, *blunt force traumas*. One wasn't as… fresh… as everything else." The words cut her as she freed them from her lips.

He knew the question that ran amok in her mind. The one thing she would've had running through her mind since he fell into her house. He knew it was stabbing the tip of her tongue right now, trying to force her mouth open and jump out into his ears. He could see it in her face, her eyes already asking him as she scanned her broken boy. But a part of her didn't know if she wanted to know either. It would hurt her. It might even hurt him, to relive it all.

Knock knock.

Just before he could speak, a visitor had arrived. His mother headed over to the door, curious but very defensive. She was ready to fight for her son.

He heard the door open as she held it ajar. She peeked through the gap and seemed to just stop, as if someone had hit the pause button. She didn't even know the worst of it yet, but she was already ready for a fight.

"Eve." She turned her head back to Adam, closing the door again. "I can tell her you're not awake."

"You're gonna wanna hear what I have to say, Adam." She yelled sing-songy through the door.

His mother lacked any subtlety. She stared daggers back at Eve. She wasn't going to let her near her son, and she had no idea how right she was to be his guard.

He closed his eyes, preparing himself for the worst. He still wanted to report her, expose her for everything she was, but he was in no state to do that right now. The hospital visit would be useful, though, as evidence against her. He didn't know if his mother had called the police, but he wasn't far off it himself.

He reopened his eyes with a short exhale and nodded ever so slightly. He was as ready as he could be, just glad his mother was there to protect him. He watched the fire light in her eyes as she turned back to the door and left it opened slightly. His mother walked away before the door opened, back to Adam's side, hoping she wouldn't have to watch Eve helping herself in.

He watched the door, waiting for her to enter. What was she waiting for? She wanted to come in, why was she hesitating? Unless she was just trying to be cruel, which he wouldn't put past her.

Before he could get his hopes up, before he could be thankful she'd left, there she was. As the door eerily opened, and she walked into his vision, he could only pray the machines keeping him alive would suddenly fail.

She stepped in, closing the door behind her, and stood beside Adam. She was right across his mother, staring her down, knowing she had venom bubbling at the back of her lips. Eve was ready for the vitriol, she could take that, she expected that, but his mother held back. She deemed her not worthy, and hate is too strong an emotion to spend on someone you don't like.

"I need to talk to him alone." Eve demanded, a confidence about her similar to a criminal with a hostage.

She *was* a criminal, and Adam had been her hostage. He would never be able to forgive her. She'd gone from being his hero to being his captor in no time at all. She threw it all away, and for what?

"Over my dead body." His mother replied.

Adam wanted to lunge forwards; he didn't want Eve to take that as a challenge. "Can you give us a moment, mum?" Adam's mouth reflexively threw himself in front of the bus.

His mother looked down at him, no longer caring for the staring contest. She seemed understandably reluctant, but Adam couldn't back down. He was saving her life and she didn't even know it. He just nodded to her, and she sighed, stepping away.

"I'll be right out here if you need me." She looked at Adam once more, as he nodded back at her again, and she closed the door behind her.

He refused to say the first word, he didn't even want to look at her. He was adamant on not entertaining it, he just couldn't get out of it. He hoped she would lose the confidence she feigned as she stepped into the room, the false strength she used to stare down his mother.

"I know you want to go to the police, Adam, but you can't." There was a tinge of nervousness in her voice, and he sensed it. "You can't, Adam."

"Why not?" He looked at the walls, trying his best to avoid her.

"I have too much to lose right now, Adam. I-."

"*You* have too much to lose?" He spat back at her. "*I* had too much to lose. *Rose* had too much to lose. We actually had something to lose. You've got nothing, Eve." He could feel the erroneous strength from the addictive adrenaline pumping through his body, his blood beginning to boil.

"She didn't deserve you. You were mine first! *You were mine.*" Her voice was cold, no remorse to be found. "I gave you another chance, you can give me another chance."

"You didn't *give* me another chance, Eve, you *took* it." His voice was getting weaker, no longer able to sustain the violence his words demanded.

"I fucking get it, Adam, you don't love me." She threw her hands up, defeated. "But you can't turn against the mother of your child."

"You killed my ch-." His darting eyes noticed Eve place a hand on her belly.

He shook his head, still refusing to look at her. He didn't want to believe her. He didn't want this to be the second chance she meant. This wasn't the child he had dreamed of. Not like this. Not with her. Not after them.

"I don't believe you." His skin had lost all colour, returning him to the calm, broken state she'd found him in.

Eve reached into her bag and retrieved a paper bag. She emptied it out on Adam's lap. The numerous familiar sticks tumbled against him, each one prodding against his thighs and then clacking against each other as they lay to rest. She had taken a bunch of pregnancy tests, from a bunch of different brands. His mind raced to try to justify them away. She probably faked them. They're not hers. They're not right. Every single one of them was either wrong or defective.

"I took some tests last night. I could just feel something was different. They were *all* positive." She shrugged him off.

"It's not mine." He was desperate for an out.

"There's nobody else it could be." She wasn't letting him escape. "You're the only person I've been with in *months*."

He wanted to throw an insult at her, but he knew it would be for nothing. It wasn't his style anyway. She didn't deserve the energy, and he wouldn't lower himself for her.

A warm palm slid under his chin, caressing his soft skin as her palm engulfed his lower jaw. The gentle touch swiftly became a harrowing grip. She noticed he was refusing to look her in the eyes, but she needed him to understand what she was about to say.

With no regard to the bandages and appendages smothering and scattering across his skin, she forced his head in her direction as she leaned in real close. She gave him no room to avoid her now, he would be allowed no escape this time.

"You might think you can save this kid if you rat me out to the police, but if I go down, I'm not going down alone. This child won't see the light of day. Not without me." She didn't flinch or waver as she uttered those words. "That'll be two dead babies on your head." She almost threw his jaw away from her as she let go, retreating herself from him.

He stared at her, stretching his jaw a little, bewildered by what she'd just said. He felt the chains slithering their way all over his body, clamping him down, rattling their curses against him. She'd trapped him again, and he had no chance of escape.

"You need to prove that kid is mine, else it's not my problem." He didn't believe that, but he was looking for an inch in the miles of interlocked steel that smothered him.

She locked eyes with him. "Do you really wanna take that risk?"

He knew he didn't mean it; he knew he didn't want to play this game, but it didn't stop him from squaring his eyes back into hers. He didn't want to back down. He couldn't back down. He needed an out, any out.

She waited for him to break, unable to read his eyes. Anything he was feeling, he was doing his best to hide, and it was working. She had laid all her cards out on the table, and here he was still trying to build a hand.

"Fine." She eventually gave in. "But you say nothing until then. I'm not going down alone, Adam. Just remember that. I know where *she* lives too. I know when she sleeps, I know where she sleeps, and I know where a spare key is…"

It took Adam a second to understand what she was saying, but he got the message. He trembled, knowing his life was about to become a hell he couldn't have nightmared up for his worst enemies.

"We're gonna be one small, happy family." She smiled. "You're gonna be a great dad, sweetie." She leaned over and kissed him on the side of his head.

It was like a switch had been flicked in her. She went from a cold, scheming, cruel witch to a sweet and loving admirer in the blink of an eye. From a pure lack of empathy, a shattering void of humanity, to a hopeful bundle of joy.

She turned and headed towards the door, stopping halfway. She leaned forwards a little, emphasising her pose, as she turned her head towards him.

"Maybe if you behave, we can be a big, happy family." She winked at him.

Adam was repulsed, slamming his eyes shut until he heard the door close. His mind was already racing, begging for his brain to find a way out. He needed to escape.

"What happened?" His mother had rushed back in the room, rubbing his head. "You're sweating like you've been running for days."

He opened his panicking eyes, only slightly relieved to see his mother. He knew she had to know, but he didn't know if that would endanger her more. She wasn't feeling very passive at the minute, and this could set her off.

"I need you to sit down." He forced a calmness in his voice for the seconds it took to utter that sentence.

His words had a sombreness to them, one his mother wasn't used to. Her brows peaked towards each other as she pulled a chair from behind her, as close to the bed as she could, and took a seat beside him.

Adam lifted his hand, his elbow resting on the bed. His mother cradled it between both of hers, waiting for him. She could see he was preparing himself for something heavy. She knew this was going to hurt, but she didn't know just how bad.

As he began unravelling the events of the past few days, her heart sunk lower and lower. It was falling. As he explained everything, piecing together a puzzle she only knew a corner of. A corner she thought was the whole thing, turning out to be nothing more but blissful ignorance.

It was as if you could hear the pieces of her heart hitting the floor. Each piece bouncing a few times before it came to rest. Some pieces breaking off into smaller ones. He watched as every part of her began to break, crumbling into a dust that just begged to be carried away or forgotten with a careless wind.

As what was left of her shattered into specks, he watched for where they landed, as if he could put her back together again. He had done this, he repeated to himself. She'd warned him enough times. He did this to her, to Rose, to their daughter, to himself. And now, he had done it to his mother. How many more victims would he claim, all in her name?

As she felt her atoms being ripped apart, she could only blame herself. She should've done more; she never should've entertained the thought of them being together. She could've kept him closer; to hell with worrying about smothering him. At least he would've been safe. She had failed him. She had failed to protect him. His father would never have allowed this, but she had. She'd let them all down. Adam, his father, and his grandfather. All of them betrayed by her ignorance and total incompetence.

As they tore themselves apart in a pleading silence, they vowed it couldn't end like this. Not at her hands, not on her terms, not like this.

Chapter 38

She no longer knew the difference between good and bad, just knew that some things did what others couldn't.

"His mother..." She paused.

"Hm?" He acted like he didn't know what she was asking.

"She must be really strong, to let a woman like that be alone with her son." She paused. "I don't know how you can let someone get away with so much, especially when they had such little to gain. There's no way Eve could've known she'd get pregnant."

He didn't know what to say. "She cared more for her son than she did for revenge. She wanted him to be safe."

"Were any of them safe with her around? Were her own parents even safe?"

"They didn't die so... probably. They were probably safer the less they knew, and one of them had already been cursed with knowledge. That's why it was imperative for him to act ignorant." He answered.

"But to have to even wonder if they were safe, the fact that it's even a question. That's a problem." She stated.

He nodded in agreement; he couldn't really say anything against it. "Some people would set the world on fire and give you a reason that only made sense to them, that's how they survive themselves. Otherwise, what's the alternative? They're evil, corrupt, tainted? Nobody wants to feel like they're the problem."

"Someone *has* to be the problem, usually the ones causing pain." Her tongue wanted to be cruel, but it was tempered.

He could sense the air around her getting warmer. He placed a hand on her back, moving it slowly up and down. She wasn't wrong, but she was at risk of becoming wrong.

It took a month before Adam was released from the hospital. Adam's mother had refused to leave his side the whole time. She had been cautious while he was growing up not to smother him too much, not to coddle him to the point where he couldn't become his own person. But now she felt she'd given him too much space. He was his own person now, he'd had his time to spread his wings, but now it was time to tuck them away and let her protect him.

Eve was definitely pregnant; she hadn't been lying about that. She sent Adam pictures of her belly, even though she wasn't really showing. He ignored her wherever he could, but sometimes she made it impossible.

He counted down the days to her first scan, knowing it wouldn't be too long after that for him to get the paternity test. Better to do it sooner rather than later. This pregnancy was more of a countdown to his impending doom more so than a celebration of something new. A new start, a new hope, a new dream. Instead of it being a chance at a new life, it felt like a suffocating death that just gave him the tiniest specks of oxygen to keep him teetering on. It wasn't just the beginning of a new life; it would become the end of another.

Despite their best efforts, with some from his mother too, Adam hadn't spoken to the police. He feared Eve and what she might do. Even though it was all preventable, he was worried about what she could achieve. This new Eve, this Eve that lived without fear. There was still a hint of her former self in there, somewhere, he just had no idea how to coax it to the forefront. It was as if she'd held herself hostage. A demon taunting its host, maybe. It was easier for him to believe her not to be human, it justified all the brutal thoughts he had about her.

He'd dreamed about calling her father and hatching a plan to capture her before she could do any damage. Tie her up, secure her arms, put her on safe. Clear the barrel and render her clear. Even though she would forever be a loaded gun, especially if he attempted to render her harmless. He didn't want to take that risk. She was right. He wouldn't take that risk.

Ping.

He looked at his phone. The grey hues against that empty blackness. He didn't really know what it was, couldn't make sense of it without someone explaining it to him, but he knew what it meant. He was familiar with what was to be expected of this blight that had befallen him; this twisted sickness that had infected Eve.

He still had the scans Rose had sent him. He had no idea what the earlier ones showed, but they filled him with joy. Well, they once did. Now, he just felt an ache. Eve's scans, though, they just filled him with disgust. That child, to him, was tainted, impure. And it wasn't even its fault. To that end, he felt guilty, pity, sorry. But he couldn't stop feeling disgraced by her child.

Test when?

He waited for her response, knowing she wouldn't be too pleased.

ur so impatient hon...

He felt his whole body recoil as he read that. *Hon.* She didn't get to call him that. She didn't deserve to call him that. But she would take every privilege she could, trying to make it seem like they were something they weren't. She had to keep up the façade, it was the only way she could justify any of this to herself. He hoped, at least, that that's what she was doing. He hoped there was a part of her that knew she was wrong, but she just kept trying to prove herself right.

meet me at mine tomorrow

She added, signing it off with a little yellow face that seemed to be mid-eyeroll. That was good enough for him. He didn't really know how it was going to be done, but he just wanted it to be done. He just needed all of this to be over. In one way or another, he wanted to be free again.

It was the longest night of his life. He lay in his bed, twiddling his thumbs as he stared into the wall beside him. Everything was becoming more real, unavoidable. And she was really getting away with it all. Somehow, she had escaped.

What would he do if it was his child? What would he do if it *wasn't*? He knew he couldn't just walk away. He was prepared to be the father of a child that wasn't his before, with this very same woman. Although, she didn't feel like she was the same person anymore. She definitely felt like someone new, in all the wrong ways.

The child was innocent. As much as his insides twisted whenever he thought about it, he knew that was more to do with its association with *her*. He didn't hate the baby, he hated their mother. He couldn't leave them in her contorted care. That would be just as bad as killing them himself. Who knows what kind of mother she would be?!

His mind was restless, but his body was exhausted. It won out, succumbing him to a tranquil blanket of darkness for a few hours. It would be a new day when the light returned. It would be a new life.

He didn't eat any breakfast, or even any dinner the evening prior. He felt wrong, the threat of throwing up constantly tickling his throat whenever the thought of food entered his mind. He decided to play it safe and just not eat as he headed out the door, at her beck and call once more.

He stood by the gate, not wanting to go into the house that now seemed so evil. Even being this close was a miracle for him, but he knew she wasn't going to make it easy for him. He had to find some middle ground, but it always seemed to be on her turf. For now, Eve was calling the shots, and there was nothing he could do about it. He had to dance to the beat of her drum, all which she shot at his feet and whipped him.

"Hey cutie!" She squealed, running towards him eagerly.

She wrapped her arms around him and tiptoed up to kiss him, lips puckered and demanding like a bear trap. He didn't lower his head, even lifting it slightly, keeping his own lips safely away from her. She huffed and settled to kissing his collar bone, determined to win him over one kiss at a time. As her lips pressed against his, they burned his skin. He was being branded. He could smell the flesh burning at her touch.

"Okay Mr Grumpy, play hard to get. I thought you'd be in a good mood today; you are getting what you wanted after all." She puffed as they started to walk.

"I didn't want any of this, Eve." He sighed, knowing she was playing ignorant.

"When you find out this baby is yours, just do me a favour?" She asked.

"As if I owe you any favours." He snapped back at her.

"Just give this a chance, give *us* a chance. We could be happy, Adam. I thought that's what you wanted. Don't you want to be happy anymore?" She seemed like she was begging.

He shook his head. "Happiness is an ideal only the rich can afford."

She just rolled her eyes, opting to stay silent as they walked to the clinic. She'd had enough of him bringing down her mood. She had picked up a case of baby fever and was permitted to be for the next however-many months. She was adamant he'd come round eventually. He's always wanted kids and he wasn't the type of guy to pass that up – even they weren't his.

The doors of the clinic curtsied open, welcoming them in. Adam followed slightly behind Eve, looking around the building, taking it all in. This was real and it was happening. He wasn't dreaming.

They were guided into two separate rooms. Adam didn't like how white everything was. It reminded him of worser times. He would probably hate Heaven. He had accepted, though, if they did exist, he'd end up in Hell. Why else would all this happen to him, if not to punish him for some sin he'd committed?

A nurse sat across from him and explained what was going to happen. They just needed to take a couple swabs from him and some blood from Eve. Knowing she'd be shedding *some* blood was disturbingly relaxing for him. He caught himself getting excited at the thought but didn't scold himself. He wrote that one off, letting him have that little bit of pleasure in the moment.

The swab samples didn't take long to collect. He waited outside for Eve, knowing she was afraid of needles, refusing to go in there to comfort her. He wanted her to suffer, even just the littlest bit, knowing it would never be enough to atone for her crimes.

He lost himself in the walls. He'd watched other duos walking in and out in the short time it took Eve to get her part done. He thought about their stories, how they may have ended up here. How many ex-lovers murdered new partners? Surely, he couldn't be the only one to have been stuck with a narcissistic serial killer.

She stormed out of the room, not waiting for him. He snapped back to Earth as her back broke his connection to the far wall. He followed behind her as she hurried outside.

"Did you do it?" He asked as they exited the building.

"Yes, and fuck you too." She roared back at him, not stopping her charge.

He slowed down, eventually coming to a standstill. He just stood there, knowing he didn't need to follow her. It was either almost over or almost just beginning. And, even if it were almost over, he knew it was just the beginning of something else.

He had a week before he'd know if he was tied to her for at least the next eighteen years or not. He had a week of chained freedom. The prison yard was his for a week, and he did well to ensure it wouldn't be taken away from him. This week of liberty was the restitution he needed, but it would give him a false hope that he would grow attached to.

An impatient knock on the door. He had barely been given enough time to get to it before the flurry of knocks became pounds. Whoever it was – and he had a fair guess – was not familiar with knocking etiquette.

"You have to give at least three seconds after the first knock before you go again." He scolded her as he opened the door.

"Here." She shoved a closed envelope into his chest, wasting no time.

"Is this...?" Both of his hands covered it, protected it, as if she might try to steal it from him.

She nodded, crossing her arms. She seemed disappointed, as if something were ending, even though he had only really had minimal contact with her since that day at the hospital. He just stared at the envelope in his hands.

"Are you gonna open it then?" She scoffed.

"I... I will. Just not right now." He kept looking at it.

"What was the point then?" The agitation in her voice grew.

"Did you have a look already?" He asked, still studying the envelope as if he could somehow read through it.

She shook her head. "I don't need to, Adam. I already know who the father is. You gave me a gift, this is yours."

She had done it now. That was enough to break him away from the only thing he'd looked forward to. Whether it was intentional or not, she really knew how to get to him, how to get under his skin and make it crawl until he wanted nothing more than to just rip it off.

"I didn't *give* you anything." His eyes were cold and blank as they met hers. "You *stole* this from me. You stole *everything* from me."

For the first time since her newfound confidence, it seemed like she felt guilt. It looked like he had cut through her false armour and slashed her. It was a sign the Eve he knew still existed, somewhere in there.

He watched her stew in his words for a moment, his eyes now burning. He was getting sick of looking at her. He turned around and slapped the door behind him. It didn't click its usual click. There was a thud where the click should've been.

He turned back to see her hand holding it open. "Do you want to know the gender?" She asked.

His head swivelled back towards her, stunned by her reaction. He didn't really know how to respond. He hadn't anticipated this interaction would last this long. He thought on what she'd asked, as his body turned back around and sank.

He sat at the front door; his head bowed. He shook his head. He didn't know if he could handle knowing that information. It would become more personal; he'd be that little bit closer to this. And all he wanted was to be anywhere but.

He had a feeling she was going to drag this out, but he wasn't going to invite her in. As if she were a vampire, he knew all she needed was an invite and his day would be hijacked. She'd hold him prisoner and ruin his week with ease.

"Do you know?" He asked her, his gaze digging into the slabs beneath her feet.

"No." She whispered. "No." She clarified, leaning against the wall.

He didn't want to make conversation, but she wasn't leaving. He didn't really know what she was waiting for, or what more she wanted from him. Was she waiting for him to open the envelope? Or was she waiting for him to say something to her? Something he was supposed to say that he had no idea about?

The truth is, he didn't want to know anymore. It's not like it would change anything. If it's his, great, he's just trapped forever. If it's not, great, he's still not going to let a child die. Knowing doesn't change anything, it doesn't make anything easier. But still, he knew he would hold onto that envelope. He knew he couldn't let it go, not yet.

"Have you thought about names?" The silence faded into his raspy voice; his throat having dried up from the anxiety.

"Not yet. Have you?" She asked, her voice a little more human than he'd experienced as of late.

"No. I'm not one to plan that far ahead. I'm more sporadic. I just do things as they come to me, as my heart dreams them up and my brain makes them possible."

She chuckled at that, smiling at the ridiculousness she remembered from their past. "You don't have *any* ideas? Not even from..." She caught herself.

That stung. He felt that one reverberate through his entire being. He hadn't seen that coming. He wanted to believe she was trying to hurt him, but he could see it in the way her body retreated. She didn't mean it; despite everything she'd done.

"It wasn't my thing; it was more her thing. I never told anyone, but Rose had been talking about baby names…" He drifted off into his memories. "Well, only partially. She said she wanted a girl so that she could name her Lily. And then another girl called Daisy, and one more called Buttercup. She wanted to raise a garden that would be filled with the most beautiful flowers… I told her I'd get her an actual garden as long as she didn't name any of our children Buttercup." He managed to laugh, letting it trail into a sniffle. "She always felt guilty for not preparing for if we had a boy. I told her that as long as she doesn't want to call him Buttercup, we should be fine." He smiled through the wave of sorrow that crashed into him. "She would've been a great mum."

She didn't know if he was trying to hurt her, trying to make her feel guilty by tugging at heart strings. He was using her pregnancy as some sort of shared experience to make her feel sorry for him. For *her*. She granted him the mercy of letting him grieve alone.

She walked away, not knowing how to respond to that. It was the space he needed, the comfort of her steps fading away into the distance.

He sobbed at the door, not letting the tears cross the threshold. He grieved for her, for what they could've had, for what he could never have again, and for all he was about to lose.

Chapter 39

She could feel the end nearing, a small void beginning to form a gap that had once been filled.

"Something tells me we're nearing the end, aren't we?" She asked.

"It doesn't have to end if you don't want it to." He answered.

"Really?" She seemed to perk up a bit.

"You can continue writing the story yourself. You can even rewrite it if you so wish." He knew that wasn't the answer she wanted.

She shook her head, confirming his thoughts. "It's not the same."

"Nothing ever is once you know the ending. We could just leave it, and then you can let it finish however you want to." He proposed a compromise she probably wouldn't accept.

"We'll see, I'll let you tell your version first."

He looked down at the envelope one more time. Still sealed. He could open it at any moment, including right now, but something just held him back. He wanted to know, but he also knew he didn't. He tucked it into his back pocket and began navigating the maze of corridors.

He wanted to witness it. It's meant to be a beautiful moment that makes you appreciate life. A moment that fills you with love. He felt nothing but dread, though, as he walked through those hallways, closer and closer to her ward.

The midwife and her parents surrounded Eve as they coordinated themselves. It was a well-oiled machine; instructions being called out and met with a swift response. Adam walked into the room and just stayed away from the crowd, as far away from her as possible, watching them all work when all he wanted to do was run away.

It didn't take long until he heard it. The cries. The frantic screaming of a newborn child. He watched as the midwife checked her over. His heart pounded, wanting to jump out of his chest. He looked at Eve, then at the midwife, then at Eve, then at the baby.

He was congratulated by a passing nurse as the centre of all attention was escorted into Eve's arms. She held her against her chest. Eve just looked down, smiling. She cried tears of happiness for the first time in a long while.

Adam watched, a confused concoction of emotions flowing through his body. The anger in his fists that she got away with it all. The pain in his heart as he could feel it wanting to love. The hollowness in his chest that refused to be filled. The churning in his gut as it wanted to burst.

"Can we be happy now?" Eve sought him out through the bodies, tired but happy, looking directly at him.

He stepped closer to her. He wasn't looking at her, though. He looked at the bundle of innocence that slept in her arms. He wanted to reach out, to grab her and run away. To save her from this wretched world, this faltering fate that she'd been cursed to.

"We can try." He answered, painting a smile on his face he didn't believe in.

"What shall we call her?" Eve asked, looking back down at her.

His mind drifted, those words triggering the memories of the last time they'd attempted this very conversation. It was only a couple of months ago, but the hurt flooded back through him like it were yesterday. In what was probably a desperate attempt to get Adam more engaged in this joy that was meant to be theirs, she had tried to talk to him about names again. She was trying to pull him back in.

She went over a few names as Adam had ignored her. He didn't care, he wanted nothing to do with it. Knowing there was only one way to get him to pay attention, to love their child like she did, Eve brought up *those* names. *Her* names. And then, *her* name entirely.

"I always liked the name Lily, or Daisy. We're Adam and Eve, and they can be our Garden of Eden. Maybe even Rose, I've always liked roses."

She had tried to steal their garden. After she'd stolen so much from him, still she looked to steal some more.

His nails dug into his palms, just like they had done those months ago. His eyes skipped, as images of her flitted across his mind. Images of her staring up at him, eyes bulging red, her mouth wide open as she screamed. His hand behind her head, pulling her by as many strands of her hair he could grab, his nails clamping into his palms to make sure his grip wouldn't falter.

He remembered dragging his head close to hers, as she yelped and whined in pain, like an injured and scared puppy. She had played with the fire she had started, and the fire was ready to consume her. He could see the fear return to her eyes. The fear she once knew. The fear she was once familiar with. And just like he did back then, his lips subtly mouthed the words he had sworn to her.

"If you ever speak of her again, I will kill your child. I'll do it while you're alive, so you can feel how *she* felt. And when you get over the physical pain, I'll make sure you suffer the emotional torment too. I'll make sure you know how it feels to lose everything. And then, just when you think it's all over, when you think I've punished you enough, I'll kill you too. And I'll enjoy it. I'll bathe in your blood, like how I was covered in hers, but I will enjoy it."

He could hear those words ringing in his head. He could feel them. And he meant them. That was a promise. One she knew he intended to keep. She could see it in his eyes, and she'd learned her lesson. She hadn't been keen to test his patience with that since.

"Adam?" Eve could see he had gone to a place in his head.

His fists instantly unfurled as she pulled him back to the room. He could still feel his nails digging into them, the violence that roamed his veins just begging to be released. He looked back at her; his head had drifted to the ground. With all the effort he could muster, he calmed himself, saving the aggression for another day.

"Eva." He seemed pretty set on the name already.

"Eva." She repeated, letting it settle on her lips. "I love it." She held her baby against her cheek. "Hello, Eva! You're my second chance at life, and I'm gonna show everyone how great of a mum I can be."

A few quiet hours passed. Eve had eyes only for their child. Adam's eyes were facing them, but he wasn't watching them. He was lost in his own thoughts, trying to figure out where they went from here. She didn't notice, though, too smitten with their child to care about him.

"Eve." He cleared his throat, watching her rock their child.

"Hm?" She replied, keeping her eyes on the baby.

"I've packed a suitcase at my mum's, it's filled with a bunch of decorations. I want to decorate our home with it before our parents can see it for the first time. I don't want them to get any hints though, so can you say it's your stuff when I grab it?" He seemed nervous.

"*Our* home?" She asked not looking at him but confused.

"Our home." He confirmed. "The empty one that's waiting for a family. It's not completely done, but it's ready enough to move into."

She looked up at him, a massive smile on her face. "Of course! You're too sweet, Adam." She blew him a kiss. "I knew you'd come around." She looked down at Eva. "See that? We get to be happy now." She cooed.

That confirmed the theory that had been nipping at him for some time. He had wondered how Eve knew where Rose lived, and how she was just always at that park when he was. It couldn't have just been coincidence. He knew she'd been stalking him, and he hated himself for not having eyes in the back of his head.

He scribbled a smile on his face, reciprocating hers. He seemed relieved, like a massive weight had been lifted off his shoulders. Eve noticed his body relax.

"Do you want to hold her now?" She asked.

Adam's eyes widened as he sat up. "N-... No. Not yet."

"You haven't held her at all." She pouted. "Don't you love her?"

"Of course I do. I just..." His mind raced, he didn't want to panic her. "I want you to have as much time with her as possible. After all, once we leave this hospital, the grandparents will be all over her. And then you'll need time to heal, and I'll be all over her for weeks." His mind had saved him once more.

Eve turned back towards Eva. "I knew he'd be a great dad. You're so lucky." She rubbed their noses together.

"Ready?" He asked, walking back into the room.

"Ready." She answered, getting up from the bed.

Adam slung a bag over his shoulder. Eve made her way over to him, the giddiness riding all over her face. She kissed his jaw. He grinned with his mouth, but it didn't carry over to his eyes. She didn't notice though, her attention went right back to cooing their baby.

They headed over to Adam's mother's house – all the parents were waiting there. It was risky, but Eve had the protection of a new innocence now. It was Adam's way of trying to show her they were getting a new start. Eve knew Adam's mother hated her, but if she was welcoming her into her house again then it must be the start to repairing their relationship.

Eve smiled at him as she carried their child through the door. Adam's mother was happy to see her grandchild. She paid no attention to Eve. She tried to be as welcoming as she possibly could, but the bitterness was there with every breath, and she struggled to hide it. Eve's parents had two roles: welcoming grandparents and peacekeepers.

A few hours had passed. All attention was predictably on Eva, and luckily so. Adam came down the stairs lugging a suitcase. He stood at the door, staring at the collection of bags on the floor.

"I've got your stuff, Eve." He peeked through the door.

"What stuff?" Eve's mother asked.

Eve turned to her mother. "Just some of my things to take to our house. I just want everything to be sorted as soon as possible." She turned back to Adam. "Thanks honey, I'll come help you." Eve started to get up.

"Don't be silly, I can help him. You stay and rest." Eve's father got up.

Adam stared at Eve, a worried look on his face. Eve stared back, unsure of what to do. Eve's father flicked between both of them, realising they weren't expecting this.

"Am I interrupting something?" He broke the awkwardness.

"They probably just wanted a quiet moment to themselves before their lives change forever." Eve's mother chuckled. "Let them go together."

Adam forced a smile on his face as he laughed with her. He shrugged and nodded, accepting her reasoning. Eve joined in with him, following his lead, and then walked over to Adam.

"We'll be back in a bit!" Eve yelled from the front door, but the grandparents were already back to focusing on Eva.

"Leave your phone here, I've got a surprise for you, and I don't want anything to ruin it." He placed his phone on the small table by the door.

She nodded as she left it beside his. Adam grabbed the handle of the suitcase and readied himself for the trek ahead of them. She opened the door for him, waiting for him to guide them. She was trying to hide the fact that she knew where it was already, even though they both knew she knew. He looked back into the living room, his mother watching him. He gave her a nod as he turned to the door. She swallowed her prayers and turned back to Eva.

He stepped out in front of her, dragging the suitcase with him in one hand and holding a bag over his shoulder with the other. Eve grabbed the remaining bags and closed the door behind her. She lightly jogged to be alongside Adam, already set in his way.

Adam was quiet, whilst Eve started talking about their future. How to decorate the house, what schools Eva will go to, how she'd love for her to become successful in whatever career she chooses. She didn't need much encouragement from Adam to keep talking about their new lives. He let her talk to herself, as she filled in his parts of the conversation too.

"Follow me, I want to take a quick detour." Adam said as he turned into a field.

Eve hesitated for a moment, seemingly confused. Adam kept moving, though, not waiting for her to question his path. She rushed behind him, not wanting to be left behind. Maybe he really did want to spend some time alone with her. Their lives were about to change, they might not get much time with each other soon.

The field led to a large hill. It was open and the cool night sky bit their skin as they trekked closer and closer to the crest. As they closed in on the top, the monument began to reveal itself, its tufts of hair revealed by the moon's light.

Sat at the top, all by itself, was a lone tree. The trunk seemed a little short, but Adam was pretty sure it was an oak tree. From a distance, it looked mighty and full, a plume of its leaves not dissimilar from the peaks of a mushroom cloud, allowing nothing through it. As they stepped closer, though, its fingers began to reveal the breaks in their chains. The moon was able to break through, its gaze sneaking through the twisting limbs of the formidable tree. Perched upon its watchtower, this lone, great oak tree watched over the town.

Silhouetted in the near distance, the world they'd just walked away from. Lights in the distant houses as people carried on living their lives, oblivious to the part they played in the scene. All of it surrounded by a dark, peaceful sky. It was deep purple, empty with a single, wandering cloud dancing in front of the moon. The stars were distant and few, faded and mysterious in their own glory.

He stood below the tree and rest the suitcase against the trunk. Then he took a step back and turned slowly, admiring their surroundings. Eve was looking around too, wondering why he'd brought her here. She smiled, taking in the beauty. Adam dropped his bags on the ground. The sound pulled Eve away from the sights, as she mirrored him.

"This tree..." He patted its hard wrinkles and let his fingers run along its frozen rivers. "This is my favourite tree. My grandad brought me here when I was a kid. He showed me this place. It was where he'd come when he needed to think… And it's where I used to come to think. I haven't been here in a while…" He studied the tree from below, tracing its far-reaching arms to their tips as if he knew each one. "He used to say this tree was me and throw a bunch of different things at me to lift me up. Caring, with all the shelter it provides and how it watches over our little town. Strong, despite its short trunk, 'cos it had to be to grow this big. Stunning, but that one's self-explanatory." He smiled to himself. "He always forgot one thing though…" His head fell to the ground beneath them. "Lonely. This tree has always been lonely…" His lips disappeared towards his mouth as he failed to hide his disappointment. "Anyway…"

He turned as if he'd never said anything, looking towards her. He took a few steps to close the distance between them, looking to the sky as he reached her. He stood behind her, arms wrapped around her waist with his head resting on her left shoulder.

"What do you think?" He asked her.

"It's… It's…" She couldn't find the words.

"Yeah, that's what I thought too the first time I came here. And every time afterwards. I will never get sick of that view." He smiled, a genuine smile for the first time in what felt like forever. "I wanted to share this with you. I wanted you to see this."

"Thank you, Adam. I'll never forget it." She turned, breaking free from his hold, to face him.

"I'll give you one more reason to never forget it." His voice was calm.

He reached behind him and retrieved a small, black box. It was hard to see in the night, as it sucked in any light the moon offered, but it was just visible. He held it between them, letting Eve know it was hers to take. She recognised the box. She knew what it was. She took it from him, he got to one knee as she did.

"Can we be happy now?" Eve asked, opening the box and staring at the ring.

"Only if you'll marry me." Adam answered.

Eve did not hesitate. "Yes, yes, yes!" She squealed, jumping with joy.

"Then I guess we can be happy." Adam smiled.

She smiled. It felt like forever since she'd heard his voice. His actual voice. Not the cold robot he'd become. She slipped the ring onto her finger, admiring it and then showing him.

"It looks good on you." He nodded.

"You've made me the happiest I've ever been, Adam." She threw her arms around him.

He wrapped his arms around her tightly too. "Good. I hope I can keep you this happy for the rest of your life."

"You will, I know you... will..." Her voice trailed off.

His words filled her with warmth amongst the cold night. His arms warmed her as they held each other. But it wasn't enough to mask the shiver. A coldness breezing past her, into her, through her.

Her eyes bulged. She slowly reached a hand behind her and felt a dampness. She brushed against a cold, hard, thin object too. She already knew what had happened. She brought her hand in front of her, between them, to confirm her doubts.

Barely, against the moonlight, she could see the black blob on the end of her finger. As she turned her hand slowly to study it, she caught the moon's reflection. Surrounding it was a recognizable dark red she had grown accustomed to.

"I'm sorry, Eve, it's for the best." Adam whispered as she looked at him.

She jolted back as he pulled away from her, retrieving his hands, as the bitter winds enveloped her. His right hand made its way to her belly, filling the gap between them. He placed his left hand behind her neck and leaned forward as he pulled her forehead against his. Before she could begin pleading for her life, he pulled her body towards his. The noise of a swift, sharp cut hung in the air.

A single tear left Adam's eye. She winced, feeling it this time. She couldn't move. She was at his mercy. She moved her hands to her belly, wrapping them around the cold steel. They were too weak to do anything, though. She couldn't stop him. With a single, brutal motion, he twisted.

She flinched and grimaced, the swift violence of his hands vibrating through her body. She looked down, her vision blurred from her tears. The knife winked up at her as its glint hit her eyes. She could make out the partial reflection of the moon in the small pool of blood behind the metal that protruded from her.

She saw it there, sticking out from her belly. Her eyes flickered from the knife to Adam. She didn't know what to do, what to look at. She was helpless. Adam just stood there, holding the handle, and trying to push it further.

She faded. Her eyes faded. They remained open but they were lifeless. Blood poured down her body. He finally extracted the knife, dropping it on the ground beside them. He watched her, with a bitter numbness.

Her body collapsed, no longer being supported against his body. He caught her and held her tight against him, crying as his grip on her tightened. He didn't have to worry about suffocating her anymore. He fell to the ground cradling her, her body folding into his.

"We could've been so good together." He began rocking harshly with her. "We could've had it all. A house somewhere quiet but convenient. A nice neighbourhood to raise our kids. Maybe even a few pets. But no. You just couldn't do it. You couldn't love me. Not properly, not enough." He cried. "Why could I never be enough, Eve? Why? After all I'd done for you, why could you not just love me? What didn't I do, Eve?" His rocking had slowed down. "I gave you everything, and you took it all until I had nothing left. And when I had nothing left to give, you took me. My body, my mind. My soul. I tried so hard to give you the world you deserved, but you just made mine worse." He stopped rocking and held her below him, staring into her open, dead eyes. "You took all of my love. You took everything and left me with this angry hate. You took everything from me. You just couldn't let me be happy. You didn't love me enough to let me be happy." He was shaking her by her shoulders, as if it would get her to respond. "But I can't let you take her, too. You can't ruin her, Eve. It's for the best." He kissed her cold lips softly. "It's better this way."

He held her for a few minutes longer. He wiped the crusted trails from his cheeks and knew he had a long night ahead of him.

Adam had prepared for this, yet nothing could stop the pain. Despite everything she'd put him through, he knew he still loved her. You're never prepared to face how much you cared for and loved someone when they're gone. And by then it's too late. You can't bring them back. There's no magic kiss in this world.

He lay Eve down on the ground gently and pulled himself up to his feet. He grabbed a shovel from one of the bags. Quickly, he dug a grave, making sure it was deep enough to not get discovered.

He stripped her down and threw her clothes into a separate bag. He allowed her to keep the ring, as if it was the least he could do for her. He remembered how happy she looked, how he told her he'd keep her that happy for the rest of her life.

He wrapped the sullied bag within another bag. He would do his best to cover his tracks. If she could get away with murder twice, he could get away with it too. Except, he only needed to get away with it once. That was enough for him.

He held Eve's body one final time, staring at her face. Such an innocent, beautiful face. No-one would think she could be such a destructive force. He closed her eyes and kissed her forehead. He said his last goodbyes before he gently lowered her body into the panicked hole.

He pulled off his shirt, wiping off any blood he could. He cleaned himself quickly and methodically, as if he'd practice this. He retrieved a small flashlight and searched the ground for drops and puddles of blood. Any he found were scooped up with the dirt they'd tainted and chucked in with her.

He stripped the rest of his clothing and threw them into a bag too. From the suitcase, he pulled out a jug of water and a bottle of cleaning alcohol. He started to wash himself over her tomb, letting the dirt stain Eve's skin. He cleaned the knife over her too, letting her blood return to her body.

He began covering her up, reminiscing on everything. How they'd met, all the great times he shared with her, everything he loved about her. He focused on the good times now, his tears scattering all over the ground as he worked.

When he was done, he washed off any remaining dirt and headed to the bag he was carrying; his spare change of clothes, identical to what he was wearing when he left.

Nobody would miss her, nobody would notice she was gone. It's not difficult to hide a ghost. To all but his conscience.

He surveyed the work he'd done, trying to make it look as untouched as possible. He reached down, grabbing Eve's bag with one hand and pulling it up to him as it dangled limp in the air. He foraged around inside of it, trying to find something he could use as a gravestone. He felt a slight thump near his foot. Something had volunteered itself. He leant down to find it. An apple fallen, landing just above her. He gently grabbed it with his free hand, loosening his grip on her bag and letting it slump away from him. He lifted it to his face to inspect it.

It was ripe but infested with holes. Why would she keep a rotten apple? Unless it wasn't rotten when she first chucked it in there. But there was something within it that gnawed away at it, took away its purity and corrupted it. Something about the apple felt right. As if it were Eve calling to him one last time. He kissed it where it seemed purest and placed it over her, letting it be a temporary gravestone.

"I'll watch over you both." He spoke, his head turned to the lone tree right beside him.

He walked away to a quiet place by the river and put some gloves on. He threw the contaminated bags into a pile and doused them in a fluid. He pulled a match from a small matchbox and held it to his lips.

"You lit a candle in my heart." He kissed the match and then struck it against the matchbox.

"Then you set me on fire." He flicked the match onto the pile.

"I just want to stop the burning." He threw the knife into the fire.

He watched as the last parts of her turned to ash. The raging inferno turned to embers, until the embers too died down. That had been her life. Passionate and warm. Fire and fury. He scattered the ashes on the ground, initially trying to kick them into the river but eventually resorting to just dispersing them.

With a gloved hand, he grabbed any remaining lumps. He turned and shoved anything remaining into the suitcase. His right foot rest on top of it, as he took a moment to take a few deep breaths. Then, with one final exhausted effort, he tipped it into the river.

He took off the gloves slowly. He dipped them in the alcohol and then began filling them with some rocks and dirt. He couldn't afford to leave any fingerprints behind, and these held just that. He threw them far in opposite directions into the still water. It was done. He headed home to *his* daughter.

"Where's Eve?" Eve's mother asked as he entered the house.

"She's gone." He sighed. "She panicked on the walk to the house. The suitcase she had me carry was her escape plan. Seems she had given this some thought, it might have been her plan all along." He bowed his head, covering his eyes with a hand.

He caught her father's eye as her mother began to worry. Adam watched a wave roll down his throat. Her father bowed his head, ducking slightly behind his wife.

She got up and paced back and forth, he followed her lead. Her father tried to call her. The faint ringing led them to find her phone by the door. They started to panic. This was her chance to start a new life and she had abandoned it; she had ruined it. Again. She had destroyed it.

"It's okay." He walked over to them, sniffling. "I told her it's okay if she needs to leave. She's been through a lot, and I think she just needs a break to collect herself, to piece herself back together to be a proper mum. She's not a kid anymore. She needs to do this bit by herself. She needs to figure out who she is and what she wants to do with her life. I've already told her I'll be here; I'm not going anywhere. We'll all be here waiting for her. I think it's best we just give her some space and she'll come to us when she's ready."

For the first time in a while, he was ready for his future. His life, his love, his happily ever after. It was finally here. And she was finally over.

He stepped towards his daughter, who lay in his mother's arms. He reached out to her, ready to accept her. He hadn't held her a single time in the days she'd been born. But now, he was ready. His mother lifted her to him, as he wrapped himself around her.

This was his new beginning. She was safe. And she was his. She couldn't hurt him anymore.

Chapter 40

Her whole life crashed before her, flittering through everything she'd known, as she questioned all of it.

He waited for her to piece the puzzle together, watching her as she'd quickly figured it out.

She took some heavy steps towards him. She stood in front of him, studying him for a moment. Without any warning, she pulled up his left sleeve. The skin on his wrist showed no signs of the letters that once lay there. Instead, they'd been replaced by a far more obvious sign.

On his wrist sat a tattoo. A withering rose. Sat perched upon it... a swan? That didn't seem... Oh, no, it was a butterfly. She traced the familiar arched neck of the swan around the wings of the butterfly, all the way back to its body. A butterfly carrying a lone swan, sucking the life out of a wilting rose.

"The letters were almost completely faded by the time she was... Well, by the time she had faded. But I still wanted to remember. I needed to remember. Both of them." He was blunt but soft.

She just stared at the coloured patch of skin, hoping this was some sort of prank. A sick, twisted, conniving long con to get back at her for something she did, even though she knew that conspiracy made no sense. She pictured the letters still there, burning against his skin.

"Did you kill her just because I'm your child?" She asked quietly.

He knew what she was trying to imply. Would she have suffered the same fate if they didn't share blood? Would he have let the police take her away and force her to rot behind bars?

He knew he had to be careful with how he answered this. This potential question mark looming over her entire existence. He didn't want her to think there was a world where he didn't want her, never loved her. That there was a world where she didn't exist because both of her parents used her life for an ulterior motive.

He gently grabbed her wrist with his right hand and removed her grip from his left sleeve. He leaned forwards a little and slid a hand behind him. He was reaching into his back pocket, this moment he had waited for and rehearsed many times in his own head. He pulled her right hand between them, turning it so her palm now faced the ceiling. His left hand glided round his body, up in front of him and came to rest in her palm.

She felt a warmth in her palm that wasn't from him. It was something else. He closed her hand around it and gifted her hand back to her. She pulled her hand close to her and unfurled it, revealing an envelope that was unfolding itself poorly. Years of being folded in the same way had forced it to take a new shape, but it yearned to return to its former glory.

She unfolded it completely and looked at it. She knew what it was. She turned it over to its unbothered side, bar the creases from the folds. She read her mother's name and her address, recognising the street. It was becoming harder and harder for her to try to explain this away as some sort of prank, which made turning it over to reveal its contents even harder.

She closed her eyes and inhaled deeper than she ever knew she could. Her innocent and naïve childhood flashed before her. The troubling teen years quickly disrupted them. Those years of bullying she faced for not having a mother. Her first steps into adulthood seemed to hit her harder now too. He was there for it all, but it didn't stop the aching from a world where he never wanted her. She knew it was unfair, but she wasn't choosing for it to hurt.

She exhaled slow and steady, thoughts of what her future might look like from here darting around. She turned the envelope and opened her eyes.

She pulled it closer to her, not believing what she was seeing. She ran a finger over the lip. Still sealed tight, even after all these years. Time had run its course on the envelope, but it was obvious. He'd never opened it. The confusion, shock and disbelief shone through her eyes.

Now she knew how he'd felt all those years ago. She wanted to know too, but the answer had a different meaning for her. Where he believed it wouldn't have changed anything, for her it would change everything.

"It didn't matter to me, Eva." The statement sent a harsh pulse through her body, the pain from her doubts being carried away. "I knew it didn't matter to me, I never doubted that for a second, but I knew it would matter to you. So, I made the choice all those years ago to let you decide."

"I don't know if I want to know, but at the same time I do." She lowered the envelope, never breaking eye contact with it.

It was staring back at her. Intensely, wistfully. It was filled with either an answer or more questions. And neither would feel satisfying.

"You don't have to make the choice today. Or ever. Don't feel you have to." He tried to reassure her. "Whatever it says in there, you'll always be my daughter and I'll always be here for you."

She looked up at him, then back at the letter. It was inviting, but its smile seemed deceptive. This was her poisoned fruit. Deliciously murderous.

"Grab your coat." He got up, seeing the conflict in her face. "I want to show you something."

She'd been snapped out of her thoughts as she followed him outside. He headed for the driver's side door as the car beeped and flashed itself unlocked. She followed behind, not sure what was happening, as she made her way to the passenger's side.

She watched the familiar scenes pass by her, thinking about how different these streets may have been when they were growing up here. She pondered on how her world had changed just as she was growing up, her thoughts drifting to how his world may have transformed too.

He didn't say anything for the short drive, and she didn't complain about it. She didn't have anything to say either, the questions in her head seemingly reluctant to become a craving nuisance.

He pulled into a car park she recognised but couldn't quite place in the darkness. He sat in the car for a few minutes as she waited on his cue. She wasn't sure what was running through his head, but she could see there was something bothering him. Before she could offer him a penny for his thoughts, the click of the door handle broke the silence.

He led her onto the grass. She realised where they were. She could see the hill not too far off in the distance. And on top of that hill, she saw a small gathering of trees silhouetted against the dark sky.

As they reached the congregation of bark and leaves, he slowed down. He hadn't been up here in a while. A slurry of emotions mixed poorly in his belly. He could feel the scratching in his throat as he wanted to expel them from his body. He pressed on, knowing this wasn't for him.

The trees were in a small, poorly-drawn circle, as if a god had free-handed it with the accuracy of a toddler. He stepped into the middle and spun around slowly, getting his bearings. The last time he was here, there was only a single tree here. She watched from the edge of the cultish ring.

He stopped as his eyes fell on the biggest tree, sat right in between them all. His old friend, smiling back at him through its crinkled skin. He walked towards it and knelt beside it. She approached slowly from behind, watching dirt being thrown behind him. He was digging.

When she reached him, the digging had stopped. He held a hand against the tree, looking down at the ground. He patted the trunk a few times, before pulling himself up and turning to her. Between his fingers sat a dark box, still covered in the dirt it had been buried in for so many years. Some of it had gotten stuck around the gap it tried too hard to keep closed.

"There's nothing in it." He held out his arm. "I really did let her keep the ring. There was a mixture of reasons why... But the box was always here as a reminder."

She took it from him and wiped it as clean as she could with her bare hands. It really did suck in any light it could. She flipped it open. Just as he said, bar some dirt that had crept in, completely empty.

"Your grandad knows. I offered him the box, as a keepsake, but he told me to keep it with her."

"He wasn't mad?" She asked.

"He was a lot of things. I think what hurt him the most was that he understood. He didn't want to think about it any more than he had to." Adam looked at the dirt, a sense of hidden shame and guilt hitting him.

"Did nan ever find out?" She felt weird calling her nan, even though it was correct.

"No. He didn't want to burden her with that knowledge. It was a curse burdened to him, and he never even asked me about it. He just knew deep down. He could see it in my eyes, and I could see it in his. But he never confirmed. I think a part of him still wanted to believe she had just left, that she's out there somewhere to this day living her own life."

"I don't remember much of them." She looked at him, sadness in her voice.

"They moved away after a while, they wanted to leave it all behind. They did send me money to look after you, though. They still care. You can reach out to them if you want."

She looked down at the empty box and then nodded to herself. "I might do that."

"Your gran is still in touch with them if you want to ask her."

"Does she know?" Eva asked hesitantly.

Adam nodded. "The same way your grandad does."

Eva sniffed, as she moved away from him. She didn't know what to say. She had grown up without a mother, but they'd done their best to make up for it where they could. It didn't take away all the experiences she could've had, or even change the ones she did.

It wouldn't undo the years of being picked on for being the motherless reject. Everyone thought her mother had run away, that she wasn't worthy of a mother's love. She had come to believe that too, despite all their efforts.

"Did you kill her because I didn't deserve a mum?" Her voice was frail, her past coming back to haunt her.

"No. I did it because I thought you *did* deserve a mum, but I had no idea what kind of mother she would've been. She wasn't the same person I fell in love with, I don't think she ever would've been again." He stepped towards her.

She nodded, trying to accept his answer. "Did you want to kill her?"

"Truthfully?" He asked, as she replied with a nod. "A part of me did. I had my own family, I didn't want one with her. She didn't give me that choice. I *hated* her for that. A part of me did want to kill her, but it wasn't the part of me that did." He stepped closer to her again.

"Is that why you proposed to her? Were you trying to mirror what you had before? A fiancée and a child." Her voice had hardened now.

"I don't really know why. A part of me wanted her to feel the loss I did. I wanted to give her everything I had and then snatch it away, just like she'd done to me. But I did want to marry her at one point. I did want her to be happy. Whether it was with me or not, I did care for her. I don't know which part of me proposed to her." He was behind her now.

She tried to thank him, but the words failed to materialise. She just looked at the box that had housed so many emotions. For the first time in her life, she was holding a part of her mother.

She walked past Adam and looked into the hole he had dug. What remained of her mother was somewhere below her. Her body gave life to the tree in front of her, and maybe a few more beside it.

It was a strange feeling, standing over her murdered mother with her murderer standing behind her. She didn't feel scared, or even angry. She knew how her grandfather felt. She understood, and that's what hurt the most.

She reached into her back pocket and pulled out the envelope. She studied it again briefly, contemplating her choices. Did it really matter? Would it really change everything? Or was it just something that would only ever be a source of pain?

She folded it neatly, as small as she could, and stuffed it into the box. She waved it goodbye with her eyes, shutting the lid and dropping the box back into the hole that once housed it. As he had taken, she would give. She knelt down and covered it up, the little black box returning to its slumber once more.

Just as he had done, her hand rest against the trunk of the tree as she whispered some words to the wind. She allowed a single tear to darken the ground below her before she wiped the rest away with her wrist. She patted the trunk a few times and got back to her feet.

She turned to him. His arms were crossed as he observed her. He gave her a nod. She replied by nodding back.

Thud.

An apple fell by her feet. She turned to pick it up, rubbing it where it landed as if it were a bruised child. It was ripe, pure, calm. The final gift from her mother.

She walked past him, back towards the parking lot. The uncertainty over her future, over his past, over her, had settled. He murmured an apology, a final goodbye, and turned to follow her.

She sat in the car, waiting for him, as he trailed behind. He allowed her to walk ahead, giving her some time to let things sink in. When he finally made it to the car, he noticed the apple sitting on the dash in front of her, its skin still undisturbed.

"Where did all the other trees come from?" She asked, staring at the apple.

"I planted them." He answered, his eyes dropping to the space between them.

"Why?"

"I didn't want it to be lonely anymore." He shrugged.

She didn't say anything in response, just nodded a little as she watched the sheen from the moon against the apple.

"Are you going to eat that?" He asked a minute later, pointing to the apple.

She shook her head. "No, it's special."

"What will you do when the apple starts to rot?" He queried.

"Bury it and wait for a new tree to be born. Just because it's bad, doesn't mean good can't come from it." She replied.

He nodded at her as he dragged the seatbelt across his body. "Is that why it's special?"

She shook her head again, turning to him this time. "No. It's special because it's beautiful. Even when the world around it was ugly, it still managed to be beautiful."

Acknowledgements

Shakur: The greatest friend anyone could've asked for. I hope we'll meet again.

Tara: Thanks for giving me the inspiration I needed to start writing again, I hope you've found your peace.

Resources

If you are a victim of domestic or sexual abuse, please seek help. You are not alone. Some useful resources below:

24-hour National Domestic Abuse helpline: 0808 2000 247

https://www.nationaldahelpline.org.uk/

24-hour Victim Support helpline: 0808 1689 111

https://www.victimsupport.org.uk/